I0657969

Other Titles in this series by Julia Caesar
(arima Publishing)

Dawn of Darkness

THE TAPESTRY OF TTEN

BOOK 2. THE CURSE OF NIGHT

JULIA CÆSAR

Published 2010 by arima publishing

www.arimapublishing.com

ISBN 978 1 84549 465 0

Printed and bound in the United Kingdom

Typeset in Garamond 11pt

Swirl is an imprint of arima publishing.

arima publishing
ASK House, Northgate Avenue
Bury St Edmunds, Suffolk IP32 6BB
t: (+44) 01284 700321

www.arimapublishing.com

Dedication

This book is respectfully dedicated to the tutors that supported my desire to be a writer. Throughout my life they will always be with me.

Miss Clarke,(Hordle Cliff House)
Miss Elphinstone,(Private Tutor)
Evelyn Shiner
(Burcote Grange High)
Stephen Loveless,(ACE)
but most of all
Rosaleen Croghan
(Open University)
who finally convinced me.

CONTENTS

Pronunciations.

Note: Emphasis or stress should be placed on the underlined syllables.
Characters shown **bold** should be hard, e.g. **g** as in **g**o, rather than g as in
gesture   Syllables in brackets are soft. e.g. (g) as in gesture.
Characters separated by an underline follow the previous syllable with no
change of emphasis.

Word	Pronunciation	Description
Ahnell	Are <u>nell</u>	Daro's foster brother
Adruna	A <u>droon</u> a	Sorceress Elect (Amethyst)
Anempor	Ann em <u>paw</u>	Capital of the Azure Sands
Arriera	Arry erra	Daro's birth mother
Ashgenar	<u>Ash</u> **g**enn are	Wilderness
Beddick	Bed ic	Ilkella's brother
Beneva	<u>Ben</u> evver	Guardian of Knowledge
Buerchan	<u>Booer</u> Chann	Capital of the Amethyst Sands
Caranchar	<u>Caran</u> Char	The Town above the Low Pass
Carolus	<u>Carol</u> us	A wandering Apothecary
Czerezin	<u>Cherra</u> Zin	Clan of the Cynabarr Sands
Colonth	Cuh <u>Lonth</u>	Large town
Cynabarr	Sinna Barr	4th Sand of Pelshar
Dinajh	Dinnar(g)e	Invisible water tracts in the Sands
Diras	<u>Deer</u>ass	Daro's bodyguard
Djellim	Jellim	Library established in Selesh
Dolcan	Doll_kan	Small monkey-like creature
Drecon	Dreckun	Dragon (legendary animal)
Errish	Ehrrish	The Master Builder of Selesh
Feydora	Faydrah	Mysterious Sandsinger from the past
Gresshe	Gresh	Clan of the Malachite Sands
Greenfruit	Green fruit	Grean peaches
Greeeyn	Gree <u>yain</u>	Academic caste, city dwellers
Guaradeign	**G**arra<u>dane</u>	Governor
Ikella	<u>Eye</u> kella	Sorceress Ruler of the Opal Sands
Inahana	inner harna	Member of the Council of Nine

Inesh	In <u>Nesh</u>	Second Clan of the Opal Sands
Iscatan	Iz Cat Tan	Ruined Gattarene Temple
Irix	<u>Eye</u> rix	Antelope like creature
Ivinish	<u>Eye</u> vinnish	Beast Master
Jentaroth	Jenn ta roth	Winter Rite of Passage
Jhirrelle	<u>Jirrelle</u>	Clan of the Amber Sands
Kora-Mai	Corra My	Clan of the Onyx Sands
Koth	Koth (as in moth)	High Priest of Gatta
Lushens	Blush ens	Mango like fruit
Malos	<u>May</u> loze	Capital of the Malachite Sands
Maraken	Marra <u>ken</u>	Trail stop where the story starts
Mihort	My Hort	Bear like creature addicted to berries
Miokinish	<u>My</u> ock innish	Boy killed at Tearchan
Myst Cat	<u>Mist</u> Cat	Puma sized feline which can disappear
Nahamida	Nuh <u>Hamm</u> idda	Sorceress of the Onyx Sands
Nishanawa	nih <u>SHANN</u> awa	Mysterious sect of the Ashgenar
Nishan	<u>Nish</u>un	Dedicated to the Guardians as warriors
Othervoice	<u>Other</u> voice	Magically empowered voice
Olneth	Oll_neth	Sybillsce Guard Commander
Patris	<u>Pattriss</u>	Felmin Wagon Master
Pelaquins	Pell ackwins	Pineapple sized cactus fruit
Pretulish	Pr'_Toolish	Small Prickly Melon
Ruenath	Ruin_arth	Ikella's brother
Sandsinger	<u>Sand</u> Singer	Extinct class of mage
Skythe	<u>Sky</u>_th	Flowering herb which promotes fertility
Shadushantesh	Shaddu Shanntesh	Ritual mask of a Sorceress
Shalhanhi	Shallarni	Ruling clanof the Opal Sands
Shenamai	<u>Shenna</u> my	Caverns with strange crystal roof
Shiarjha	<u>She</u> ara	Sorceress Elect of the Opal Sands
Skyrrh	Skirr	Cavern system, Temple of Gatta

Soloria	Soll orya	Late Sorceress of the Amethyst
Suraya	Surr rah yah	Baby Sorceress born empowered
Sybillsce	Sibillsh	Clan of the Amethyst Sands
Tearchan	Tier shann	Hospice at the crossing below Maraken.
Tirjhinar	Tier rinn are	Fabled lost city of the Sandsingers
Tuennis	Tue enniss	Inesh woman Guaradeign of Caranchar
Usticus	Us_tick_us	Daro's pet Dolcan
Vetali	Vitt arly	Trifoliate plant with magical properties
Zeglurs	Zegglures	Donkeylike Pack animal
Zenitheon	Zenith_ee yon	Summer Solstice
Zephryn	Zefrin	Legendary single horned storm horses
Zurias	Zurry ass	Clan of the Azure Sands

Opal Sands South

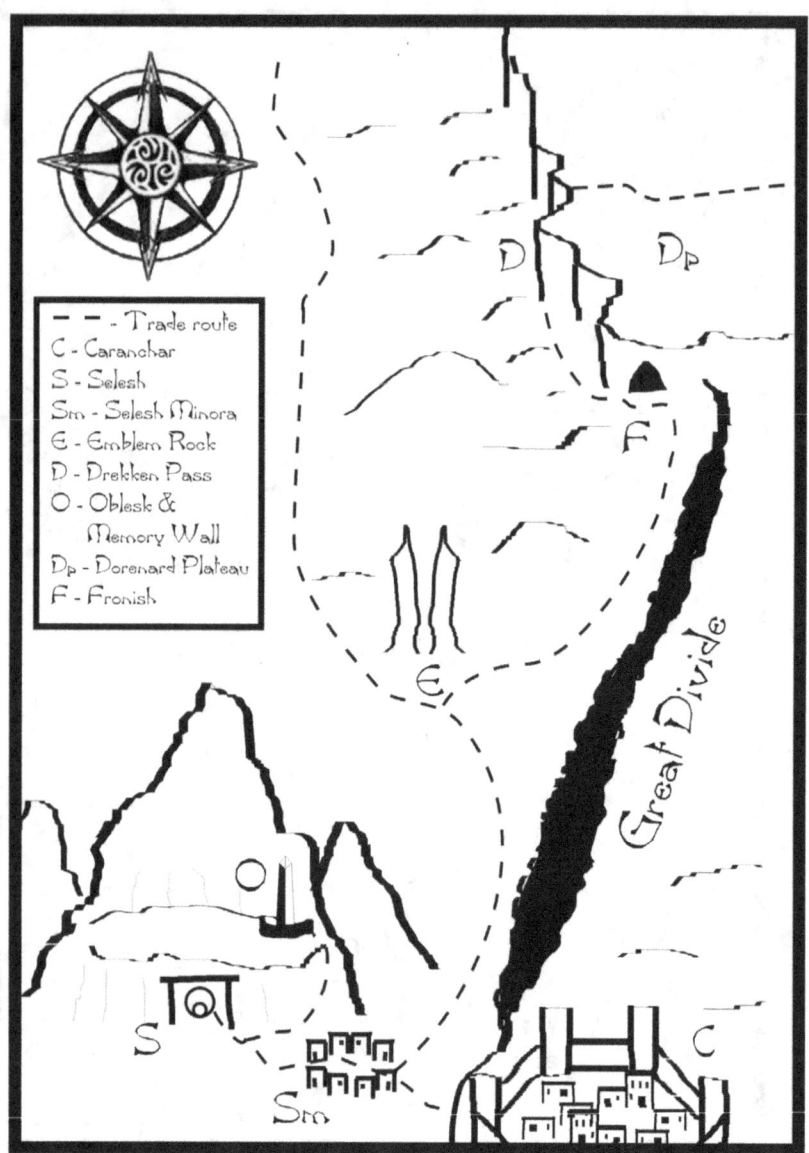

Opal Mid Eastern Borderlands

Amethyst Sands showing Sherrol Pass

PART ONE - THE PARTING OF THE WAYS

Prologue

Foreword by the hand of Brannith, scribe.

Following the terrible events of these last few ninenights, we are safe at last in Selesh, the retreat of my Lady Sorceress, Ikella te Syrene. Now, I will be able to consolidate important notes for my Master's use and document the strange savagery of the Storm as it struck these Opal Sands. I will record the lost, recount the twists and turns of the changing Way, (the pattern by which all men live), as the harness of Sanctuary falls to our Sorceress to shoulder. Within this great and ancient place however, I observe that my Master is welcomed, seems lest restive and more willing to remain a while, if only until the end of this Rotation of Pelshar, our deeply divided, but still Beloved world.

"From the Chronicles of Carolus.", It has been many Rotations since I have been in the heart of the Clan. During this time I believe because I have distanced myself from these hallowed halls, all reference to my previous infamy has been forgotten. Selesh, the holiest shrine of our Sands, still whispers to me of ephemeral things that jar oddly with what I recall of my life. Here, I can't help but remember my earlier residence, but nowhere can I find any trace of those times or people. I have quietly walked its corridors in the footsteps of our Sorceress and once or twice felt that I should encounter some evidence of my youth, but those paths have changed beyond recognition, fled into the night with the images that once palely haunted my dreams. Now, I rejoice that ever blessed with speed of thought and action, I was able to revive the child that was rescued from the Storm, because of this, I have found myself being treated as an intimate of Lady Ikella, admitted to the innermost secrets of Selesh and appointed as an Ambassador for the High Council. From this, it would appear that little account had been paid to my earlier digressions from the Way, I am once more, welcomed in our ancient Hall.

Over shadowing joy at the safe return of the Sorceress, has come the fall of Sanctuary. I find it strange that I had no suspicion that I would never see that magical place again. Of the day that I departed from its walls I only recall with sorrow, the vivid Colours of those I left there. My friend Jocasta, the "little sisters" in her care, Miriniva, solemn Guardian of Power, not to mention the Nishan. All gone to the Sands and the Winds, as if they had never been. The bright promise of their power and purpose vested in the deliverance of the Sanctuary Chest and the survival of one scrawny child wrapped around with incoherent prophecy.

His deliverance, into the hands of an austere virginal Sorceress with no maternal instincts, seems hardly an auspicious start to the Second Age of Mystery. That they know nothing of the past that defines our future is certain, but they must learn of it, supported only by an assorted bunch of Healers, a wandering Apothecary and his herd of Zeglurs! If it were not for the survival of Beneva, Guardian of Knowledge and her installation at Selesh, I would probably sink into a despair, but I am convinced that the whispering walls of Selesh will once more speak to me and where that Voice leads, I will again, follow.

Chapter 1 - Apprehension.

Ikella, Sorceress of the Opal Sands, rose early and padded swiftly to her ablutions, having learnt over her long life, that this was the only time she could be truly alone with her thoughts.

She scrunched her hair up in one hand, examining her face in a polished glass, considering the Eve of Conclave and the forthcoming Gathering of the Clans.

Never had such a Gathering been held. Her green eyes darkened as she contemplated the catastrophe that had befallen them. Feeling as if the walls of Selesh groaned under the weight of her burden, her thoughts turned to the foundations of her faith, to the Mother House of Sorcery.

Sanctuary, in the far north of the Eternal Snows, represented centuries of stability to all Pelshar. Here, the Sisters of Sorcery trained to rule the vast deserts of this arid world, under just three Guardians, who presided over the accumulated knowledge of their lost and secret past, the governance of their current culture and the use of magic. She stared into the mirror unseeing, knowing that today a new history would be written in the start of a new age without Sanctuary, for Sanctuary was no more.

It had seemed so permanent, stood like a beacon of hope on the Heights of Surrandel. Its soaring turrets and delicate towers poised on the edge of a dramatic precipice, crossed only by the Bridge of the True Believer. No-one knew how it came there, or who had built it, but all knew what it stood for, stability, permanence, the Way by which they lived. Now it was gone, taking their protectors into the dark with scarcely a murmur, leaving her to pick up the mantle of Guardianship without faltering.

She set her jaw experimentally, refusing to allow sorrow and loneliness to dominate her expression. Lifting her silver hair, she bound it back from her face, absently noting how taut the skin over her cheekbones seemed as she cast her mind back over the turmoil of the last half Rotation of Pelshar.

Savaged by a storm of unprecedented ferocity, townships had been reduced to dust. Whole societies had been destroyed and it was her task to reveal their losses and lead the survivors by example. She could never give in. Not to death, not to disease, not to despair, however understandable that might be. She raised her eyes and stared critically at her reflection. She was Sharall deir Opal, absolute ruler over all Sands and she would go on, regardless.

Her thoughts turned to the celebration of Jentaroth, two daybreaks from now. This annual festival of the Clans was the imperative behind her decision to call her Sisters in Sorcery to Conclave at Selesh. Now beset by doubts, a frown creased her brow, as she continued her morning routine. Mechanically shrugging off her nightgown, she collected a few salve pots in a rush basket, mentally reviewing the laborious preparations for the festivities. Her mind touching here and there, still stubbornly skirted the issue of this morning's Audience and an outcome still too painful to contemplate.

She soaped her body and slipped into the pool, letting the gentle heat relax her, until at last she could keep her troubles at bay no longer, sitting bleak-eyed and expressionless, as she wondered what to do about Daro. As desert law demanded, she had rescued the orphan from the Storm, but his tiny fingers had woven themselves around her heart.

Only a few ninenights ago she had ruthlessly dismissed his claim on her. Recognizing that his frail hold on life posed a threat to her emotional balance, she had decided that he must return to his own family, if any survived the Storm. However, no-one had responded to her Seeking Spell, though it was a powerful lure, weaving together known elements of his history, catalysed by an object belonging to his mother. Winged eyebrows drew together, as she remembered the tiny carved gemstone she had used, then, she shook herself out of indecision and reached for drying cloths.

Climbing out of the pool, she reviewed the situation, Just when she had decided to adopt Daro as her own, just when she had surrendered her cool virginal heart, her mind quavered, "Just when I decided to love him, someone decides to claim him.".

Choking back a sob as she towelled herself dry, Ikella ruthlessly crushed her emotions back under control as she recalled the evening before.

A late arrival had sent her a token, stating that he sought a baby and its mother, lost from his trek train on their Western borders. This was indeed where Daro's mother had been found, about to give birth in the heart of the Storm. Ikella, resolutely pulled down the barriers and faced her pain, using breathing exercises to quell the emergent tears. Abruptly, rejecting the garments laid out for her, she selected an ornate overobe in rare and costly Opal weave, (if only to steel her nerves). The intricate magical weave shifted and shimmered comfortingly beneath her hands, until she sighed and turned back to the business of the day.

Wandering into her day room, she found the glowstone fire alight and her maid Trinet, waiting to serve a light breakfast. Trinet glanced at Ikella's clothing, but said nothing, being used to her mistress, who often made the most fractional of changes for obscure reasons beyond her attendant's understanding.

Still running her mind over ceremonial preparations, the Sorceress asked absently, "Did they find enough material for all our new robes?".

She was determined not to think about her impending loss until the very last moment and Trinet beamed, "Yes, my Deshun. They hang ready in the Syndarial.", Trinet continued, briskly folding garments away as she spoke.

"The cloth is Opal weave of great antiquity, stored in chests that preserve such things. Seris Beneva said that there were too many treasures to examine before Jentaroth, but the material was yours to command.".

Silently, Ikella thought that too many discoveries had followed the Storm and decided that things lost millennia ago, could wait until these Rites were over.

Reviewing the agenda for Conclave, she decided that certain revelations wouldn't be shared. Her mouth turn down at the thought of such duplicity, but she resolutely took up a cup of stemmis, sweetening it with honey-cream and drank absently, her mind still racing.

Into the age old traditions of Jentaroth, she must, as celebrant, weave her own Rite of Accession to Guardianship. Beneva, sole survivor of Sanctuary would conduct this and for a moment she felt a flutter of panic in her stomach and Trinet saw her pale and her hands clench. Entirely unaware of this anxious scrutiny, Ikella turned her mind to the ceremonies of succession. Fresh from their novitiate at Sanctuary, three young women would be raised to the full status of Sorceress. Without the usual benefit of a long apprenticeship to strengthen their resolve, without the inherited memory or the song-spells of their predecessors, they would be truly alone and at that thought she shuddered.

"These unfortunate circumstances, will involve me in a deal of extra work.", she thought ruefully, realising that she had only met one of them during the many Rotations of their training and finally, her thoughts fastened on the dilemma of baby Daro.

With a sigh she finished her sweet drink and rose to her feet. Leaving Trinet cleaning her day room, she went into her study and sat at her desk. Taking the child's heartstone from the pocket of her shift she placed it on the highly polished surface. The fire opal gleamed, pulsing softly, reflections from the carved fruit on its surface glittering oddly, as if waiting for something. Reluctantly she reached into the drawer of her desk, where a second carved fruit glittered crystal flame.

She took it up carefully examining it as she had done the previous night, acknowledging that this was indeed twin to the stone she had used to create the Seeking Spell. She stared cat-like through narrowed, unblinking eyes at the crystal apple. She remembered her astonishment as its twin fused, almost protectively, around the opal heartstone that she had placed on the child during the casting of the spell and wondered. Could the despair of a dying woman, so influence an artefact under a spellworking? She knew nothing of motherhood. Her elevation to the Staff of Sorcery had put ordinary female dreams from her forever and she had little understanding of that precious bond. Her unnaturally prolonged life of a magic user, had taken her beyond the call of living relatives, could even take her beyond the lifetime of the child she loved. How she wished that her magic would show her one glimpse into the future, for herself, for Daro, but that way lay dangerous self-indulgence. She couldn't step from the path her feet had been set on and so her decision was made. If the man who had demanded audience was the child's relative, she would give him up. She would force herself to, even though her heart broke.

She stood, tall and austere, great calmness on her features and a storm of anxiety in her heart. She dropped the child's heartstone in one pocket and the stranger's token stone in another and slipped on the Opalwear over robe.

Trinet seemed to sense Ikella's tumultuous thoughts, keeping silent as she dressed Ikella's hair, gathering it into a great coil at the back of her head. Her hand hovered questioningly over the box containing the Shadushantesh, Ikella's ceremonial mask, but the Sorceress shook her head.

"Not until Jentaroth Trinet.".

Ikella found it difficult to keep the sudden, almost violent aversion from her voice and in the mirror glass their eyes met. However, the woman slipped two highly ornate combs into the Sorceress's hair without any comment and held up a gazing glass for Ikella's approval.

Minutes later, surrounded by her Honour Guard, she passed through a doorway, Staff in hand, a mild glamour of inapproachability cloaking her features as she made her way to Audience. Passing the nursery door, Daro's bodyguard fell into step at the rear of the party. Flanked on one side by another warrior carrying the child and on the other by Daro's wet-nurse, they processed into the Audience Chamber behind Ikella..

Many waited for her appearance that morning. She settled into the ornate chair that tradition demanded she use and made herself comfortable, while her bodyguards disposed themselves in a semi-circle flanking her to each side. Diras stood to her

left, guarding Nadra, who settled down to entertain a wakeful Daro. Ikella watching him, found it difficult to accept that it was already thirty ninenights since they had prepared his mother for burial. Nearly half way through his first Rotation, why when he had taken hold of her heart, had her Seeking Spell been answered?

She looked down the flight of steps to her dais, beyond the light cast by the day glows into the shadows and saw him, stood with his group of friends, hukvah in hand, awaiting her pleasure. He stood out amongst the other men. Taller, straighter, plainly sighted, he had an air of command, his companions deferring to him easily.

"So he is a leader.", she thought, puzzling over this strange Felmin trait, thinking, "The child will be well looked after at least.", She studied his clothing, while the last petitioners were ushered in and the doors to the Audience Chamber closed. He was clothed in clean linens and his beltash the distinctive indigo blue tunic of a trader, although well worn, looked to be soft and comfortable. His boots were well shone and his desert pants were tucked in firmly, laces neatly tied. Altogether, as well dressed and clean as she would like, she mused, leaning forward on her chair, an elbow resting on her knee, chin cupped in hand. He seemed unaware of her gaze and was busying himself with his men, making sure that the elderly folk present were comfortable, fetching a blanket roll for one frail man to sit on, guiding a blind man to the rail of the steps. Ikella noted the compassion in the man, who was patently bringing his petition to her last and decided that if he did indeed claim Daro, she couldn't have hoped for more , but her heart was heavy as she looked down on those who sought audience with her this morning.

The usual petitioners waited in line, some would be wanting to know if harvest would come this Rotation, she thought over many other Audiences since the Storm. She could almost predict the requests now, would a much loved son see again? What help could Selesh offer them, what shelter? Some of this group were plainly Caranchese and she dimly remembered inviting the families of her hostages to join the Gathering as her guests and she inwardly sighed , so many problems to deal with, so many decisions to make and for a moment her faith faltered within her, then, her gaze fell on Carolus who had wandered in to the Audience Chamber and was happily chatting with some of the visitors from othersands. To her astonishment, the old man met her eyes fully and with a hint of amusement blatantly drooped one eyelid in an enormous wink. She was so taken aback by this unabashed greeting that she had to restrain herself physically from laughing and then discovered that her sense of trepidation, her fear of impending doom had fled with the strangled giggle at the ancient Apothecary's antics. Composing herself, she raised a hand to Sorrill, who stepping forward and grounding her spear with a thud that resonated around the Audience Chamber intoned, "Let all who have business before Ikella, Sorceress of the Opal Sands be welcome at this time of Audience. Draw near, into the protection of her sands, under the cloak of her spell and unburden yourself of your worries without fear of her wrath.", and so Audience began.

Chapter 2 – Audience

As the line of petitioners dwindled, Ikella dealt with matters of property, quarantine precautions and suspended tithe collections. Welcoming visitors from Caranchar, she smiled at their reaction to the simply furnished Audience Chamber, wondering what they would think of the new Hall of Welcome, proud that she had neither dipped into the Treasury of the Sands, or levied taxes on the Clan to fund its creation. privately hoping that the provision at the Healer Hall, would gain approval, as Selesh admitted more patients and visitors flocked to see them.

Carolus remained, assisting her petitioners to depart. Few choosing to hear the rest of Audience on this festive occasion and she took comfort in the old man's presence, though why, she couldn't have said. So her thoughts ran on, as she dispensed wisdom and justice, alms and assistance and then there was but one man remaining before "the Seeker", as she had mentally named him.

A blind man stood in front of her now, grasping his Staff as if his life depended on it. With a rush of sympathy, Ikella saw two small boys cowering at the rear wall, eyes fixed on their father as he slowly knelt before her. With a silent gesture, she indicated that he should be seated and a low stool was produced. One of the men helped her petitioner to sit and Ikella waited for him to regain his composure, before asking, "How can I assist you and yours this day?".

Her voice, gently enquiring, was of such a soaring bell-like clarity, that it identified who had spoken, unmistakeably. His face flushed shyly, as his voice, tremulous with suppressed emotion was made to respond.

"Lady, I am unaccustomed to speaking with those of your rank.", he hesitated for a moment, then continued, "I am not of your Sand or Clan, but my woman was.".

He paused uncertainly, until Ikella encouraged him with a comment of her own.

"I think you Zurian. From the far South if I am correct.", she unhesitatingly placed his soft accented speech and he visibly relaxed, smiling cautiously, as he began his tale.

"I am called Duvell Lady. I am travelling back to the Sands of my birth, for I am homeless since the Storm. I have lived here many Rotations, managing a Brew House in Maraken, from where this good man has brought me to your door.".

His hand moved, indicating the tall Felmin trader, who stood close by his side, ready to support him. Ikella almost nodded, just catching herself as she realised that Duvell couldn't see her, she cleared her throat.

"Go on.", she encouraged and he began again, his voice hesitant, laden with sorrow.

"My wife went to the Sands in Maraken, leaving my boys motherless.", His face was schooled to impassivity, but his hands convulsed as he spoke painfully.

"I lost my sight to Storm Plague and with it my livelihood, my independence, my home. One of my sons has been sick ever since. I thought he just missed his mother, but he had high fevers, much pain in his eyes and neck. His limbs have shrivelled, he talks in riddles and his mind wanders in some dark and terrible place.".

Even as he spoke, one of the traders men carried the boy, a lad of about five Rotations forward and laid him on his blanket at his father's feet. The child made no response, just lying on his back, eyes rolling, arms curling inwards, he seemed to be talking softly to himself and Ikella winced at the terrible damage displayed there.

Duvell's head lowered towards the child and his hands gentled and stroked him lovingly as he spoke, plainly embarrassed by his need to beg.

"He has suffered so much, with our Healer dead, I sought help at Tearchan, but it has gone, so my trader friends took me on to Caranchar.", He made a physical effort to control his emotions and Ikella, walking mentally in his footsteps, sighed as she remembered her own journey of despair, taking in his shabby clothes and bare feet. His children drew together, the older boy soothing his frantically agitated brother, as, oblivious to his surroundings, he rocked to some internal rhythm that only he could hear. Duvell was still talking and she focussed with difficulty, suddenly aware of his voice again.

"That new Healer at Caranchar was wonderful with my boy.". Duvell confided, then

"She advised me to come here for help Lady. She even fed us, without payment and loaned me a blanket for the boys.".

Ikella took note of this, as Duvell struggled to his feet and addressed her in a clearly rehearsed manner, so formal that it was piteous in its dignity.

"Lady, I beg leave to try and earn a little money in any inn that will take me. I was Master Brewer by trade. May I apply for permission to take work here, so that I may pay for my son to be treated by your Healers. I ask your mercy for both my boys were born of your Sands and of a woman of the Clan.".

Ikella drew in her breath with an audible hiss.

"Had it come to this?", she thought in shock.

"Did people believed they had to have permission to take work here? Why should they think that they had to pay for their children to be treated?".

She leant forward, catching one of the blind man's hands in her own.

"In my Sands, children are the future. No man has to ask permission to work, only save he reports to his Guild Master, where that Guild is represented. As a Master Brewer yourself, you may ask for hospitality in any settlement of the Sand and there is no charge for treatment of any person young or old, of any Sand, caste, or belief. Take your children to the Infirmary immediately Duvell and yourself, for you are exhausted, malnourished and those eyes should be examined.".

She clapped her hands imperiously and two of her guard stepped forward, "Gather their possessions, carry the children to Hannah immediately. Tell her that they are to be admitted to the infirmary, I will come as soon as possible to treat the young one myself.". She turned aside for a moment and then said, "There are clothes a-plenty left by those we lost. Dorra has them washed and stored ready for such an emergency. See that they are fed, bathed, shod and clothed. They are to be put together in one room so that the children are not frightened. Give them a mild sleeping draught, they should rest before I divine the treatments needed".

As the little family was gathered together and shepherded away, the purpose for this Audience stood before her at last. For a time, she realised, she had forgotten the baby altogether in the execution of her duty. She shuddered with the effort not to look at Daro, who was cooing at her. The soft little sounds, a precursor of real speech, were special. He had developed a kind of questioning tone that he used when she picked him up and her heart thudded painfully, as she realised how much she would lose, if this man had a legal claim.

Then the Seeker stood before her, flanked on either side by his men, bowing his knee and doing her obeisance. She looked down, into his eyes and recognised him instantly.

"The man at the trail stop, the one I was compelled to warn against travel, the night of the Storm!", she thought and a momentary frisson of awareness touched the mind that was schooled to recognise in synchronicity the working of the Way. In that moment of mutual recognition, they both uttered a single word, "You!".

Then, slowly and deliberately, he prostrated himself at her feet, followed by his men.

Ikella found herself kneeling to raise him, until he stood, uncertainly twisting his hukvah in his hands and muttering, "Lady, I don't know what to say, for I owe my life to you already.".

His deep voice although melodic, was loud from Rotations of shouting orders down the line of a trek train, but Ikella knew he was trying to thank her, and replied.

"Few traders know the Ways of our Sands Harmeister. They shift oddly from time to time and I couldn't see you go unknowingly to your deaths in the Winds of that night, to add to our sorrows.".

She paused, aware that as she spoke the group around her touched lips, forehead and heart, in the ritual recognition of some Higher presence, at which she said lightly, "Now that you know who I am, may I know your given name?" and he replied gruffly.

"My name is Patris. These men are Rowbet my lead driver, Somner my wagon Master and Ivinish his brother, who is our beast handler. We still have a company of sorts under my Guild papers, although in truth, I should no longer call myself Harmeister, as I no longer have forty wagons, crewmen or beasts left alive. I have only three wagons, two of those stranded in Caranchar for repairs, the central routes are impassable with Biron carts", he continued, saying harshly, "I can't take paying passengers into the Sands to be killed by freaks of weather.".

Ikella noting obvious distress realised that Patris had lost friends on this journey. He carried sorrow like a coat, perhaps some guilt accompanied him, casting a long shadow across his Way. He met her gaze through respectfully lowered eyes, his whole manner and expression guarded, but she finally made the first overture, saying softly, "You sent me this?".

She drew out the crystal apple from her pocket and extended it, on the palm of her left hand. Patris blinked and looked at the little stone and then said doubtfully, "In your hands it seems to glow more lady, it looks the same thing, but different if you know what I mean?". The Sorceress glanced at him sharply, but decided that there was no hint of false flattery here, no attempt to curry favour, not a whisper of artifice. Noting that he made no attempt to touch the jewel, or take it from her hand, she questioned him, curiously.

"How came you by this pretty thing?".

Patris, voice schooled to neutrality, explained his encounter with Arriera. Gradually the tale emerged, coloured by vivid verbal sketches, till Ikella saw her. Tired, anxious, the burden of advanced pregnancy, the Colours of Clan Jhirelle. She heard the whine of the Winds again, felt the Sands on her skin once more, but she still suspected that there was more behind this Search.

As his voice tailed away miserably, Ikella suddenly saw that open Audience was not the place to establish who had more lawful claim to Daro. Though, since the Storm, she had shared many of the sorrows and joys, of her people, she could wish fewer witnesses to her own. She touched Patris lightly on the arm, "This is a matter for private Audience Harmeister Patris. Will you and your men accompany us to where we can take our time to settle our business?".

She rose and abandoning all pretence at maintaining a diplomatic distance between herself and Patris, signalled to Carolus to join them, as she remarked, "Dealing with this here is unutterably silly. Let us go to the comfort of the Djellim, where Beneva can see we are not disturbed. Nadra can take Daro back to the nursery to feed him and we can eat while we talk.".

Patris froze in the act of rising to his feet. Momentarily, insecurity surfaced and Ikella laughed, saying lightly, "Oh come along man, I am no different to any other old lady. I like to meet people who have travelled strange places, talk about shared experience and I don't like to starve while I do so.", Shrugging aside the discomfiture of the trader she gathered Carolus into her retinue and made her way briskly to the Djellim, where Beneva, warned by a Guard was waiting. Root broth and plain bread was set on a hot table to one side, places were laid at the study table and soon they sat together and shared their midday meal.

Carolus observed the traders discreetly. He was impressed by their solidarity and their leaders sense of purpose. There was initial fright but no panic in the face of the Sorceress's unusual invitation. He noted how Patris closed his eyes when Ikella gave thanks for their food, which was to his mind, a clear demonstration that this man had faith and practised it. He nodded approval and at that moment Ikella knew that Daro was safe in the company of this man.

She broached the subject of the traders search, choosing her words with care. As Mina and Beneva brought warming sweetdrinks for them, she questioned Patris closely.

"How is it that you still search for this woman Arriera?", she asked. "You said that she was of the Amber Sands, but I think not of your caste, for she wore the Colour and the woman I found was certainly of the Clan Jhirelle.". She saw him wince as she added sombrely, "Although by the time I found her, she was already dying, far beyond lucid speech.".

Patris nodded, he warmed his hands round his cup and considered what he should say. Clearing his throat and carefully lowering his voice he said, "She only travelled with me about sixty sanches, but in that time she made her presence felt. She spoke little, seemed anxious and tired and yet there was something important about her. She seemed to have purpose, an aim and I had on board my trek train many who seemed to have no purpose, no Way or Path to their lives. She simply shone amongst them and I felt, no still feel.", he amended hastily. "Responsible for her loss.".

As silence fell, Ikella felt the stones in her pockets pulsing and took them out, laying them on the table. The Trader's crystal apple and a large fire opal, bearing an engraving, created when another crystal apple had fused to Daro's heartstone, during the casting of the Seeking Spell.

For some obscure reason, Ikella had placed the crystal in one pocket and the heartstone in another. Now, as she placed them on the table, they rolled together, striking as softly as a kiss and coming to rest in front of the Apothecary. There was a soft sighing sound, a breeze touched Ikella's neck and she knew with certainty that magic still commanded the stones. As the trader's men gazed at them fearfully, there was an audible "ting", a shimmer, then the heartstone quivered as though some glamour dissolved. and the first crystal apple disengaged itself, rolling clear to lie resting against its twin. The Sorceress, gathering up the heartstone and returning it to her pocket observed the bewildered men. Not that she thought Carolus was that bewildered.

"He seems remarkably pleased with himself.", she thought irritably, but catching the trader's eye murmured softly, "Now that is very strange, don't you think?", and he nodded silently, obviously unacquainted with magic so she returned to safer subjects

"I understand your distress at the loss of your passenger Patris, but you don't have any blood link to her, or to the child do you?", she asked solemnly, continuing, "I sought Arriera's bloodline. Mother, father or other responsible relatives only. I believe that you came of your own volition, or that the stones sought each other. Either way, if you are not bound to the mother or child, what do you seek here?".

He hung his head, a little embarrassed by her question, "I had hoped that Arriera might be found and wanted to return the jewel to her, it was all she had to give and her child might have need of the money it could raise.".

Ikella, unaccustomed to finding such honesty of feeling amongst men, persisted, "Did you search for them in Quinnox? Wasn't her sister there? She has a call on this child's Sand rights and her kin should know of her death!".

Patris bit his lip and said nothing, but Rowbet sitting to his right, smiled bitterly, saying, "Lady, we searched Quinnox in vain. The city was devastated, many houses ruined, but it seems that they have deep shelters which housed every inhabitant. They were insistent that not one of the "true caste". had perished.".

A scornful look crossed his face, twisting his fine open features into a mask of absolute distain.

"They thought it quite a joke that any Sandsworn girl should have sought shelter amongst them. They allow no exchange or friendship between themselves and any other caste. I think they wouldn't even trade with us if they could survive otherwise. They told us that no Sandsworn could enter their Inner gates or homes, even to birth a child.".

His face darkened as he continued, "We nearly got thrown out for asking. After this, I believe they will withdraw from all contact with other castes. They appear to fear anyone whose background they don't know.".

Somner examined his left fist with interest and the scars and bruises told a story to the Sorceress, who was not head of the Guild of Healers for nothing.

He commented seriously, "One man told me that the city "father's", had to remain pure of the "vermin of the Sands.".".

His contempt was mirrored on the faces of all his company, until Ikella said thoughtfully, "I must visit Quinnox one day very soon!", to a backdrop of shudders as they registered the sudden chill in her voice.

Patris said slowly, "I admit that I thought her lost then. I had lost my beasts at Maraken, where so many died. Those Greeyeyn passengers, sought to evade paying me, as if the Storm was my fault.".

He sounded weary, dispirited and Beneva leant forward encouraging him to finish his tale. He looked up, smiling awkwardly. "I was reduced to hiring three beasts, just to transport those travelling from Maraken, to Omnel. After waiting for guides, I got my original passengers to Quinnox but made twelve journeys in all to deliver my goods and theirs.".

He touched his fingers lightly to head, lips and heart. "Thank the One that I don't carry perishables, or I wouldn't have been able to pay the hire, let alone purchase some new beasts of my own.", He ran a hand through unruly hair unconsciously, as the sorry tale ran on.

"When I returned to Maraken the last time, I salvaged what I could from my own wagon, which was destroyed during the Storm. It was only then that I recovered my clothes and my purse, in which I had placed the jewel. I admit that it gave me quite a turn, a deal of sorrow, for I see her still, just as she was when she gave it to me. I never knew that it had a partner.".

His eyes dropped to the pair of carved stones, reluctantly.

"Every journey since has had its own search built in, until my men think me mad. It is at their insistence that I came here, now you tell me that you found her. Is it true?".

Mina, returning to the table settled to listen, as Ikella told Patris the sorry story.

The Sorceress, noting the discomfiture of the men when magic was mentioned, decided only to relate the basic facts. The discovery of the girl collapsed and dying, the birth of her child and his deliverance out of the Sands, to safety in Selesh. Of the strange cavern they had found, she said nothing. Not a word was spoken about visions, the alteration of her Staff and no detail was spent on their stay in Caranchar.

Out of care for the men, Ikella described the simple rites that had been performed for Arriera, saying simply that she had been laid to rest where she had born the child.

For a long moment, there was silence and they all pretended not to notice discreetly applied kerchiefs, or Somner's sniff of misery.

Here Mina took up the tale, describing for Patris the child's allergy to animal products. To the child's near death experience, she made no reference, earning herself a nod of approval from her Sorceress, who sat listening intently. Patris took it all in, but looked heartsick and sad when she eventually finished her tale

"What will become of her child now?" he asked pensively and Ikella said, swiftly and decisively, "If any of his family survives, they should have answered to my Spell by now.".

She drew in a long quivering breath, "A decision must be made. Now, before Conclave, before Jentaroth.".

"I will claim Daro's sand rights before the Clan at Jentaroth.", she said clearly.

"I found his mother dying in child birth. I hold his life to be mine. Our law says that I must rear him if no-one else claims him. Does anyone here claim his sand rights for him?".

She paused, looking about her, "Do you have anything to say against that idea Patris?".

The large man shook his head, "No Lady. You can give him far more than I, for he is born in your Sands. I have no wife to mother him, I am not of his caste. If the Clan Jhirelle acknowledged him, he would still be a fosterling and I would want a proper mother for him. No Lady, I must earn my keep, for my men depend on me. I would like to see him though, if you will permit?".

There was a slight bustle as orders were given and during a natural break in the proceedings, Patris who seemed to be waking from a dream, murmured to Mina.

"I have been quite mad with my sorrow for a girl I didn't know a ninenight, quite mad. I would have served her to the end of my days I think, if I had found her living.".

He said wonderingly and Mina lent forward, pressing his hand sympathetically.

"Not mad Patris, be assured that you are not mad, just in love. She must have been a very special person to have affected you so deeply.".

His company made small sympathetic murmurs, whilst they awaited the arrival of the child and soon afterwards Diras appeared, holding Daro to her shoulder.

She fell to one knee and presented him to the Sorceress. He was sucking a finger busily as Ikella reached for him. He came to her happily, snuggling his warm little body close to hers. For a moment, she allowed herself to feel his warmth and the love that suffused her for this tiny orphan, was there for all to see.

She turned Daro so that he faced Patris, who left his chair and knelt so that his face was level with the child's.

The Sorceress spoke simply, "This man who knew your mother, sought you out my son.", and the baby cooed at Patris happily, as Patris extended a huge finger to the child, who gazed unblinkingly at the trader.

"He has her eyes.", the big man whispered, a catch in his voice. Leaning over the child, he spoke softly in Darvish, the language of his mother's Sands. Raising his face to Ikella's, he smiled saying simply.

"I told him that I would ask you, if I can stay Lady? I am a trader born and bred. Selesh may have need of my skills in bartering for the food he needs. I have travelled far and wide, am welcomed in many markets. I trade in weavers threads, bolts of material, tools, leather and information from many sources. My men say they wish to remain in my service, whatever I choose. If you will permit it, I wish to remain here, so that I can see the baby grow, perhaps put my sorrow from me?".

Ikella nodded, grateful for this solution to the problem and so it was decided that Patris could embark on free trade in the Opal desert, returning to Selesh with goods and produce as he found them, transporting passengers and patients as required and keeping a watchful eye on Daro as he wished. They talked for a little more about living quarters and work for his men and to Ikella's delight Ivinish offered to open up the disused covered pasture, take care of visiting beasts and run a market in the village for herders to bring in their young animals for sale.

They parted company and it was a relieved and happy Sorceress that carried Daro now sleeping back to the nursery, handing him to Nadra with a smile of relief. The welter of emotions that she had experienced left her exhausted and it was well into the sleep period after height of sun when she finally left Carolus and Diras with Nadra and returned to her rooms. She was grateful for the drowsy peace that filled that space and slept a little, in preparation for the evenings of High Ceremony to come in the next ninenight.

In her dreams great amber eyes were fixed on her face, there were no words, just a warm feeling of gratitude, of peace. In her pocket the child's heartstone pulsed gently and in the nursery, strung on a cord two crystal apples danced and spun, creating little scatterings of light on the face of the sleeping child.

Chapter 3 – Premonition

When Ikella woke to the echo of a recurrent dream, she was shocked to discover that the entire afternoon had gone. Rising swiftly, she realised that by now, preparations must be well underway for the Rites of Succession. The immense Hall of the Healers was already prepared to welcome her Sisters in Sorcery and she had no doubt, that despite the ravages of the Storm, large contingents of visitors would make their presence felt.

With the organisation falling to the new High Council, she had watched as their Master Builder and Mina, (Senior Healer) were thrown together, as ritual preparations were made. All nine symbols of power were displayed in order of precedence. Seating was set out, and rooms had been allocated for local dignitaries . She washed briskly, thinking all the while about the forthcoming ceremonies. Space had been found in the Syndarial for new robes, somehow, the Hall of Welcome was fully supplied. Her Clansmen had taken over the preparation of a tented village outside the Gate in the Rock and Carolus and Satra had announced that sufficient produce had arrived for the five-day festival.

Her worst problem lay in gathering her Sisters in Sorcery to Conclave. As she approached that task, the immensity of it caused her eyes to darken, her face to pinch with anxiety, as she sat staring into her looking glass, before summoning Trinet. She indulged Trinet's love of face paint infrequently, but the reflection in her mirror, told her that she looked pale and drawn. Unable to use her habitual glamour of magical illusion whilst working with the High Magic by which she intended to gather her Sisters in Sorcery, she relented and Trinet picked up her face paints glancing at her Sorceress quizzically. Unaware of this scrutiny, Ikella sat on a tall backless stool, gazing intently into the mirror and reluctantly permitted her attendant to redden her lips.

Trinet was using coramin, a salve created from crushed skythe, combined with essential oils from the Carnelian Sands. Absently, Ikella noted that the pot was nearly empty and the desperate plight of her people became clear, as she reviewed the produce and medications that they could be deprived of, if even a quarter of their own trade routes were blocked. Again she felt a trickle of apprehension. Somewhere a door banged and she flinched. From elsewhere, she heard the steady tramp of passing feet as her guard mustered. Her eyes met her own in the mirror and she bit her lip, quivering as she controlled an impulse to run.

With Sanctuary gone, it was inevitable that all eyes would turn to Selesh for help, for advice. Since the time of her revered ancestor, Adaria te Syrene, Selesh had been known as the Mother of the Sands. Now, it was essential that Selesh should remain in contact with the other eight Deserts.

It had taken hundreds of lifetimes to create the routes that connected the Sands, making it possible for the differing Clans to coexist in peaceful harmony. She found herself shivering apprehensively, for she knew that there had been a long history of conflict between the Sands before unity had come. She realised that even she only knew the half of it and that history had a habit of repeating itself. With that thought came a memory of Jocasta, telling her to be careful of what she investigated, once she came into her powers at Selesh, and she found it hard to shrug off a feeling of impending doom.

However, she understood that if nothing else, the members of the Council of Nine had to be returned to their homesands, families and lives. The very thought of their departure, planned to take place when their Sorceress returned home, made her scowl, for she would miss them, but catching the look of anxiety in Trinet's eyes, she smiled at her reassuringly. However, her mind skittered on, refusing to acknowledge that this premonition was linked to her intended use of Jocasta's Door.

Now, however reluctantly, she forced her mind to face her presentiments head-on and realised that she couldn't deal with this alone.

Somehow, her Sisters in Sorcery had to be conveyed to Selesh before Conclave and the only practical method of managing such a feat, was to take her Sisters in Sorcery, through a process, that she had only recently discovered.

Of late she had woken in the night, her heart racing, the sound of marching feet in her ears. Since she had first travelled through the glass to the grazing land just outside the Gate in the Rock, she had even experienced waking dreams, in which she heard the tramp of many feet marching through the corridors of Selesh. Several times she had woken in panic, with a litany of terror running through her mind.

"Invasion. Jocasta's Door makes Selesh vulnerable to invasion.".

With that very thought bringing a dew of swept to her forehead, she realised that she would have to find a strategy to counter this problem. As Trinet continued with her preparations, emphasising her eyebrows, dusting her cheeks, she considered the use of Jocasta's hand glass.

Using this, the ancient Guardian of Sanctuary had viewed the entire planet from a distance and totally unaware of her scrutiny, many potential leaders had been selected, amongst which it was entirely possible to include herself. She had no way of knowing whether Jocasta had been able to activate the "Travelling Glass". Considering this, she began to wonder whether the artefact, that had manifested itself in her Council Chamber, was not the one and the same thing.

"Of course! It must be in some way connected to the Sanctuary Chest!.", She shifted restlessly under Trinet's hand as she realised this.

"Had it not been the repositioning of the Chest, that had provoked the appearance of the innocent looking glass, that was no glass?".

She sighed and submitted to having her hair redressed, without enthusiasm, but felt better when clad in simple day dress, she could regain the privacy of her study and think in peace.

She pondered her course of action, pacing backward and forward to no avail. Even Nadra, bringing Daro to see her, failed to raise her spirits, though she freely admitted to a great feeling of relief now that Daro's future was settled.

She still had a frown creasing her forehead, when Beneva arrived, to coach her through the final steps of the ceremonial in which she was to play centre part.

"Whatever's the matter Ikella?", the sole survivor of Sanctuary exclaimed. "I thought to find you in high spirits. The High Council say everything is proceeding well. The Hall of Welcome is open, Mina and Errish are already receiving guests. Whatever ails you my dear? Will you not share your worries with me?".

Her words finally penetrated, for Ikella looked up smiling faintly, "I have been guilty of a great oversight Beneva.", the Sorceress of the Opal Sands said slowly, "I was contemplating the use of Jocasta's Door to gather our Sisters. Now, I find myself frozen with trepidation.".

She caught the long slow glance at Beneva ran over her before continuing, (voice and diction sharper with the intensity of fear).

"If this is not a premonition, I don't know what is, but I suddenly awoke and I heard, well, it sounds stupid now I come to think of it...", her voice trailed away miserably and Beneva was forced to encourage her, until she eventually whispered.

"I hear the tramp of many marching feet!". She continued hurriedly, "All I can think of is, "Invasion!". The word simply won't leave my mind. I don't know whose voice I hear, it could even be my own, but it is there, waking and sleeping!".

Beneva sat very still and Ikella realised that every sinew in her friend's body was taut, her eyes closed as though she was listening to something from a long way away. The last living Guardian of Sanctuary, drew a long ragged breath and spoke, her voice emphasising her own concern.

"Then Seris Ikella, I suggest that we do something to protect ourselves. Undoubtedly, this is a warning! I half expected to receive something similar myself, but it seems you have been signally honoured. I suspect that the voice you hear is none other than Adaria's. We Guardians have heard it in times of great danger. It is for that reason that I yet survive!".

Her wide grey eyes met Ikella's with a distinct warning not to probe too far, or too soon. Then she turned away, picking up and straightening a loose pillow before she asked somewhat mischievously, "May I use this room to commit an act of benign conspiracy?".

With great relief, Ikella saw that although the Guardian's face was sober, her eyes danced with laughter and something in her relaxed, as Beneva began to explain.

Chapter 4 - Benign Conspiracy.

Beneva continued, "While we discuss Sanctuary business, I'll enforce absolute privacy.", Turning to face the door, she made a slow, descending gesture with both hands and a faint glow emanated from the latch, followed by a swift flash of light which traced the edge of the architrave. The door appeared to shimmer, as if seen through a heat haze and Ikella felt a disconcerting sensation in her ears and caught herself thinking, "So much for Guardians, not actively practising magic!".

However, she didn't doubt that anyone seeking them, would be dissuaded from knocking, or, might even assume that the room was empty. Returning to her chair, the Guardian instructed, "Proceed!"

Ikella, mindful of the short time in which to examine her premonition, or find a solution to her problem, spoke rapidly.

"Beneva, I am convinced, for reasons of security, that the existence of Jocasta's Door, must remain a secret. Since we knew of it, I have been troubled, waking and sleeping with a single thought of invasion and am persuaded that I must seek your help.", Struggling to convey the depths of her anxiety, she caught hold of Beneva's hand, in total breach of protocol and as they touched, a clarion call rang out nearby. Silenced by dread, they clung to each other, listening to the strange sounds around them. Another brassy summons, a clash of arms and the resounding thud of marching feet echoed round the room. Hardly daring to breathe as an uneasy silence fell, they stole hand in hand, to peer from the window overlooking the Gathering Square, where normal activities prevailed. Trying to gather their thoughts against the outlandish beat of war drums, Ikella hissed and abruptly disengaged her hand from Beneva's. Normality resumed and as their alarm evaporated, they sat, contemplating this oddly shared experience.

Beneva looked at her pupil enquiringly.

"Is that what you've been subjected to Ikella? For the sake of the One! Why didn't you confide in me sooner?".

The Guardian, palely imperious in the traditional silver robes that marked her out amongst the Opal Order, stood staring out of the small deep set window at the increasing traffic in the Gathering Square. Then she prowled soft footed, to the door, where she paused listening. Raising a silencing forefinger to her lips, she conjured a palely flickering window, through solid iron-bound Torrenwood, revealing Ikella's faithful guards stoically stationed, backs to the door. Returning to her chair, she sounded puzzled, as she said, "I see no reason for you to reveal the existence of Jocasta's Door.", and flinched at Ikella's sarcastic chuckle.

"Oh Beneva! You are so embedded in study, you seem to have lost the thread of reality! How can I use it to Gather my Sister's in Sorcery without proclaiming its existence?" as another thought struck her, she whispered the codicil, "Worse still, demonstrating that I can use the door, might see charges of excessive ambition levelled at my head.", she leant forward, eyes glittering as she exclaimed, "These premonitions have become so powerful, I fear to use it altogether. Yet, as I must, tell me how can I render my Sisters unconscious of the means by which they travel?".

Beneva rose, pacing backwards and forwards, until she said thoughtfully.

"This is not an insurmountable problem, but I am disturbed by your lack of trust in your Sisters!" Her gentle voice took on a note of censure as she came to a momentary stop in front of the Sorceress and Ikella looked up. Never a tall woman, Beneva nevertheless bore herself with the dignity of her high rank. Now, arms folded across her bosom, head bowed, footsteps eerily silent, she wove her considering way between the window embrasure and the door, covering their problem from every angle. Coming to a halt again, Beneva demanded.

"What is your argument for not revealing the existence of Jocasta's Door?"

Ikella, feeling as if she was back in the classroom, replied.

"Because Seris Jocasta neither revealed or concealed it, I should, at least for the time being follow that lead, lacking as I do her wisdom and experience in matters of High Magic. My experience is in Healing and the One only knows that my skill in that is needed to keep the Union of the Sands alive. The Ways change my Beneva and we must prepare to change with them!" Beneva nodded quietly, taking a seat on a nearby stool, as Ikella spoke pensively.

"Again, there may be some objection to my remaining Sorceress, whilst taking up the reins of Guardianship. I don't expect a universal vote of confidence!".

Beneva nodded saying acidly, "I was not aware that the position of Guardian was achieved through election!", to which Ikella had no reply. Eventually Beneva said solemnly, "Now that we stand alone, we must prepare a new Way. I know I have to re-establish a new Sanctuary, here in the heart of Selesh. I must seek out a Guardian of Power and then, only then can we function as we did before.".

Astounded, Ikella stared at the older woman , blankly, then Beneva smiled and said briskly, "So it begins.", Around her wrists there was a silvery glow and startled, Ikella lifted her hands, feeling in her wrists a warmth, similar to what she had felt, when Beneva clasped her hand earlier.

The room seemed suddenly lighter. As she stood and joined Beneva, who reached out and took both Ikella's hands in hers. Between them, suddenly was a surge of multi coloured fire and Beneva lowered her head, closed her eyes and whispered, "A Catha moi, noiye doushen, noiye solishen, noiye lepsos.".

As the last words left her mouth, there was a soft shivering note, like some great deep throated bell and a profound silence fell. In the well of peace that enfolded them, Ikella's memory took her back to the Ceremonial Hall of Sanctuary, the sand-glass that dominated the day of those committed to its service. She lifted her head recognising this profound silence for some magical state and her eyes questioned Beneva. The Guardian of Knowledge, raised a hand as Ikella moistened her lips, preparing to launch a barrage of anxious questions.

"Not now, not here, my Sister!" The Guardian cautioned her, "I have not stopped time, just to have a cosy gossip! We must go to work.", she began.

"For the last eight Rotations, I have been permitted to research objects, scrolls, diaries, notes and recipes found by Carolus on his travels, after his own studies of these artefacts revealed an ancient threat to our very existence.".

Ignoring Ikella's hiss of protest, the Guardian quoted from Adaria's Rule.

"To assume proprietary rights to any field of endeavour is to step aside from the Way.", Blushing furiously, Ikella murmured, "I am so used to him being an Apothecary for our Healers, that I quite forget his other function, but why, in the face of natural selection, did they pick a man?", Beneva grinned wryly and suggested in a sly voice, "Because he could hardly seek to control any of the secrets he retrieved?" and Ikella faced with the breathtaking scope of the suspicions rife in Sanctuary, remained very quiet. Beneva said thoughtfully, "As a Guardian, you may have to entertain suspicion in a manner that quite goes against the grain of your Order and Calling. It is hard enough when it is all you have to concentrate on, but for you in your dual capacity it will be harder.", that said, she returned to the topic saying in a carefully neutral voice, "There is no threat from those already sworn to the Staff.", She paused for a second to permit Ikella to respond, but when she didn't, the Guardian returned rather grimly, to her discourse.

"Where the danger lies, is in the group yet to be raised to power. I pray most sincerely that they have not come under negative influence since they returned to complete their induction. As you know yourself, having your elect in place, is no guarantee that she is ready to be called to the Staff.".

Ikella blushed, acutely aware that she had not welcomed Shiarjha until recently. They stared at each other, understanding at last, that the danger lay, not only in whatever triggered the premonition, but in voicing their suspicions.

Eventually, Ikella raised her head and regarding Beneva soberly, asked, "How much worse would it be my Beneva, if we don't take precautions? We must begin in the same manner employed by Jocasta. Anyway, can I gather our Sisters using Jocasta's Door, or not? If not, you'd better have a good back-plan!", she set her jaw belligerently and Beneva chuckled.

"Perhaps I should show you my solution.", she smiled mischievously, as she dragged from her pocket an Apothecaries twist, made of some dark coarse leaf, saying, "This, I think, should suffice my dear.", She untwisted the wrap, extending her hand to Ikella, who looked at the particularly nauseating green crystals within, grimacing as she asked, "What is it? Plant extract? Mineral salt? Other?", wetting a finger to pick up a single crystal.

Beneva said quietly, "It is a plant based compound, which has gone out of use. Carolus found a recipe which told of Healers using it to induce sleep of a type that permitted bone-setters to work on a sleeping patient, but it is tricky to handle. Generating these crystals, by straining the result through a mineral filter resulted in a more stable compound which has other properties, which we Guardians are trained to use.".

Ignoring the scathing glance that Ikella threw at her, Beneva sat back to see what she would make of the crystals. Bringing her hand to eye-level, Ikella began the required examination. The colour was vividly unnatural, so she proceeded to smell, half expecting something unpleasant, but there was no scent discernible. She was about to taste it, using just the tip of her tongue, when Beneva placed a restraining hand on hers, halting her instantly. As she raised a quizzical eyebrow, the Guardian said dryly.

"Unless you wish to sleep through your own Rite of succession, I should desist immediately!".

Ikella, curiosity thoroughly aroused, swiftly returned the crystal to its wrapper demanding, "How is it used?".

Carefully folding the wrap, Beneva answered her question, voice throbbing with power.

"Exodias. Exodias mi ento!". ("Remember! Remember the Searching.")

Obediently, the Sorceress remembered. Without effort or conscious control, her thoughts turned back, until she was a child again, travelling around the Irix herders with her family, buying animals to trade. She recalled the progression of events that led her to Selesh, the Irix buck who no-one could heal, her father's desperation and that first long night of Healing, a child of eight Rotations, stroking and singing the stricken animal from the brink of death. From the wisdom of her many Rotations, she reviewed her father's pride, her mother's increasing anxiety, the inevitable decision. They made the journey to Selesh and the annual celebration of Jentaroth in her tenth Rotation, embracing the concept of separation with obvious relief.

The Rotations streamed past as she recollected classes spent in looking, touching, tasting substances gathered from all Nine Sands of Pelshar. Surrounded by sixty giggling girls, she felt more isolated than ever before, her "difference", estranging her from her companions. With no friends to confide in, she went alone to the special test, that would set her apart from those she treasured for the rest of her life.

As she journeyed in memory, far from the luxury that surrounded her, Ikella almost felt the rough surface of the wall she trailed her hand along, following Dessidera, then Senior Healer of Selesh. She remembered the woman's rough sympathy, recalled the sound of her voice saying briskly, "Come along child, if you would but hurry, this would soon be over. The sorceress won't eat you, she is a good and kindly woman who only wants to know if your voice, that is, your *othervoice* matches your undoubted ability with herbs and medication.".

Almost one hundred and twenty Rotations later, Ikella could feel the compassion in Dessidera's voice and understood that everyone other than herself had known how special she was, how lonely and secluded her life would be.

She would never forget Selection, the feeling of achievement, the joy of knowing that the things that interested her were not unusual, that she would have friends who thought as she did. That of course, was before Sashandra tested her *othervoice*. Her memories accelerated, taking her past the ceremonial acceptance of the Healers, the lights hanging over the Sacred Circle and the faces of the Council as she made her curtsy to her Sorceress. Her body trembling, Sashandra drawing her gently away into the Cavern of the Singers. She saw again events long past, Sashandra, small, a delicate woman of limitless power and she grew restless, filled with a kind of poignancy for those times when she had known to a heartbeat what each day contained.

"Remember 'Kella.", a familiar voice whispered in her mind,. "Remember.", and she was there.

Taking that first breath, she launched her *othervoice*, thinking only of the Opal surmounting the Staff of Selesh. Peering into the depths of the stone, she modulated the note until the Opal began to resonate and the Source opened to her. One part of her knew that she stood in that secret shielded room, her eyes focused on the Staff. The other, knew nothing, but that she was magnetised, flooded with warmth and filled with indescribable joy. Somewhere a contralto voice Sang, then, the Opal of Sashandra Staff fluoresced. The brilliance of it took her breath away, she was mesmerised, a deep pulse engulfing her, hands and body cloaked in Opal as she basked in the light of the Source. Then it was over. Caught close in the most sisterly of hugs, Sashandra's gentle hand laid on her forehead in blessing and then, there was, Beneva!

Ikella came to herself and remembered. The Guardian entering the secret chamber, Sashandra and Beneva conferring, a crystal flask, a shimmering glass, then...

"You must be very thirsty!" Sashandra had commented and for a moment Beneva's hand had hovered over the glass before she passed it to Ikella. She remembered drinking thirstily and then nothing, until she woke at Sanctuary.

Ikella was jerked back to her present and found herself demanding, "But how did I travel? Was it through Jocasta's Door?".

The Guardian blinked, but smiling said, "No my dear, we had to wait for you to discover that particular aspect of its use! You travelled sleeping on the shoulder of a Nishan warrior and you never stirred, until three days after we arrived back at Sanctuary!"

Ikella eyed her askance and muttered to herself.

"Powerful stuff!" and Beneva nodded cheerfully.

"Sashen is a very powerful compound, but it is dangerously unpredictable. We believe that the original plant has been altered in some way, since our forebears used it in the outlawed practise of body cutting.", Ikella wracked her brain and then said in a horrified voice, "Healers used to invade their patients bodies?" and Beneva continued quietly, "Oh yes. They had the understanding of many techniques then, but they were not dependent on wild plants either. We grew medicinal plants and made compounds under special conditions. The Greeyeyn provided the technology, the Felmin the plants and the Clans the Healers that could use them.", and before Ikella could denounce this rank heresy, Beneva continued.

"Now only we have the secret of the process and a safe supply of both plants and filtering mechanisms. Sashen has become too unpredictable to use in what was once known as "surgery", so we have abandoned the process and have lost that thread in the weave of our world.", Ikella frowning deeply said, "why have I never remembered this before?" and Beneva smiled.

"Possibly because we Guardians, didn't wish you to do so!". She suggested slyly and Ikella's brow creased with sudden tension.

"Are you telling me that Sashen is a hypnotic?" She demanded in outrage!

"Beneva! The use of hypnotics was outlawed in Adaria's time. How can the Guardians rule on one thing and do another?", she queried looking directly at Beneva, who said in a matter-of-fact tone.

"Very easily my dear. Wild Sashen is dangerous. Thankfully it does not occur in the open and only a few of us know how to distil it. I am practiced in its use, which is just as well, a little too much can cause nightmares from which no sane man has ever returned and yes!" She held up a hand to silence Ikella, "It can be used on men or women, young or old. It has been used safely for many Rotations by bone-setters for example, but only at the last resort, only in the right hands and only if Carolus has distilled it.".

Ikella wrinkled her brow as she replied doubtfully.

"Does it always take so long to wear off?" and Beneva shook her head, "There is more than one way to confuse a Myst-cat my dear! Sashen's hypnotic properties can be used to promote what I call walking sleep. In this state, subjects can be induced to perform actions that they don't remember afterwards. Prior to rousing them, I can plant in their minds a command which, when activated, can bring back total recall of the event. I can even plant a false memory, say of a journey in the mind of someone and I, subject to your agreement, plan to use that to protect Jocasta's Door. "

Her tone was solemn as she added, "Sashen is a powerful tool in the right hands, removing pain and fear from the minds of patients. However, I am certain that even our use of it should be limited. Although tonight we use it for a different purpose, by even this benign conspiracy, we step from Adaria's Way! I would prefer to seek the source of our alarm and neutralise it, but tonight Sashen is my solution.".

Ikella exhaled in relief, "I am in agreement with you.", she murmured and Beneva lifted her hands, clapping them softly, as something around them, undid.

Just before the bustling sounds of a busy day came to her ears, it seemed to Ikella that somewhere in the far distance she heard the tolling of a bell. For a moment, they eyed each other, Guardian and Guardian elect and Beneva raised an arm in blessing, softly intoning, "Deis moyus adreo! In faith this is completed!" and the day moved inexorably on towards the evening, towards the Gathering in of the Sisters of Sorcery.

Chapter 5 - The Gathering Begins.

As that extraordinary afternoon progressed, Ikella became convinced that far from stopping time, Beneva had speeded it up. Emerging from her study to the guard's consternation, they parted company. Beneva to the Djellim to rehearse the rituals, Ikella, returning to receive last minute reports before Sundown. Feeling oddly detached, Ikella had the strangest impression that she was just part of the pattern that was Selesh and caught herself thinking, "If I vanished into thin air, this would still go on without me!", as she settled to business. She was still struggling with a sense of impending doom as she accompanied the last Council member to the door and went to change her clothes.

When Beneva returned, emerging into Ikella's study from the secret passageways that riddled Selesh, Ikella was dressing to go Gathering. As Beneva opened a panel in Ikella's study, the Sorceress felt the discreet tingling in her wrists that announced the presence of the Guardian and called softly, "I'm in my robing room Beneva.".

Finding Ikella poised on one foot, the Guardian observed her elaborate costume sourly, as the Sorceress turned to meet her gaze. She wore an Opalweave tunic over loose pants, casually topped with a sumptuous over robe.

"That's too gorgeous to travel in!", Beneva stated, but Ikella smiled serenely and continued to dress, as she spoke.

"I know! It is one of my favourites and has rather special properties. I won't be a moment, then I can show you". She was bent over, tucking lacings into the soft bleached Irix hide of her boots, while Beneva cast a wary eye, over the hooded cloak that glimmered like a living Opal from its hanger nearby. Ikella, voice muffled as she bent over her travel pack said, "I wish Trinet had heard that!".

The Sorceress spoke appreciatively. "She made all the new robes you know, but I sent her to summon Jashell and Indeera. Shall I show you, why I particularly like this weave?".

She glanced at the Guardian's pursed lips, explaining hurriedly, "It restores my confidence, it never seems to get dirty and I can change my appearance at will.", and proceeded to demonstrate as Beneva circled her.

Visualising the simple, drab garb of a roving Healer, Ikella overwrote the shimmering garments, with that dull illusion as she flung her cloak around her, transforming it into the rough homespun of a winter traveller and Beneva, clad in something remarkably similar, gave her rueful approbation.

"Yes, you can certainly project the image of one who has been travelling for ninenights.", The Guardian remarked, "The smell seems authentic too!". The Sorceress, slid a familiar hand-mirror into her pack and refused to be abashed, walking into her day room with the Guardian in tow.

They found Jashell and Indeera waiting, shrouded in the dark uniform of the Night Watch, veiled and hooded, calm and inscrutable. Looking at their spears thoughtfully, Ikella held out an empowered hand for her Staff. As it materialised, to Trinet's dismay, it changed shape, taking on the aspect of an ordinary walking Staff. The shaft shorter, thicker, the delicate wings along with the Opal power-stone absorbed into the head. Trinet scowled, turning troubled eyes to her mistress, as Ikella commanded, "Trinet, I don't want my absence advertised, during which Somishen Shiarjha holds the Staff, while we Gather our Sisters in Sorcery. They and their attendants will be exhausted and will need no gossiping tongues around them, so I rely on your normal discretion. Although, I welcome reports on anything unusual, all information is for my ears only, you understand.".

The woman dipped an obedient curtsey as Jashell assumed responsibility for the Sorceress, followed by Indeera, who slung a spare flask across her body, leaving her hands free to protect the Guardian. With no more ceremony, they passed out, through the Gate in the Rock and into the Opal Desert beyond, turning before the village, to take a little-used track towards Torrenesh.

The path twisted and turned, overshadowed by the twin pinnacles of Emblem Rock, an immense outcrop, which soared into the Sundown sky. In its shadow, Ikella conjured the flicker of handfire, commanding her small contingent to gather around her and in the unnatural light that lent the hollows and peaks of their Sands, a distinctly sinister aspect, they drew close and seemed glad to do so.

"Jashell, Indeera.", The Sorceress called them forward and somehow it didn't seem unusual to any of them that the Inesh found themselves facing two magic users, whose clothes now pronounced them both to be Guardians of Sanctuary. Ikella felt the shift as Beneva willed it, but Maintained her poise as the Inesh knelt before her. They remained totally impassive, no hint of curiosity in their gaze and once again Ikella felt marginally unnerved by the thought that, somehow, her faithful guards were aware of far more than she was.

She drew a deep breath and in her hand the unusual wooden staff she carried transformed back into its usual shape, the Opal at its head casting only a subdued light over the group. Before she could speak however, Beneva stepped forward, the insignia at her wrists glimmering and a subtle glow outlining her body. The Guardian's voice was low, vehement and the very air about them tingled as she spoke.

"What I tell you now, Jashell of the old path and Indeera of the true faith, remains under the Seal of Sanctuary.", she intoned solemnly.

"I have come to Selesh, not to end my days in the memory of Sanctuary and all it stood for, but to assist at its rebirth, here in Selesh.", - at which momentous announcement, neither Jashell or Indeera even glanced at each other. Beneva continued huskily, "The Ways of all true believers change forever tonight and it is your destiny to protect Selesh and our Sisters who have yet to hear about that change. In your strength and honour we trust, but your silence must be bound by oath, taken under the Seal of Sanctuary. Will you so swear?".

Both knelt before her willingly and spoke solemnly, wide-eyed with wonder as the great Seal of Sanctuary, seen by so few in life, suddenly blazed from the sheltering cradle of the Guardian's hands.

"We do so swear, on the lives of our Clan, that our eyes, ears and tongues be sealed in the service of both Selesh and Sanctuary!".

Over the bowed heads of the Inesh women, Ikella's eyes met those of Beneva and then the Sorceress took her travel pouch, extracting Jocasta's hand glass and cast a reflection, using the dimmed light of the desert evening, as she drew strength from the Source. As her aura encompassed the group in a circle of light, she summoned Jocasta's Door , saying softly

"Arish solishen, open our way!" and once more she stood before the misted frame, commanding, "Hannan's Valley.", Ignoring the hiss of surprise from her guards, as the "Door" was revealed, she guided them through from the dim shimmer of the Opal Sands, to the pitch black of the Onyx Desert, re-disguising her winged Staff and their clothing as she did so.

As soon as she set foot upon the midnight Sands, Ikella turned to her companions. If she expected to see any fear or bewilderment in her guard, she was to be disappointed. Jashell acted as observer, while Indeera quartered the shadowy arena in which they had arrived, spears at the ready.

As she stepped through the portal, Beneva herself looked more worried, but a swift glance around put her mind at rest, for, as Ikella had planned, they had arrived close to Hannan, home settlement of the Onyx Desert. However, just as they had left Selesh, they were in the shadows of a small cliff and unlikely to have been seen arriving by any chance observer.

As if she had been doing so all her life, Ikella closed down the visible image of Jocasta's Door. It simply winked out of existence at a gesture of her hand. Almost in the same movement, she stowed the small hand glass back into her travelling pouch and straightening, surveyed their surroundings. Having journeyed here many Rotations ago, to attend Nahamida's accession, she remembered this place because of the strange disposition of the rocks which looked like the teeth of some snarling beast. Huge soaring formations in obsidian, provided curving "canines", which lay at bay, half buried in the rippling black Sands of the Onyx.

Relieved that she had unerringly brought her small contingent through the portal, she carefully examined the cliffs soaring above them. If only her personal knowledge of the trail to Hannan was as good, she mused, watching her guards casting about for visible signs that would lead them on to the trail.

Jashell came to stand at her side, shaking her head as she relayed their lack of success.

"Lady, there are no way marks I can understand and this sand is too fine to hold a print for long! Can you help us?".

Ikella, ever reluctant to use small magic on othersands, frowned, but the two Inesh women waited quietly whilst Ikella and Beneva conferred.

Beneva murmured quietly to the Sorceress for a moment, then, carefully pitching their voices together in a rolling weave, the magic users sang a long low note. For a moment nothing happened, then the sand beneath their feet began to glow. As luminous footprints appeared, Jashell and Indeera scouted ahead of Beneva and Ikella, who strode forward, still singing, following the direction in which the footprints led them.

As they moved more certainly onto what was plainly a well-trodden path, Ikella looked around her curiously.

It was very much warmer here, so she watched where they walked, being aware of active tar-pits in this area. The unusual tinge in the sky was more noticeable against the black rocks and charcoal Sands of the Onyx. The clouds rolled, sullen purple slashed with magenta. This was a land of melodramatic contrasts, oddly beautiful, yet full of hidden dangers. With a sudden feeling of isolation from all she held dear, Ikella shivered.

They had walked into a narrow canyon. Soaring cliffs cut off the view to the right of them, but to the left, hewn out of the natural basalt wall, was a desultory range of buildings behind doors of solid smithwork. An immense archway came into view bridging the canyon walls. Shortly thereafter, they saw The Gates of Hannan. Set into a towering cliff face, which sealed the end of the canyon, they rose fully forty spans high, even Beneva was awed into silence. With a gesture, Ikella turned into the shadows for a brief moment. Glancing around to make sure that they were unobserved, the Sorceress threw back the hood of her cloak, exposing her great mane of silver hair and her pale skin, so luminous in these dark surroundings. She glowed before them, gesturing to Beneva to do the same and as she did so, Ikella dropped the image she had imposed upon herself and stood revealed as no ordinary traveller. Her hands flickered in a gesture and the Staff of Selesh blazed momentarily as it transformed back to its usual shape, wings fluttering as though protesting their short metamorphosis.

Soon Jashell was running ahead of the party, crying out as she did so, "Ho the gate! Ho the gatekeepers of Hannan! Let the light within shine upon the daughter of the Opal, first among mages, Ikella, Sorceress of the Opal Desert, Warden of the Winds and ruler of the Nine lands.".

There was the sound of confusion from within, but soon the great gates were being heaved open by a party of six men, straining to haul on immense ropes. Each harnessed to the other, they came stumbling into the sands as they did so and Ikella saw with a sense of shock that they were all to a man, blind.

"So the Storm plague has struck here as well!".

She acknowledged silently and almost as if she had spoken aloud, Beneva nodded her agreement, continuing in the same vein.

"Hanna has an interesting theory about Storm plague.", she muttered under her breath and the Sorceress made a mental note to get Hanna to explain her ideas on her return to Selesh. As they entered Hannan, Ikella became aware that Beneva's robe had taken on the dull, silver glow that made the Guardians stand out against any background. Jashell and Indeera, close to their heels, padded along in the sinuous flowing manner of their kind, spears held upright in unforgiving hands.

To the right and left of her, huge Kora-Mai men stood with arms folded across their chests. These ceremonial guards were clearly sighted and Ikella felt her spirits lift as she took in the number of men who had not succumbed to the blinding plague.

As she progressed down an impressive walkway into Hannan proper, she was overwhelmed with the lavish decoration, the painted walls, carved statues and plants. Everywhere she looked there were plants and she had difficulty in concentrating on anything else. They were in full bloom, every one healthy and fresh and yet here they were growing inside a massive cavern complex where no sunlight had ever penetrated. Hanging above the plants however, were unusual smithworked glows that burned with a steady, white light far superior to anything Selesh had. She made another mental note to find out more about these and Beneva nodded!

Everything here seemed larger than life. The Kora-Mai were tall people, some of them exceeding seven spans in height, but she had not realised that they were seemingly built on a totally different scale. Amongst them she realised she must appear small and insignificant, however, they bowed respectfully as she passed and, despite feeling dwarfed, she began to relax.

They turned into an immense cavern, inside of which a regular city had been built. Huge, public buildings had been constructed on terraces - tier upon tier climbed dizzily above her. A wide avenue supporting a cluster of houses clung around the base of an enormous building in front of which a crowd was forming and she realised that she was being escorted towards the Sorceress's palace and Hannan's Gathering Square.

Ikella marvelled, this was certainly new to her and she looked about at the spacious dwelling houses. She could see a number of people, drawn from every Clan or so it seemed, including (she noted with immense surprise) a sprinkling of Greeyeyn boys and some Felmin youths as well. They all seemed to be occupied and were apparently supervised by an adult. Assuming that they had an extremely active fostering system, she failed to see Beneva's compassionate glance at this group, nor the compressed lips, or the stiffening of the Guardian's neck. Ikella was mildly puzzled by the sheer number of fosterlings, but then everything here seemed so huge that it became difficult to relate to normality.

In the next moment, all of these thoughts fled to the echo of Beneva's voice sounding urgently in her ears.

"Ikella, Indeera, Jashell, we are about to be signally honoured in true Kora-Mai fashion! Stand still. Don't react I beg of you. Don't move, not a muscle!".

The warning was so abrupt, almost shouted, that Ikella could hardly believe that the Guardian's lips had not moved, but she caught the gently inclined heads of her guards and knew that they had heard it too, with relief.

As they entered the Great Gathering Square of Hannan, a number of Kora-Mai warriors sprang into action, running towards Ikella and Beneva, spears lifted to throw. These men, wearing little other than the fearsome trophies of ancient victories and elaborately applied body paint, threw themselves forward in a little rush that placed them centrally in front of Ikella's party. She swiftly put out a hand to each of her guards, steadying them, as the booming voices of the men echoed in the cavern, challenging the Sorceress and her escorts.

Nine men dressed in animal skins shook their fists and glared wild-eyed at Ikella. They were chanting hoarsely, almost growling out the words, as they performed a ritual, stamping dance, which left observers in no doubt that the visitors had been challenged. When the warriors paused, eyes and muscles bulging belligerently, Beneva placed a hand on Jashell's arm and Ikella and Indeera heard the warning, "Keep absolutely still!".

For a moment, the leader of the spear party turned his back on them, but almost immediately whirled to face them again. Grimacing hideously and bringing his spear up to the throw, balanced on his shoulder, he ran directly at Ikella.

At what seemed to be only two spans from her, he slid to his knees and grasping his spear in both hands, broke it against his forehead. Arms raised, he proffered the broken spear to the Sorceress, head bowed submissively. Struggling to remain serene and impassive, Ikella took the spear from the warrior, bringing the broken shaft to her own forehead before returning it.

Honour satisfied, the warriors slipped away, melting into the crowd.

The Sorceress, who had schooled her face to rigid impassiveness, was nearly undone when Jashell muttered under her breath scathingly, "Men are such fools!".

Just then, acting as a welcome distraction, from the crowd stepped a stately woman, dressed in flowing robes and wearing a veil. She bowed low before Ikella, extending her hands to them and then, wordlessly turning, she led them into the interior of the great palace building where the clan leader awaited her.

Thankfully the ceremonial stopped here, ahead of them in the corridor stood Nahamida herself, dressed simply in the long straight black robes of her people, her hair unadorned but elaborately braided and carrying a small travel pouch. She was accompanied by a Kora-Mai Healer, both women dressed simply for travel as Ikella had instructed and ready to leave immediately. Ikella accepted the ritual greetings of both women, who bowed low in deference to her companion, touching their foreheads almost to the ground as they did so and then she swiftly held up a hand to Nahamida.

"My dear Sister, forgive me I pray you". Ikella knew that given the opportunity to gossip, Nahamida, would command the conversation until the following Rotation.

"It is time to Gather.", she announced seriously. "The Way is long and treacherous. We will need all the help you can give me, to get back home to Selesh safely.".

Beneva smiled thinly, "What help does Ikella need to succeed in anything she wishes to do?", she thought cynically of the powers that she had witnessed for herself since her own arrival in Selesh. Piously, she bowed her head and intoned softly, "If the One wills our safe return, so must it be.", to which Nahamida was swift to respond in kind.

"Then let his will be worked.", as they departed.

In the gathering gloom, the party left the gateway of Hannan. Cloaked against the chill of the desert night, they walked into the sands. They walked closely together, talking in soft voices, the black sands beneath their feet glittering before returning to its normal opacity, as they passed on their way.

Soon they drew into the shelter of great soaring rocks and the dim light still left in what passed for day, was obscured by the height of the outcrop towering over them. Dwarfed in its shadow, they stopped and sat on the dark sand, as Beneva poured water into a travel cup, which was passed to Nahamida first, according to custom, returning to Beneva by way of Nahamida's companion and Ikella, who didn't drink. The guards ever observant watched, as first one then the other of the Onyx-sworn nodded gently to sleep, then Ikella stood and took from her travel pouch a small hand glass.

Using the mirror, she cast a reflective circle on the sand and empowered, called Jocasta's Door to her, while Beneva encouraged her dozing companions.

"Come Nahamida, come Sylina, I know you are both exhausted and hungry, but there is not too far to go now. See, we are near the path to Selesh, we must go on for it is very cold in the Opal at night.".

Slowly, sleepily, the Onyx-sworn rose and tottered wearily, guided by the guards, towards the Door. Cloaked in her aura, Ikella commanded, "Emblem Rock, Selesh!", as she stepped through.

She disappeared from view, followed immediately by one of her spear bearers. Yawning and staggering as if in the last stages of exhaustion, their Kora Mai visitors followed, then Beneva and the last guard.

For a moment, Jocasta's Door was left alone, then it flickered and disappeared as if it had never been. In the Onyx Sands, the wind moaned softly and the tracks of their passing vanished, until the dark Sands slept under sullen skies.

Chapter 6 - Jenta Rising.

When the travellers were sighted approaching the Gate in the Rock, they had abandoned their disguises. Flanked by Indeera and Jashell, Nahamida, followed by Syrena, managed the last few steps with grim determination. Mina had posted a look out and as Beneva and Ikella led them forward, it was clear that the Senior Healer's services would be welcomed as both the Kora-Mai visitors already suffering Sashen-induced exhaustion, shivered in the unaccustomed chill of the evening air. Ikella was relieved to see the welcoming committee forging their way towards them against the tide of pilgrims laying claim to their seats in the Hall of the Healers.

All around was hustle and bustle and for once Ikella was grateful to hear the stentorian tones of Jashell bellowing to clear the way in front of them, even though the sudden blaze of the Opal Staff had alerted pilgrims moments before the Guard's voice rang out.

"Ho there, make way for your Sorceress, Ikella de Syrene, most honoured lady of the Opal and her guest Nahamida, sister ruler of the Onyx Sands!".

As Indeera steadied Nahamida, who looked almost grey with weariness, Ikella was grateful to see Mina and her team close at hand. Smiling and bowing to the visiting Sorceress, Mina was anxious to remove their guests to the private rooms set aside for the Sisterhood.

"Nahamida, I can't remember the last time I saw you!".

The bubbly little Healer exclaimed, in so familiar a tone, she might have been addressing a younger sister, rather than the Sorceress of the Kora-Mai, first daughter of the Onyx Sands.

"My dear friend, you must have had a terrible journey! You look exhausted and you are so cold.", Mina continued consoling their guest. For a moment Ikella held her breath, wondering what Nahamida would say, but she caught Beneva's supremely confident glance and composed her own features, as Nahamida replied through chattering teeth.

"Oh Mina, it was a dreadful trek, so dark, so cold. We seem to have travelled without rest and I am so very, very hungry!".

Mina soothed her, determinedly steering the visitors into the peace of the guest wing.

"Just a little further dear friend and then there will be a warm brick, a soft bed and some small fancies to ease your hunger.".

Ikella, looked at the height and ample girth of the Kora-Mai and thought cynically.

"Small indeed.", as she saw trays of food being taken ahead of them by two Hall servitors.

In no time at all, warming blocks had been brought to thaw Nahamida's feet and hands and once the shivering had subsided their visitors visibly relaxed.

Nahamida rolled dark, expressive eyes at Mina and said in a wheedling, little girl voice.

"Mina, Mina of my heart, there is not the remotest chance of honey cake is there?".

Smiling, Mina fetched a bowl into which she had ladled the soft, brown, even-textured cake for which the Highlands of Trazorn, far to the west of the Opal Desert, was renowned. Poured over the cake was a liberal helping of honey cream and, with a soft sigh of anticipation, Nahamida drew her spoon from her belt and, with a blissful expression on her face, began to eat.

It was clear to Ikella that her presence was no longer needed, so she marshalled the Gathering party and slipped away discreetly.

They stopped only to gather another flask of water from a well-stocked bench in her study, placing the travel mug (considerably contaminated by Sashen) in the wash bucket for later attention. Taking up a clean travel mug, Ikella asked Beneva curiously.

"Have you enough Sashen?".

To this enquiry, her companion silently half-withdrew a cloth bag of a curious, brown hue from the capacious pocket of her cloak, indicating its full status, before returning it with no further comment.

The Gathering party, went back into the Sands and headed for Emblem Rock once more, Beneva and Ikella talking quietly.

"That went remarkably well don't you think?", Ikella said softly, "I am amazed by how you suggested such weariness, when plainly none of us had travelled any real distance on either side of the departure point. It was clever of you to suggest hunger to Nahamida, she is such a baby for sweet things!".

Beneva blushed, saying lightly, "It is nothing really, but it is a skill that I have had much time to develop and many reasons for doing so, I just wish that I could do as much without Sashen, but we magic-users are almost impervious to suggestibility, unlike others.".

The Guardian's face softened, recalling the numerous sleeping children that she had taken to Sanctuary for training, as she kept pace at Ikella's side. She continued enthusiastically. "You'd probably be good at it yourself my dear. It only takes the ability and the confidence to imagine what you want your subject to experience, including that subject in that event, not only in your own mind, but in theirs and the job is done!"

She paused saying thoughtfully, "You definitely have the confidence to use illusion, your clothing proclaims that fact, although I believe some trick of ancient weaving techniques advance the easy way you approach the matter. You have in a very short time, both understood and learned to use Jocasta's Door. Visualising your destination and taking us there as if you were born with the "command of glass" in your hand. Yes, many can use their imaginations, but no-one I know has quite your skill or power.".

Noting the ease in which the term "command of glass" came to Beneva's lips, Ikella's own suspicion that this ability had been foretold deepened, as the Guardian explained more.

"I simply think what I want the subject to feel, not in any great detail mind, just a general impression of completing their journey in the normal fashion. I thought of the empty villages and deserted settlements, the tracks half-buried. Remembering a physically exhausting journey in increasingly low temperatures for Nahamida and her handmaiden was not that hard.".

Ikella snorted derisively, "Handmaiden? Sylina? She is High Priestess of Hannan and no servant! Next to Alaylia, Nahamida's Elect, she is the most powerful woman in the Onyx! She is Nahamida's right hand, much as Mina is mine and has her ears and eyes in everything! However, let Nahamida think we don't know. It will be interesting to see what Inahana makes of it, when they meet.".

They were fast approaching Emblem Rock and the shadows on the undercliff were lengthening. Ikella drew them all into the encompassing circle of light cast from the hand glass and her own aura, complaining to Beneva momentarily, "Please try not to include hunger in your next illusion Beneva, we have enough troubles without running out of food.".

Then as Jocasta's Door appeared again, she added commandingly, "Shenamai Cavern, Malachite Sands!".

The mist within the "doorway", glimmered green, as the Sorceress and her companions stepped through, disappearing from view. A second later, the portal itself vanished and a chill wind touched the Opal Sands, erasing any trace of their passing.

Deschima, warrior Sorceress of the Gresshe, awaited them on the trail to Malos, chief settlement of the Malachite Sands. Lying to the far North East and sharing a long border with the Azure Sands, this trail was very familiar to Ikella, who encouraged her party to stride out now, anxious to lose no more time. Beneva, less certain of the way, was trying to keep up with the group when a cheerful greeting rang out from ahead of them.

"Ho Seleshani, greetings my Sisters.".

In the pearly green light that penetrated the mist that obscured the track, they saw a movement and the ever battle-clad Gresshe women, jogged into view and came to a grateful halt. A party of four, their Sorceress in the lead, followed closely by another wearing light, silver, smithworked armour. Their travel cloaks swinging from her shoulders, shimmering, blonde hair flowing in the breeze.

As the parties drew level, Deschima held up her hand and the group trotted to a halt, while salutes were exchanged and greetings given as tradition demanded. Ikella was less than delighted when, with her own guard dismissed, Deschima wanted to run the short distance to the Shenamai Caverns, through which their route passed. Yet, considering briefly how else she could persuade her guests to rest and take a drink, the solution evaded her.

The caverns, which nestled into the foothills of the Drekken Heights, hid from casual view one pass into the Azure Sands and, thinking of that, a ghost of a plan touched Ikella's mind.

She fell in with Jashell and Indeera matching Deschima pace for pace in the lead, followed by Graine, Deschima's attendant. Behind them, Beneva panted along miserably, supporting her precious flask with one hand and keeping her cloak from under her feet with the other. However, at the cavern it was Deschima who held up a hand of caution saying.

"We have not travelled outsands since the Storm, knowing that there were falls in the Caverns. They are treacherous places my Sister, to be negotiated with care and not at speed.".

Soon enough, they came to a fall of greenish, blue rock, glittering with little glances of gold and pearlised swirls of indeterminate hue. Ikella slowed with a grimace of concern and Deschima, not knowing that they had not recently passed that way, said with concern in her voice.

"We endlessly warn travellers through here to take care. The cavern has been shedding for Rotations, but this must have happened only a short time ago. Ikella, think you that the walls are worse than usual?".

Trusting the One, Ikella said evenly, "I really didn't notice Deschima, I have my mind on so many things at the moment, with Conclave, the Gathering, Jentaroth, end of Rotation and I suspect much more to juggle!", crossing her fingers as they turned into the main passageway which flickered uneasily with a low, misted light.

Beneva catching up from the rear said breathlessly, "That looks as I recall it Ikella. If Jashell and Indeera scout ahead of us, we can stop to refresh ourselves once we are back through the pass.".

Ikella, noting that Deschima looked impatient to be on the run again, spoke persuasively, "Deschima my Sister, I must age you by fifty Rotations or more and I have been ill myself of late. At least spare some seconds so that Beneva and I can take a drink before we cross the pass back to Selesh. Tirjella is already on her way to our designated meeting place and I shall have no time to refresh myself once we return home.".

Deschima responded immediately, "I had no idea that you had not been well my Sister.", she said swiftly, "Forgive my haste, I am so surrounded in Malos that any excuse to get away, any excuse to run is welcomed wholeheartedly.".

She shook out her mane of white gold hair and stretched deliciously, saying almost to herself.

"I so love to run that my mother told me she thought I was half Zephryn.".

She chuckled richly at the memory, her voice setting off a zinging and pinging through the crystals on the roof of the cavern. She lifted a warning hand at that and turning to follow Ikella's scouts, the little party collected themselves and, with caution overriding their amusement, continued on their way slowly. Indeed, it was no time until Jashell and Indeera drew them from the caverns and into the opening where below them the vast expanse of the Azure Desert rolled away into the darkness of the closing night.

They stopped at the cavern mouth, the two Gresshe standing at the ready, while Ikella sat with Beneva who had now thrown back the concealing hood of her cloak, revealing her identity to the confusion of Deschima.

The Guardian took out her flask and filling the travel mug offered it to Ikella, who waved it away temporarily, "Thank you but let me get my breath first.".

As protocol demanded, Beneva offered the flask itself to Deschima, who drank thirstily from it, saying gratefully, "Aah, that is truly the water of the Opal, I thank you Beneva. It has been a long time since we last met.", as Beneva drank from the mug. Passing it back to Ikella with a meaningful look, as Deschima called her attendant.

"Baine, come drink before we get into yon blue sand.". Baine, looking a little intimidated by the presence of a Guardian in their midst, said uncertainly, "My lady, I have my own water.".

Ikella held her breath for a moment, but Beneva said easily, "Perhaps the water you know, is the water of choice?".

Deschima said nothing, but her brows grew together in a scowl of ferocious proportions and her body servant stammered hesitantly, "Oh, thank you. I couldn't refuse such generosity.". at which Beneva passed her the flask saying, "You will find that lasts longer! Opal water is carried for many crossings, as people seem to need less of it than the waters of the high grounds, or even of their own Sands.", and Baine ceased to argue and drank.

Jashell picked up the point as Beneva called cheerily, "Let's go then!", and, still stowing the flask at her hip, she led the party at a steady trot down a gentle slope and on to the Azure Sands.

Hardly had they reached the blues of the Azure, when Deschima faltered slightly and Beneva caught her arm.

"Gently, gently. We don't need any falls.", Beneva crooned in a soft, sing-song voice that Ikella was beginning to recognise as her "Sashen" voice.

"It is much colder here and we shall have to keep moving if we want to get to Selesh safely. Even at a run, we have at least three days journey with no real stopping places in between. We are certainly going to need all our strength to make it.".

She threw a wicked grin at Ikella continuing, "Don't you think our Sister in Magic looks glorious? She loves to run too but our people would think her position is above such activity.".

They drew to a halt as Baine staggered and Ikella, casting the light of the handglass on her Librarian, scowled as Beneva planted hypnotic suggestions in her subjects.

"Thank the One, we brought plenty to eat.", she crooned reminiscently, "I am so full I can hardly run another step.".

Even as she spoke they were running out of the shade of Emblem Rock in the Opal Sands. Jashell and Indeera catching the arm of Baine as she doubled up gasping, smiled as Ikella (closing the "doorway" behind them) said decorously,

"If I am to keep my reputation we should walk to Selesh my Sister! Baine has hiccups, and I must be getting old, for indeed I am weary.".

On the track just below Emblem Rock there was a brilliant gleam as the Staff of Selesh lit their way home. The whispers passed through the village as Deschima's spear transformed into her own Staff, flaring at her touch into a soft, steady green.

"Something's happening this Jentaroth! Here is the Lady with another of her Sisters.".

Thus, the second Sorceress was conveyed to Selesh where much news awaited them.

Handing over her tired charges to Mina, Ikella established that Nahamida still slept and, leaving Beneva to gather another flask, she directed Jashell and Indeera to take a brief rest while she cleaned the dust off her feet and found out how matters progressed in Selesh.

In her own dayroom Shiarjha was dictating to a flustered Andria.

"Kerisima, Elect of the Tourmaline, is safe and travelling.".

She broke off as Ikella entered briskly, "Oh Mother, you are back again, thank the One.", Dropping a belated curtsey, she said swiftly, "I know that you are gathering our sisters, but I have news that could save you much footwork. Sit, while I tend your feet and hear what I have to tell you!".

She drew out a low chair and Ikella gratefully sank into it, allowing her acolyte to minister to her sore feet and tired legs. Quickly, applying strong, even strokes, Shiarjha smoothed cooling tannisbalm into her Sorceress's feet, working the knots out of her calf muscles, while she elaborated.

"A runner came through saying that our sister Tirjella set out from Darnesh, bringing with her Idirina, Elect of the Amber Sands. She was studying at Anempor when the Storm hit. They had no sooner left, when they were recalled, because Kerisima, Elect of the Tourmaline, had arrived at their gates. She had worked her way through to the Azure Sands, having been on a period of retreat when the Storm overtook them. Apparently there is no direct way through to us from many of the Southern Sands. The poor girl travelled up the Amber, then right across the Azure, seeking a way through to Selesh. All she knew was that she couldn't get home. Without help she couldn't contact Maranniah, Sanctuary or us. She was so overwhelmed by what Tirjella told her, that they thought it wise to medicate and bring her in a litter. They have already travelled more than half way from Caranchar and Kerisima has almost recovered from the shock. May I send Driss and Sorrill and the second watch to escort them in? I thought that any party with three of our Sisters in it, should at least have that honour!".

Ikella mechanically corrected her acolyte.

"One of my Sisters and two of the Elect dear.". but made no more of it than that, murmuring.

"Ohh, that is wonderful Shiarjha. I had forgot what a skilled Healer you are.", as the deep ache faded from her feet. Soon she was clutching a drink and muttering almost to herself.

"What about Adruna? How shall I gather Adruna?".

Shiarjha's head came up, a shadow in her eyes, just a flicker of a glance in Andria's direction was enough to still Ikella's tongue. As Driss and Sorrill of the second watch received their orders from Shiarjha, their Seconds took the watch at Selesh and for a moment all seemed clatter and bustle as the Inesh left on escort duty.

Jashell, Indeera and Beneva appeared and Andria bobbed in acknowledgement to them as she departed.

Ikella stood to return to her Gathering and was passing Shiarjha, when her acolyte said quietly, "Adruna sent a runner to say that she will travel here unaccompanied. She needs no-one to meet her and seems to know our timetable very well!".

Her voice was low and tense. Ikella, sensing discord, said gently.

"Problems child?" and Shiarjha could contain herself no more.

"I don't like or trust her Mother. She was impossibly rude at Sanctuary, openly questioning our Guardians about everything.". Ikella was disturbed to see Beneva nod in agreement, as her own Elect continued.

"She was, however, greatly skilled.". Shiarjha admitted reluctantly.

"Yet we found her aggressive, bad tempered and willing to take risks, no matter who paid the price! She treated us like her personal servants. She is spiteful and cruel, cares for nothing and no-one. In fact I am afraid of her and what she will do when she comes to power, for that is all she wants, nothing interests her except power!".

Now the dam had burst, Shiarjha the meek, Shiarjha the silent, couldn't stop. Hot, angry tears tracked down her face as she remembered Adruna at Sanctuary. Beneva and Ikella listened with mounting concern as Shiarjha complained.

"She is greedy, self seeking, a disgrace to the memory of Soloria, who was so honest, so kind. Her every sentence started with, "When I am Sorceress" and seemed only to once continue in the vein of her glory, her power, her will. Never once did she think that to become Sorceress, Soloria must die. Never did I hear her talk of what she could do for her people, only of what her people would be made to do for her when she was raised to the Staff.".

Ikella felt a thread of fear touch her as Shiarjha elaborated. Kind, gentle, forgiving Shiarjha with reluctance in her voice was saying, "Guardian, she used to say dreadful things, like celibacy was for those who wished to stifle power, that to truly experience power one needed the release of union.". She whispered this last as though she committed blasphemy and Ikella saw the painful flush on the cheeks of her novice.

"I asked Guardian Jocasta of beloved memory, if she could stop her saying such terrible things, but Jocasta smiled and said that there were many paths to the truth and that exploring those paths in thought and voice was not wrong in itself. She told us that even evil had its place in Pelshar.".

She rubbed her moist eyes, whispering painfully, "Mother, I am afraid things are never going to be the same are they?", as Ikella patted her hand.

"There, there child, you are tired and worried and no, nothing will ever be the same again, but you and I walk the same path and you know that Adruna must be pure, whatever her wild statements meant. Sanctuary would never have let her pass out into the sands if she was impure when she left the Eternal Snows.".

With those words of reassurance, Ikella passed on her way out into the sands again, to Emblem Rock and beyond, Gathering her Sisters for the first conclave at Selesh. A frisson of alarm touched her as she left the Hall and her acolyte, watching her depart from the Gates a moment later, was bleak-eyed as she whispered.

"Take care my Mother. With Jenta rising, so your power wanes, yet a new Way lies before you. Let not the glass lead you onto the pathway of Night.".

Chapter 7 - The Songfathers

Night had fallen when Ikella brought the aged Sorceress of the Carnelian Sands into Mina's care. On the path above Selesh, she considered her task grimly. This time, local traditions had nearly confounded them, for both Eshima and her servant Yani, had committed themselves to a ritual of silent fasting until Jocasta's successor was named. Taking the frail, old Sorceress by both hands, Ikella explained quietly, "Eshima, dearest Sister, although I honour your sacrifice, Seris Jocasta's dying command was to Gather at Selesh. In obedience, Seris Beneva has opened the secret paths of Sanctuary, but can only protect us, if we drink this preparation. You must break this fast, or you may never see your native Sands again!" To Ikella's relief, Eshima and Yani drank and soon thereafter fell into trance.

In a discreet walled garden, Ikella called Jocasta's Door, passing as before, into the shadows of Emblem Rock. Quietly reinforcing the "memory", of their journey in Sashen laden minds, Beneva remarked, "Wasn't it painfully cold in the Amber Sands? I admit I long for my warm bed after such a tortuous trek!"

Eshima, too frail to resist this suggestion was shivering, as Jashell and Indeera lifted the tiny Sorceress on linked hands, carrying her tenderly towards Selesh and Beneva relaxed.

Ikella, finding Medrana's sigil scratched on the boundary marker to announce her presence, was relieved. Even Jashell and Indeera were pale with exhaustion and Ikella acknowledged that she would never willingly, travel through Jocasta's Door so many times in one night again. The village lights dimming behind them, they approached the Gate in the Rock, where the Welcoming Committee claimed Eshima and Yani and Beneva escaped. Taking report from her Guard Commander, Ikella saw the ceremonial tents of Medrana's Clan in the pilgrim's camp and was turning towards her own bed, when Shiarjha appeared, pale with excitement and bursting with news. Suppressing a sigh, Ikella followed her Elect into the Hall of the Healers, relaxing, as its scented atmosphere closed around her like a pair of loving arms. Quietly walking the Way of Challenge, she exclaimed at the sight of the flowering vines climbing gilt poles.

"Jenta's Stars! Shiarjha, how are they still blooming?", she exclaimed in delight as she bent over the delicately perfumed blossoms.

"Master Carolus thought the shelter and the hotfloors might support these through winter, we might extend this principle to growing food in the underground pastures all Rotation round.", the girl replied, "However, this isn't what I brought you to see Mother.".

The Sorceress followed her to the Sacred Circle, drinking in the ambience, until they stood gazing at a ceremonial stand, from which tomorrow, three new Staffs would answer their Calling.

"That's odd!". Ikella ignored Shiarjha's nudge and leant forward staring at a Staff of great antiquity, already in place, disregarding traditional procedure. Her gaze ran up the elaborately carved Blackwood shaft, from the silver stop to the sleeping power stone surrounded by an incredible spiral cage. Skeletal hands and contorted faces fashioned in silver metal, embraced an Amethyst shard, like some cold, angry flame. An arcane image of horrible fascination. She shuddered, moistening suddenly dry lips to whisper faintly, "Where did that dreadful thing spring from?".

Shiarjha drew her away, hissing urgently, "Not now Mother!" as she dipped respectfully to the Book of Rule and fled. Nerves already at breaking point, the Sorceress followed, anxious to escape the sinister Staff and her sense of sinuous movement in the shadows beyond. Exiting through a guarded vestibule, they encountered a huge man in lilac robes. Every visible body part was covered in symbolic tattoos. Although he smiled amiably enough, bowing deeply and placing his hands together in ritual greeting, Ikella was horrified by the tongueless grimace that passed for his smile. His lips were deeply pierced, with an arrangement of silver studs, that obviously could be locked together. Shocked, she acknowledged him silently, following Shiarjha into the corridor beyond, where a concealed stair led to her apartments.

They fell in through the study door, almost into the arms of Beneva who waited quietly for their nervous laughter to subside.

"Praise the One!". Ikella touched her hand to her heart, lips, forehead in relief. "Who is that extraordinary man? What is he doing here?".

Shiarjha, her voice low and strained said, "That is what I was trying to tell you Mother! Adruna has arrived accompanied by Koth, High Priest of Iscatan, who brought that hideous Staff.", She flung out a hand in appeal, "Now, I am really afraid. I suspect he has some dreadful influence over Adruna! He terrifies me and we have already had to medicate the guards who believe he is cursed!".

The young woman shuddered and Beneva reached out and touched her soothingly.

Brain whirling, Ikella sank into a chair. She was exhausted, beyond exhaustion really and this last was too much.

She vaguely remembered studying an uprising at Sanctuary. Anarchy had swept the Sands, the Gattarene cult proclaiming their dark moon Gatta as the font of the Source. Violent disturbances had preceded demands to transfer all the Rites of Jenta, to its twin. Her childhood studies, mentioned acts of depravity, so vile that her revered ancestress Adaria, had sought retreat. Discovering the abandoned settlement at Selesh, Adaria founded the Sisterhood of Sorcery, under whose influence order was restored. Thinking about Beneva's belief that history had a habit of repeating itself, Ikella stood purposefully.

"We can't undo what is done.", she said firmly. "I won't demand explanations at this hour and without those, talking and worrying serves no useful purpose and we all need our sleep!"

She glanced towards the flask of Sashen-laced water saying, "If only we could induce peaceful rest and a refreshed wakening on ourselves!" She yawned, adding wistfully

"I would like to take a hot sweetdrink before I go to bed though. Shiarjha, perhaps?".

Her voice trailed away suggestively, but then she came to a halt, looking stricken, "Deo me, I had forgotten Daro.".

Rising swiftly, she nodded to the Inesh guards and silently sped along the corridor to the nursery, Beneva in tow. More guards stood outside the nursery and Ikella lifted an interrogatory eyebrow, at a young woman sporting an elaborate arm band.

"Diras, what is the meaning of this?", she enquired and the tall warrior grinned at the bemused Sorceress.

"Somishen Shiarjha doubled the guard on Master Daro as other Clans arrived in Selesh.", The young woman explained, "I wrestled the whole Chapter for the honour of carrying my Lady's son tomorrow and won, so my command will stay with him day and night, until end of festival.".

Ikella was beginning to feel light-headed and thinking better of rousing sleeping babies, she turned in her tracks, muttering under her breath, "I shall never undo the tangle I inherited with that child!".

Ignoring Beneva's poorly stifled giggles, she sipped the sweetdrink that Shiarjha served, until wracked with a prodigious yawning fit, she struggled wearily to her feet, wishing Beneva goodnight. Shiarjha looked up at them, her eyes glowing as she said sweetly.

"You two look absolutely exhausted. You really need to go to bed and sleep!".

As Jashell and Indeera appeared to escort the tottering Guardian. Ikella heard her Elect, through swimming senses saying softly, "Why don't you stop worrying about tomorrow Mother? Go sleep. and wake refreshed and ready for anything.".

Ikella paused, peering at Shiarjha suspiciously, before walking on strangely leaden limbs to her bed, where she curled obediently and slept.

Trinet woke her grumbling softly.

"My lady, waken now my lady. It is the day, such as this dark dawn gives us. I must fetch fresh water for your morning drink, my last night's blending was all spoilt and curdled by the One only knows what!".

Ikella opened her eyes reluctantly. She was comfortable and warm and very loathe to move. Stretching, she discovered no hint of the devastating fatigue of the previous night and rose, making a mental note to interrogate Shiarjha further about that, she went to the small table and picked up her morning sweetdrink, sipping it slowly, her brow furrowed in thought.

By the end of this day, she must tell her Sisters in Sorcery all she knew of the fall of Sanctuary and the death of all their hopes. Beneva must guide them through the blended rituals of Accession to Guardianship and the Calling to the Staff for three young candidates, as well as marking Jentaroth. This Rotations sorrows contained in the enormous roll of the Dead, yet to be read to their Clansmen. She considered this night would mark a turning point, without any presentiment of just how dramatic that change would be, though she recognised the tricky path she must tread.

Ikella, along with all her Sisters in Sorcery, had accepted that her days would pass, one after another, performing her duty as her predecessors had done. Every day prepared for carefully, from garments to meals, from ceremonial to tradition, never altering by so much as a whisper of inflection, the words used, the invocations chanted. Overnight, it seemed that she had lost all that certainty that was the Way and if the Way had been the root of her confidence, how much more was it her people's? Reflecting on the changes, she took her morning bath, thinking that this too was part of the same ritual, part of the Way, her Way. She brought herself up thinking, "I shall wear the snowberry incense today" and realisation dawned with a shiver of apprehension, she had always been able to choose, possibly had always believed in self-determination just never practiced it. Feeling somewhat reassured by this revelation, she ate the morning meal provided by Trinet and then, dressed simply in an over robe of light Hanka wool, made her way to the nursery.

Daro was sitting on a rug watching Ahnell with the steady fascination that she had come to expect of him. His hair had thickened and was attaining that true brown-blackness associated with the Shalhanhi, curling on to his neck. Swiftly, she stooped and placed a kiss in the angle of his jaw. He leaned back confidently against her and lifting his arms above his head he tangled them into her own hair, gripping tightly, until she was forced to pick him up to dislodge him.

Nadra was folding clothing into piles, separating by size tiny robes for the evening ceremonies, for both boys their first nameday. At end of Rotation, Jenta, (their smaller brighter moon), abandoned its dark partner to its own lonely orbit, rising to dominate the nightscape. Gathering on the Eve of Jentaroth, the Clanswomen brought the children of that Rotation to the Sorceress, to name, entering them in the great roll of the Clan for all time.

Boys, passed this one time only, from parent to Sorceress, through the artefact known as the Eye of Jenta, in the ritual that prepared male children for a semi-nomadic life in the Sands. With their foreskins removed and their nictating membranes freed, they passed into the Sacred Circle, borne aloft in the arms of the Sorceress, to be named, in the place where no male otherwise ventured, on pain of death. Girls entered the Sacred Circle by right of their gender. This night marked the start of many ritual lives. Their nictating membranes freed themselves during the first Rotation of life, but this was, for all children of that Rotation, their Nameday when the book of the Clan would list them for the first time. Ikella struggled to remember her first time in the Sacred Circle, but it wouldn't come to her, although one point she hadn't considered did.

"How can I offer Daro as Mother and receive him as Sorceress?", she questioned herself, , knowing that even her command of magic wouldn't permit her to be in two places at the same time. She cradled him protectively, wondering if the boy child felt any discomfort in the process that the Eye of

Jenta performed? She had no evidence of any pain. No outcry, no tears accompanied the children who came into her arms. She thought back along the Rotations, hearing the voice of Sashandra her predecessor instructing her.

"Hold the child firmly but gently. When he comes from the parent into your arms, remember that each child is our investment in the future, but he is theirs in particular. Great care and respect for their risk must be shown. Lift him above your head for all to welcome and say clearly, "This is the son of our clan, brother to all present. His name shall be…" then say the name that the parent will speak as the child comes through the Eye. Say it loudly three times, naming the parents of the child first, then his family name and lastly his Clan, thinking as you do so on the One and his will. Pray for the life of that child as you have never prayed before. If there is one boy or one hundred boys a Rotation, dedicate each life to the working of the Way and yours to their service. This is your most solemn duty, so see that you carry it well, for it is a day that every parent remembers for each child. Remember, many of those children will return to the Sands before they grow to maturity .".

Cradling Daro, Ikella thought solemnly of the huge responsibility that came with parenthood. She had not been given the pain of birthing this child nor any other and therefore she couldn't feel the primordial drive of the mother who strives only to protect her son. Yet she had been given the responsibility for bringing this child to adult status, for assuming the duties of his dead mother and in her mind she heard a deep melodic voice saying.

"Look after the child for he is your future". Then she remembered that she was also to be known as "Honoured Mother", but in truth she didn't feel honoured by the trust placed in her. She felt frightened, uncertain of her Way and then she saw with piercing clarity that, as it was with the child, so it was with her world - the world she must lead by the hand and teach a new Way. She stood holding the child in numb arms, hearing only a roaring in her ears, feeling each heartbeat like a frightened bird trying to escape its inexorable fate and she wept.

Nadra seeing her distress, silently indicated the nursing chair. Ikella sank into it gratefully, realising how heavy Daro had become as he curled against her. She brushed the dampness on her cheeks away and gazed down at Daro, noting the healthy bloom of his skin, the baby fat dimples on the backs of his hands. As Nadra prepared two bowls of food, avoiding the adventurous Ahnell, who crawled around her feet, Ikella thought about the evening ahead. Inevitably, some women never saw their children come to their Nameday. She recalled receiving countless infants through the Eye of Jenta from their nearest male relatives. This tradition would suffice for her purpose she thought, gently easing Daro into a more comfortable position, but who would stand for him?

As no-one had answered her seeking spell, she had to assume that he had no living relatives. A reflection sparkled across Daro's face, from the crystal apples left by his mother and the answer came to her. She would ask the Gathering, citing the lifebond that tied them together, rescued to rescuer as a reason for claiming his sand-rights. If there was no objection to that, she would adopt him and she knew just who she would call to be Daro's Songfather!

He woke and she leaned over him, studying his face. He stared solemnly up at her and then his lips quivered into a huge smile as reaching for her face, he patted her gently. She caught his hands, dropping a kiss into the palm, until his gaze shifted to Nadra. Seeing the clean wrapper in her hand, he began to cry.

Swiftly, Ikella took the wrapper, scooping the baby up and on to, a padded shelf . He kicked and gurgled with delight, fast changes of mood flickering across his face as Ikella scolded him gently while she stripped and bathed him clean again.

"Now, what is this? You can't cry because Nadra must change you!". She tickled the soles of his feet and he struggled to get away from the torment, gurgling happily as he did so.

"Hold still young man.". she dictated, deftly substituting the clean wrapper for the old and tying it. She lifted him against her shoulder, which he promptly mouthed, trying to bite the seam of her garment with baby gums.

"He is teething Nadra", the Sorceress diagnosed, as she ladled milta gruel sweetened with honey cream into the hungry, little mouth.

"He is thriving, but I think a simple Shanroot chewing stick could do him no harm and might ease his discomfort. Send to Hanna for some and watch his temperature doesn't rise. ".

It was a disagreeable moment when the duties and rituals of her high position reclaimed her attention once more. Beneva stuck her head around the door enquiringly and smiled at the domestic scene in front of her. Ikella sat folding clothes away. Daro lay on a blanket, busying himself with the "swimming" movements of a child about to crawl. Beneva regretted having to break the moment, but this day would give her little chance to speak to Ikella. She cleared her throat discreetly and the Sorceress swung abruptly in her direction, her face clouding as she did so.

"Ah Beneva, I thought my luck had held for too long.". she said, slowly getting to her feet. Stooping over Daro, gently touching the crown of his head, she said gravely.

"Goodbye baby, be good until I see you again.". And, with a pricking at the back of her eyes, she speedily stripped off her over robe to reveal flowing Opalwear robes that matched Beneva's sense of occasion perfectly. Following the Guardian, Ikella went back to the duties that bound her to the Opal.

They headed for the Djellim, where four Inesh stood guard side by side to the left and right of the double door leading into the library. They had adopted the uniform of the secretive shadow warriors of that distant past. Ceremonial daggers, thrust into belts, encrusted hilts glittering in the light of the glows. She gazed into inscrutable eyes, noting that in covering their tightly braided hair above their traditional half-veil, they had completely depersonalised themselves, becoming the epitome of a single force, bearing only Ikella's sigil on the oath-cloth bound to their foreheads as identification. At the sight of such honour,

Ikella felt her flagging spirits rise in wholehearted approbation. Countering their reaction to the terrifying, tongueless Koth was essential and she smiled as she passed those who guarded the Djellim so jealously. The doors opened and Ikella and Beneva passed within to discover that they were not alone.

Within the high-vaulted room, Carolus waited with Tuennis, Guaradeign of Caranchar and Ikella welcomed her warmly saying, "I didn't think to find you here Tuennis. Why haven't you been to visit Ahnell?", and instantly regretted her words for Tuennis, mother of her other fosterling, grew stiff and defensive.

"My Deshun, I would be both presumptuous and arrogant if I sought to visit a hostage without obtaining your permission first. What I came to ask may tax your patience further, yet I crave your indulgence for this is Ahnell's Nameday also!".

Ikella stood silent, appreciating the struggle going on in this woman. Recently bereaved, responsible for the rebuilding of Caranchar and its daily management.

Tuennis continued, her voice thin and strained with emotion.

"I come to stand for Ahnell, to see that he pass into the care of his father's Clan and to give him his father's name, to dedicate him to Mirayen then to leave him with you. As Head of my husband's Clan, I appeal to you directly to honour the child's Clan rights. I brought our marriage contract to show the Clan Council the truth of what I say.". She bowed her head and waited for Ikella's response.

Ikella considered carefully. Ideally, she would have liked Ahnell to have been brought up in Caranchar, but he was a hostage, along with eight others from the town. It was too early to return any one of them to their people or her actions regarding Caranchar would have no meaning.

Nadra, herself recently bereaved of her entire family including two children, was acting as both Daro and Ahnell's wet-nurse and they were too young for that situation to change. Besides, she needed to stay here and heal as well. The Sorceress drew a breath.

"What you have requested of me is yours by right Tuennis, Ahnell is indeed entitled to the protection of both Clans, his father's and his mother's as well.". She held up a hand against any protest.

"Tonight you shall also hear me change the Way for all Inesh and for that reason I demand your presence in Hall at Rise of Jenta. I will accept Ahnell only from your hands and will minister to him as a mother should, for the days that you define. I shall teach him of Caranchar, his parents and their love for him as well.".

The woman nodded briefly then spoke in a low voice.

"It would be better for him to know only of his father, of his life as Headman, of what he achieved. Of me, he need only know that as a widowed Inesh I couldn't support him and so gave him to his father's Clan.".

She paused and Ikella saw her gulp and swallow.

"You asked me to be your Guaradeign Lady. This is more than Headwoman, more than Headman. I attend Councils for this, Councils for that. I have Sadorin working night and day. Your Healer has people clearing and cleaning everything and it is to me that they turn for advice. Pah! I sometimes think they believe I have your great wisdom, even your power, but I have only the same experience as they!".

She spread her hands expressively, saying.

"I must attend to their needs, even if I don't know how to. I can't say, "I am sorry, I can't come right now, I have to feed Ahnell!" Do you not see my Deshun, Ahnell is safer here with you than in Caranchar with me?".

She dashed angry tears from her eyes. "I am Inesh, I live to serve and so serve I will, without the child I should never have borne.". As she turned away she whispered in an agonised voice.

"I told Donnesh that no good would come of our union…", and before Ikella could move she fled from the great library.

Carolus looked at Ikella gravely, "Another sorrow on the Sand.", he murmured heavily, but brightened as Ikella, refusing to speculate further on the outcome, addressed her own problems with Daro.

"Carolus, I am persuaded that you must be the Elder of our Clan.", she announced without preamble. "Although I heard about "Carolus of the Nine Sands" in Caranchar, I think that there is some reason for that fine Opalwear belt that you sport today!".

The old man's eyes twinkled as she explained. "You may have journeyed far from here and you say that nowhere is home, but I believe you to be Shalhanhi, born of these Sands. You took your oath to the Opal too seriously for me to believe otherwise, am I not right?".

She sat down, watching him with one hand supporting her chin and Carolus nodded, "I truly don't know my parentage, but I remember the Sand of my childhood and some of the places I have been. I feel comfortable here, some of the corridors of Selesh are very familiar to me, though.". he admitted with a wry chuckle, "some of my memories of Opalwear belts are not happy ones!". Ikella went on.

"Whatever the rights or wrongs of it, you are the sole reason that Daro survives.". - she reminded him. "I must have an elder to stand for him. to pass him through the Eye of Jenta when the time comes, a man to teach him the Ways of men, this night and for all the nights that they can.".

She eyed him gravely. "You restored his life to me, I would repay you some of that debt if I could. Will you stand for the baby if no-one claims him before sundown?".

"What about Patris?", the Apothecary demanded.

"He has no claim, being Felmin, but he knew Daro's mother and befriended her just before her death. He comes from the Amber himself and having sacrificed so much to find the boy, he surely has a part to play too?".

Ikella paused, thinking until Beneva grew impatient.

"What about both of them? There are no laws against having two "Songfathers".", the Guardian stated categorically.

"You could ask for anyone who is kin to Daro to claim him, failing which you can invoke the tradition of eldest male of the Clan present and nearest male friend to become the child's Songfather. It has been done before and I can't see Patris refusing the honour. He asks after Daro every day. ".

So the matter was settled, Carolus departing to tell Patris the joyous news, leaving the women alone together.

Ikella opened the Council Chamber's hidden door and, without dispelling its magical field of protection, she surveyed the preparations with a critical eye.

"Nine seats at the Council Table, tablets and enscrasures prepared.", and discovered the air redolent with busybugs wax and perfumed with dried flowers. She noted that the Sanctuary Chest was missing and raised an eyebrow at Beneva, who murmured.

"Removed to the Sacred Circle this morning. I had it placed by the Book of Rule and encircled it with a binding that I doubt the shade of Jocasta herself could break!" Further than that, she wouldn't comment, other than to say.

"With the Chest out of the Council Chamber, the access to Jocasta's Door can't be accidentally triggered. I have quartered every inch of the room with Carolus and Errish, none of us could trigger it, by weight or movement, individually or together. Carolus says that he is certain that something binds the door and the Sanctuary chest together. That where one is so goes the other and I agree. That dreadful man Koth still guards their Staff from the standpoint just outside the Circle, where even he won't dare to enter. The Sanctuary Chest is safe enough from human threat, the Inesh have doubled the guard, outnumbering Koth four to one!".

The door opened into the Djellim quietly and a small procession entered, under escort. At the doorway Jashell intoned.

"Welcome to the most high, the most exalted Sisters of Syrene. Enter into the presence of Ikella, Sharall deir Opal, our revered Mother of the Sands, Tirjella Sharall deir Azure, Deschima, Sharall deir Malachite, Medrana, Sharall deir Cynabarr, Nahamida Sharall deir Onyx and Eshima, Sharall deir Carnelian.".

In the sombre faces of her Sisters in Sorcery Ikella saw the initial impact of their losses, as they entered the Djellim. There was a small pause in the procession, then four younger women, entered.

"Shiarjha, Elect of the Opal Sands, Idirina, Elect of the Amber Sands, Kerisima, Elect of the Tourmaline Sands, Adruna, Elect of the Amethyst Sands.", intoned Jashell once more, as they entered. Led by Shiarjha, they curtsied to Ikella. who saw beyond the shadow cast by the cowls of their traditional mourning cloaks, to the tensions and grief within those who would accede to the Staffs of their Sands without the precious memory spells of their predecessors.

Acknowledging their obeisance with a gentle inclination of her head, she took a breath and let the party see the Chamber beyond the protective barrier. With satisfaction, she heard the gasps and whispers of wonder as she drew on her own connection to the Source. Extending an empowered hand she summoned her Staff silently. It hovered before the assemblage of the most powerful women on Pelshar, before swooping to her hand. The Opal glowed brilliantly and her aura swirled with power as she intoned.

"Shalonthi, shanushek, adreo opus.".

The field of pure energy that separated the Sisterhood of Syrene from the Chamber, flickered and dissipated. Ikella, encompassing them all in the glow of her Staff declared.

"Welcome my Sisters. Welcome my Sisters elect. Remembering only your duty to your Sands and to each other, let Conclave begin!".

Chapter 8 - Four Free Men.

Carolus made his way from the quiet of the holy community of Selesh out into the Gathering Square. Stepping from the smothering silence into the busy hum of normality, he felt his spirits lift as the doors closed behind him. The immense courtyard fronting the Hall of the Healers was alive with drudges running to and fro, carrying trays of hot pies, buttercakes and savouries. Here and there he heard the bawl of a harassed cook calling.

"Honeymead, look quick now, we have no time to lose!" then, "Where is that sandblasted boy now? I sent him for grain half a Rotation ago!".

Carolus grinned as he recalled his own youth, settling his hukvah jauntily over one eye as he made his way across the Square to the Hall of Welcome. Making enquiries at the kitchen for Patris, he discovered that the Wagon Master's entire company had left the Hall several days before. A friendly serving girl remembered only that they had taken to eating with new Beast Master Ivinish, directing him with a smile.

"They were at the village inn last night. Do you know "The Cross Eyed Zeglur" Master Carolus?".

For a heartbeat, the old man had struggled to bring each of his large herd of Zeglurs to mind, then he remembered this new custom of naming village inns.

"Do you mean the one to the right of the market? The inn with the green shutters?" The woman shook her head, laughing.

"No silly, that's the Roaming Apothecary! Far too high class for that lot. I meant the one next to the barracks, where the Inesh women drink.".

"Ah.", Carolus took his leave of her and set out in search of his friends, muttering faintly as he departed, "The inn where the Inesh women drink! Obvious really, I should have known!".

The door closed on the serving girl's giggles as he made his way through the Gate in the Rock, out into the sandy path that led to Selesh Minoria.

It was not far to the inn that he sought, but already the path was thronged with pilgrims. He found himself weaving through a sea of Clansmen gathering in many cases for the first time after the Storm. He noted the number blinded by storm plague and realising that all over Pelshar this story was being repeated, he pressed on.

This Jentaroth, all eyes would focus on Selesh. while their Sorceress Elect represented those Sisters attending Conclave. Three others would be plunged into solemn mourning, yet in Selesh, somehow, Ikella had successfully imposed a sense of normality. His mind dwelt briefly on the punishing schedule set out for Ikella this night and he briskened his pace, anxious to find Patris and his companions.

All about him the market traders were setting up. There would be no trading today, but stall holders were erecting tents, storing their wares, stowing bedding under their tables in readiness for the Gather Fair tomorrow.

Here and there, a child ran crying for his parents and, noting increasing numbers of children just wandering around unsupervised, Carolus frowned. Then abruptly a door opened on his left and, laughing, a pair of Inesh women drifted out, arms entwined.

They acknowledged him with a chorus of, "Master Carolus.", then vanished in the crowd that filled the street. He stepped carefully round a group of men crouched over the tiles and dice of a game of Nine Winds and made his way into the blissfully cool inn, spotting his quarry the instant he did so.

Patris was holding court at a corner table. Rowbet and Somner, heads drawn together, were nodding in agreement to something he was saying, as were Errish, Arkneth, his Master Woodsmith and Beven who sat with his father Timoran, the Master Smith, at the next table. Timoran was very animated, contributing a flow of technical information to the conversation despite his recent loss of sight.

Carolus edged nearer to the bar of the inn, nodding to traders who hailed him cheerfully then glaring at one who called.

"Let the old-timer through Idaven. If you don't move your oafish self, this old boy is likely to go to the Sands while he waits.".

The Apothecary gratefully accepted the gap that opened up for him nevertheless, calling for a jug of his favourite Honeymead.

Beaming at the brightly polished bar and catching the familiar tang of fennish soap mixed with a blend of warm spices, brewing mead and Hoshen liquor, he said happily, "Ah, now this is what I call home!".

Stretching out a hand to pay, he encountered the soft yielding bosom of a tall woman, propping up the bar to his right. Sorrill turned, catching his hand in hers in such a manner that the conversation around him died on a single intake of breath, as the traders waited to see what the Inesh warrior would do to the ancient. However, seeing who had touched her so, Sorrill grinned amiably and to his chagrin replaced his hand on her breast, saying, "I am sorry Grandfather. I am not used to the ways of you medical men. Do you need to feel more to make a diagnosis?".

Carolus dropped his marker on the bar, grabbed the jug and drinking vessel proffered and amidst the good-natured catcalls, made his way to the table where the group he sought sat chatting, happily oblivious to his embarrassment.

He sank into the seat offered, engrossing himself in taking that first joyous gulp of Honeymead, until, draining his cup, he turned to Patris who demanded.

"See this Carolus.", The Wagon Master pointed dramatically, "Errish is designing a new type of wagon.".

Carolus examined the sketch thoughtfully. The group was brimming with excitement which he was reluctant to dampen, but his own task was pressing. He broke into the conversation.

"I congratulate you Errish, but I am sent from the Sorceress with an invitation for Patris. Can we talk?".

Drawing Patris to one side, Carolus left the others discussing possible ways of transporting goods across the Sands where proper trails didn't exist and explained his mission to the incredulous trader.

"Our Sorceress has asked both you and I to become Songfathers to young Daro today.". Pitching his voice so that it carried only to their table and ignoring the dumbfounded expression on his companion's face, he finally told Patris what was required of them.

"She appreciated what you sacrificed just to find him.". Carolus spoke firmly, "She also understood your pain, your determination to try and find his mother and wishes to acknowledge that you have a bond and a right to the child. She obviously thought that our advice would be of use in Rotations to come. Have you ever been a Songfather before?".

The trader shook his head, uncertainty creeping into his voice. "No, it is not a practice of my people Carolus. We Felmin have no great rituals like this.", His voice trailed off, returning more desperately.

"I can't! I don't have any decent clothes! My own Gather cloak was used as shrouds for the dead, bandages for the living, I would shame the Gathering and my Guild.".

Carolus, sensitive to his friends dilemma, said comfortably.

"You need new under-linen, but that is available in plenty. We will visit Mistress Dorra at the Linen Room to see what she can find. Where are you staying now? Have you moved out of Selesh?".

As they stood to leave, the Apothecary discovered the tightly knit team had moved into the underground pastures, with Ivinish. He listened intently to the description of the strangely glowing cavern roof above the lush grazing. They strode out into the street, discussing the harness and tack room and Timoran revealed that a locked door led to the forge, itself based in another of the underground caverns. The Master Smith admitted apologetically.

"I knew it was there but just never used it. It never occurred to me how useful it would be. Beven could do with access to running water for some of the things Errish wants forged.", Weaving through thickening crowds, they worked their way back to the Gate in the Rock. Here pilgrims were beginning to enter the Gathering Square, at the invitation of the Summoning Bell.

It was well past the Height of Sun, as they passed in through double door set directly into the rock. Beyond, a passage widened out into the most astonishing place. Underfoot was a lush pasture, growing a softly blued green grass. Around greyed bronze walls were wooden barns and buildings, some plainly fitted for human use, some for animal shelters and above all of this, the eye-catching splendour of a crystalline roof stretched away into the distance.

As they progressed down a well trodden "path" in the pasture, he looked for his own Zeglur herd and to his astonishment, saw the irritable creatures placidly grazing alongside the Biron. He had hardly seen the Biron at first, taking the huge trek beast for some rocky outcrop so closely did its coat match the cavern wall. He questioned Ivinish eagerly, almost before the gentle beast master had invited him into their quarters.

"I have never seen the herd so settled. What has induced such tranquillity do you think Ivinish? Is it the grazing or the light from this cavern's roof?", As Carolus spoke, they were seating themselves around a large table which plainly doubled as a desk. The beast master considered the question for a moment then shook his head.

"I don't really know the answer. When I brought them in from the outer pasture to free up the land for the Gather, they were still very skittish. I brought our three great lumps in under cover.", He chuckled suddenly, the humour lighting his solemn features momentarily. "They had already frightened yon daft Zeglurs, so I put them in the back pasture and they settled immediately.", he added cheerfully.

"Once I got the first group in and settled, the others just trotted in. They've grazed together ever since.", He indicated a group of baby Zeglurs, who ran and played together oblivious of the enormous male Biron munching placidly at close quarters.

"The coltings that were born in the last ninenight like the Biron. The other night I surprised young Karmarek, our male, playing chase with them!".

A shy smile lit up his face as he recalled the comical sight and then he grew more businesslike, reporting happily, "Yes, that is another thing Master Carolus. We now have eight live births. No complications, no need for assistance and all feeding well. Your dams are in good health and I suspect that we will see your herd increase rapidly under these conditions. It could be to do with the light in here, it could easily be the good grazing, or even the company! Whatever it is, Zeglurs and Biron seem to go together remarkably well!".

"Which.", Patris explained. "Is what put us on to the idea of redesigning a wagon that would allow us to harness them together! However, we digress and I have an announcement to make.".

The large man stood carefully and taking his drinking bowl he raised it to the table.

"It is my pleasure today to make an announcement which will be posted at the gates of Selesh.", He fumbled in his pockets, eventually withdrawing a curl of some rough, pressed paper.

"As it concerns this company, this is where I wanted to say what I have asked a scribe to set down in writing.", He flushed before continuing formally.

"Stand up Rowbet, Somner and Ivinish, Felmin of the Far Reaches.", and the three men stood in bewildered silence, staring at their Wagon Master apprehensively, as Patris cleared his throat.

"Rowbet you are my journeyman and so I will discuss your further service first.", Rowbet tensed, his face anxious as Patris spoke solemnly.

"You have served me for six Rotations out of the Nine. Fought for my honour and rights, helped me dig a way out of Maraken and helped me bury my sorrows along the roads and paths of our Way. I have in mind to reward that loyalty, so I will sign your indentures and declare you Wagoner in your own right.", Ignoring the gasps and sighs of his men, Patris faced them, eyes half closed as if he recited a well learned script.

"Somner, you have been there to offer consolation and counsel. It was your thought to follow to Selesh the faintest of trails. For supporting Rowbet, Ivinish and me, we owe a debt of gratitude which I will repay by setting aside your indentures and declaring you Freeman Driver of my employ.

"Ivinish, you have chosen to remain here with the people of the Sand and to work your own magic with animals within this community. As the Sorceress requests your service I relinquish it to her, just as I give up the rights of free trade to serve her myself.".

He paused, looking into the faces of each of his men a trifle anxiously, "I can't carry out my service to these Sands without business partners. I will have to find at least two drivers, a base with decent quarters, a Master Beast Handler to start off with. After that I will need, close to hand, a cart builder with craftsmen at his disposal, a smithy nearby and an Apothecary to assist the Beast Handler when sickness strikes. Does anyone present know of a better place than this?".

His voice dropped as he tentatively placed the parchment on the table for all to see.

At the top of the page was a drawing. Depicting a group of men with a wagon, it showed one very tall man, not unlike Patris himself. The other three were much of a size. one held a whip, another held reins and the third held a baby animal in his arms. Significantly, they had all been drawn standing on the same level, as partners. Under the picture was a sigil which showed a wagon standing on undulating Sand, surmounted by an eye. On the side of the wagon were four bold lines.

Patris pointed to it saying softly.

"Trade safely at the sign of the Four Free Men, citizens of Selesh, official traders to the household of Ikella te Syrene, thereto I set my seal!".

Reaching into a capacious pocket, he brought out a seal similar to the one that Ikella had used to stamp their official appointment.

"This is ours.", he said proudly.

"Drawn by Somishen Shiarjha herself and given to me by the hand of our Lady Sorceress. We are now the official traders for Selesh. We have all had the freedom of these Sands conferred on us and you no longer serve me as apprentice to master. Your papers have been signed and counter-signed by the Sorceress. I have given my word that if any of you decide to leave I will allow you to depart when Jentaroth is over. However, I would like you all, as partners, to join me and profit from walking in the next path of our life together.".

He raised his drinking bowl hopefully and solemnly Rowbet lifted his own until the rims touched, followed by the entire company as they drank, saying quietly.

"On the new path – together!".

They rested in the drowsy fall of Sun, Carolus wandering into the pasture to inspect his herd. The new coltings substantially increased his stock and he discussed their dispersal with Ivinish, watching with approval the Beast Handler's gentle but firm handling of the frisky, baby Zeglurs.

The shaggy, brown man of the Southern plains whistled gently as he ran his hands down the leg of a Biron dam, sucking on his teeth sharply as the great animal shied away.

"Trouble?" the Apothecary queried, but Ivinish only grinned saying, "Nothing we can't deal with Master Carolus.", Ivinish bent to the task of inspecting the sore limb and Carolus observed his slow, confident manner. Examine by sight, examine by touch, examine by smell, he remembered his own Master demanding and watched as this was duly carried out. Ivinish straightened, patting the animal soothingly.

"If you have any saltberry extract in your stock, I could provide a draw to remove infection.", he said thoughtfully.

"They all ran around as if possessed last night, about the time that the new elect of the Amethyst arrived. I only stepped out for a moment to see the Inesh women welcome her and they just took off! I expect she got kicked or knocked into something.".

Promising to look in the generous space allotted for his own goods, Carolus took his leave of the traders, smiling at the homely picture that they made. Rowbet and Somner, plainly holding their former master in high affection, had turned out their own clothes and were sorting through them in search of garments suitable for his use. Ivinish was ladling fresh milk from the small herd of Dorrowen that grazed the high Plateau above Selesh into a great double-handled pan and in the pasture the herd grazed sleepily.

His duty to Ikella discharged, the Apothecary made his way to his own rooms - a small washing cubicle and a sleeping area provided along the corridor leading to Ikella's suite, near to the sparse apartment occupied by the guard commander of the watch.

Everyone was resting, the heavy skies above concentrating the heat in great, sullen, airless waves. By the time he reached his room, Carolus regretted the urge to move. His clothing clung to him and he thought wistfully of the cool interior of the pastures. He lifted the latch and instantly knew that there was something wrong before he saw the destruction of his few possessions.

He detected an acidic smell, as if he inhaled the very scent of danger. A faint rustle attracted his attention and then the weird impression of something that he couldn't quite see as it glided past him. He turned, trying to make it out in the shadowy interior, but then a terrible blow literally rocked his brain in his skull, sending him into oblivion.

He woke to find his head pillowed comfortably on someone's lap. Cool water was being trickled on to his forehead and a calm voice was saying, "Keep still for the moment, a Healer is coming. We have penned your man.", He became aware of a dull pounding pain in his head and whispered, "Someone was in my room!".

He attempted to struggle upright, but was restrained with ease by powerful hands and the strange lassitude of his own body. She, for it was a woman, soothed him saying.

"Master Carolus, you must keep still until a Healer sees to you. You are not a young man and you can't suffer a blow like that without dire consequences.".

She was bending over him now, gently applying a cool cloth to his forehead and Carolus forced his eyes to open, hissing impotently as the room danced and swayed before him. He waited for it to settle before attempting to see his rescuer once more, but now sandaled feet were slapping briskly on the tiled floor outside his room. His vision blurred as the Healer entered so he closed his eyes wearily while the women conferred.

"What has happened here Driss?" He was instantly able to identify both his rescuer and Mina as she deposited a basket filled with cloths, bandages and ointments on a low shelf near his bed. Through a sudden roaring in his ears, he caught a few sentences from Driss as she made her report.

"Koth, servant to Somishen Adruna. At full alert, we saw no one pass. Someone will pay for that, but he will answer to our Deshun for this! We have sent word to our Deshun, she will come to him.".

Sudden terror gripped the Apothecary and he moaned, sweat breaking out on his forehead as he rolled his head, frantic to get their attention.

"No, no!" he cried out loudly, his voice suddenly harsh to his own ears.

"She must not leave the Chamber while Conclave is in session!".

His agitation plainly alarmed Mina who bent over him, catching hold of his frantic hands. He panted for air, mumbling in a low voice so that only the Healer could hear him.

"She must not leave Adruna in the Chamber alone.", He gasped as Mina applied cooling sithabalm to his poor head, carefully checking the position of his skull bones, rotating his neck carefully, all the time talking softly.

"Just relax Carolus. Driss has gone to the Djellim herself to pass your message on to Ikella, she will do as you say. Relax.".

Strangely he did so, hearing a quivering sigh from his own lips. Powerless to prevent it, he relaxed into her healing hands.

Someone was singing. Carolus tried to locate the sound but couldn't - it seemed to float in his head somewhere, while a thousand cooling hands massaged his sore brain, neck, shoulders. He felt himself being lifted, turned, floated on the Source, washed through with power the like of which he had seldom met before and his eyes flickered open to see Ikella, hands raised above him, power flowing through her, working her will on the Source, on him!

He protested.

"No, no you should be in Conclave. You are all in danger, you must not leave the Chamber! I am of no account.".

He woke, lying on the floor of his room, cushioned by throws and pillows, her voice still in his ears, chuckling.

"Don't be silly I am still in Conclave and safe. I won't leave until Koth is sealed in my cage.".

An icy anger coloured her voice and he shivered as she said, "When I return, I shall want answers.", Her voice faded and cautiously Carolus raised his head, testing his neck gingerly, feeling foolish. Mina came to support him as he rose, stretching stiffening limbs.

"I beg of you, at least lie down on your bed for a while man.", she grumbled and for once Carolus was pleased to obey her, drifting immediately into healing sleep.

When he eventually woke, he was alone again and quite well, but for a soreness at the nape of his neck none of his peculiar afternoon might have happened. He rose, made use of his small but private washdown and necessary and found the clothes that he had set aside for tonight, none the worse for wear despite being dumped in an unceremonious heap on the floor. He racked his brains trying to recall what he had left in his room but there was nothing. Everything he treasured went with him, small but significant items dotted about his person. He listed the evidence. The strange scent he had detected, the soft, swift, sibilant sound that told of some presence sliding surreptitiously past and the crushing blow that had felled him and realised that he had actually seen nothing while standing in the same room. He pondered these facts as he dressed, tying an elaborate knot in his ceremonial belt, turning down the cuff of his boots, knowing that Ikella would demand answers.

Carolus for once was at a loss and decided that it would all have to wait as the first Summoning Bell of the evening rang.

There was the usual buzz of conversation around him but he didn't join in and, seeing his distraction, his neighbours left him to his solitary biscuits, his lonely sweetdrink. He ate and was ready to leave for the Hall of the Healers when the entire Sisterhood of Syrene swept in and, despite the low whispers of surprise, went to the High Table and sat.

Beside his chair, Ikella paused fractionally. Her eyes swept over him in a fiercely diagnostic stare and then, with a miniscule widening of her eyes, a silencing twitch of the lips, she was gone.

He left the dining hall silently and made his way slowly out against the steady press of those coming in, crossing the Gathering Square to look for Patris and his company.

They were nearly ready when he joined them. Ivinish resplendent in the strange, short, rough skirt and even rougher jacket that proclaimed his craft, Rowbet and Somner wearing tanned, hide jackets over the gaitered leggings of free men and lastly Patris, who proudly sported a full length Gather cloak of a subtle, golden shade over his newly adopted Opalwear tunic and pants. His clothes, all new, fitted him like a glove and he wore his hair freshly washed and flowing over his shoulders. A clean hukvah bound in place with a topah made of trace strips and whip thongs surmounted this vision of beauty and Carolus softly applauded. He felt pleased with his own decision to wear his ancient but lavishly decorated Colours, the fine Opalwear subtly enhancing his flowing, white mane and beard.

"We are indeed fitted to our new standing are we not?" he cried in delight and the group of men stood admiring each other, before the next Summoning Bell of the evening drew them into the Gathering Square to join with the crowd waiting for the immense double doors to open.

Above the sullen roll of cloud, the annual alignment of the twin moons commenced. As it did so, some unseen mechanism set the great Gate in the Rock in motion. With a deep groan then a series of grating sounds, the outer ring of the door started to rotate. Slowly, ponderously, it swung the symbolic representation of Jenta away from the symbol representing Gatta at the base of the door where it normally rested.

Up and towards the top of the door it moved until, with a distinct click, the rotation stopped. A single chime was heard and the crowd turned to find that the double doors to the Hall had smoothly and silently swung open to welcome them. So they came, ancient leading newborn, the sighted leading the blind, from every Sand those who followed the faith, each wearing their own Colours, like a veritable tide of humanity. They came silently and knelt before the Book of Rule and Ikella welcomed them all to her as the Sisters of the Order of Syrene, the House of Sorcery founded in the distant past of Selesh, filled the Sacred Circle behind her.

Chapter 9 - The Rites of Jenta.

The Great Hall of the Healers was full to bursting point. Visitors thronged the aisles, striving to remain with others of their Clan or Sand of origin, so that, as the eye swept the crowd, patches of Clan Colours radiated like the spokes of a trek cart wheel amongst the Opalwear of the Shalhanhi, who lined both sides of the Way of Challenge, as was their right.

The Zurias, who wore Azure blue like their Sand, ran down the lower left flank of the Hall, the dark green Malachite flash of the Gresshe was overlaid with their traditional silver half armour, in the upper left quadrant of the same section, fronting the Sacred Circle.

Separated by another smaller aisle from the left side of vast Hall, another bank of seating provided three tiers of benches. On these sat local dignitaries and special guests. These well-raised seats commanded a particularly good view of all that took place, from the Circle to the great double doors. Today, it was perhaps significant that the lower left of this seating was commanded by the second Watch of Jashell and Indeera's Guard.

To the right of the Way of Challenge, the Shalhanhi again stood nine deep. Next to these, a number of paler greens showed where the Quexoni from the far-flung Tourmaline Sands stood to do their new Sorceress honour. In their rear, keeping to themselves as usual, the Sybillsce formed a bright amethyst splash, lighting up the area next to the entrance.

On the far right of yet another aisle, Amber-clothed Jhirelle flowed into the dusky Kora-Mai: their traditional black Colours shot with gold, forming an elegant background for the narrow ribbon of the Clan Jedrun, followers of Deschima, from the Carnelian Sands.

Down the length of the Way, a line of soft cream identified Clan Cereczin, whose turn it was to act as Gathering Guides. As the Hall filled and everyone found their places, they had fallen into a narrow band bordering the Shalhanhi Clansmen. With their brilliantly-hued feather headdresses and elaborately beaded garments over copper, scythe-stained skins, they appeared a fiercely proud people. This Gathering, they wore painted symbols on their faces, honouring their own forefathers and proclaiming their mourning for those recently lost.

Around these brightly-hued visitors flowed the Shalhanhi. Clad in the colour of their Kind, they flickered as one with the natural rock opal from which this immense Hall had been hewn. Created in another age with skills that were as yet unmatched, the natural stone was now dressed and oiled until it gleamed. Around the outer walls, a decorative band revealed all the shades of blue, green and flickering fire that opals conjure. Even in the walls surrounding the Sacred Circle, where the background colour of the rock wall changed from milk-white through bronzed gold to black, the fire flickers shot the walls with shades as yet unseen in this hallowed place. As Carolus and his companions approached the seats reserved for them, they eyed the splendour of their surroundings with deep satisfaction.

Along the entire length of the Way, flowering vines bloomed, the brilliant, white flowers spreading their heavy perfume on the night air. Underfoot, the new hotfloors gleamed as though lit with a warm, white light. The floor felt warm to the touch and Carolus caught, in the ghost of a smile, the Master Builder's relief as he surveyed the newly caparisoned Hall with a craftsman's eye.

Great swathes of golden Torrenwood, from the dwindling forests on the heights above them, provided bench seating for the main Hall. Golden, smith-worked ceremonial Staffs lined the Way of Challenge. Golden flames flickered in the glows from the sconces on the walls to those hung on chains above the Sacred Circle, around which a rim of the same metal was set denoting the point across which no man could step on pain of death.

In the centre of the Circle, a lectern stood holding the mighty Book of Rule, waiting for the day when one who could read from it, would appear.

To the left of the lectern now stood the Sanctuary Chest, gleaming softly luminescent. Although its lid was closed, it seemed to be lit from within, radiating power over the congregation of the Sands.

The ambience, warm yet solemn, welcome and ostentation mixed, caused mouths to open in wonder and lips to quiver in delighted smiles. Tired bodies relaxed in the comfort of their surroundings and the fear and grief that had recently so afflicted them dropped away in sighs of relief – and the Gathering was done.

The Shalhanhi were as one again, their endless wanderings over for this night above all others. They came in family groups, from far and wide sharing experiences, sharing emotions in the bosom of the Opal, safe and warm, gathered to the arms of their clan and their Sorceress.

Standing just a fraction above them, centred to the Way of Challenge, she waited silently, watching until all were Gathered in and the great double doors closed. Behind her in a semi-circle stood her Sisters, all clothed in the high ceremonial fashion of their own Sands, each holding their Staffs of Office where the peoples of their Sand could see them clearly. Here and there, amongst those who filled the Hall below, mothers were touching daughters, gently compelling them to gaze on their own Sorceress with love and pride. Little whispers escaped them, carrying to the Sacred Circle by who knows what magic.

"See little one, see our Colours there, yes there. Look up. That is Tirjella, Mother of our Sands, come all this way so that you can see her.".

To one side of the Circle, ceremonial robes cloaked in mourning black, three candidates sat shrouded in contemplative misery, awaiting elevation to the Staff of their Sands. Behind them, their unawakened Staffs glowed softly with the power reflected from within the Circle.

Beside the lectern, Beneva, last Guardian of Sanctuary, came into view and at the sight of her silver-shot Colours, her unmistakeable authority, the Hall quietened until a delicate cascade of chimes was heard.

A collective sigh went up as two of the Healers appeared to the right of the Hall. Between them, mounted on an ornate stand, they carried the Eye of Jenta.

Placing it centrally between the boundary of the Sacred Circle and the Way of Challenge, they slipped the feet of the stand into slots on the floor with a soft click.

Above the table, from a square bronze-coloured base, rose two silver, sickle-shaped "horns" about a man's arm length high. They swept elegantly up to form an arch and the space within that arch would allow a child of less than two Rotations to pass from parent to Sorceress. As the Eye of Jenta was locked in place, a low vibration ending in a loud click emanated from the direction of the Gate in the Rock. A bell chimed softly within the Hall, then from somewhere behind the Sacred Circle, a disembodied voice proclaimed.

"Thus ends the Second Stage of Jenta.".

Obscured from view in the Syndarial, Shiarjha read aloud. Each name had been gathered from the communities in which lives had been lost. Every name verified before this solemn hour. Interspersed by a low, sweet chime, Shiarjha's solemn voice intoned the ritual reading of the names of the dead.

For every man, woman and child who had gone to the Sands this Rotation, the cybron chimed. For every chime, a scribe wrote a name in the roll of the Clan and this Rotation's list would be unbearably long, employing many more than one scribe, many more than one record roll for not only their own, but for every Clan whose members had been lost in the Opal Desert.

Ikella closed her eyes and prayed for strength, for herself, for her people, as she heard the roll of the dead. Those she had known within Selesh first, then the Clansmen from other villages and towns.

Errish, Patris and Carolus bowed their heads in solemn thought as the names rolled on, accompanied by the muffled sobs of widows and children, the choked murmurs of men in prayer. Many and more were the names that flowed like the Sands themselves, like the tears of their loved ones. On through Jenta's third stage, through fourth and then the last name was spoken, not by Shiarjha, but in a low, grief-stricken cry from the Way of Challenge.

"Donnesh! Donnesh of Caranchar.".

Tuennis, his widow, stood proudly dressed in all her Inesh warrior finery, the late Headman's Obesh on its original red sash now used as an oath cloth bound to her forehead, marking her out as Ikella's woman Guaradeign.

There was a distinct buzz of interest, heads swung in her direction as everyone tried to peer at the woman who marked the Changing Way and then came a cascade of tiny tinkling chimes as the Book of the Dead was closed.

Now, every head lifted as Ikella stepped forward, standing directly below the great Vault of the Hall.

Raising ornately tattooed hands glittering with the symbols of her power, she called softly.

"Jenta, let your children bathe in your light.".

A low chorus of delight filled the Hall for, as though she made some divine signal, a single light poured down from the Vaulted roof above. The beam strengthened, pouring down on the Staff of Selesh, lighting the Opal, leaping in a silver stream through the empowered hands of the Sorceress, bathing the Eye of Jenta in a glowing field of energy. It filled the arch between the horns in a glowing mist which rippled, then steadied and cleared, until only firebright flecks revealed its presence.

Ikella raised her head, opened her hands to her people and spoke the ritual words of invitation.

"Holy light of Jenta, light the way of all women, draw them to you and allow them to conceive in the glow of your light. Dedicate their manlings to your service and render them safe amongst the many Sands of their wanderings, until they return to the Sand once more.".

One by one they came, though many familiar faces were missing this Rotation. All too soon, she was receiving small babies from wifeless men still struggling to comprehend their loss.

To the right and left of her, Mina and Hanna, the Infirmarian, took the babies that she blessed and handed them back to the parents, directing them back to their seats with the help of the Inesh and the Gathering Guides. She mentally committed to memory all the names and families that had come to the Eye, until she found herself facing a small boy. Only about ten Rotations himself, he held a baby in his arms as he approached her hesitantly.

One of the Inesh, whispering urgently, pointed him back down the Way, directing him to return to his place. He sidestepped her, dogged determination on his face, as he came to the Eye and found himself facing Ikella through the arch of the artefact. His lower lip quivered.

"I don't know what to do.", he muttered and then, "But I promised Mother, I promised that I would bring him.".

He raised fearful eyes to Ikella, who sank to her knees so that their eyes were on a level. Never had she been so glad that she had resisted the urge to hide behind the Shadushantesh as custom decreed, but she had been concerned that the impersonal mask might frighten Daro. Now she reaped the benefit of that decision as she took a deep breath and asked.

"Is he your brother?".

Her voice resonated sympathetically and the boy nodded, wide eyed because the Sorceress was speaking to him. Gathering courage, words flowing like a torrent, he continued.

"Father died when our house blew away. Mother still carried Jethen, but she and I walked until we found water and a little food. When Jethen came, Mother got sick.", Sudden tears tracked his face as he whispered.

"She made me promise on her songbeads to bring Jethen here.", His hand opened and Ikella saw, with a rush of pity, the Opal songbeads of a healer.

She wondered silently if this was the story across the many Sands of her world, looking past the boy, down the Way of Challenge, to the vast doors and beyond to the unfeeling Sands that she ruled. It was then that she saw the small forms slipping into the Way like shadows. At first in ones and twos and then in small waves centred on her as she knelt at the edge of the Sacred Circle.

Many carried babies, the crowd on each side encouraging them to come forward and her heart sank. She found herself standing, directing Dorra to fetch all those who wanted to bring male babies to her. Muttering to Mina, to Hannah.

"So many orphans. So many in despair.".

She waited for the small crowd to settle down and then directed them carefully.

"You are all the children of a Clan. Do you all know your Colours?" and the children nodded, calling out so that soon she was in no doubt.

"I will receive the boys of the Opal Sands first.", she announced.

"Then the others will identify themselves and their own Sorceress will receive them when this ceremony is over.".

There was a hum of appreciation from the floor of the Hall and Ikella stood again, cloaked in a sparkling mist of Opal power she spoke to Jethen's brother softly.

"Give me your name first, then the given name of the child you bring and then your parents" names, that we might tell them that their children are safe in the hands of their own people.".

The boy tipped his head on one side as he regarded her through the sparkling field of energy.

"You are very pretty when you sparkle like that.", He remarked ingenuously and Ikella found herself smiling at him, as with the confidence of innocence he handed his brother to her through the shimmering energies of the Eye.

"My name is Villith and I bring you Jethen, child of Marrat and Adena.", Ikella lifted the child high above her head, calling out as she did so.

"Welcome Jethen, child of Marrat and Adena, safely received into the House of Selesh together with his brother whose name he shall bear.".

She swung the baby up to face the congregation of the Clan, holding him firmly as she said.

"Jethen app Villith bin Selesh, we bid you welcome in the name of Jenta.", and the congregation responded.

"Jethen app Villith bin Selesh, we welcome you.", Child after child followed, until all that was left were two Zurias girls and their little brother who were received by Tirjella. It seemed that all the other children had brought their baby sisters with them and so she instructed them.

"When the last baby boy has been received, then I will call you all forward. Will you wait until then?" and the remaining children subsided, seating themselves comfortably on the warm floors as she stood once more and called forward the last two male children of the Opal Sands.

"Welcome Tuennis, Guaradeign of Caranchar.", she called and, flanked by Sorrill and Merrith of her own Honour Guard, Tuennis stepped forward cradling Ahnell to her. Regretfully, Ikella received the child from his mother once again.

"I pass into the care of the Clan Shalhanhi, Ahnell of Caranchar, son of Donnesh, Headman of Caranchar and Tuennis, Inesh woman of these Sands.",

Tuennis said steadily and Ikella, noting the odd inflection of her voice, took the boy and held him high above her head.

"Welcome Ahnell of Caranchar. Welcome into my protection orphan son of Donnesh, Headman of Caranchar and Tuennis, Guaradeign of Caranchar. I name you Ahnell app Donnesh bin Selesh.".

Tuennis her head held high, met the eyes of her Sorceress throughout this statement and as the child was returned to her she turned swiftly and, dropping a kiss on the boy's head, handed him gently to his wet-nurse who bobbed respectfully, melting back into the crowded Hall. Tuennis paused, lost for a moment, until Sorrill instructed her to return and stand with the Honour Guard. She nodded, satisfied that at last her child's place was ensured and, head held high, made her lonely walk back to the ranks of the Inesh.

Ikella watched her go sadly, certain in her heart that Tuennis had made the decision to relinquish her child permanently but, unable to do anything other for her, she bowed her head in acceptance and continued with the concluding part of this ceremony.

From the rear of the Hall came the soft tramp of feet and then, with Diras at their head carrying Daro in her arms, came an entire chapter of the Honour Guard. Dressed in their ancient illusionary uniforms, their eyes the only visible part of their faces, they flowed down the Way of Challenge and came to a pause by Patris and Carolus, who rose and flanked Diras one on each side of her as she approached the Eye of Jenta.

Daro was wide awake and was staring fascinated at the glows set into the vault of the ceiling above the Sacred Circle. He made no fuss as Diras relinquished him to the arms of the Felmin trader. He simply stared into the man's face with interest, twining his fingers in Patris" clothes as Ikella began the ritual greeting for an unknown orphan.

"Welcome stranger child of these Sands.".

A little ripple of interest swept the gathering as women craned forward, anxious to see this baby. Little, murmured comments passed along the Gathering and Ikella watched with troubled eyes as Jashell, Captain of her Honour Guard, announced, "If anyone present wishes to claim this child, son of Arriera bin Jhirelle, let them approach and declare the same. If anyone claims Clan or Sandrights by reason of being blood relative of Arriera bin Jhirelle, let them come forward and prove their claim. Lastly, if any man felt drawn to this place and time without conscious choice, then know that our Lady has cast for him a Seeking Spell, that any living relative may be given a chance to claim this child as their own.".

A stern note of finality entered the stentorian voice.

"Otherwise, let it be known that Ikella, Sharall deir Opal, claims Sandrights for this child from this time forth.".

A long silence fell over the Hall.

Somewhere a bell rang out and Ikella, who had waited the long, silent allotted span for claims, started in surprise and then met the grinning faces of Patris and Carolus through the arch of the Eye of Jenta.

"Who presents this child, for the family of the lost?".

She demanded, carefully listening for any quiver of emotion in her own voice, surprised that she could speak at all, so dry was her throat.

Patris stepped proudly forward. He turned, carefully rotating, holding Daro above his head for all to see and spoke. His voice, so used to carrying above the noise of a trek train, boomed round the Hall.

"I am Patris, trader of the High Sands South.", he declared.

"I gave free passage to a Jhirelle woman, late in pregnancy, as far as Maraken on the night of the Storm, in which she vanished. This child was born of such a Jhirelle woman in the sands below Maraken on the night of that same Storm, his mother having been found by Ikella, Sharall deir Opal and the Council of Nine returning from Song Walk. She rescued the mother, birthed the child and when his mother passed into the keeping of our Sands, brought the child safely to Selesh and had him fed, clothed and housed as her duty dictated.".

He paused for breath, declaring roughly.

"I stand for his mother, Arriera of the Amber Sands, sleeping here in the safety of the Opal where she birthed her child.".

He ceremoniously handed Daro to Carolus, who looked earnestly into the child's face, taking the baby's hands in his and kissing them in some silent dedication, before turning him to face the crowd, holding Daro's back to his chest so that the child faced the assembly.

The Apothecary spoke quietly and yet his voice carried to every part of the Great Hall as he said.

"I stand for the Clan of these Sands in which this child was birthed, to whom he has been gifted by the rite of blood bond. Do I as an elder of these sands have your oath to succour this child who has lost his birth mother? I will teach him the duties of our Way and encourage him to find the true path that he may walk in the Light of the One.".

A collective sigh of agreement rolled around the Hall as Carolus turned, paused only for a fraction and then carefully passed Daro, wide eyed and watchful, through the Eye and into Ikella's welcoming arms. As he handed the baby over, Ikella felt his hands trembling and swept him with a measured glance before she lifted the baby high above her head, holding him aloft for all to see, declaring.

"Welcome Daro, welcome son of Arriera, welcome son of our Sands.", The Hall echoed.

"Welcome, welcome."

Ikella continued.

"As first finder of his mother, I claim the blood bond that binds him to me, Ikella, Sharall deir Opal. He shall be known as Daro app Syrene bin Selesh!"

Ignoring the wave of consternation from her Clansmen, Ikella continued defiantly.

"He shall be regarded as the Son of the Sorceress of the Shalhanhi and for his guidance I will take Patris bin Selesh and Carolus of the Nine Sands as his Songfathers.".

There was a short silence, then murmurs of approval augmented with discreet applause and so it was decided. Reluctantly, Ikella handed Daro back to Nadra who was seated on the right of the Sacred Circle, backed by a full Chapter of Guard. Ikella, eyeing the arrangements for her with approval, found the time to speak quietly to Mina.

"Mina, look after Carolus. He was trembling when he handed Daro to me and, although he appears indestructible, he may still be suffering from shock.", She withdrew discreetly, forcing herself to continue the ritual as somewhere another cascade of bells chimed. She waited for the Eye of Jenta to be ceremonially removed again and then she beckoned the people forward.

"Bring me your girl children, Mothers of the Sands. Bring me those who would enter our Sacred Circle, that I may know their names.".

Scarcely had she finished speaking, when the aisles filled with the women of the Sand, all anxious to hand their daughters to their own Sorceress themselves and for a while time slipped by as she invited baby girl after baby girl into the Sacred Circle.

She passed back into the arms of the Sisterhood those too tiny to stand and positioned those who could walk in order of height, so that for a brief instant the great Circle was filled with the new generation of their Clan for all to look on. This time there was no ritual, each child was here by right of being born female or of these Sands. They would always be admitted here, they would walk into the shelter of the Circle many times in their lives. This was simply the first occasion, the time that she would personally welcome them, every child carried in her arms or gently led hand in hers so that every parent would remember, so that she could commit to memory every last name.

Gradually, the parented ones slipped away back to the arms of their mothers and grandmothers, fathers and grandfathers and then once more came a little patter of feet and the orphans approached her again. Girls of ten or twelve were carrying their younger sisters, handing them to her with shy murmurs.

"Mother called her Tegris.".

"My father never saw her and mother died birthing her. Can I call her Shevi?".

Until both Ikella's arms and heart grew heavy they came. Then, there was but one more, a baby of about the same age as Daro, carried in the arms of a boy, who stood shyly, a distance from Ikella, his eyes on the metalled rim of the Sacred Circle. Ikella smiled and to the surprise of all knelt, indicating the place that the boy should stand.

"If you stand right there young man, I will take your sister for you.".

She dictated and the boy, barefooted, wearing neat but ragged Colours, came up to her. He was no more than eight Rotations himself, she suspected, his tears tracking his face as he gazed down on the baby who lay perfectly relaxed in his arms, gazing back at him. Ikella coaxed him gently.

"Why do you cry little one? Tonight is the celebration of your sister's birth. Tonight, your parents will know, from beyond this Plain of Tears, that you and your sister are safe in the heart of the Clan. Don't weep, we will look after you both.", Tremulously, he handed the baby to her, saying simply.

"My name is Hanno. My Father's name was Morra of Sesil on the Southern Border. My mother was Fennima, formerly bin Selesh. Father died in the Storm, Mother not long after, but before she died she said that this baby was special. She told me that I should give her to you and no other, that you would know her for whom she is. Mother said that I wouldn't be able to stay with her, but that it was my duty before the One, worth more than my own life to protect her, until I give her up to you.".

He sobbed suddenly, knuckling his eyes and, at a gesture from Ikella, Carolus gently drew the boy to his side.

Hanno's eyes fixed on his sister as she came into Ikella's arms. As she stood up and moved back into the Sacred Circle, Ikella felt the power touch her, sweep through her and looked down to see a sparkling, Opal aura cloaking the baby. Her own aura blossomed about her, lights bathing both of them in a confusion of opalescence, the baby raising her arms and cooing happily as Ikella stared in utter confusion, delight written across her face as she proclaimed for all to hear.

"Welcome, she who shall be Suraya, who already knows her truename!".

An astounded silence filled the Hall as all eyes turned to the Sorceress and the baby in her arms. Somehow, Ikella managed to back her own power down, to reveal the aura cloaking the baby and she repeated wonderingly.

"She who is Suraya te Syrene, who shall be to Somishen Shiarjha, Elect as she is to me!".

Traditional cries of acknowledgement rang out from the Hall as she whispered.

"Welcome, welcome to Amishen Suraya, Sorceress in waiting. Welcome to she who is the sixth successor to this Staff and Little Sister to all others of our path.".

With tears of delight sparkling in her eyes, still shaking with the untrained power of the baby flowing through her, Ikella stepped into the Circle, taking the baby to her Sisters in magic to admire.

In the body of the Hall, a small boy wept inconsolably and an old man comforted him, frowning anxiously as he caught the look of naked hatred on the face of Adruna.

As the children drooped sleepily, the Gathering Guides lifted them gently and bore them away into Ikella's Audience Hall, especially set aside this night as a dormitory. Felmin women regularly volunteered minding services for Clan gatherings so, all but the few children from the Sorceress' own nursery were installed there to sleep through the High Ceremonies of Accession. There was a bustle about the Sacred Circle as Diras and Daro's honour guard reformed themselves to accommodate Suraya and a hastily formed entourage, then Ikella came once more to the top of the Way of Challenge and a bell was chimed for silence.

She raised her hands and as if she had spoken the congregation shifted, their Colours rippling as they braced themselves for more bad news. She began, her voice husky and very gentle.

"What we have witnessed here, we must never see again.", she began, the statement ringing out as a cry of pain. "So many children who have come to Selesh for assistance, so many more who have died in the attempt!".

As Ikella voiced the collective grief of the Sands, she made no attempt to hide her own and her voice grew harsh as she continued.

"These children, in ten Rotations or less, could be apprentice craftsmen, novice Healers, the Sixth Elect of these Sands. It is no fault of theirs that they are alone, but if they remain so, it will be our fault, ours and no others!"

Pausing just enough to let her message sink home, she raised her voice in impassioned appeal.

They are kin to all of us. There are many small beds that have been emptied this Rotation. Those who committed their own children to the Sands, know what I ask. This is your chance to redress two sorrows, yours and theirs.", Her voice shook with the intensity of her appeal.

"Clansmen, I entreat you. Search your hearts and take a child home with you!"

There was a rustle and a whispering in the Hall as the congregation turned, looking over their shoulders towards the Audience Chamber, speculation lighting their faces.

Out of the corner of her eye, she caught nods from solemn-faced men, hopeful smiles from saddened women and her heart seemed to rise up, nearly choking her, it was so full. Her low voice commanded their absolute attention now, it was as if everyone held their breath.

"The continuance of our Way has always depended on training our children to follow a Path. By taking a child who has no parent living, you give yourself the chance to continue the Way. Let the tears of our Sands be washed away in the joys of guiding the next generation in the Way, in the path of our forebears.".

She turned away, hearing the buzz of whispered conversations from the Hall, couples talking urgently, women beseeching husbands and the gentle, low drone of planning men. She took herself to Beneva who waited for her in the empty Syndarial.

Slipping behind a screen to change for the High Ceremonies of the evening, she spoke swiftly, in a low voice that would only be heard by the person for whom her words were intended.

"Adruna. My voice carries only to your ears. Koth is my prisoner. He was caught after attacking a High Councillor, in my private guest rooms. Sssh! I don't accuse you of anything, yet! I want to know why that tongueless man has abused my hospitality and on whose orders! I should not have to remind you that I am Mother of all Sands and you and yours answer to me!".

As she adjusted her over robe, Ikella remembered the hideous symbols that formed the skin record of Adruna's High Priest, viewing his impotent rage, as her guards had shackled him to the cage in the shielded cavern behind the Syndarial, which was completely impervious to magic. She caught herself smiling grimly at the thought, that although far from the purpose for which it was intended, she could use that cage to restrain the actions of those determined to engage in activities that ran counter to the interests of her people.

In the magically secluded cavern of the Singers, Koth woke, mindlessly whimpering, the cage suspended from a great chain sunk into the heart of the rock above. Below him, silently gathered in predatory anticipation, the Inesh warrior women circled. Here, where no external sound penetrated, only the echo of his own whimpers pierced the terrible paralysis that had gripped his mind from the moment he had touched the old Apothecary and as his terror grew, one of the Inesh licked her lips and sharpened her spear.

From his seat below the Sacred Circle, Carolus saw a stillness come over Adruna's face and rightly divined that something or someone held her entire attention. She was not a tall woman, but she had a compelling presence. Her hair, black as night, was tightly braided in the fashion of the Sybillsce, every tiny braid threaded with rare Amethyst beads, caught up at the back of her neck. Most of her head, being covered tightly with a traditional mourning veil, showed only a hint of the elaborate styling near her smoothly immaculate forehead. In the centre of her brow blazed a pure, purple Amethyst stone shaped like a tear. What Carolus could see of her skin was flawless, a light bronze glistening in the light of the glows. High cheekbones dusted with some gentle tint drew the gaze of the watcher to her eyes and what eyes they were. dark-lashed, amethyst glows, set in deep, heavy-lidded sockets, as yet only touched with a hint of the power that they could command. However, the warmth of the colour that they held was belied by the frostiness of her stare, the haughteur of her carriage.

As though she became aware of his interest in her, Adruna altered her position and swept the great Hall with her eyes.

As her gaze stopped at him before passing on, Carolus found himself feeling as though something loathsome had touched him. The sensation faded almost too quickly to identify, then Adruna's eyes fell to where her hands were tightly clenched in her lap. Nevertheless, the Apothecary frowned and mentally filed his impressions of that gaze for future reference.

In the robing area of the Hall, Ikella was at long last dressed to Beneva's liking and with a final touch to her new robes she waited for the signal that would start the main event of the evening. Beneva, herself clad in the robes of Sanctuary, was even now taking centre stage, positioned in the centre of the Sacred Circle. The muttering in the Hall below died away as Beneva raised her hand for silence, a single bell chimed and the Rites of Accession began.

Beneva addressed the wondering peoples of the Gathering solemnly.

"Peoples of the Sand, traders and visitors all over Pelshar at this very moment, my voice reaches every Gathering on this our most holy of nights. As you and yours have been gathered to your Clan, to the Gathering of the Sands, so have I been gathered to the bosom of the Clan from which I made my journey to the Eternal Snows and to Sanctuary, more Rotations ago than even I think possible.".

She paused and came forward slowly until all the people below could see her, carefully folding back the sleeves of her gown so that the insignia of a Guardian of Sanctuary was displayed for all to see and a collective sigh went up from the audience gathered below as the wide bracelets of some clear and glittering crystalline material were revealed.

Beneva turned slowly so that each side of the collective below could see her rank clearly, then she continued.

"There is no need to tell you of the Storm for we have all suffered its impact. Many and more are the lives that have been changed forever since this second cataclysm struck our world and it is my solemn duty to reveal to you all the magnitude of our loss.".

She paused for a second and then from somewhere a deep, bell tone sounded, once, twice, three times and on the third stroke Beneva lowered her head and spoke softly, reverently.

"Jocasta, Guardian of all the Ways, Miraniva, Guardian of all Powers.".

A deathly hush fell as the terrible roll call continued.

"Ramora Sorceress Ruler of the Amber Sands, Maranniah, Sorceress Ruler of the Tourmaline Sands, Soloria, Sorceress Ruler of the Amethyst Sands.", She paused, hearing soft moans of terror from the people below, then continued, her soft, reluctant, inexorable voice reaching every part of the Hall.

"The Flowers of the Sands, our Sisters in training. Alandia of the Opal, Mikella of the Azure, Nihandra of the Malachite, Iriquesta of the Cynabarr, Adahuna of the Onyx, Alornia of the Amber Teschia of the Carnelian Andrahnia of the Tourmaline and Rihandia of the Amethyst Sands.", There was a suffocating silence from the Hall below, because although the names were well-known, those who bore them had passed far from those who had known them in life due to the magically enhanced lifespan of a magic user. However, Ikella found herself praying earnestly for these young women who were more real to her than her own family. She had never known that she might not see her family again. As her life was extended by the use of magic, she had come to realise that they would have gone to the Sands long before her return from training. Her Songbeads rustled gently as she thought sadly of what Pelshar had lost. Then Beneva spoke again, softly intoning the names of her own special friends, sorrow in every syllable.

"Timan, Leader of the Nishan Guard, Arkinah, Second of the Nishan Guard, Hundredth Honour Guard, Mineth Honour Guard, Hanama Honour Guard.".

The names rolled on, until her Sisters in Sorcery were palely shocked and soft sobs rose from the Hall below.

Beneva, coming to the end of this roll-call, raised her cupped hands and turning her wrists slowly, she conjured a stream of light in mid-air, which formed a fluidic bubble. As gasps rose from the Hall, this strange phenomenon hung where it had formed, dancing slightly in the glow-warmed air. Raising her hands until the glittering circlets on her wrists blazed with power, Beneva called out imperiously.

"From beyond the pale of death, from beyond the mists of this Plain of Tears, from the eternal rest of the long night, Jocasta, Guardian of all the Ways, I summon you one last time.".

Caught in the centre of the hanging circle of power, a mist cleared, revealing like some insubstantial shadow, the well-known features of Jocasta. As her image steadied, heavy-lidded eyes opened, as if she roused from deep sleep. The Sisters of Sorcery knelt, heads bowed in solemn homage, as the last surviving Guardian turned away from Jocasta's image-self and selected a small engraved block from a nearby table. The size of a child's hand in diameter, it bore the strange interlinked shape that appeared on the Door in the Rock.

Beneva came to stand below the suspended image of Jocasta, who spoke, to soft cries from the throng that filled the Hall.

"Is it time?" Jocasta questioned, a deep weariness in her ancient voice. It quivered and sighed through the Hall and in its wake banners moved, the perfume from the waxy petals of the flowers wafting on the gentle breeze.

Steadily regarding her sister Guardian, Beneva held out the engraved block.

"It is time to change the Way, Sister.", Beneva replied and Jocasta's face turned, appearing to peer down at the block in Beneva's hand as once more her voice whispered through the settlements of every Sand.

"I will then set my seal on Selesh, ancient home of our founder. With this seal shall Selesh become the Mother House of Sorcery once more.".

Those brave enough to watch saw the block in Beneva's hand glow, expanding to a softly, gleaming gold in which clearly visible, were both the insignia of Sanctuary and the symbolic icon of Sorcery. As this symbol of power evolved, it floated free of Beneva's empowering hand, towards the centre of the Sacred Circle and there it simply floated to the ground and seemed to meld with the opaline floor, appearing as if cast in gold metal into the ground beneath their feet.

An awed silence filled the Hall for a moment, then, once more, wearily Jocasta's voice came again and, as all eyes strained to see the flickering image of the Guardian, at a subtle gesture of Beneva's hand the Sanctuary Chest opened and the soft light within spilled out as the top tray unfolded.

Inside lay the same wide, crystalline bands worn by all Guardians. This pair, unempowered, lay dimly reflective of the light around them, awaiting their Calling to Power and the audience below sighed and murmured in anticipation as Jocasta's voice strengthened.

"By these symbols and by the Calling and wearing of the same, shall the new Guardian of all the Ways be known. There is only one wise enough to wield such power at a time, to this Path and to its true following, I dedicate our Sisterhood anew. To all who witness this Calling, today's ceremonies will seem strange and yet this has ever been the Way of Guardianship. She, who was the Guardian of the Ways, must return once more and Call the one who is to take her place to stand forth and be recognised in her stead. Then and then only can we rest, secure in the knowledge that the Way is safe.".

A low murmur ran round the congregation, at the thought of such sacrifice. For those admitted to this mysteries for the first time, this was High Magic indeed. It seemed that Jocasta's voice strengthened with each sentence and as she continued, the concentration on the faces of those gathered intensified.

"The Ways change beyond any change previously foretold. Now, we who wield the power of the Source must change to follow this new Path, or we will falter and fall. Sanctuary itself is no more, it has fallen to the Chasm of Beyond.".

At this momentous announcement, the Sisterhood of Syrene surveyed the congregation, but although pale faces were turned towards them, there was not a sound from the Hall and Jocasta's voice took command again.

"No more will those who come to wield the Staffs of the Sands be segregated while they train. It is time for the Way to change once more. It is Time for the new Guardian of the Way to be recognised and take my place.".

A bell tolled softly in the background as a subtle change in Jocasta's surroundings took place. Her face glowed with motherly love as she called her followers.

"I call upon the Sisters of Sorcery to face the Call to Guardianship.", she lifted her hands into view and at her wrists were bands of icy fire as the orb, in which her image appeared, trembled and expanded until she stood alongside Beneva once more. In the poignancy of that experience, a collective sigh rose from the people.

One by one each Sorceress approached the Sanctuary Chest. Extending empowered hands above the bands of Guardianship, while the light from the Sanctuary Chest bathed them in a silvery glow. This time there was no order of precedence, other than the number of years that each Sorceress had held the Staff. Tiny Eshima was the first. Her aged face and paper-thin skin was revealed as the glow widened to take in her outline and then a single, faint chime sounded and the light of the chest dimmed. As she turned from the Sanctuary Chest to take up her Staff from Beneva's hand, Eshima faced Jocasta sinking gracefully into a deep curtsy, before returning to her Sisters, to wait for the next Guardian to be confirmed. Time seemed to slow as they came forward. Tirjella, Deschima, Medrana and Nahamida, each in their turn making obeisance to the image of Jocasta as they also returned to their position in the Sacred Circle. Now it was Ikella's turn and she came forward, handing her winged staff to Beneva to hold before taking her stance before the Sanctuary Chest. Her face, bare of all glamour, was serene as she extended her hands, holding them above the crystalline wristlets that lay within. As the light bathed her face and touched her hands, a wild peal of bells rang out, emanating apparently from the Chest. Then the wristlets flared into life, scintillating in iced fire as they clasped themselves around her wrists. It seemed to Ikella that a pair of cool hands had grasped her lightly, but when she looked down, her eyes told her that they now glimmered upon her own wrists.

Raising her left hand Ikella took up her Staff once more and, as she did so, the Seal that had been laid onto the floor of the Sacred Circle took on a new brilliance. Ever graceful, Ikella turned toward Jocasta's image and knelt for the Guardian's blessing, hearing the distance that separated them in the faintness of the ancient voice.

"From this day forth, know that Ikella, Sharall deir Opal, is also the Guardian of all the Ways. This is her burden, this is the yoke that she must bear until the ending of her mortal days and she will shoulder it with pride. Listen to her wise counsel, heed her advice as you have heeded and obeyed mine. Upon her Staff I place my mark.".

Ikella's Staff suddenly glowed, where two crystalline bands, one above and one below the Opal, showed. All eyes were turned to Jocasta as she glowed before them. A brilliance almost too bright to bear filled the Sacred Circle as, with Ikella kneeling before her, Jocasta spoke her last words.

"Now I can lay down my earthly burden and pass forever beyond your calling, my dear ones. Though it has ever been the Guardian of the Way's choice to name her successor, there is yet one more to be Called. Be assured that when the time comes another Guardian of all Powers will be revealed.", The ancient voice trembled and the image wavered then strengthened once more.

"Great changes are upon us again, changes beyond your imagination as new paths open, new Ways are divined and new powers come to pass. Keep the peace amongst the Sandsworn, keep the pact between Sandsmen and Landsmen, avoid the temptations of pride and greed, shun those who would strive to achieve power for power's sake and treasure your children for now is the time and a new Age of Mystery is upon us. My blessings fall on Selesh and all who honour this ancient place of power. My thoughts are with you all. Ikella, don't fail my trust.", Abruptly, the image wavered, faded and was gone, the banners fluttered faintly and the glows guttered then steadied as a stunned silence filled the great Hall of Selesh.

Chapter 11 - Curse of Night.

Gradually, as the Gathering Guides made subtle changes to the seating, under the direction of the Inesh, the congregation were rearranged so that the visiting Clansmen of the Amber, Tourmaline and Amethyst Sands, could witness their candidate's elevation to the Staff.

Amongst the celebrants, Beneva closed the Sanctuary Chest and with what seemed an insignificant movement of her hands, contrived a subtle shift in the threads of both her own and Ikella's robes. As another gleam suffused the gown, Ikella felt the throb in her wrists and knew that her new role as Guardian, had overwritten her position as Sorceress, in much the same way as her Opal robes had transmuted to dull silver. She raised her hands for Beneva to slide the wide sleeves back, revealing her wristlets as well as the fiery glitter of the tattooed symbols of power on the backs of her hands. Never before had a serving Sorceress been elevated to the rank of Guardian and, almost as if the very sight of her own empowered hands confirmed her own understanding of the degree in which the Ways had changed, Ikella paused, staring in mute wonder as the wristlets flared and the lacy tracery on her skin blazed with them.

Now the Sacred Circle glowed softly, the combined Seals of Sanctuary and Selesh gleamed golden on the floor and around the edge of the Circle the other Sorceress leaders, positioned themselves in order of precedence, Staff's planted in the floor mounted holders, as they assumed their own powers.

As the Circle was bathed in the light from the power-stones on their Staffs, it radiated to the centre of the Sacred Circle, where of right Ikella's Opal Staff was planted centrally, only the gaps in the wheel of colour behind that, marking the path of their mourning, where soon the newly empowered Staffs would shine. To the left of this setting the Candidates shared a prayer stand, to the right, their Staffs awaited First Calling. At the forefront, besides the Sanctuary Chest the Guardians chanted softly, their othervoices entwining in a slowly growing wall of power. As the power within the Circle multiplied, layer on layer, it touched the combined auras of the Sands with tiny, lightning-charged sparks. To audible gasps, now, between the Guardians, there spun a vortex, eddying around their highlighted hands.

Feeling the weave between them alter, at a quiver in the Source, Ikella felt a thread under her fingers. With a tiny shift of her magically empowered hands, she detached a single, glowing orb. Balancing this on one hand, Ikella's powerful *othervoice* began the ritual chant of the Calling, only dimly aware of the spellbound audience below.

"So waken to the one who will wield you.", She commanded, addressing the three sleeping Staffs of Power, turning an encompassing gaze on the kneeling figures at the prayer stand, recalling the joy of her own Accession to the Staff before continuing.

"Waken to the warmth of her hand and hers alone. Set her on the Way of enlightenment and guard her steps every day of her life, until she wends her Way to the Sands once more.".

She faced the kneeling candidates, gesturing them to rise, as she sent the Source-birthed orb in a graceful, curving arc toward the Amber Staff.

It flared into life, causing a little ripple of gratified murmurs from the watchers in the Hall. Twice more, she and Beneva raised the power whirling between them, twice more Ikella's orbs bathed a Staff in the fire of the Source, but the sullen gleam from the Amethyst Staff aroused much trepidation in her and the anxious glance that Nahamida threw at Adruna did little to reassure the new Guardian, who frowned.

Not knowing whether to be relieved that she was not the only one alarmed, or more worried still, she walked thoughtfully to her allotted place within the circle and paused, studying those who knelt before her. Idirina, eyes closed, lips moving as she prayed. Kerisima, hand over her eyes, leaning against the prayer stand, thoughtful and introspective, then Adruna, kneeling submissively enough, but with a look of triumphant anticipation in her eyes, which jarred Ikella's sensibilities more than she would have cared to admit. Sworn to the practice of Sorcery before ever they left Sanctuary, these three had already studied for Rotations with their predecessors. However, in the sudden violence of the Storm, there had been no chance for an orderly transfer of power. The Songspells of generations had gone to the Sands, with the three Sister's taken from them in so untimely a manner and Ikella's heart ached for their loss.

As Beneva prowled the Circle, sprinkling incense at the Nine Points of Power, reciting the age-old prayers, Ikella heard the gentle click of Songbeads, the rustle of robes, the perfume of Jenta's Stars and felt herself bathed in the light of the Opal Staff. Thus Beneva blessed each serving Sorceress in turn until she reached the sixth point of Power and the Amber Staff. Here the Guardian of Knowledge paused and said Softly, "In the blessed memory of Ramora, dear Sister in Sorcery.", and to a grief tinged silence, Idirina rose and came to kneel at Ikella's feet, readying herself for the moment she both yearned for and dreaded.

Beneva's voice rang out like a call to arms, reaching every member of Clan Jhirelle, wherever they were in a litany of hope.

"Protect the Clan Jhirelle against despair. Bring the strength and wisdom of those who went before to Idirina, who willingly shoulders the burden. Guide her always into the Light, where she and her people belong.".

The Guardian paused for breath, looking at the fervent face of Idirina with affection, noting that Kerisima had raised her own face and was now quieted and prepared. Of Adruna, Beneva could see little but the top of her head, yet she raised an eyebrow at the irritated twitch of the Amethyst - elect's shoulders and wondered as she continued.

"Protect all the peoples of the Amber Sand. Guide, guard and keep them faithful to the worship of the One. Let not petty jealousies and spite set Sand upon Sand. Shun the ways of the unbeliever and guide those you serve to the service of their Sand so that the light may shine on them and theirs forever.".

A bell rang out deliberately and Ikella counted silently until the sixth stroke was fading before she began the Oathtaking. In the body of the Hall, Idirina's Clansmen leant forward, holding their breaths as the new Guardian of the Way asked solemnly.

"Idirina, Elect of the Amber Sands. Do you still desire entry into the Order of Sorcery? To seal yourself forever to the Sands of your birth, in the service of all who pass therein? Do you still foreswear all familial relationships, all bodily ties, keeping yourself virginal, sanctified and celibate, dedicated in service, to your people and their Sands?".

Idirina lifted her face to Ikella, Looking steadily into her eyes, she replied firmly.

"I take my solemn oath, so to do.".

At the ritual response, Ikella felt her wristlets sparkle spontaneously as she extended her hands in blessing, as from each of the Sisters of Sorcery came a stream of light tinted with the shades of their own aura. Caught in this glow, Idirina's own aura woke, enfolding her in soft, shades of Amber shot with flecks of gold and bronze. Almost as a reflex, the joyful girl raised an empowered hand and summoned her Staff for the first time.

There was a soft, thrumming sound, a sort of sigh and the Amber-tipped staff came to her hand lightly, easily, with a familiarity that caught at Ikella's throat, so fitted was Idirina to her new position. For a long moment, Ikella held Idirina's gaze, noting the dewdrops trembling perilously on her lashes, then she drew her forward, presenting her to all in the Lower Hall. Hands upraised for attention, she called out.

"Behold the true Sorceress of the Amber Sands! Idirina is confirmed as the ruler of the Sands of the Jhirelle. From their farthest point to their nearest, across their wandering places, their dwelling places and the places that the dead lie sleeping, she rules alone. As she has given freely her fealty to me, so do I swear to serve her and her peoples in return all the days of my life. I promise to guide and protect the Jhirelle as I protect my own and to support Idirina as she sets her feet upon a new and untried path, that of Mother of the Amber Sands.".

Ikella drew the smiling girl to her and kissed her formally on the forehead as signal of her acceptance of Idirina as a full member of the House of Syrene. Then she led her to join her Sisters, filling the empty space at the sixth Station of the Sands, the appointed position of the Amber Sorceress. Ikella watched the unselfconscious grace of the new Sorceress with pleasure, before turning back and catching Beneva's eye.

"Now we are seven.".

Beneva murmured as Ikella called the Circle to order and proceeded to repeat the ritual of Accession for Kerisima. Shy, shrinking Kerisima, now waiting with admirable composure for her own elevation to the Tourmaline Staff.

This time, when confirmation was sought and returned, when the prayers had all been uttered, it seemed to both Guardians, that the girl who faced a cheering congregation had finally become a woman. As she stood to summon her Staff, Kerisima seemed taller, more robust than the fearful child who had entered Selesh, tearful and distraught. She was pale but determined and as her Sisters bathed her in the light of the Source, she found a tremulous smile. Scarcely had Kerisima's aura surrounded her in a pale green shimmer, when her Staff launched itself, a crooning note in the air following it to the girls hand. Ikella, watching her closely, saw the pure mischief lurking in the delighted eyes of the new Sorceress as she demurely curtsied to the Guardians, before taking up her position at the eighth Station of the Sands and was relieved enough to think, "Thank the One. Normality returns.", before she turned to face Adruna.

Redoubling her efforts to ignore the voice of alarm running through her body, Ikella found herself struggling to pronounce the words of dedication clearly. Nahamida's puzzled eyes demonstrated that she too had picked up some vibration and with relief, Ikella saw her most sensitive of Sisters, delicately adjust her position to shield the nursery group, including Daro.

To be true, Adruna knelt before her just as the others had done. alone, head demurely bowed, still sheltered in the all-enveloping mourning cloak, her own Colours muted below the sheer, black cloth. Wishing that she could have interviewed this Candidate previously, Ikella tried to dampen the unusual antipathy she felt and strove to light the Amethyst Aura around the newest Sorceress, so that she could summon her Staff as the others had, but she was forced to admit defeat. In the face of all the People of the Sand, had her powers failed?

As she watched, the Source flowed in slick eddies around Adruna, as though an invisible barrier protected her, then Ikella felt an ancient thread of power. It was so old, so incredibly cold and alien, that for a moment her sanity seemed to hang on the edge of a dark precipice. Then, silently, Adruna rose to her feet.

The mourning cloak unwound in a sinister, sinuous manner that made Ikella's flesh crawl with revulsion. The veil fluttered from her face, sinking into the ground like some fluid spill, as people flinched in collective fright, repelled by the malicious glee etched on the girl's face.

Adruna already empowered, was elevating. A darkly pulsing Amethyst aura simmered, as it repelled the combined power of Sorcery. She hung in mid-air, surrounded by all the Colours of the Sands, yet cocooned in a halo of dark fire. Ikella felt the strength of her own aura, snap protectively around her and glancing swiftly at her Sisters in Sorcery, she saw them form a protective huddle around the newest additions.

Beneva grasped Ikella's hands, directing her so that their combined wristlets were aimed at Adruna, who hung some four spans above them radiating darkness, a secretive smile on her face. Ikella studied Adruna. Eyes closed she seemed enraptured as the dark Amethyst crystal at the heart of the ancient Staff flared into life.

From the floor of the Hall, the Inesh came running. The entire congregation radiated fear. It spilled out in a tangible wave, as Adruna opened her eyes and caught Ikella in a chilling glare. They glowed, sending smouldering tendrils of hatred into every part of Ikella's body. In her mind she heard Beneva chiding her, "Ikella resist, stand firm. Ikella, you are the Guardian here. resist, resist or we all go to darkness.".

Abruptly, as though she turned a key in a lock and put a hand to the Sanctuary Chest itself, she found a residual memory of light. A pure, crystal light, with powerful waves pulsing in its depths, seemed to surround her mind.

She heard strangely deep voices chanting, then higher tones carrying the Song. The chiming of a million crystals surrounded her and she drew a deep, cooling breath, eased her fear-constricted throat and cried out.

"Mirayen, Avantorish scionectish dimash!".

There was a howl of affronted fury as a gale blew through the Great Hall, sending glows guttering in their stands. As the wind prowled the edge of the Sacred Circle, Adruna blazed her aura more darkly, against the corona of brilliance that surrounded the Guardians.

Ikella felt the wash of power hit her, sending the shadows that surrounded her fleeing back to the far corners of the Great Hall. Extending this emanation as far as she could, Ikella threw out a graceful hand, bathing her people in its protective brilliance.

Adruna was speaking, her voice harsh and angry, her words as terrifying as the twin snakes that now wrapped the hand which gripped the ancient, amethyst Staff.

"I, Adruna of the Amethyst Sands, take my power as is my birthright. I, take, my, power, for no other has the right to bestow my power on me!".

There was a sibilance that made the flesh crawl in that voice. Terrible were the writhings and gesticulations of the faces and hands that embellished her Staff and the flickering power stone at its head, as feeding on the fear that it engendered, that sinister voice spoke again.

"I swear no fealty to this Sand nor any other. In the light of the dark and forgotten one Gatta, the source of all true power, will I rule. I don't bend the knee or kiss the hand of this holy society, for I will rule by right of my own power! My power, mine!" She floated darkly dreaming, just out of reach, venom trickling through her voice.

"I won't swear to you Guardians, nor bend the knee to another Shalhanhi. I won't follow the Way of this or any other Sand, nor pay lip service to outdated customs. My Way is the dark Way and I walk alone!"

Huddled fearfully below, her Clan heard their strange new ruler's ranting, as she screamed defiance at the Order of Sorcery.

"Who are you to assume the role of Guardianship?", she demanded of Ikella.

"Mother of all Sands? I have no Mother, no Sisters and want none. I won't share what is mine by right and mine alone, so Shalhanhi beware! Enter my Sands at your peril.", If Ikella was shocked into silence by this, worse was to follow. Adruna levelled an accusatory finger at her, spitting her words like venomous darts.

"You hypocrite! You, who preach sanctity and virginity, yet suddenly have a child? You should have been stoned to death for such sacrilege. Ikella the Guardian, who preached one thing and does another. Mother of the Sands? Liar! More likely the birth mother of that incubus!".

She turned but before her angry glare could fall on Daro, Nahamida gave a defiant shriek and extended her gold-shot aura around the child, his Guards and nurse. Unable to find a chink in this all enveloping shield, Adruna contented herself with threats.

"You can't hold me. You can't stop me for you know I am as powerful as you. I shall work to the end of my days or yours to bring you down, Sharall Deir Opal, to the dust that you should have become Rotations ago.".

Ikella struggled to remain composed, but her control was wearing very thin, as her thoughts raced.

"What had Jocasta said?", she reviewed this nights advice, reluctantly resisting the temptation of engaging in a senseless battle with the heretic.

"Shun those who seek power for power's sake", was that the answer? Break the Union of the Sands that had withstood the last five hundred Rotations against all comers? Could she do that? Would it work?"

In reply, she heard a clear, calm voice reciting.

"To shun corruption it must first be clearly identified. Secondly, like disease, that corruption must not be allowed to spread. Thirdly, a segregated place for that which is corrupt must be found, for unless that corruption can be healed, it can never be freed to corrupt others. Fourthly, all parts or parties to that corruption must be shunned equally or, like water finding its way, it will escape and cause havoc once more. In the hands of one insane or drunk on power, the adoption of more power is a dangerous thing. For one who does not have the clarity of mind to shape the power they wield, stilling is the only safe answer. for the one who has the ability to wield corrupt power, shunning is the only way. If power has corrupted the user completely, to remove that user from all contact with others who can be corrupted is the ideal solution, but it is not always achievable.", The voice carried on like a memory in Ikella's mind, as she strove to disregard the fanatical voice of Adruna.

"From the heart of a storm, such as our world has never seen, you bore that child, that unnatural child whom you call son.".

In the Hall of the Healers, the heart of Selesh seemed to slow, to falter at the implication of Adruna's words. There was a soft hiss, as a thousand appalled Clansmen gasped at their effrontery. Piercing stares, levelled at the Sybillsce now huddling together in abject misery, sent Sorrill and the second watch to surround them, effectively placing them in protective custody.

"Is it any wonder that nature itself rebels against the Sands when one called holy, one called Mother of all the Sands, steps aside from her vows and creates a child for herself?".

Ikella could barely believe her ears.

"What in Nine Dry Sands was Adruna hinting at?"

She found herself blushing furiously, but forced herself to concentrate on the malicious voice as it continued.

"Indeed, one would suppose in a woman of your age, the power of a cataclysm would be needed to create a living, human child! The power behind the Storm perhaps?".

"There. The accusation is out in the open.", Ikella thought grimly. Now whatever she did to protect her people would smack of retaliation, unless she was very careful. The poisonous filth continued to drip from Adruna's mouth, filling Ikella's ears, numbing her brain and still Adruna continued to rant.

"Even if you went about it in the normal fashion, at your great age the weave that would carry you to term would require the Source to have quickened the infant.", Now, Adruna rotated in mid-air, her eyes glaring down as she pinned Daro with a gaze so full of hatred that Ikella's heart jolted in her chest. Adruna's lip curled scornfully as she spat the words in Daro's direction.

"Is this unnatural child the one?", she pointed a at Daro, but couldn't resist goading Ikella once more.

"Still call yourself celibate? Holy? Sorceress? Where then is your One to protect you?" Her voice, dripping honeyed poison, seemed to reverberate in Ikella's heart.

"See, I have you all in my thrall.", She waved a hand wreathed in the hissing heads of vipers and, to a woman and child, the entire body of the congregation got down on their knees and keening and groaning banged their heads on the marble floor.

As Adruna's voice rose to a frenzy and the banging of heads on the floor of the Hall reverberated in Ikella's mind like the thudding of her own heart, she heard Adruna's voice, slick with cruelty.

"As you have committed your Sands to light, I will commit mine to darkness - the eternal darkness which has fallen on our world, that fills the valleys even in the Height of Sun, the eternal shadows of the caverns below.".

Her voice rose to a fever-pitched, fanatical chant.

"In the heart of the Amethyst, let the dark light of Gatta shine. Let it shine on the face of Pelshar, the world that no longer sees the light of Seleus, the sun who has been driven from the skies by her mortal sin. Let the unnatural one, he who is called the son of the Opal Sorceress, be cast into Gatta's holy darkness and let the Curse of Night fall upon you all, forever!".

As the drumming of heads in the Hall increased and cries of pain and terror rose around her, it seemed to Ikella that she stood on a very high place. She felt remote, isolated from fear, from anger and pain, where a cold light bathed her and serenity claimed her thoughts. She spoke, crystals chiming in her voice as she found herself assuming a mantle of icy fire. At a single gesture of her hand, centred above the Sacred Circle a portal appeared. Through this a darkly glowering, amethyst cloud could be seen which seethed and bubbled, shuddering to the crystalline clarity in Ikella's voice.

"Begone!" she commanded, absolute and unshakeable authority in her ice-cold voice.

"Begone from every Sand of this world other than the Sand to which you are bound.", A concerted groan of terror arose from the ranks of the Sybillsce but Ikella continued, inexorable and terrible in the certainty of her power.

"Begone from the tracks and valleys, paths and byways, from the Fringes to the Highlands. Begone from the eight Sands remaining in our Union, keeping only that which falls to the Amethyst as your own. You and those who follow the tainted path of Gattarene worship will be shunned from this day on. You and your followers will be turned back at the Pass, confined to the Sands of your birth, confined to the Sands of your death.".

Fully aware of the horrific implication in that sentence, she continued soberly, "Those who choose to follow the Path of the Gattarene are to be segregated from all outside contact. Without fear or favour, those who practice the worship of the Dark One, who lend themselves to believe in ritual sacrifice and other acts of a heretical nature, must be forever shunned.".

She paused, hearing agreement from her Sisters in Sorcery. Deliberately schooling her features to impassivity, Ikella, every inch the Guardian of the Ways, began to chant. Drawing on every power, her low-toned voice found the dreadful words and heard them echoed solemnly in a swirling descant, as the spell of final expulsion from the Sisterhood was repeated for each of the Sands, for each of the Winds, until Ikella and Beneva declared in unison, "Daryan, ever watchful of the Eternal Snows, ever Guardian of Guardians, take this heretic and confine her and her followers to the Amethyst, the Sand of her birth, the Sand of her Death, until her Sands be run through the counter of time!".

Now Ikella stood alone again, fortified by a strange calm, the pain of breaking the Union of the Sands far less than the pain of trying to control this wayward Sorceress.

"Adruna te Syrene, Adruna of the Amethyst Sands, we have witnessed your heresy, we have witnessed your rebellion against the Rule and traditions of this House. As the true inheritor of Soloria te Syrene of blessed memory, you have failed in the full view of the Sands of the Union. You have brought pain and isolation upon yourself, upon your people.".

She raised a hand in command and said, slowly and decisively, "You are shunned, excluded from the Sisterhood of Syrene and cast into utter darkness with those of your followers who support your heresy. We convict you, who chose the empowerment of the dark with your own will and Seal you to your Sands forever. As for the previously spotless Sands of the Amethyst, whose peoples have done us no wrong, whose peoples we can no longer protect, the choice is theirs. Within the One's true faith, those who choose to remain outside their Sands we shall find a refuge, but for those of the Gattarene persuasion there can be only one solution and that is the shunning. Now Adruna, daughter of the Dark, do you regret your heresy? Do you wish to rescind your false allegations?".

Again Ikella paused, long enough to turn eyes of flame in the direction of the hapless new Sorceress who dangled powerless before her, impotent fury visible on her face. Adruna gasped for breath, caught in the beam of Ikella's power, held captive in the fierce grip of the combined Sisterhood. Her lips parted and she shuddered but she still spoke defiantly.

"Never! I shall never bend the knee to you or yours, never!" and at her words Ikella smiled sadly and the fire at her wrists flamed and the icy flame of her eyes scorched as she chanted softly.

"Then I cast you and yours into darkness, Adruna of the damned! I expel you from the Sisterhood of Syrene, no more to call yourself Sorceress, evermore to call yourself shamed. You are shunned, forever segregated from our Sands.".

Even as she spoke, the trembling congregation stood and turned their backs to Adruna, who scowled, hissing vengeance. Ikella continued.

"We, the Sisters of Syrene, shun you.", she declared and the Sisters of Sorcery turned their backs on Adruna in silence as Beneva stepped forward to join Ikella.

"We, the Guardians of Sanctuary at Selesh, shun you. Be gone and take your creature with you.".

Ikella's wristlets flared Crystal flame, searing the air around the hapless Sorceress of the Amethyst Sands.

With Adruna's spell broken, the congregation, still with their backs turned, peered over their shoulders, staring towards the Sacred Circle anxious to see what was occurring.

As the Sisters of Sorcery turned back they saw that Adruna, white-lipped with fury, was suddenly fighting some inexorable force as it dragged her towards the portal that, forgotten by all, still hung where Ikella had conjured it. A great wind was licking at her suspended form. she was being rolled, tipped, spun, shrieking towards the portal which was flared open to receive her.

A mighty thundering rang out and Adruna's servant, Koth, was hurled past her by some unseen force. No-one saw where he came from, just that, with his lilac robes entangling his frantically thrashing limbs, he was caught helplessly in the grip of the force that sucked him into the amethyst-cloaked rift. The last thing Ikella saw was his hideously tattooed face, mouth agape in some rictus of absolute terror and then he was gone.

There was a brief, thundering roll, a pulsing sensation and then the wind redoubled its efforts to dislodge Adruna. She was fighting it, hanging on with both hands to the edges of the portal and resisting with all her strength. As Ikella lifted empowered hands towards her, she cried out.

"The Curse of Night on your son Ikella! Let him suffer the Curse of perpetual Night!".

As she was sent shrieking in impotent fury into the void, the great amethyst atop her Staff flared as though struck by a lightning bolt and split in two.

At the top of the step into the Sacred Circle, the Guardian of All the Ways, crystal flame at her wrists and in her eyes, took a deep steadying breath and met the eyes of the one man left standing in the Way. Carolus the Ancient, frail with his Rotations and yet strong enough to withstand the power of the portal, the power of a spell that had driven much younger men to their knees weeping in terror, stood regarding her. Slowly and almost imperceptibly he dipped his head in respect, before turning to help a somewhat dazed Wagon Master to his feet.

Ikella felt the power that had filled her draining away. She looked down and saw her aura retreating, the fire at her wrists fading to a dim glow and behind her, as the portal closed, a bell chimed and a voice announced calmingly.

"Thus is ends the eighth stage of Jentaroth.".

The eight remaining Sorceress leaders of the Sands knelt in the Sacred Circle and mourned the loss of the Amethyst Sand and its peoples. From somewhere in the recesses of her memory, (or was it Jocasta's?) Ikella found a prayer for the peoples of the Amethyst Sands. As the light dwindled in the Hall, the gentle lament sounded poignantly, the cadences fading as the day blended into the deep night. Kneeling with the bereft Sisters of Sorcery, Shiarjha found herself thinking sadly that the morning would bring the dark dawn on the rest of their lives and for once she didn't know which way the Path of life turned.

Chapter 12. "Adruna the Terrible"

Hidden deep in the natural fault line known as Skyrrh, an ancient and secret cavern housed the most unholy seat of the Amethyst Sands. Here, at the orders of their wild Sorceress Elect the people had gathered to be put to the test, too terrified to refuse. Their children had been inspected for defects, as prescribed by their new High Priest. Mercifully, he had taken only three to the Reaper this ninenight, which was good news for all the new mothers of this Rotation, except for those bereaved of their newborns, who mourned their loss in terrified, tear-stained silence.

As in every Sand, they could hear the ceremonies at Selesh, but here none prayed openly. No Songbeads rustled through reverent hands. Instead, fearful eyes watched the prowling of the ever-vigilant priests, who would silently point out any infringement of the New Rule to the detriment of the culprit. Hideously tattooed and hooded men waited to flog those who lapsed into the old way of worship and those who persisted died.

They heard in silence, the Elevation of the Amber Sorceress, then the Tourmaline girl and now the congregation hunched forward as Adruna summoned her Staff. Troubled eyes sought each other as the events at Selesh unfolded. Still there was no sound, with the exception of short terror-filled gasps as the heresy of their new Sorceress was revealed. As her vile accusations pulsed in this unnerving silence, a whip cracked, a child screamed, as Adruna along with Koth came sprawling out of the rift they had entered in the Opal Sands. As the screaming wind abated and the rift closed, there was a crack of lightning and a disembodied voice pronounced the terrible sentence of their Sands.

Despite the speed at which Adruna recovered, she was furious at her humiliation being made public. Snarling like a wild beast at bay, she rounded on her congregation.

"Clear the Hall, get them out!"

She screamed at the priests, stalking angrily to the steps leading down to a shadowy amphitheatre glowing hotly Amethyst in the darkened Hall.

"Kill them, blind them, or better still...", her voice trailed off as she appeared to consider something, then she ordered.

"I have it. Koth, show them your tongue!"

As panicking people fled screaming under the compelling goad of the priestly whips, the hideous High Priest opened his blackened, tongueless mouth in an enormous grimace of unholy joy and Adruna remarked conversationally, "Any man, woman or child who speaks, nay even thinks about what you heard here tonight, will have their tongues ripped out. I shall enjoy a dish of raw, squirming tongue!".

So saying, she summoned Koth and left the people fleeing in terror.

At the rear of the hall, a dark, cloaked figure stirred warily. Olneth, Captain of Soloria's Household Guard, whispered softly.

"So begins the reign of the Fifth Sorceress, Adruna the Dark and Terrible.". The echo of his whisper was left hanging in the air like some ghostly prophecy, as he slipped into a niche in the wall. His gaunt features softened as he slipped from around his neck, two items on a thin chain of some dark metal.

His hands shook as he opened the heart-shaped locket and looked longingly at the curl of dark hair it contained, picturing in his minds eye, the gentle grey-eyed girl he had married only two Rotations ago. He sighed deeply, wondering where she was now. She was heavily pregnant and he had hidden her with Soloria's women, in the hope that the elderly Sorceress would protect her, if anything happened to him. Now he had nothing, no wife, no child, no hope in his Sands and in sudden resolution he tucked the locket away and hurried through the short dank passageway he had entered, with a twist of his passkey.

It took him lower, through dripping caverns, twisting and turning, until he saw the glimmer he had half hoped not to see. Stepping into the small cavern beyond the passage, he faced the truth. Like all those remaining in the Sands of the Amethyst he was trapped.

His hands clenched and he found that he still held the other object. He had forgotten it when he rammed Telandra's locket into his short cloak. He eyed it suspiciously, remembering how Soloria had given one to him, the other to his wife to hold for him.

"This is a little something I conjured up a while ago.".

Soloria, never one for protocol grinned at him amiably.

"Let us just say that this is the key to the back-door into my Sands.".

She chuckled wickedly, saying quietly.

"It is keyed to you, or your kin. Only you can use it and you must use it only one drop at a time. It can only be used in the right place and you will know the place, if you think long and hard. Choose a dark night, hide yourself in dark clothing, but bear my symbol on your wrist to show good faith.".

She had reached out and grasped his wrist, her eyes closed and around his wrist a band of pure Amethyst had gleamed suddenly.

"Think of me, think of our conversations and the band will light!".

She had peered at him closely and for a moment Olneth saw her again. A tall woman, a little ungainly, hair straggling from a carelessly pinned braid, her near - sighted eyes kindly. Now just the memory left him breathless, grief-stricken, as he realised that she had a presentiment of her own fate and had chosen not to tell him, in case he refused to leave her.

He leant against the wall, his face wet, his breath coming raggedly. In the distance, he heard a grating sound and knew his time was growing short. He looked at the small vial he held and almost angrily drew the cap off.

The liquid was oily, ice cold to the touch, but as Soloria had suggested, he transferred a drop on to his finger and whispered her name.

"In the name of Soloria te Syrene.".

He flicked the drop off his finger, into the whirling whining barrier, that prevented him passing and the barrier dropped as he strode forward into an unknown future.

Chapter 13 - Partition

In the aftermath of terror, Ikella regained control. As the frightened congregation spilled out into the Way of Challenge, her voice soared above the clamour, compelling their obedience.

"Still yourselves. Be calm. The danger is past. Sit for our Healers to tend you.", she commanded, aware that all eyes were fixed unwaveringly on the small group of Sybillsce surrounded by the Second Watch. The Sorceress, reassured of their immediate safety, turned her attention to her Sisters in Sorcery.

"Is anyone hurt?", she demanded and although her eyes sought for Nadra's nursery group anxiously, it was Medrana who answered her.

"We are well enough Sister... Mother...", her voice trailed off uncertainly, then Beneva suggested slyly, "Ikella?", which produced a relieved chuckle as the others reported themselves unhurt.

Nahamida's cheerful face relieved her most pressing anxiety, as she came forward with Daro in her arms and Ikella wasted no time in sending the children back to the nursery, for they should all have been in bed. Watching Diras's Chapter surround the most precious of her hostages to fortune, her eyes grew bleak as she turned back to the Hall and other responsibilities.

The Gathering quieted. Her Sisters in Sorcery returned to the stations of the Sands, where alone, the ninth station stood bare of its representative. Beneva, reluctant to engage in clan politics, stood by the Sanctuary Chest and waited for Ikella to guide the Union of the Sands, towards a new Way of Life.

She spoke in measured tones, her voice devoid of all emotion.

"This night has been a night of revelations, of remarkable changes, of challenges that we had never considered. The pieces of the old Way are scattered like the many peoples of the Sands, who must now decide a Way for themselves. Each of your Clans has sent its gifted daughters to Sanctuary and accepting the guidance of Guardians, has joined the Union of the Sands voluntarily. This has been the Way, our Way since Adaria te Syrene, from whose family I am also descended. Now it is my task to ask each and every one of you to search your inner hearts before you reply. With the exception of Clan Sybillsce, will the Elders of each Clan present stand.", She waited, slightly amused by the number of Clan Elders revealed amongst the travelling companions of her Sisters in Sorcery, but schooled her features to sobriety as she said simply.

"Amongst our people we have a pact. We agreed to support our Clansmen and women, Sand to Sand across this our beloved world. In the light of what has occurred here tonight, I have been forced to act in defence of us all and have expelled the Gattarene, her cult members and their Sands from the Union. It is not possible to permit normal interaction with such heresy and so I have confined its practitioners to the Amethyst Sands. However, we are not blameless, amongst the remaining Clans, there must also be fundamental change.".

She caught the swift glances amongst the Elders standing, but continued relentlessly.

"The Storm of this Rotation didn't see Sand assisting Sand! We were all confined by the devastation to our own problems, our own repairs. Now we have buried our dead, we can see clearly that passes are closed, markets are bare of produce and Winter is upon us. We all have resources, some more than others and yet we don't share. We don't share our knowledge, but guard it jealously and yet lives could be saved by bringing together all that would help the Union of the Sands survive.".

She looked sternly down, glowing, imperious in the silver of her Guardianship.

"If we still have Union in the Sands, that is?", she challenged and the Hall below erupted.

She forced herself to remain still and unemotional but the tingling at her wrists told her that Beneva approved and a swift glance behind her showed every Sorceress quivering with suppressed excitement at the growing chant from the Hall.

"Union. Union. Union!", the chorus rippled through the ranks. They cheered each other on, they clapped, they stamped in rhythm to the words. The Shalhanhi rocked the aisles, the Zurias growled and stamped, the Gresshe howled the words as a call to arms. Ikella stepped forward, watching the tumult grow. It ran through the massed Czerezin, Kora-Mai and the Jhirelle like wild fire. Even the placid Jedrun clapped and rattled bangles in approval, the Quexoni swayed and nodded, calling "Union. Union. Union.", and when Tisanna got to her feet amongst two others of the disenfranchised Sybillsce, she finally held up her hands smiling.

"The People of the Sands have spoken.", she announced as silence fell. "The Clans remain committed to the Union of the Sands and a new Way of my devising.".

The congregation forced themselves to sit while she continued soberly.

"There will be many Clan meetings in your own Sands, in which I will take enormous interest, but for now we will engage in organising only the most basic changes.", She eyed the Sybillsce warily, as she explained.

"I can't recognise the Clan Sybillsce, until the fall of the Gattarene. However, we do have a duty to care for the Sandless funded by the Treasury of the Sands.", Her eyes sought Tisanna's. "You must submit to the Truth search, obey the laws under which you live, but mine won't be the hand that decimates, for you are not a Clan in rebellion. The Gattarene and her cult bear the blame for your loss of status. You are innocent refugees, in need of protection.", her voice took on a severity none had ever heard her express.

"The Gattarene, her Cult and its followers are damned and for them there can be no forgiveness, no return. I am not a vengeful ruler, nor do I seek to restrain any from returning to the Sand of their birth, but if anyone is so minded, they should know that I can't allow them to leave again, until she is brought to her knees.".

Hopeless sobs rose from the Sybillsce, but Ikella was focussed on Tisanna, of the Council of Nine. Tisanna who had laid Daro's mother into the birthing basin just six journeys of Jenta past. Tisanna of the merry eyes and a peal of giggles for every occasion, Tisanna with an endless Sand of Sorrow to walk, alongside her exiled Clansmen.

Savage anger flickered in her voice and in the wristlets of Guardianship as she spoke.

"Now hear my words clearly, for they can't be unsaid. As Guardian of the Way Changed this is my edict. Let the name Adruna be struck from the records of Sanctuary and consigned to the Roll of the Damned. Let no child ever bear that name again, let it be expunged from the memory of all Pelshar. Let every Gattarene know that they are condemned, their names removed from the record of the living and consigned into utter darkness. Brand their sins on their faces. Let them be forever expelled from the society of our world, penned within the Sands of the Amethyst, the borders closed, even upon our own, for fear that such wickedness may escape.", Low moans of grief accompanied this statement as Ikella whispered softly.

"Every evening for the rest of my life and beyond, prayers will be said for the innocents in her hands, for their eventual release from fear and tyranny, as we invoke the power of the One and the mystery of the Source, to their aid and protection.".

She knelt, hands clasped in silent prayer for those that she had doomed, as tears flowed from the congregation of the Sands.

With her religious duties done, Ikella took quick counsel from Beneva and then returned to the Way of Challenge. The Colours rippled as the Clansmen settled again and she spoke quietly, watching Shiarjha and Carolus's clerk scribe for her.

"From now on, Rotations will be named for the events that you have borne witness to tonight. The Rotation that ends with first Light will forever be remembered as the Rotation of all Sorrows, to mark our lost ones and the passing of the Way that was. At Dawn the Rotation becomes Partition and each successive Rotation will be numbered so that events can be pinned to the Rotation in which they occurred. Do you agree?"

Amongst murmurs of assent from the Clan elders, Ikella continued saying gently.

"The remainder of this celebration will continue. There are markets tomorrow and a feast before departure. I wish you a less turbulent day tomorrow, we will meet at Fall of Jenta, before you return to your own Sands.", and as the glows in the Hall brightened, Ikella formally bowed to the people, then bending her knee before the Book of Rule, she gathered her Sisters and departed, shepherding them all back to the Djellim.

She gazed at them all affectionately, remarking gruffly.

"You must be exhausted my dears and though we could talk all night, I doubt that would repair our society. We should eat supper and sleep and to that end, I suggest a mild sedative, for the night, although eventful, is still young. Now is the Gathering of the Inesh, who celebrate the Cleansing of Women.".

She eyed her Sisters in Sorcery doubtfully. They came from far flung cultures and she hoped fervently, that no offense would be taken by her elders, used to their solitary, celibate state. She broached the matter delicately. They are not always known to be silent.", she admitted. "It is their night, a time of freedom and I don't begrudge them that. However, I must join them, for I have an announcement to make. I will go presently, but for now, my dear Sisters, gather near, look after our young ones, protect our ancients...". Her eyebrows rose as Eshima, the oldest amongst them by far interrupted, cackling merrily.

"Yes, yes, get you gone young Ikella! Go and drink redberry wine with your guards. I'll cover for you and no, we'll not go to refectory! We'll go to my room - it is the biggest. And Mina won't bring a sleeping draught, she will bring our supper and something to drink, and, while you have fun, we will sit up and tell stories of Sanctuary when I was young. Stories to curl the hair of new, young sisters.", She clapped her old hands briskly.

"Go, get you gone woman.", Her voice raised, she bawled.

"Mina, where are you? Bring cushions for my room so that we can eat and talk together. No, you wretch, I am not in need of a Healer. Bring food, bring wine. How sad that we have no men to wait on us!".

Smiling at the shocked expressions on the faces of her youngest "Sisters", Ikella gratefully fled to her own rooms.

Although guarded, the nursery door stood wide open as she came along the corridor and she stepped inside, bewildered briefly by the bustle of Healers that surrounded the third crib bed in the corner. A small voice was heard protesting in the ablutions room set aside for Nadra's use.

"I don't care who you are. Even if youse a Sorceress, I not going in there, I not. I never had to for my own mother, she didn't say I had to be drownded to look after Suraya. No, no!".

The piercing shriek that followed this last was enough to set the teeth on edge and Ikella bypassing Healers who should have intervened, went to investigate.

Nadra sat drying a naked Daro, while at her feet, Ahnell lay kicking on a wide drying cloth. Focussing her attention on the scene around the sunken bath, she could see a small boy running rings around an Inesh warrior, an old man and her own Sorceress Elect. Having assumed that they had the evening schedule of the nursery would continue, as normal, Ikella's brow drew together in a thunderous scowl and then she saw where the problem lay. To the untrained eye, Hanno's eel-like agility let him evade them all, as he fought valiantly to avoid the necessary bath. Ikella's lips quirked as she watched the humiliating failure of so many adults to contain one child, before she drew their attention to the opal flicker touching his skin and raised her voice above the furore.

"You will never catch him you know.", she remarked acidly. "Not while his sister protects him. Shiarjha, do something sensible for a change. Go and feed Suraya, play with her, distract her while I bathe this monster.".

With a discreet movement of her hand, Ikella, (she who disdained to use small magic), conjured a tall tub of warm, soapy water, whisked the still protesting boy into it and thrust a soaped cloth into the bemused hands of Carolus.

"Now it is up to you.", she remarked. "Once I have taken a look at Daro, I will continue with my duties, which is what you should all be doing. Nadra, bring Daro, I want to see for myself that he has suffered no ill effects from this night.".

Collecting her wet-nurse, she turned, preceding them all into the spacious nursery, calling the Healers away from Suraya's crib.

"Hannah, Andria, I sent you here to examine Daro. I need to be certain that Nahamida was able to protect my son from the Gattarene's Curse.", Studiously avoiding all further reference to the revelations of the evening, she concentrated as the Healers subjected Daro to a rigorous examination, smiling with relief as Andria commented.

"He is a little lighter than I would like, but then he has a strange diet for one so young. Other than that there is no obvious cause for concern. As you must well know my Deshun, next to you Nahamida is the most powerful in Sorcery.".

Her voice tailed away as she caught the bleak look in Ikella's eyes.

"Next to the Gattarene, Nahamida's power looks like the random dabbling of a child at play.", Ikella commented grimly. "I shunned her because she was wicked in her thoughts and motivation, I shunned her to protect the people.", Her voice dropped to a whisper. "I shunned her because I was afraid.".

She hugged Daro to her then kissed him before handing him back to Hanna, who began to dress him for bed. He yawned, relaxing against the Healer, eyes half-closed and abruptly Ikella stood, calling out so that everyone in the suite could hear her.

"Fare thee well, I am for my last duty of the night. Shiarjha, you hold the Staff. Carolus, can you care for the boy? His sister will sleep if she can see him beside her. Andria and Hanna hold the nursery and have charge of Daro and Ahnell. Tuennis, I have something to say to all Inesh before I rest, meet me in the Square at Gathering time.", She consulted her infallible sense of time and without waiting for any answer, she swept out of the nursery and entered her own study. Hardly had she grasped the scroll that Shiarjha had laboured over all the previous night, when the door to her rooms opened and she heard the voices of Jashell and Indeera, with others of her Honour Guard. She opened the door to the ante-room and peered out demanding.

"What are you doing here now? I need no guard to walk down to the Gathering Square. Did you think to escort me?".

Jashell, seeming to seize on that suggestion, said briskly.

"After this night my Deshun, it would hardly be right for us to desert you. We will go together if you like.".

She clapped her hands for the six Inesh with her to form up. So they went forth, Ikella and her Honour Guard and along the hall where they had been listening at the nursery door, merry eyes smiled at ancient ones and Shiarjha said comfortably to Carolus.

"It won't hurt her to have some fun. She needs to relax, to let her hair down and they are right, you know, she is the Mother of the Sands and very fitted for new experiences.", She smothered a giggle when the old man remarked.

"Whether her hair will be let down or not, she should share in the "joys" of the night, but I do hope they don't overdo the redberry wine. It is very potent, she is not used to it and I have absolutely none left.".

Chapter 14 - The Ninth Stage of Jenta

Unaware of the innocent plot forming around her, Ikella went out of the slip door to the Gathering Point. Already, the Square was filled with women, waiting for the Ninth stage of Jenta to begin. Starting when Jenta reached the top of its annual separation from Gatta, this stage celebrated in Inesh culture continued until sunrise of the following day. During these all-female rites, women of all castes shared their common bond, that of motherhood.

Persuaded by Sashandra her predecessor, that this ancient tradition was seen as a solemn duty for mothers from all castes, Ikella had permitted its continuance, for many Rotations, encouraging friendly relationships between her Guard and the villagers of Selesh Minoria, by contributing both wine and food for the feast that followed. Now, with a mounting sense of curiosity, she joined the growing throng in the Gathering Square, for the remainder of the night was women's work.

Jashell, glancing around and apparently satisfied with the numbers present, raised a hand and silence fell as Ikella stepped on to the dais, scroll in hand and with a glad heart, launched into her last duty.

"Tonight, I also bring the Inesh a new Way.", she said steadily and a hiss of indrawn breath greeted her from her listeners.

"Though we don't know your origins, for Rotations, this the second Clan of the Opal Sands, has been sadly neglected, in our writ of rule.", She paused as a buzz ran round the women, then, as silence fell once more, she continued, looking deep into the eyes of the one Inesh woman who had spoken out against the fate of her people.

"Whilst I can't undo the past, I can soften the burden that you carry and change your lives for the better. To this point, I have brought you a new Charter. It will be posted at the Gate in the Rock tomorrow and a scribe will remain there so that any who can't read can have the charter read for them.", She firmly ignored the sidelong glances and continued.

"Whilst the Shalhanhi rule here, so shall respect be shown to the Inesh who free us to rule. From now on, the slavery of the Inesh Clan is ended.", There was uproar, tears, questions, bewilderment, fear and lastly an uneasy silence while Ikella dwarfed by her Guard waited for peace and then at a nod from Indeera, she spoke again.

"We have shared our Sands for too long to abandon you.", she said simply, allaying fears she could already hear being expressed. "We need you, far more than you need us, but I will elaborate so that you can see what I offer clearly. You will be able to remain in service, if that is what you choose, but you will have the right to settle amongst us and follow your own Ways also. You may form a Clan Council, hold land, own property, marry, have children, be a free people again. We ask only that you agree to maintain the security of the Sands until this current crisis is over.", She paused, looking up at the intent faces of her Guards and finished softly.

"The Inesh shall have a right of vote upon the Clan Council of this Sand and they will elect one of their own to speak for them after the next circle of moon.", The silence from the gathered Inesh was so deep that it was tangible. Unbelieving eyes looked back at her as she reached up to the Summoning bell and chimed it just the once.

"As customs alter one thing remains absolute and that is my Source-empowered right to dispense justice to all. In recognition of their time of service to us the Shalhanhi, inheritors of these Opal Sands, so I set my word and hand on this Charter of the Inesh. From this night forward, so may it be! I have spoken on this and my word is my bond and the law of this Sand.".

Even as she finished speaking, she was prevented from stepping back by the presence of her Honour Guard who had closed around her, protectively she thought at first, as Jashell lifted a hand for attention.

"My Deshun, though not elected as you would have it, I speak for all here as I would have done before your great act of generosity was made known to us. We welcome the gift of your justice and celebrate it on this the Ninth Stage of Jenta, in the Rotation of Partition.", The Guard Commander's clear voice carried over the heads of the other women, who nodded, smiling at each other and Ikella.

"However, there is one item of special interest to us tonight that you can't rule on, for the time is past and even as you speak I, Guard Commander of those here gathered, must take action to detain one who has evaded our justice for many Rotations.".

Bewildered, Ikella tried to gain a better vantage point, but the guards to left and right of her had gently seized her arms, compelling her to stand quietly. Disconcerted, she attempted to engage her powers in vain as she was forced to face Jashell, who smiled down at her, saying softly.

"Oh no my Sister-ruler, as Jenta alone rides in the unseen heavens, your power over us has faded, gone until Jenta joins her twin. We are as we ever were, free until sunrise and you can't bring even your great power to bear on us.", She paused, aware of the frightened beating of Ikella's heart as she stood powerless only a pace away.

"You have nothing to fear from us.", Jashell reassured her. "For there have been a thousand Rotations in which we were also free, in which any one of you could have been slain in your sleep. We, however, kept the oath. We kept the faith, kept you safe and yet you have ignored your duty in one respect and for that failure, I will pronounce sentence.".

The warrior turned to her people who, to Ikella's amazement, were grinning hugely.

"Ikella, Sharall Deir Opal, how long have you been a mother and resisted the ritual of Cleansing?".

Jashell challenged.

"How many Rotations have passed since you became Mother of all the Sands? Yet, still you didn't present yourself this night, to submit to your ordeal by water? This Rotation, we in truth couldn't allow you to evade your responsibility, any longer than we could evade our duty to the Sands. As mother of a male child you shall endure the ritual Cleansing. As the recalcitrant Mother of all Sands, you will be purified.".

From the crowd came a muttered suggestion.

"Nine Times?", to which witticism, a laughing Jashell reached up and rang the Summoning Bell.

Before Ikella could ask questions, she was hoisted shoulder-high. Protesting weakly, she was borne aloft by her Guards, followed by the laughing, chanting crowd. Her heart thumped, louder than the thudding step drums, as amidst the triumphant ululation of the Inesh and the shrill whistles directing the procession, they took her towards the immense, communal bathing rooms of Selesh. She thought defiantly.

"I must remember this, every part of this, whatever it costs me.", little realising that the events of that night would remain engraved on her heart forever.

The preparations went by in a blur, as she submitted to Jashell's ministrations. Stripped of her finery, robed in a loose bathing gown, plunged into a warm pool, then queuing with the others, she found herself stood, holding a sprig of Corra herb in her right hand.

"Nascus for a girl child, to give her courage, strength and endurance. Corra for a manling to make him fleet of foot, far-sighted and long-lived.", Sorrill had murmured as the herb was pressed into Ikella's hand. As intended, Ikella suddenly thought, of her baby one, her Daro, sleeping innocently in the nursery above.

Slowly, the queue wound through an archway, turning along an unlit maintenance corridor. The torchbearers went ahead of them, lighting the path, until, one at a time, they passed into a cavern that Ikella had never seen before.

Inside, a magnificent bathing pool set on three levels, dropped away below them, as they walked along one edge, heading towards the back wall from whence a narrow waterfall thundered directly into the shallows. Downward this path sloped, wending its way past ancient glows, which sprang to life, as they passed. Following closely as the path passed behind a rock wall that immediately obscured her sight of the waterfall, Ikella felt the walls close in, then the pathway disappeared. She stood in a cramped, saturated space in which the deeply shadowed roof soared above, with no visible exit beyond.

Ahead of her, Onaria, mother of twins, was disappearing through a fissure in the wall, gesturing encouragements to follow her. Nervously, Ikella glanced back, to meet the smiling faces of Indeera and Driss, who offered a supporting hand, indicating that Ikella should step down into the gap on her left. Lowering her head, she followed Onaria, into a small, dark tunnel, waist-deep in running water, that led into a pool lying behind the waterfall where the rest of the group, including Jashell and Sorrill, waited.

Bewildered by the assault on her ears, Ikella stood amongst them and felt strangely welcome. The water was cold and her resolve not to show any discomfort was sorely tested as she waded through the wash looking around her curiously. Here, it was deeply shadowed, surprisingly quiet and she could hear Sorrill's instructions perfectly.

"The Second of my Honour Guard has taken on a very different role here.", Ikella mused, hearing an echo of her own speech patterns, in the words of the Inesh warrior.

"This is the Way of the Inesh from time immemorial. We mothers, come to be cleansed of our birthblood in the heart of the waters, returning that birthblood to the Sands in which our children will live, in the hope that each child born of the Opal will make its way back to sleep in its Sands. We offer symbolically, the birthblood of each child to the Sands, before passing through the waters, to be cleansed and prepared, in the hope of another child to come.".

Naked except for a thong, Sorrill stood on a rocky spar in which cradled, dry as a bone a shining stretch of purest Opal sand. In her left hand, she held a dish. In her right, she held a long, narrow glass, which glowed a vibrant red. Next, Jashell, similarly clad except for a pendant of carved Opal, addressed the gathered women.

"When you are called, take the wine in your free hand. Speak the name of the child you commit to the Opal and then dip your herbs in the bloodbowl held by Sorrill and sprinkle the drops from it into the Birthing Sands. Pour, in one steady stream, the wine you hold onto the Sands and speak your name, that you may be reunited after your deaths. When the glass is refilled, you should drink the wine in one swallow, to represent, the restoration of your blood in preparation for the births of the Rotation to come.", She smiled gently for several of the women in the line were already blessed, the gentle swell of bellies betraying their condition. She continued, her voice strangely clear above the waterfall that thundered down relentlessly into the pool beyond.

"Walk through the waters of the Opal with no outcry to ensure true cleansing, pass beyond into the arms of your sisters who await you and submit to their care.".

As the first of the women with her was called forward by name, Ikella observed her surroundings quietly. There was something familiar about the cavern here by the Birthing Sands she thought, but she couldn't make the connection, so distracted was she by the ceremonial. That too had an echo of something she ought to remember. She wracked her brains to no avail, now not being sure of what her own personal memories were and what she had absorbed through her link with Jocasta and the other Guardians of the Way past.

She watched as woman after woman called out their children's names, crushed the herbs they were carrying into the bloodbowl and shook what she took to be blood into the natural curve of the Birthing Sands beyond Sorrill. The herbs were being gathered into two great stone urns by Indeera, manning one and Driss, manning the other. They held torches aloft and the shimmer of the darkened waters reflected on their hands and faces as the women drank their wine and passed through the waterfall, silently returning to the gathered Inesh beyond who were not silent, their claps, whistles and cheers as each woman rejoined them, startled Ikella who was used to more formality, more spirituality about her ceremonials.

All too soon, Onaria was being called and Ikella realised with a little nervous start that it would be her turn next. She watched with interest to see how a twin birth would be celebrated.

There was a murmur of question and answer from Sorrill as Onaria appeared and then Ikella's question was answered. Onaria was dipping the herb in her left hand into the bloodbowl, scattering the drops and calling "Dispa", a male name, before crushing the piquant-scented leaves and giving them to Driss to place in her urn. The herb was Corra, to make the child fleet-footed, farsighted and long-lived and as the perfume of it came to Ikella she remembered the scent. It was the heart of the incense that was burned in the room of a new bridegroom-to-be for nine nights, his body oiled in it to make him more potent. Ikella blushed, for her memories suddenly touched on things no maiden lady should think of and she looked up into the laughing, challenging eyes of Driss as Onaria took her wine and passed through the waterfall.

She was confused. The Sorceress knew that both babies lived, yet what of Sorjia, the girl child? Then there was a splashing and a swift body slipped past her and Onaria once more approached the Birthing Sands below the waterfall, this time scattering the red liquid from the bloodbowl with Nascus in her hand, thoughts of her girl child gaining in courage, strength and endurance in her heart. Again, she sprinkled the sand, handing the herb this time to Indeera to place in her urn and then she poured the libation of wine into the sand, draining the second glass before passing beyond the waterfall to a roar from those waiting.

Now it was her turn. Ikella shivered, but stepped forward steadily, taking direction from Jashell, a Jashell who seemed to have grown even taller than her usual statuesque height, a Jashell gleaming with the water reflecting in her eyes. Ikella listened quietly to the instructions.

"Ikella, you that have given us a new Way. Now, we give you a new path, new knowledge in the privacy of the birthplace of the Inesh. Within the heart of the Opal, we freely admit you to the Sisterhood of Free Sands who's High Priestess I am. You must first take upon yourself the duty of the cleansing of the Sands, for without that cleansing there can be no recovery from the Storm of Storms, nor can you protect those Sands against the predations of the Gattarene. Every Sand of which you are the Mother must be represented in the cleansing. Without this cleansing, evil and wickedness will walk the dark canyons and caverns with impunity, for the division of the Opal Sands will cause the memory of this cleansing to be lost and the dark penetrates every place no longer lit by Seleus our sun, father to the light.".

There was silence beyond the waterfall and Ikella was suddenly certain that every word that Jashell spoke was heard even through the thundering water, as the Inesh woman continued.

"We can't be certain if the Sands have male or female attributes or both and so you will use both herbs, name each Sand in order of precedence and proceed as we have with our living, breathing children. This will engender courage, strength and fortitude amongst the innocents of every Sand. This will engender swiftness of body and mind, clarity of vision actual and spiritual, and, in longevity of rule, the continuance of our great faiths against whatever is to come. Now, in this Rotation, is the time of the return of trust between the peoples of the Opal and to this purpose I invoke the rites of Cleansing for the Nine Sands.".

Speechless, Ikella received the Nascus, adding it to the Corra in her hand and plunged both herbs into the bloodbowl that Sorrill offered her, relieved to see that it contained nothing more sinister than red wine. She crushed the herbs, thinking that mingling them was a curiously symbolic combining and suddenly found herself compelled to reach forward, capturing Jashell's hands with her own, making the Inesh warrior assist her to crush the herbs and scatter the wine drops into the Birthing Sands. The flashing wonder in Jashell's smile spoke volumes as Ikella spoke in a husky whisper.

"The Sands of the Opal Desert.", carefully handing the Nascus, the Corra to Indeera and Driss. The Sorceress took up the glass of wine and poured it steadily into the Birthing Sands, speaking in a low voice.

"Ikella te Syrene, Sharall deir Opal and Mother of these Sands".

She took the second glass of wine and, with her eyes fixed on Jashell's, she drained the glass in one long draught, feeling it bloom in her throat, suffusing her with a rare flash of warmth as she stepped into the heart of the waterfall and managed, just, not to shriek as the fierce, biting cold of it struck her unprepared body. Just as her brain turned to ice, she felt welcoming hands grasp her, drawing her out of the freezing downpour into the shallows of the great, stepped pool beyond.

From Daro's self appointed Chapter of guards, Diras, Miyani and Brey led her stumbling feet into the mid-pool into which she sank gratefully, feeling the numbing ache of the ice shower receding.

"Not too long my Deshun.", Diras warned. "You must return through the steps to the right of the fall, turn left and back through the tunnel.", and so it was. Like some arcane torture. the shivering return through the shallows to the inner cavern, the ritual of the herbs and wine, the invocations, the naming of each Sand in order, after Opal, Azure, Malachite, Cynabarr, Onyx, Amber, Carnelian, Tourmaline and lastly, Amethyst.

The very name of the proscribed Sands stuck in her throat, but Sorrill whispered to her.

"You must! You are still Mother of the Amethyst. The Sands themselves don't sin! By doing this you may protect the innocents, strengthen their resolve to endure. Ikella, you must!"

So Ikella crushed the herbs for the ninth time, poured the wine into the Sand for the ninth time, drank the ninth glass of wine, then went fuzzily through the waterfall, for the ninth time.

She was drawn through the last of the downpour by Diras, who looked at her closely as she cleared it. Her legs felt as though they no longer belonged to her, the deluge no longer felt cold. Hugely relieved that she didn't have to go through the ritual again, she sank shivering into the warmth of the mid-pool, until Diras was dragging her up again, pressing a single spray of Corra herb in flower, into her hand and hissing, "Deshun. Deshun Ikella! You must go through again, for Daro. For your son!".

She staggered to her feet, looking at the Corra in her hand totally bewildered, as Diras said, "I will take her.", and found her reluctant legs being forced to move again as Diras marched her determinedly back round into the cave below the waterfall.

This time there was a clear sense of urgency. As she crushed the Corra herb, she heard Diras" voice saying from somewhere, "I found the only piece in flower on the plateau. I knew you would want the finest, the most potent for our baby.".

Ikella knew that she had to hurry for some reason. However, she found herself slowed internally, concentrating, remembering every movement, every sense tingling, every sight, every scent as if it was being recorded. She forced her hoarse voice to obey her as, scattering the wine from the bloodbowl, she called out.

"Daro, born of the Opal Sands, in the heart of the Great Storm.".

She crushed the wine-soaked Corra in her hands, drinking in the heady perfume of it as she handed it to Driss to add to her urn. She watched unsurprised as the Inesh woman set her torch to the pile of Corra on her side of the Birthing Sands and at last Indeera set her torch to the Nascus herb of the girl children on its other side as Ikella poured her libation into the sand and said firmly.

"In birth, Arriera child of the Amber Sands, laid to rest in the Opal and, by adoption, Ikella, Sharall deir Opal, your most humble servant, stand as mothers to the child Daro bin Selesh.".

As she turned away, a fleeting memory touched her, another pool, another waterfall and was gone as she took the last glass of wine from the hand pressing it on her and walked steadily through the waterfall once more to the cheers of her people, her other people, the Inesh of the Opal Sands.

Beside Ikella and holding her hands were Jashell and Sorrill, behind her companions followed Indeera to the right and Driss to the left, Diras kept pace immediately to her rear as she cleared the thundering waters above and as she did so the waterfall ceased to flow. Suddenly, Ikella remembered where she had seen something like this before, far away and in the heart of a storm.

Her shivering limbs had only started to come under her control, as the warmth penetrated the chill, but against the wine she had imbibed, her brain felt as if it had no chance, as she tried to grasp the enormity of what she had seen. She found the noise and presence of so many others bewildering. She stood, staring in amazement as the Inesh played games in the waters, pulling one another under, swimming like some school of water-born creatures.

She noticed that along the side of this great, central pool, were women who had left the waters, some lying on drying cloths, some of them taking a massage from the hands of their friends and neighbours, others just lying, resting and drying their naked bodies. Ikella's head was swimming with so much noise, so much confusion, she was grateful to feel gentle hands directing her and tried to focus in vain on the faces of the women who were leading her stumbling feet into the precious seclusion of a small and almost private cove to the right side of the pool.

Here, the green-tinged waters bubbled and swirled. There was a place to rest here, leaning against the rocky basin's edge, a place to sit even some plinth-like structures on which first Jashell and then Sorrill laid themselves, extricating themselves with indecent ease, from the breast-high waters.

Ikella eyed the high edge of the basin and decided to remain, floating, waiting for the roof above her to stop spinning. Indeera and Driss waited with her and Ikella was grateful for the support for she was tired, strangely light-headed and her limbs didn't seem to belong to her at all. Thus, she drifted just within hands reach of Driss, of Indeera, with a blissful expression on her face.

A group of young women, armed with drying cloths, flagons of oil and other treatments, had descended on Jashell and Sorrill. Jashell submitted willingly to what seemed to Ikella to be torture, allowing them to roll her on her stomach, pummelling her back, moulding the deep muscles of her body. Slapping with brisk chopping movements of trained hands, oiling shoulders, breasts and stomach with the easy intimacy of sisters. While Ikella floated and watched, Sorrill also underwent similar tortures, allowing the woman pummelling her, to disrobe her completely, abandoning even the narrow thong, parading herself in glorious, abandoned nakedness like some happy child, trailing her legs into the warm springs.

Indeera and Driss stood waist-high in the bubbling spring and gently towed Ikella in her hazy, drifting dream to the water's edge. Lifting her simultaneously over the rim of the pool, they left her stranded and gasping with outrage in the hands of the masseurs. Somewhere between water and massage couch, another glass of wine was produced and the stumbling, protesting Sorceress was encouraged to drink and behave like a woman.

Someone was beating her back, another someone had hold of her hands and was massaging her fingers with a combination of oil and salts. Deep, cleansing things were being done to her shoulders, hip and calf muscles and Ikella found herself giving soft, growling groans. She thought of protest, but found herself querulous and disappointed when the massage stopped.

She raised her swimming head and stared into Jashell's face as the warrior maiden dipped her hands again into the oils, soaking away the cleansing salts, smoothing her palms, with a strong, polishing motion from hands to insignia-branded wrists. Ikella blearily peered at her fingers and, remarking on the new brilliance of her tribal and symbolic tattoos, suddenly found her tongue thick, her words slurred. Stumblingly muttering, she managed to say.

"It is not permitted... I can't think.", then confusedly she complained.

"I think I'm drunk.", in such a mumble that the amusement of the other women was complete.

Totally naked and happily unembarrassed, Jashell raised a single eyebrow in a remarkable mimicry of Ikella's own facial habit, calmly remarking, "And?".

to the laughter of all those in earshot.

They insisted on carrying her through the winding tunnels of their knowledge, taking her deeper into the ancient heart of Selesh than she had known of. She was paraded - now dressed in the finery that Sorrill had lavished on her. With her body still singing from the deep massage, her brain still befuddled with the potent wine that she had imbibed, at the head of the throng of new mothers, many of them here at these celebrations like herself for the first time.

She remembered little of where they went, or what she saw, save that there was a hall, bedecked with what greenery the darkened hillsides above Selesh had furnished. She was placed on the amassed cushions that covered the floor and beside her resting place she saw a beautiful beaded and woven bag, which was handed to her with great ceremony. Ikella looked at it bewildered, as Onaria, mother of the twins, haltingly made a speech, of which she remembered little, her head spinning and the assembled company appearing to surge in waves of sound, that faded to a dim murmur then surged forward again.

Slim Miyani, the youngest of the Honour Guard, was smiling and speaking now and Ikella forced herself to concentrate, to grasp the very words that the girl was speaking.

"That you will use this gift as we have used it, to carry your precious new ceremonial robes in.". She was saying, as Ikella, looking down, saw that the robes she had worn to this gathering were even now carefully folded and locked in the cunning embrace of the beautiful carrier that they were placing in her hands. She took it uncertainly and said slowly.

"But I have nothing to give you in return.", Then Tuennis stood and spoke softly.

"You have nothing to give us in return?" She sounded disbelieving.

"Ikella, this day you have shown me a person I didn't know existed. You have revealed yourself to be what I have prayed for - someone we could all trust, someone who would remember the things that were told her and act upon them. Today you have given us back our birthright. Today you have given every Inesh the right to live, love, bear children, die and be buried in the Sands of our birth and to have our names known, our Name Days celebrated, our memories honoured and you say you have nothing to offer in return?".

Ikella fell silent at her words and then, thinking of what physical thing she could offer, she giggled suddenly and found herself blurting out.

"No, it is alright, I forgot that I gave you the wine!".

To peals of hilarity, Jashell raised her glass solemnly and Ikella's last clear memory was of Jashell, High Priestess of the Inesh, Captain of her Honour Guard, saying firmly.

"That's alright then, seeing as you have drunk most of it.".

Looking up into her eyes, seeing in them a hint, a reflection of a power she had never noticed before, Ikella found her head was spinning, around her a tingling and a buzzing in her body, in her brain a numb void of darkness beckoned. Her throat was incapable of speech, her hands were relaxing, her cup was falling. Still Ikella seemed to hear a voice - was it her own? - saying.

"Well I paid for it.".

There was a momentary silence then a chorus of laughter as the darkness rose in her exhausted body like a wave. As she struggled to her feet, she knew intuitively that it was too late, she had no power to repulse this and, reeling into the arms of her trusted Honour Guard, she slipped into the spinning depths and knew no more.

Chapter 15 - A New Way begins

When Ikella woke, she was in a dark and strangely confining place. Every part of her body hurt, for she lay on a bare rock floor. Her head felt as though it was split, but reaching up to investigate, she struck the back of her hand against a hard surface and retreated sobbing. Eventually, biting back the tears, she attempted to open her eyes, instinctively screwing them shut again, when she discovered that they felt burnt to their sockets.

She explored carefully, deciding that nausea and pain prevailed over cramped cold lethargy, subconsciously diagnosing her own dehydration before a harrowing thought struck her. She cowered whimpering, alone, in confused misery, wondering if she was alive or dead, worse still, had she by some dreadful mistake, been buried alive?

Slowly, neck and back tortured, muscles protesting, she stretched, persisting, until she had regained one elbow and could lean into a corner, achieving some relief from pain.

Cautiously, she opened her eyes and winced as the lids grittily parted. It was too dark to reveal the nature of her entombment and for a brief, panicky moment she revisited the theory that indeed she had died in the subterranean chambers of Selesh and her body had been hastily concealed. Sense prevailed, though she choked back the sob of dismay that rose unbidden to her throat at the thought of Daro, orphaned twice.

"If indeed I am dead.", she thought blearily, "I would have been brought on a bier, to lie in the Sacred Circle. not tumbled into some dusty corner and hidden in the dark.".

Into this melancholy reverie came a sound, a small regular sound, the sound of feet approaching. Despite her aching body, Ikella cowered into the corner and desperately tried to still her frantically beating heart and calm her breathing while she hid herself from the unknown.

She heard the sound of a latch being lifted, a hiss of indrawn breath and then a sort of greyed light penetrated her hiding place and she peered curiously at the drapes that covered the entrance to this precious corner of safety. A voice spoke.

"Deshun?", it called questioningly and then into her restricted view came a pair of feet. She looked at them uncomprehendingly, but then she recognised Mina's new Gather shoes. Made of dyed Irix hide, they were currently the love of Mina's life. With relief, Ikella realised that whatever terror she had hidden from, with Mina present she was safe and before she remembered the tight confines of her hiding place, the Sorceress stood up, crashing into the firm, wooden base of her bed!

Reeling back to the floor, she lay clutching her wounded head, sobbing with the progenitor of all hangovers.

There was a brief period of confusion as Mina directed the removal of the bed, lifting the trembling Sorceress, in solicitous arms, restoring her to the bosom of her Healers who took her into the private bathing room. Gently, Inahana bathed her face with some delicately perfumed liquid that soothed and refreshed her dry skin. Mina, quietly tutting under her breath, examined her scalp for signs of damage.

"You have been very lucky my Deshun, for there is not a break in the skin.", Mina said disapprovingly, as she placed a cold, damp cloth to Ikella's bruised scalp, as Ikella, who didn't feel lucky at all, groaned involuntarily and submitted to being put to bed. Smiling and nodding knowingly at each other, her Healers slipped away, leaving only her guard to mind the Sorceress through the long, hot afternoon.

The deep shadows of the perpetual twilight had lengthened into early evening before Ikella re-appeared in the outer chambers of her suite. She was her mysterious self once more. Her pale, drawn face concealed behind the Shadushantesh. Her hair elaborately braided and her ceremonial robes glittering, encrusted with Opals. Jashell, who now wore her shadow warrior's garb, had her own face partially concealed behind the half veil, but their eyes sought each other and locked in a nod of recognition. Slowly and deliberately, Jashell dipped her head in obedience to the Sorceress's brisk comment.

"Again we come to Fall of Jenta and we must away to give thanks in Hall my warriors.", The Inesh followed her proudly. At the door, Ikella paused and then taking Jashell's arm, she drew her forward until they stood side by side.

"I am persuaded that this is where you belong Jashell.", she commented as they swept out of her quarters and down the stairs leading to the private entrance into the Hall, where the people waited.

"We will talk about this later.", she promised, as they struck their hands to their chests in salute and then she was gone into the Sacred Circle where her sisters in Sorcery awaited her announcements.

At last, the closing ceremony came to an end and joined by Beneva, she was able to make the most radical of her announcements. Raising a hand for silence, she stepped forward, her Opal aura engaged and spoke simply.

"My fellow Clansmen, those whom I have mothered all the Rotations of my service. As Sorceress to the Shalhanhi, my duties won't change, although I shall rely on Somishen Shiarjha much more to assist me in local or Clan matters. However, I can't function entirely as before and be Guardian of the Ways as well.", she wove quiet reassurance into her voice as she continued, shifting her ceremonials to show the silver of that exalted status.

"Therefore, as each Sand recovers, their own Sorceress will lead them, with advice from the Guardians if they need help. Every Sand should raise a High Council, so that the people can play a full part, developing answers to problems and pride in their skills, which can later be shared in the revival of the craft Guilds. Seris Beneva, the Council of Nine and I have a greater work to begin!", she smiled as agitation died and became curiosity.

"During the Winter months we will be unable to travel. This Rotation has only just permitted us to Gather and for the next five Rotations, the ice Seasons may get worse. Jentaroth must be celebrated in your own Sands, in comparative safety.", she was gratified to see Clan Elders nodding guardedly and plunged on.

"Meanwhile, I will start building, opening up Selesh once more, so that I can obey Guardian Jocasta's last command and open both the School of Sorcery and the Guild School of the Healers at the festival of Zenitheon, five Rotations from now!"

There was a stunned silence, Ikella held her breath, then there was a rustle before and behind her and she saw that not only every Healer in the Hall was standing, but her Sisters in Sorcery had come forward shoulder to shoulder and relief swept her as she realised that she had consensus.

So it was in the light of the following dawn that the Clan leaders departed, determined to make their mark on their own Sands and lead it along this untried ascent to enlightenment, Seris Ikella's brand New Way.

PART TWO - ASCENT TO ENLIGHTENMENT

Chapter 16 - Eve of Zenitheon
(Seven Rotations later.)

In the dim dawn light before Summer Solstice, a tide of humanity eagerly converged on Selesh. Tomorrow, witnessed by every Clan, Sand and Guild, the Guardians were opening a school of Healers during the festival of Zenitheon, but today was for Gathering, exchanging news and gossip, bringing their daughters to be tested for Talent.

"They are coming!" reported the runners from the villages around.

"They are coming!", sang the wind along the plateau above Selesh.

"They are here! Along with every living relative, their animals and all known forms of transport!", a highly delighted Master Smith reported, as the tented village grew in the sparse pastures at the foot of Mount Torrenesh once more.

A group of women swiftly wove through the assembling visitors. Three tall tawny creatures, wearing the uniform of the Inesh warrior guards, faces concealed by half veils, hair tightly bound. Despite the impersonal anonymity of their clothing they walked confidently towards the Guard post smiling and exchanging greetings with the visitors. Pilgrims stepped aside for them and laughter rang out, as some noted the rank armbands and Opal pendant worn by the tallest, then the throng waited patiently, as amidst a flourish of salutes, Jashell, Clan leader of the Inesh, was admitted accompanied by Indeera and Driss.

As the light grew, the Gatekeepers opened the Gate in the Rock, admitting visitors into a wide tunnel, which sloped down, levelling out into an immense Gathering Square. Here, surrounded by glistening walls and gleaming flagstones, bemused visitors gazed at doors of massive proportions, which proclaimed the ceremonial Hall beyond, as the centre they sought. Around them, other doors led to living quarters, the great Infirmary, the passage into the new School. Beyond, the vast warren beneath Selesh provided an "undercroft" with permanent Winter quarters for villagers. To the right of the Square, were the forge, the underground pastures, then the Hall of Welcome, providing guest accommodation. However, it was to the Gathering Square, where local announcements were made, Clan rulings given and secular celebrations held, that their attention returned. Today, those who crowded around the edge so hopefully, would be admitted further than any other before, as they brought their daughters to study the mysteries that Selesh had guarded for so long.

In the Square, the Inner Guard formed ranks and as the visitors settled, Jashell, flanked by Driss and Indeera, approached the dais below the summoning Bell, which ordered their days. There was a rustle of interest as a Guard Commander brought the parade to the alert, with a shouted order.

"Relief Watch stand alert!", Sorrill shouted and her Chapter drew themselves up, bellowing back.

At your command!".

Driss, her face concentrated as though she consulted some inner clock, reached up to the Bell and struck the clapper against the bronze casing once, twice, then on the third chime, in complete silence, the huge doors to the Hall of the Healers opened.

The woman who stood framed in the entrance wore the plain, tan tunic of a Healer. Behind her, eight Healers identified themselves with the Sand of their origin by the colour of the tunic they wore. This was the Council of Nine, the ruling body of the Healer Guild, who were followed in turn by a small woman wearing the dull, silver robe of a Guardian.

By now, pilgrims had advanced into the Gathering Square to stand at its far edge behind the mustered Guards. As the party of Healers advanced, a whisper ran round the assembly as mothers pointed out their leader to nervously shuffling daughters.

"That one there. Yes. The lady with the silver wristlets. See the tattoos on her hands? Yes, that is Ikella, head of the Healer Guild, Sorceress of the Opal Sands and Guardian of the Way!".

An indignant comment escaped and those whose sharp ears caught the words suppressed a wry grin as they heard.

"What do you mean she doesn't look all that special? Believe me, if you had seen what we saw at Caranchar you would understand. If you really command power you don't need to wear finery or jewels to wield it!".

Jashell's lips twitched as she solemnly relinquished the platform to Ikella's party. As they passed, the tilt of an amused eyebrow told the Guard Commander that the Sorceress was resigned to the legend that had grown out of her spell-casting, naked as the day she was born, a screaming baby bound roughly to her by a sash.

At the thought of Daro, her eyes narrowed and she scanned the throng again, discreetly positioning herself so that she could speak softly to Driss, who stood, tall and inscrutable, monitoring the junction of the entranceway and the Gathering Square where Ikella's adopted son and his faithful shadow, Ahnell, tended to loiter. Her suspicions were allayed as Sorrill gracefully inclined her head to indicate another arrival and, almost as the Sorceress reached up to touch the Summoning Bell, a full Chapter of Guard accompanied two remarkably clean and well-groomed boys into the Square.

Carefully positioned by Diras, his own bodyguard, Daro stared around him in delighted interest, beside him, Ahnell shuffled restlessly, flanked by towering guards, ready to protect or control them at a glance. Thus satisfied, Jashell signalled and the Summoning Bell rang out the Gather, summoning the Clans in order of precedence. Each strike of the clapper calling a Clan to honour its Sands, touching the fingers of their right hands to head, lips and heart, pausing wherever they stood. As the second chime rang out, visitors from the Azure Sands stood taller hands raised in salutation, followed by the Gresshe, then through the remaining Clans until at the last chime, where once the Sybillsce would have honoured their Sands, the Inesh warriors gave salutation to the Opal once more. In the shadows, a few Sybillsce refugees wept, praying for the innocents trapped in the shunned Amethyst Sands, Then Ikella stepped forward and spoke.

"In this place, at this time, let the barriers between Clans be removed for all who Gather in the worship of the One. Let none amongst you raise thought, word, hand or deed against another, save in protection of the whole Gathering. Let those who would return to the fold of the Healer Guild stand forth as one Clan, as one Guild and let them pass amongst the many Sands henceforth, freely and unchallenged, wherever their services are required.".

To one side of the small dais, a group of women approached. They each wore the different Colours of their Sands and soon this rainbow mixture began to sort itself out in order of seniority. As the shuffling ended, a scribe appeared holding a wax tablet and began taking names. These were handed up to the dais where the Council of Nine were gathered around a small bench while a roll call was being prepared. Ikella spoke again briskly, for her eye had caught the gyrations of bored children.

"Now, will all mothers with a girl wishing to enter the Guild of Healers bring their children forward and make them known to us?".

It was a command not to be ignored and soon the candidates stood nervously before the Sorceress.

"For the next few days during Gather, we will take you into the Hall of the Novices.". Ikella stated firmly.

"There, you shall live exactly as you will if you are accepted for training.".

A ripple ran round the Gathering Square as parents noted the departure from tradition, but this died away as Ikella held up her hand and spoke again.

"We have many more to welcome during the day, so to begin with I will take all the potential Healers, together with those whose promise was recognised at First Scrutiny and gather them together. Only then will I begin to sift those who are ready for training now from those who are not. This takes time and consideration, this takes skill and many tests of purpose. Would you want me to repeat previous mistakes?".

There was a collective intake of breath as the Clans remembered that last Gathering, then parents and others let out a sigh of approval and the early morning Gathering was done.

The Sorceress and the Council of Nine drew aside with those charges that had been placed in their care already. Beneva took brisk charge of the scribe and his tablets, bearing both away into the cool depths of the Djellim to make up the initial roll of names, while a motherly, little woman trotted out of the entrance to the living quarters to collect Daro and Ahnell for their morning meal. She seemed totally unaware of the curious glances from departing visitors as the two boys danced along holding her hands with a full Chapter of the fiercely protective Household Guard marching in the rear of the homely party.

As visitors made their way out of the Gate in the Rock and back to their tents or lodgings, a small caravan of travellers approached. A wagon was hastily directed in through the Gate and down the entrance into the Gathering Square, where it was plainly expected. the doors to the underground pastures swung open the instant that wheels were heard in the Square. Even as a number of travellers descended from the wagon, it was drawn inside by a weary-looking Biron. Before the doors closed, a small herd of Zeglurs was driven in behind the wagon and then an ancient Apothecary appeared, a younger man at his elbow also dressed in Apothecary's Guild leathers. For a moment they seemed to hesitate then the elder drew the younger man to him with a companionable arm around his shoulders. Thus entwined, they made their way across the Gathering Square and through the doors into the living quarters of the community.

Just inside these doors, the younger man gave a choking laugh and, despite his elder's protestations, lurched and then slid to the floor in a dead faint. Immediately, his companion delved into a capacious scrip and was busy selecting remedies when a tart voice remarked from the staircase to his left.

"Carolus, I despair of you. What is the use of a brand new hospital if you insist on draping our floors with your waifs and strays?".

Ikella, as full of concern as she was of sarcasm, continued down the stairs directing her personal Guards swiftly.

"Call Mina and Hanna. Get those porters with a carrying board to come here directly.".

Then to the Apothecary, she said in a slightly uncertain voice.

"What has happened to him?".

Reaching forward to turn the patient so that she could see him clearly, she grew very still as she took in the terrible injuries. Something had scalded the man's face, turning healthy, sun-bronzed flesh into a reddened mass of suppurating tissue. One eye had disappeared into this mess, the other was closed in unconsciousness. She hissed in horror as more damage was revealed under her exploring fingers. His neck and chest were badly torn as if some animal had mauled him.

The Sorceress clapped her hands together and sang a long, low note, conjuring more light by which to see the injured man better and, as she did so, a long, traditional plait of hair draped across his shoulder caught her eye and she paused for a moment, examining the elaborate twist of Amethyst beads at the end of the braid. Her lips pursed, she reached forward, gently lifting the eyelid on the one undamaged eye. The pupil swam into view as he struggled to regain consciousness. Ikella knew that peculiar shade of blue, for she had seen no other with eyes like this in her long lifetime.

"Olneth!".

She identified him unerringly and Carolus nodded.

"Found him pegged out on the Sands, just south of Maraken, where the crossing trails meet.". He spoke shortly, all his attention on his patient.

"Can't put him in the Infirmary until we know how he came there. Can't let any Sybillsce know he is here either, just in case they have breached the Pass!

He's badly injured, he's full of poison, his mind wanders, but he wanted to come here.".

As the old man spoke his hands worked quickly. He had prepared a bowl with a number of powders to which he was even now adding water from his gauche, carefully returning the leather stopper to the ancient medicine flask one-handed. He continued to talk as he mixed a stiff paste.

"Must stop the air reaching whatever is still burning his skin. I have dressed it twice since we picked him up and it gives enormous relief, but lasts so little a time.".

She heard the sound of tramping feet as the porters arrived yet she concentrated on holding Olneth still as Carolus applied the compound which thankfully served to mask his identity further.

"I dressed him in my spare clothes. I thought that bringing him in dressed as the Commander of the Gattarene's Household Guard might not contribute to his longevity!".

The Apothecary's wry chuckle was echoed from the litter that Olneth had been gently placed in. With horrified sympathy, Ikella realised that their patient was awake and aware of every excruciating movement as the litter bearers made their way to the private sickroom set aside for the Sorceress herself.

Twice they had to stop on the way through the labyrinth of corridors. This was forced on them by the increasing distress of the patient, whose low whimpers gradually increased in volume until there was little choice. Both times Carolus took charge of the situation, attending Olneth diligently, carefully raising the younger man and administering a few drops from a flask, dribbling them cautiously into one side of the ruined mouth.

As she paused beside the litter, Ikella glanced down at the stricken man. He was sweating, grey with pain, his lips drawn back from his teeth in a rictus of agony. Yet there was sanity in the one fierce eye that turned in her direction. His voice, low and strained, managed a hoarse gasp.

"Lady, I have... much news...".

Carolus interrupted him.

"Not now lad, hold on!".

The bearers lifted the litter once more and set off on the last leg of the journey, the one that took them into what was now the Sorceress' own floor. They passed the offices allotted to Jashell and the Inner Guard Commanders. Then the doors to the Apothecary's own suite and turned into a new passageway that drove between Beneva's rooms and the nursery suite, where childish voices were raised in some exhortation.

As the litter turned, a door opened and something came squealing and skittering along the floor, hotly pursued by two small boys. The litter bearers hoisted the litter out of the way as Ikella and Carolus each reached out and retrieved a child, pulling them to one side of the corridor with abrupt admonishments to take care and not to chase Dolcans in the corridors. They swept on and out of sight, leaving the bemused boys staring after them, wide-eyed with amazement.

"Phew!" exclaimed the taller of the two.

"I thought we would catch it that time, but she didn't even pull our ears!".

Daro stared after his mother speculatively.

'she's worried.". he announced quietly.

'something's really wrong. She had her "magic" face on too.".

A chittering sound interrupted them just then. Ahnell darted past Daro and paused in the doorway of the Guardroom uncertainly. Driss was holding their pet aloft, her powerful hands restraining the frustrated Dolcan easily.

"Don't hurt Usticus!".

Ahnell danced anxiously in the doorway, protesting their pet's treatment, but Driss grinned maliciously at the almost human features of the Dolcan.

"I won't hurt him, but you must pay a fine to get him back.", she admonished.

"I saved all week to buy myself a ripe pretulish at the market.".

She sat, still holding the wretched Dolcan aloft. The boys shuffled under her gaze as she continued.

"This Usticus of yours has stolen my fruit, eaten it and I think that boys who will have a Dolcan should learn to restrain it from stealing their friend's food.".

She eyed the boys sternly.

"I had a Dolcan when I was a girl and my mother fined me every time it stole from her. So young masters, your task is to find me a ripe pretulish in time for supper!".

As the boys hesitated, wondering where in the Sands they were to find such a thing, the Inesh warrior commented.

"I believe that Master Patris brought a net of them down from the Heights of Maraken only this morning.".

She lifted the hapless Dolcan into a cage that hung on the wall of the Guardroom and closed the door on the chattering monkey-like creature.

'seems a shame to sell or exchange him in order to replace my fruit, but…"

Her comment was never finished, for when she turned back to the doorway where the boys had jostled for the right to view their pet, they had vanished.

Driss grinned as she returned the baleful look that the Dolcan bestowed on her, stare for stare. The fruit that it had eaten was far from ripe but, as the warrior figured it, the Dolcan wouldn't be telling anyone the story any time soon!

Outside, new arrivals replaced the earlier Gathering quietly. As the Summoning Bell tolled at

Height of Sun, the second wave of entrants were admitted into the cool sanctuary of the Hall itself, where they were encouraged to leave their markers on seats for the evening ceremonies. Progressing from there to the Audience Chamber, another harvest of novices was Gathered for the school.

This time, Shiarjha, Sorceress Elect, greeted her Clansmen and their daughters, in the same tradition practiced at morning Gather. The Council of Nine took charge of a gaggle of would-be Healers, another scribe entered their names to a growing roll-call, with Beneva overseeing the entire ritual.

The day grew hot and heavy. Selesh and its pilgrims slept under a sullen roll of cloud, except for the two small boys who carefully folded and rolled the bedding from the wagon to stow it away in the hayloft that served the underground pastures. Daro glanced thoughtfully up at the sign of the "Four Free Men" and whispered to Ahnell.

"That looks like an innkeeper's sign!", he observed the freshly painted sign scornfully.

Ahnell gave the offending item a cautious glance, then whispered impishly.

"I think their office smells more like an inn than an office for transport drivers!", he confided with a grin which vanished as a voice remarked conversationally.

"I heard that young man.".

Daro's mouth turned down at the corners.

"Henbane! How does he do that?" he hissed. "We can't say anything without Master Carolus overhearing. He's got ears as long as his Zeglurs!".

The boys couldn't see the Apothecary anywhere, until movement in the pasture attracted their attention, to where Rowbet and Ivinish were rubbing down a tired Biron. As the animal moved they saw Daro's Songfather watching the animal closely.

"That's weird.", announced Ahnell. "How can he hear us from there? He has eyes in the back of his head as well. Nadra told me that.".

A mutinous lip stuck out as Daro heaved a sigh. Brows drawn together, he put his hands up to his face to draw Ahnell's attention to them and then he signed in the quick hand-flickering code of the Inesh warriors.

"Bet he can't read this!"

The flurry of gestures comparing Driss's antecedents with those of their pet, drew a smothered giggle from Ahnell, then forgetting the adults, the boys bent to their task once more. Gradually. wagon drapes were removed, mattresses beaten, blankets brushed, rolled and stowed in the barn. Daro eyed the dust strewn barn and went in search of a broom. In the tack room, Somner was oiling the traces, hanging them so that they wouldn't shrink. The great Biron's halters hung nearby, looked as though some invisible team still wore them, as they shifted in the humid air. Not for the Nine Sands would Daro venture in, on that account, so the net of ripening pretulish, hanging from a rafter was safe from pests of all varieties and Somner grinned as an apparently disembodied hand, first collected, then returned a broom stealthily.

As if to himself, the driver remarked.

"Anyone who wanted a really ripe pretulish, might sweep the wagon floor also. A deal of dust must be on that now!"

The broom mysteriously disappeared again. Then, shortly afterwards, aggrieved voices were raised as the boys quarrelled vociferously.

"Its mine! I saw it first Ahnell.". Daro's voice rang out, followed by a shrill complaint from his companion.

"Didn't too! It's on my side of the wagon Daro! You said so yourself.".

The wagon creaked rocking back and forth and the men in the pasture started back at a run, as Ahnell said triumphantly

"Daro! Don't pinch! I'll show it to you, just don't grab, you might break it!", followed abruptly by a cry of pain, a gasp of fright, as the adults arrived at the tailboard and took in the scene.

Daro was holding a hand to his forearm, which was bleeding copiously. Ahnell, his eyes round and horrified, was staring at a curved object clutched in his hand and the last man to arrive hissed an oath as he saw what the child held.

"Help me up Rowbet.", Carolus snapped and as he was lifted over the tailgate, he reached an emergency medical scrip from a hook near the rear of the wagon.

His face white, skin bathed in sudden sweat Daro was faltering, wide frightened eyes turned to Carolus, as the Apothecary grasped his injured arm fiercely.

The old man spoke gruffly.

"This is going to hurt.".

He announced and then drawing a brilliantly tempered blade, he made two swift incisions into the child's arm, above the wound. He examined the blood that bubbled in the wake of the blade.

"Good.". He announced, glancing at Daro who far from fainting was taking deep interest in the procedure.

"Here.". The Apothecary turned to the greenish faced Ahnell.

"Hold his arm up, so.".

He abruptly elevated the wounded limb level with Daro's head.

"That's right, hold him steady while I apply this twist above his elbow.".

Carolus held out a hand, into which Somner placed a trace strip. The leather was tied tightly above Daro's elbow and as the Apothecary thrust a short piece of wood through the tourniquet and tightened it, for the first time the boy blenched and cried out.

"Hold still my lad!".

Ivinish the beast handler, had quietly mounted the wagon from the other side, setting Ahnell to one seat, he encouraged Daro rest against his massive frame.

He supported the boy as the Apothecary wiped his mouth with a large leaf coated in a pale green cream, which he also applied to Daro's arm, before bending his head and sucking out the blood, spitting out the poison that flowed from the wound in a sinister black stream.

Somner questioned Carolus anxiously, speaking in the Darvish of his far distant homeland in the Amber Sands, so that the boys wouldn't understand him.

"That looks deadly! Shall I fetch Ikella?".

To their amazement, there came a strangled cry, from Daro.

"No, don't disturb her, she'll be angry with me.".

Followed by a weakening mumble as the child collapsed.

"No, Somner, no Ivinish, I must not spoil this Gather for her.".

Daro wrestled fiercely with the Apothecary's strong hands.

"Let me go Carolus, let me go. It was an accident. Ahnell didn't mean anything by it, we both saw something we wanted, it isn't poisoned, it isn't!".

His struggles were of no avail. Ivinish restrained him with the ease born of fighting recalcitrant Biron. Carolus steadied the boy's flailing arm and returned to the task of sucking out the poisoned blood, while Somner ran to their bunk room and roused Patris, spilling out the story almost too fast for the wagon master to follow.

Even as they spoke, a shadow fell across the doorway and Jashell appeared looking mildly concerned at the air of confusion within. Shadows crossed her face rapidly as she took in the scene then she bent her head, twisted a thin chain from around her neck and handed it to Carolus.

"Take it.". she ordered gruffly. "It contains the water of the Opaz, the underground river on which my people came here during the Cataclysm. It is pure, sanctified by his own mother when she took his oath to the birthing sands. It may help him survive until I fetch her!".

Not waiting for a reply, the tall Inesh Commander, herself High Priestess of her people, turned and ran across the Square, driving all before her as she sought Ikella.

She tried the Hall of the Healers then took the shortcut to the Sorceress' private rooms, the nursery, the Djellim - all without success. She fled into the secret places of Selesh, her feet making no sound, only the pounding of her heart loud in her ears, until, returning to the Djellim, she encountered Shiarjha leaving the Council Chamber happily unaware of the impending tragedy unfolding just across the Gathering Square.

Seeing Jashell's distress, knowing that the woman couldn't talk and get her breath back as well, Shiarjha, who had spent many hours with the Inesh women, lapsed into their flickering hand code.

One word was all it took.

"Daro!" Jashell signed. She followed this with the swift tap on her forehead to denote the Sorceress's sigil, a shake of the head preceding the question in her eyes.

Shiarjha shrugged, they both knew of Jocasta's Door. If the Sorceress was not to be found, she could be anywhere. they must act for her and quickly.

'show me!".

Shiarjha was no longer the shrinking Sorceress-Elect that she had been. Now she was strong and decisive, schooled by Ikella herself and she brooked no delay. She followed hot on the heels of the Guard Commander, a hastily packed scrip in her hand containing many items of magical power. Yet she paused outside the nursery for long enough to lay a silencing hand on Jashell before slipping into the somnolent darkness that should have held two sleeping boys. Bending over the bed that Daro habitually occupied, she rummaged for a moment, bringing out from under the pillow a large Opal heartstone and two crystal apples strung together on a silk cord. Slipping these into her pocket, she left as swiftly and silently as she had come and, turning, followed Jashell at a run.

The doors to the underground pastures were closed when they arrived, but Ahnell had been placed where he could get a view out across the Gathering Square through a convenient knot hole in the wooden doors. His pale face, grimy with tears, lit up as he saw Shiarjha running alongside Jashell and he hurriedly pulled on the cord that opened the heavy door so that as they approached at a dead run the door swung open to admit them. Shiarjha went straight to where she could see the Apothecary at the rear of the wagon, his face drawn and weary in the light of the lantern slung high above the tailgate. The young Sorceress Elect paused briefly to survey the old man and then, low-voiced, she called back to Jashell.

"Quickly now, summon Beneva and tell her we need the book of mysteries.".

The Inesh warrior paused only a minute and then with a quick nod turned and made her way back to the Djellim to summon the Guardian, her face deliberately expressionless, but her eyes grim.

Shiarjha bent over the child huddled in the wagon. She noted that his hand drooped into a pile of suspiciously Amethyst-tinged sand and she made a swift decision.

"We must move him, somewhere we can work on him more effectively, somewhere that no contamination can affect what we must do.".

Her eyes sought those of Carolus, delivering a deliberate warning as her eyes stared directly into his. Patris roused himself to suggest.

"An Infirmary tent in the far pasture?" and the choice was made. The wagon emptied, leaving just Shiarjha and Carolus locked in some silent rapport and the tentage was soon erected by the practised hands available. The door to the pastures opened silently while this was going on and suddenly Beneva was there, one arm lightly draped about the heaving shoulders of Ahnell who wept hopelessly as he took in the slight, almost shrunken form of his unconscious playmate.

'show me!".

The Guardian commanded and in her voice was a sudden throb of power. Hiccupping, the boy explained the series of events that had brought Daro and himself into this coil and, as if she was seeing the events replayed before her, Beneva nodded. Subsequently, her eyes took in the spillage of sand that Shiarjha had noticed and she sucked in her breath.

"Take him away from that, now!".

Her command was abrupt and obeyed just as swiftly, Ivinish having just returned from the far corner of the pasture where a tent had been erected. The quiet man with the gentle hands lifted the boy, supporting his wounded arm along his own shoulder and with his long, loping strides, the child was conveyed into the Infirmary tent, Beneva, Carolus and Shiarjha in tow.

In the dimly lit tent, Daro was laid on a raised bench padded with a mattress for his comfort. Carolus extended the arm once more, carefully wiping it with a few drops of some spirit from a pale blue flask, while Patris gently stripped the child, laying him on a clean blanket and wiping every inch of his body to cleanse his skin. Shiarjha examined the wound which seemed oddly puckered as though the child's own blood had scalded him.

Beneva observed the twin slashes above the initial scratch that ran across the boys forearm.

"Thank the One you realised that the boy had poisoned himself.". she remarked placidly. "What colour was the blood you removed?".

She shook her head, eyes narrowed as Carolus made his report and when he mentioned that, even though he had coated both his mouth and Daro's arm with sithabalm to neutralise the poison, he had noted a tingling around his mouth and tongue, she insisted on examining him immediately before continuing with the boy.

She then turned her attention to the strange object that Carolus had retrieved from Ahnell. It was about the width of a small boy's hand - a smooth glassy curve with a sharp, pointed projection at one end. Beneva pursed her lips, soundlessly whistling through her teeth with surprise as she viewed the strangely sinister object.

"May the One protect us!" she exclaimed, right hand invoking the power of the Sand in the ritual gesture to head, lips, heart.

"A Drecon's claw.".

She muttered and Carolus blinked as he examined the object cautiously. Shiarjha reached out to touch it, but the Apothecary whisked it out from under her hand, slipping it into a pouch with an unconscious shiver of apprehension.

Beneva heaved a sigh and brought from her pocket an elaborately decorated book encrusted with silver smithworked designs and furnished with a lock and hasp that kept it firmly closed.

Carolus stared at it curiously and, frowning, said slowly.

"I brought that to Sanctuary didn't I?".

Beneva nodded as Shiarjha brought from the chatelaine that was looped over her belt a small silver key. Together the Guardian and the young Sorceress Elect performed an elaborate ritual, fingers linked. Then they disengaged and, with a final gesture of Shiarjha's hand, the key raised itself and sought the lock to the tiny book.

There was a sudden brightness in the atmosphere, a gently cascading chime rang out from nowhere and the pages of the book that Beneva had laid next to the child started to turn. Faster and faster the heavy vellum flickered until, towards the middle of the book, the motion slowed and finally ceased as the book fell open at one page. There had been no evidence of writing visible, so fast had the pages turned, but now, glowing from the page was a drawing identical in every way to the strange cause of Daro's illness. Under this drawing was the picture of a plant with fruit strangely reminiscent of the object itself.

Carolus grunted in recognition.

"Humph, Minimosa drekonis.". he pronounced. "Dragon's claw pepper plant! I hope that the kitchen can provide some!".

Shiarjha frowned, asking quickly.

"Would kitchen quality produce all that we need? Don't we need the living plant to collect leaf, stem, fruit and root, Master Apothecary?".

Carolus grinned, appreciating just how far this previously timid, young woman had come since Ikella had recognised her and taken her under instruction.

"Precisely.". he answered her.

"Mistress Shanigah has come with Nahamida to cook for those of a more fiery disposition and I happened to catch sight of the living plants that they brought with them. I am planning both a medicinal and culinary herb garden further into these pastures and hoped that they might remain with me. I will go and see if one plant can't be spared for an emergency.".

Rowbet, Somner, Ivinish and Patris waited solemn-faced outside the tent. Patris spoke heavily as the Apothecary emerged.

"We have failed him. That wretched Gattarene has succeeded in bringing that curse to bear on him, for he was standing in a pile of those sick sands when the Curse struck. We should never have let him sweep the wagon. We have failed in our duty of care as Songfathers I fear. Where in all this is his Mother? Why has she not sensed his danger and appeared to save him?".

Carolus faced his friend calmly.

"I have the child safe for the moment Patris, though you may be on to something when you mention the Sand of the Amethyst. I will include that in my calculations. As for his mother, her many duties prevent her from being there morning until night for our boy and no, we have not yet failed him. He is very sick, he is very fevered, but he has huge resilience, he is young and strong, don't despair. We have the means to cure him and I will go now to collect the plants I need.". He broke off thoughtfully.

"It just occurred to me that the crystal in the cavern here could be preventing our Deshun from feeling the disturbance around young Daro, which could work to our advantage.".

He opened the door slowly, aware of the crowds filling the Gathering Square.

"The Nine Winds rise.". he cursed as he realised the lateness of the day. Beneva and Shiarjha would be needed in Hall, Jashell even now mustered her Guards in the Square. He fled to the kitchens, taking in the flicker of hands that told him that Ahnell had been returned to the nursery and that Nadra was aware of the situation, as were all the Inesh.

He returned swiftly, bearing a tall plant which swayed perilously close to his face as he made a discreet gallop back to the covered pastures. He put the pot down just inside the door and closed it firmly against the proceedings, aware that both Beneva and Shiarjha must get into place before the sounding of the Summoning Bell.

Collecting his tools and a stone grinding jar in which to prepare the plant, he made his way to the silent tent where, bleak-eyed, the magic users looked up from Daro's makeshift bed and four men prayed for the child's safe recovery.

Chapter 17 - First Rite of Zenitheon

In the Square, the Guard shepherded a growing throng in Clan Colours, all unaware of the crisis growing beyond the pasture doors, as Beneva, Shiarjha and Carolus fought for Daro's life.

The child was delirious. His head turned this way and that, restlessly searching, fingers prowling as he muttered continuously.

"Light a glow Nadra. Its so dark, cold and dark.", Yet his temperature soared. His arm was swelling ominously, icy water failed to cool him and even Shiarjha and Beneva's soft chants were to no avail. As Shiarjha extracted fiery juices from the peculiar plants, Beneva (with more determination than hope), followed the prescription in her silver book, before reluctantly drawing the others aside.

"Daro should be in the nursery Carolus.". The Guardian looked at the unusual crystals above. "If that roof inhibits Healing, he is lost. For the fever to break, the poison must be drawn. However, it is not yet time and we must fulfil our duties in Hall.".

Her hand hovered over the closed book, but she left it lying on the bed, saying firmly, "No, that is too precious to risk in public. Keep him cool. I will retrieve it later, when we bring his mother to treat him.".

They slipped away, parting the crowd in front of them with a flicker of empowered hands. Setting the doors to open on the pull of a rope, Carolus returned slowly to the fire, sunk deep in memories that took him far away and long ago. Patris, watching him, spoke sombrely.

"I have never seen Carolus so withdrawn. If the child dies, I dread to think what she will do to us. If we have done all we can, we should go and pray for him..".

Somner stood willingly, "I'll tell Carolus where we're going. We can take his apologies to the Council.", So saying, he sought the Apothecary, carrying a sweetdrink in one hand and a small flask in the other. The animals had drawn together, heads down, sleeping where they stood, but Carolus was pacing pensively. Low whimpers of pain had drawn him to his patient, who writhed fretfully, eyes closed, sweat-soaked hair plastered against his skull. Shocked by the child's appearance, the tall driver stared at Daro's arm in horror. Blackened and bloated as a ripe gourd, it hardly seemed salvageable, then the Apothecary said slowly.

"The crisis will come soon I think.", and Somner turned, aware, as never before of the gulf of skill, education, intellect and authority, that yawned between them.

Self-consciously, he held out the flask, muttering, "I brought my father's holy water, blessed in Sanctuary. It might help if we ask Mirayen to cool his fever!"

Carolus had never suspected that a devoutly religious man lay within his drinking companion, but his eyes brightened and he produced a coin.

"Buy me some of those isabane sticks from the dealer in the Square will you? Perhaps familiar scents can hold his attention. I like not this searching in the dark!".

The driver headed for the stall and securing his purchases, returned swiftly saying that the Hall was packed to overflowing.

"I spoke to Master Errish and he will cover for you.", he commented. Setting a light to the pot of isabane sticks. They smouldered, bathing Daro in sweet, soporific perfume. He muttered drowsily, one hand clasped the crystal apples that Shiarjha had left on his bed and sighing, he slept.

Carolus spoke, as the Summoning Bell rang out.

"You must go my friend.", He indicated the fire and the stacked ingredients in pans.

"I have work aplenty. Everything I need is ready and you can do little to help. Slip in by the Audience Hall so as not to attract attention.", and Somner departed, leaving the Apothecary staring into the heart of the fire.

He sat, as one entranced, until a brightness in the crystal roof roused him. A chorus of voices whispered through the pasture, wavering on a strong, chill breeze that caressed his cheek and clung curiously to the fevered child, fluttering the skirts of the tent. Rising, he went to stand by Daro's bed, hooded eyes glowing brilliantly. Stretching a hand towards the child, he seemed to grow in stature, as a high, singing tone surrounded them. Smoothly, the silver book rose from the bed, unlocking itself as it sought the imperious hand that summoned it. In that moment, the shadows that cloaked the Apothecary quivered, there was a mercurial flash across the crystal roof, then light poured down bathing the child in its glow. It sharpened, streaming down the wound, bubbling fiercely along the injury, with a subdued hiss. As it died away, a sweet, melodic tone filled the tent with a shivering intensity that drew a sigh from the man, who stood whipcord slender, tall and powerful, hands extended over the child's forearm. In one hand the mysterious book locked itself once more and in the other a minuscule shard of matter and a grain of Amethyst sand materialised.

Returning to reality, as though he woke from a trance, the Apothecary replaced the book and dropped the debris he held into a bowl. Turning, ready to make up the potions he needed, he was astonished to see that the fire had all but burned out. Pots and pans stacked neatly, were empty and washed. Lying beside them, was a jumble of jars and pots, stoppered and sealed with red wax bearing besides his own stamp, the universal sign for "Danger". Grinning, he selected a small pot. Leather gloved hands worked the lid cautiously and as the seal parted, his eyes watered, stung by the fierce energies contained in the innocuous-looking paste within. Returning to the boy, the Apothecary examined his arm, as he tore two strips, off a long roll of clean linen. He folded a neat square no bigger than a child's hand and using a horn spatula, carefully scooped the paste on to it. He talked to the child soothingly as he worked.

"Well young man, you have given us all a nasty fright, though I don't suppose you meant to do that.", he laid the compress on the wound gently, binding the swatch in place, explaining rapidly.

"Now, that is magic paste. No-one else must dress your arm, because the paste might make them ill, unless they were trained in its use.".

He observed the boy for a few moments and then Daro asked languidly.

"Can I have the Drecon's Claw Master Carolus? I never saw such a thing before Ahnell swept his side of the floor.".

Carolus sighed, speaking seriously.

"As your Songfather, I don't often refuse requests my boy, but that is one souvenir of this escapade that you can't have.", the Apothecary continued cautiously.

"Those ancient beasts were deadly poisonous. So is the remedy that I used to save your arm.", The old man saw a thrill of horror run through the child and chose his words carefully. "Things that lie in the Sands for Rotations, stay just as dangerous as they were, before. They can still hurt or even kill us. You must never touch, let alone fight over, something that you don't understand. Ask Beneva or me before grabbing anything. Now, how do you feel?".

"My arm throbs, I'm tired and hungry.", Daro complained.

"Well.", said his Songfather, a subtle pass of his hand making the fire leap into life.

"Come and sit with me by the fire, I have a sweetdrink just warm enough for you and we have bread and cheese for supper.".

It was there, that the returning group found them curled together companionably. Lifted in his bodyguard's solicitous arms, Daro was borne away by his strangely reticent mother. A silver book was discreetly returned to Beneva and Shiarjha loaded a cane basket with remedies to study. Gradually the pasture grew quiet as everyone departed to their own quarters.

However, as Patris and his crew performed their last rounds, there was a sudden disturbance in the Square, then the door to the pastures opened to admit Jashell, who shepherded a young couple before her.

"Ho, the pasture, where away the Master?", she demanded and Patris rose to meet her.

"Master Patris.", Jashell smiled at him. "I have come to beg your indulgence for a "cousin" of our Clan.", She stepped aside, revealing a graceful woman, wearing an unusually tinted armour and carrying a plumed helm under one arm.

Jashell spoke with uncommon pride.

"This is Viness, from the Temple of the Winds, wife to Rowin of Jerritol, They attend the Guardians tomorrow. They need accommodation tonight and I thought of the tent. Could they stay here for tonight?".

Amazed, Patris could hardly believe he was seeing one of the reclusive Nishanawa. However, a discreet nudge reminded him of his manners and he made a bow, profoundly aware that the Ways had indeed changed if the keepers of the remote Temple of the Winds were travelling abroad. He found his voice.

"Welcome my friends, We can provide you with everything you need for the night, aye and privacy too.", he added hospitably, knowing that the woman would appreciate this more than anything else. Aware that his team were making up beds in the tent behind him, he wished their unexpected guests a good night and withdrew to let the pasture sleep.

Closeted in his own quarters, Carolus studied an unusual ceramic game board, on which was a game of Nine Winds. Once square, it had lost a corner, although that apparently didn't impinge on the game. Arranged in a complex pattern, hand made tiles impressed with symbols, were stacked. Mixed with these were native stones of various hues, polished by many Rotations of use. The Apothecary frowned at two stones that lay to the left of the current pattern and he sat, thoughtfully stroking his beard, "This is not the strategy I'd planned.", he thought mildly intrigued in the way the tiles and stones had tumbled. Then thoughtfully lifting the two new stones, he moved them until they butted up against the central pattern. As they fell into place however, a third stone was revealed. It glimmered. A small polished shard of lapis lazuli. Carolus smiled, pronouncing softly under his breath.

"Thus ends the Eve of Zenitheon. In the far depths of night when Seleus starts his journey back to us, so starts the day of the Zenith, when all works are dedicated to Seleus, the bright one.", Lifting the candle lantern that lit the table, the old Apothecary, left his game and went thoughtfully to bed.

Early the following morning, the nursery was unusually subdued. Nadra greeted the Apothecary with a finger to her lips, so Carolus slipped quietly past her and peered into the sleeping rooms.

The first stood open and empty, the bed neatly folded back, piles of small clothes laid out ready for the boys when they woke. The old man peered into the dim recesses of the next room and saw rumpled bedclothes stripped back as though some urgent summons had fetched a child out of bed in a hurry.

The Apothecary obeyed the instruction in Nadra's pointing finger and carefully opened the door into the last room, which was somewhat larger than the other two, having an outer play area before the screens that sheltered Daro's bed. Carolus stopped in the entrance listening to Daro's voice declaiming seriously.

"Ancient things can be very dirty. They have often been buried for many Rotations and carry diseases. After he mended me, Songfather Carolus told me never to touch anything that we found before asking the advice of a senior.".

There was a sleepy protest from Ahnell and Daro's voice took on the gruff, lecturing tone of Carolus's own voice as he reiterated sharply.

"Never touch or fight over things that you can't identify, particularly if they are found in a place you have no control over, like outside, in the desert or in someone else's place!".

Ahnell questioned sleepily.

"Like Patris's wagon?".

Daro corrected him. The authority in the younger boy's voice surprised even Carolus.

"Particularly in Songfather Patris's wagon. It travels many ways and takes up many different people who could drop things where they ride or sleep. It would be impolite to steal from those we don't know and could be dangerous, even deadly. If we had been alone in the pasture, I could have died while you fetched help. I was really lucky that Songfather Carolus was actually there..." Carolus decided to interrupt before he could hear his own praise sung too devoutly.

"Yes.", he agreed from the doorway, unslinging his medicine scrip from his shoulder as he spoke.

"I can't be sure which caused the illness and infection , it could have been the shard of Drecon's Claw that I removed from the scratch, or the grain of Amethyst Sand that I flushed out of the same area, but neither would have been clean in any case and infection of wounds kills more people than the wound itself.".

He arranged a clean rella towel on a tray, took out a bowl from his pouch and called back to Nadra.

"Can I beg some freshly boiled water dear heart?".

To which a delighted Nadra responded tartly.

"Dear heart is it this morning, after I sat with this scamp worrying all night? Dear heart indeed!" The usual bantering rights established, she went away to fetch water, certain now that her precious charge was restored to health.

Carolus continued his preparations, methodically laying out cunning, smithworked pincers that Beven had constructed at the forge. He produced a stoneware bowl and a flask, with a mutilated tanbark stopper. Withdrawing this with his teeth, to the delight of the boys, he poured a liberal quantity of a pale, straw-coloured liquid into the bowl and placed in it, a blade, his pincers, a metal spatula. Ignoring Daro's sudden pallor, Carolus took a piece of linen from his pouch and saturated it from the flask, proceeding to wipe his hands with the liquid.

Ahnell looked at him scornfully.

"What has putting magic water on your hands got to do with making Daro better?" he challenged, but before Carolus could answer another voice chimed in.

Ikella had approached so silently that even Carolus was surprised, but the Sorceress slipped around the end of Daro's bed, pushed Ahnell's legs over and sat quite naturally, a mother concerned to see how her son was being treated.

"That is quite a clever question Ahnell.", she commented without censure and proceeded to explain.

"That is not "magic water" that Master Carolus is using. It is a spirit. It evaporates so that when you wash your hands, they dry by themselves. You then don't carry infection from your own skin to someone else. Practical medicine demands absolute cleanliness. Healing on the other hand can be used alongside practical medicine or instead of applied remedies and such healing can only be used by women and trained Healers at that. Sometimes more than that is demanded and then magic is involved, however, no man has ever used magic to heal or for anything else for that matter!" Carolus, glancing at Daro, met a gaze so perceptive that he flinched, but when he looked again, the boy was lying against his pillows, eyes carefully veiled, surveying his bandaged arm ruefully.

Ikella's voice sharpened suddenly, seeming more severe than usual as she turned to Daro.

"You, my boy, should have known better. I was most shocked to hear that you had touched this strange object. Have I not told you often enough that Selesh is very ancient and holds many strange things not of our making? How many times have I to tell you not to explore on your own, or interfere with things that you don't understand? Have I to appoint Diras to follow you like some tame hound to stop you getting into trouble?".

Daro spoke swiftly.

"No Mother, please don't! We didn't realise how serious you were before.", He lifted his sore arm and said in a mollifying tone.

"I shall have the memory and the scars to remind me now!" and for a second he paled, remembering the terrible burning pain he had suffered.

Seeing that her words had struck home, Ikella shooed Ahnell off to get his breakfast, while she and the Apothecary examined Daro's arm.

She reached into a pocket and donned the shantana of her calling, masking her nose and mouth so as to prevent contamination from her breath. Carolus carefully unwound the bandages that he had applied the night before and, using the pincers, he cautiously lifted the square dressing that he had slathered with the plant paste.

A sigh of relief filled the room, as Daro withdrew his arm, flexing it carefully. The limb, no longer blackened, was still far from a healthy pink, but it was nothing like the scar his mother had expected. It wasn't puckered, although it was still livid and the Sorceress and the Apothecary nodded in approbation.

The Sorceress thoughtfully examined the two slashes inflicted by Carolus himself.

"If I didn't know better, I would say that this was worked magically.", She sounded interested rather than accusatory, so Carolus said smoothly.

"Well, I could hardly believe my eyes when I saw what had caused Daro's injuries. I knew enough to believe poison was at work, if not infection, so I sent for Beneva to identify the cause. She knew the minute she saw the vile claw that she would need Shiarjha, so I let them get on with it.".

He spread his hands disarmingly, conscious that the Sorceress had straightened as she realised that just about everyone except herself had been involved in saving her son's arm. The Apothecary continued apologetically.

"I smothered him in sithabalm to kill infection and sucked the poison out before it climbed higher. They sang for half Sundown, while Jashell and the others offered everything from the living water of the Opaz to holy water collected from Sanctuary itself. I finally finished the job using a tincture of

Drecon's claw pepper plant, a rare enough plant in our circle of the Sand but which just happened to come to hand to make a draw for the arm and this is what I recovered.", He held out a small pot and the Sorceress uncovered it carefully. She stared into its interior curiously, seeing the Drecon's claw for the first time, then the shard and finally focussing on the grain of Amethyst Sand. She shuddered and blindly held out the pot to Carolus who retrieved it and closed it soberly.

His innocent expression met her penetrating gaze and after a moment the Sorceress said gruffly.

"You never thought to ask where I was?".

Carolus considered, then lightly said.

"I assumed you were looking after another guest.", and Ikella, realising her son's interest in their continuing conversation, simply nodded.

"Our traveller could do with your attention. I think that something of this sort was practiced on him, though to what purpose I have not yet put my mind.", Carolus frowned grimly, but forbore from mentioning the word "torture" in front of an impressionable boy.

He carefully re-dressed Daro's wound before telling Ikella.

"I will indeed see him, though I fear his chances are slim.", He broke off aware of a pair of inquisitive eyes and turned the conversation skilfully, saying more cheerfully.

"Right, now young man, you must keep your arm bandaged today and, because the paste I used on it is quite dangerous itself, you should not run around outside. I think you need some more sleep anyway and when you are able to play, you will find that Usticus has been restored to you.".

Ikella leaned forward and brushed the hair back from Daro's forehead. For a moment her eyes surveyed him anxiously, then she said firmly.

"You can have some breakfast now, then you should sleep a little longer. After your midday meal you will rest through Height of Sun and then and only if Mina thinks you well enough, you can go, with Diras and Ahnell and thank your good friends for their care. You have caused quite a stir and right in the middle of Zenitheon, after I told you to behave!".

The Sorceress however, had a light tone to her voice and although he cast a doubtful glance at her, Daro ventured.

"Mother, I am sorry. I didn't mean to worry or upset anyone.", He hesitated for a split second and then continued.

"I should not take advantage of Driss. Usticus stole her pretulish fruit. He ate it before she could catch him and I willingly agreed to try and earn one of those that Songfather Patris brought back from Maraken yesterday. I didn't complete my task, so I was not paid and now I can't earn a fruit for Driss.".

He thought for a moment and then asked tentatively.

"Could you buy one of the ripe ones and give it to Driss for me and thank her for returning Usticus? Ahnell couldn't sleep last night without him, so he came in with me instead.".

This last comment vastly amused the Apothecary, who said happily.

"I bet that sleeping with Usticus would be more peaceful.", and at his chuckle the Sorceress nodded.

"I am glad that you remember your responsibilities Daro. You will tidy the main nursery for a ninenight and I will buy the Guard a pretulish from Patris, which will suit him well and serve her right!".

Daro stared at his mother in confusion as she rose to depart.

"Child, pretulish are so large and filled with water that they ripen slowly and only come to harvest just before the Storm Season. Some however, fall from the bush early and are harvested for animal food. If a ripe fruit ever fell into Driss's hands at this time of Rotation, it would lack flavour and might even give her stomach pains, a bit like the ones that brought Usticus to my door late last night! However, a bargain was made and will be fulfilled.", A sudden wicked grin crossed her face and Daro had to bury his face in his pillow to stifle the sniggers that threatened to escape.

"Did it ever occur to you, that you and your revered mother both have a peculiar sense of humour?".

Asked the Apothecary, but there was a twinkle in his eye as he departed to the pastures and breakfast with his trader friends.

Outside the Gate in the Rock, the pilgrims patiently mustered, filing through to the Gathering Square grouped together in families. From young to old they went to see where their sisters, nieces, daughters and in some cases grand-daughters would be training for the next four Rotations of their lives. Slowly the queue wended its way in and then, returning, made its way, as instructed, up a side track and on to the great plateau which had been used to grow food and herbs for the community of Selesh.

As they reached this area, a collective sigh of wonder came from the crowd, for where Torrenesh continued to soar above Selesh, hard against the sheer rock face stood a great obelisk. Around this strange object Master Errish and his men had provided a wide semi-circular pavement and around that a low retaining wall kept this area from encroaching on the precious growing fields.

The pilgrims were encouraged to find places to sit with their Clans or families. Baled animal fodder had been provided to make temporary seating - and soon the entire Gathering were collected together, eyeing the obelisk uncertainly, wondering what wonders their Guardians were about to reveal.

They didn't have long to wait, for already the air hung hot and somnolent in the embrace of this strange monument. The cloud cover, though unremitting, was somehow lighter, higher and a soft breeze sighed along the sheer rock face that backed this new structure. Somewhere on the track below, a bell tinkled and then the steady tramp of feet was heard as the expected procession came into view.

Led by her Honour Guard who carried their battle banners aloft, the Sorceress and her fellow Guardian Beneva arrived. The crowd gazed in awe as the Guardians passed, for beneath their feet rolled a most mysterious and magical field of power. They didn't seem to be walking, but were rather borne on this field of energy to the very foot of the obelisk, where suddenly there was an altar supporting a great Opal capstone. From the top of this stone emanated a flame, so bright, so clear that those near it were forced to shield their eyes against its brilliance.

Ikella's voice rang out, carrying clearly to the entire Gathering.

"This Gathering, to celebrate the Rites of Zenitheon, we offer in dedication to the One, his works and all his believers. We seek to raise our children in his light and to that purpose we dedicate this beacon.".

She paused, gauging the position of their cloud-shrouded sun then, engaging her aura until it flashed and flared around her, she raised an empowered hand.

"Behold the beacon of Seleus, who warms and lights our world.".

At her words the flame on the capstone flickered, grew taller then flared into full life. Beneva, standing opposite Ikella, stretched out her hands and almost as if the Guardians lifted the capstone themselves, it raised from the altar. The silvery stream that had floated the Guardians to their places now seemed to engage in raising the capstone to the tip of the obelisk. Slowly, steadily, it soared above the crowd, drawing level with the plinth that would lock it in place, the brilliance of the flare it sustained bathing the wondering faces of the crowd below.

There was a chorus of gasps as the capstone lifted into place with an audible click and then there came a steadying of the atmosphere, the beacon's light streamed upward, lighting the underneath of the cloud briefly before penetrating it, streaming outward, seeking beyond the confines of Pelshar's atmosphere.

Ikella and Beneva remained poised. The strange, silvery stream that had empowered the raising of the capstone seemed to have narrowed until it touched the base of the flame, sending tiny shivering flickers of silver in its wake.

For a long moment they waited, the crowd restlessly swaying as each man, woman and child jostled to get a better view of the phenomenon.

To Ikella and Beneva time seemed to have stopped then, almost imperceptibly, the silvery stream brightened, the flare changed colour to match and there came, without doubt, the toll of a great bell.

It sounded beneath their feet, directly under the obelisk and Beneva, her robes gleaming the dull silver of her calling as a Guardian, stepped forward and raised her hands.

"Thus is restored the link between Seleus and his people.", she announced and a great fanfare rang out as the Inesh warriors blew the traditional curved horns of their Clan.

Startled, the Gathering came to full attention as Beneva continued.

"Now is the Source re-empowered by the flame of the True Believer. Once more is the pathway of the Sun known to this land.".

The Gathering pressed forward as the silver streak that was all there was to see of the energy field, surged down the obelisk from the silver flare that reached skyward to touch Seleus. Only then did the crowd see the lines chiselled painstakingly into the paved apron, spreading out like a fan from the base of the obelisk. The silvery trail hesitated for a moment and then found its course into the channel directly at the base of the obelisk, rushing to its outer edge, where another channel ran around its frame. As the line flared silver, the toll of the bell came sonorously over the plateau and Ikella calmly announced.

"Once again we have a marker for the sectors of the day. At Height of Sun, the great bell of Sanctuary will toll and at its call, all who were lost to the Storm will be remembered.".

She indicated the great, sheer wall behind her.

"Everyone, man, woman, child, free or slave, will be remembered here. Selesh takes the responsibility for providing a stone with a carved name and nameday for Clan members. Those who reside in our Sands and who are not Shalhanhi may also choose to have their people named here, in the stone of their home Sands if they wish. At every Zenitheon, their names will be called, from sunrise to sundown, until all are named and have their tribute.".

It was a monumental change to tradition and for a moment there was silence and then a voice rang out.

"This is the will and the Way of the Guardians. In Selesh shall Sanctuary once more blossom. After the direction of she who was Jocasta, so let it be!".

Against the roar of approval, Ikella stared with astonished eyes at the Nishan warrior who stood suddenly framed against the obelisk and Beneva smiled in welcome.

"Viness, I heard that you had survived the Fall.", Beneva's face was animated as she welcomed the woman who stood tall, armoured in lightweight, silvery blue. The blazon of Sanctuary radiated from her belt and the crest of her helm.

"How wonderful to see you, to hear you once more.".

She grew silent for a moment, thinking of all those she would never again see in this life, then sighed and said in a matter of fact voice.

"So, you were the messenger to the Temple?".

Viness nodded shortly, disinclined to talk about their mutual loss and Beneva, recognizing the stratagem of a survivor, changed the subject smoothly, as all around them wondering pilgrims watched the almost imperceptible movement of the time trace as the silver flow tracked its way to the next time sector.

"I stayed with the Temple for a time.", Viness spoke in a gentle melodic voice and Beneva nodded.

"You needed time to adjust, as I have found for myself.", she murmured in reply.

"Then, I caught a mate!" The tall woman grinned at Beneva.

"In the custom of my people, of course.", She managed to imbue that statement with a wealth of meaning and Ikella was intrigued to see her fellow Guardian blush furiously as Viness continued, glancing shyly at the tall man who stood by her side.

"However, I am unable to catch a child so readily and so I came on pilgrimage to find out what this Healer Hall can do for me and my husband.".

She caught the look of surprise on Beneva's face and added.

"Oh yes. We jumped the trave at Darnesh, signed our names in the Sand of the Azure, sealed our lives before the Clan and still no baby comes to bless us.", A wealth of pain lay behind those words, her eyes were shadowed.

"My father-by-marriage only tolerates my presence at the Weaver's Halt because I am skilled in dyeing. He holds it in trust for Rowin, but won't release it till we have an heir. He had other plans for Rowin's marriage and will force us to divorce if I remain barren. Yet we know I can conceive, for I managed to do so when we travelled last Rotation. Unfortunately, our joy was premature and I miscarried before the child quickened!".

As they turned to follow the retreating procession back to Selesh and the celebrations, Ikella suggested slyly.

"I have a talented Healer with a remedy for such problems, Viness. If you trust me, I can provide some treatments and time away from stress. Rowin is welcome to weave uniform cloth for the Healer Hall. That would give him a reason to stay and a contract to satisfy his father. Shall you remain with us until we can rule out common failings?".

For a moment Viness hesitated, then, she replied.

"Yes, if it please you Seris Ikella.", and so the party departed to plan another turn in the Way.

Chapter 18 - The Quickening.

That night, the celebrations seemed to go on forever. They celebrated the High Council, the work of the Master Builder and his team. They celebrated the peaceful resettlement of Sybillsce refugees, the opening of the Novice Hall and the restoration of the Inesh to full Clan rights. That night, the cloud that had masked Pelshar from the glory of its sun for nearly seven Rotations seemed to lift exceedingly high and the pilgrims sat on the hillside outside the Gate in the Rock as Jenta rose, still ominously shadowed by its dark twin Gatta. Cooking fires glowed, families drew together and told stories about the days when the sun shone and all kept a nervous eye on the sullen roll of cloud that only permitted the faintest glow where they all thought Jenta should be.

In the services held in High Hall, children born since the Jentaroth of Partition were received into the Clan and by the light of the silver moon there was a strange continuance of the most precious Rite of Jenta.

As the last child came into Ikella's arms, she realised with a sense of wonder that the Eye of Jenta performed its function even though this was not the night set in tradition for such things. Privately, she confided to Beneva, that there was no evidence to suggest that a child's nameday had to be at Jentaroth. She had long supposed the winter Gatherings were more spectacular, better attended and therefore more convenient as Clans tended to keep closer to their own Sands at End of Rotation.

It was after the main service of dedication, well into the night, when Carolus sought her. Immediately fearful for Daro, she leapt to her feet, but the old man waved her back to the comfortable chair she had been sat in and said slowly, "I have spent most of my day with Olneth and am happy to say that I think the man will live. It was necessary to use a great deal of the new paste to draw both poison and contamination from his wounds. However, he is young and strong and that will stand him in good stead.".

He sounded weary, but something in his manner concentrated Ikella's attention and she spoke a little sharply as she demanded, "And?".

Carolus continued, with the comment, "I don't think saving his life, will be as hard as saving his mind! Putting it bluntly, he is convinced that a living Drecon attacked him!".

Ikella felt chilled quite suddenly. She sat pensively, a finger tapping on the arm of her chair as she stared into the fire that dispelled the cold of the desert night. Eventually, she found her voice.

"I wondered when I saw those wounds.".

She made the remark in a manner that sent a shudder through Carolus. He stared at her, astonishment writ over face, body language and voice as he declared, "Drecon's undoubtedly lived once, but I can't understand how one is alive and in our Sands now. I can't believe you wouldn't know of something so old, so evil, so alien to our world.".

Ikella considered this and pointedly asked, "Can you think of any other explanation? Olneth may be raving of course, but those wounds were of no man's making!".

She rose and paced back and forth before the fire, her face drawn as she said firmly, "I looked at the wounds with the man stripped and washed clean. There was evidence of great ferocity, ripping and tearing wounds, symptomatic of reptilian attack with teeth and talon. There was a noxious slime in the bite marks, indicative of some reptiles which inject a paralysing substance with their bite, though I never heard of a reptile bigger than a sand lizard. Then there is the Drecon's claw, which is almost conclusive evidence!" She enumerated facts on her hands as she paced and Carolus found himself nodding in agreement. He listened to her reasoning in silence and then responded reluctantly, "What is so especially horrifying, my dear friend, is that someone pegged Olneth out on the Sands! All he recalls is getting hit over the head as he left an inn near Maraken. We found him on the south side of Tearchan crossing! Wouldn't have stopped, but we had a Biron cast a shoe. We needed wood to make a fire, so Rowbet could re-shoe the beast and thought we had struck lucky. He looked just like a pile of sand-cast planks. We could hardly believe our eyes when we realised who we had found. In the morning Somner will have the place mapped and you can see that it lies not far from the shunned one's Sand!".

He sat back in his chair and belatedly Ikella summoned Trinet to make a sweetdrink for her guest. As her servant departed to go to bed, Ikella finally reacted to the last comment Carolus had made.

"A map would be useful, particularly if Somner can recall any tracks in the Sand thereabout. I can't see how the Gattarene has anything to do with this, but it could be her way of leaving a warning.".

"Mmmh.". The Apothecary quaffed the last of his drink, mumbling into his beard.

"Yes, Olneth has been very active lately, I have at least three reports that came in the last ninenight to analyse. He has been as far as Minesh in the Amber Sands, North to Trabzon and back again. I managed to get the idea that he had strayed too close to the Sherrol Pass before he became delirious.".

His sober words brought home to Ikella that whatever success they achieved in Selesh, that very close to home, the Amethyst's Sands sole exit was into the Opal Desert.

Though the Sands were sealed, its Sorceress shunned for heresy, they still lived in the knowledge that beyond the Sherrol Pass, dark powers prowled. Ikella shivered apprehensively then, with a small shrug, she threw a shawl around her shoulders and stood saying, "I suppose we must look in on Olneth and Daro before we retire?" She spoke wearily, but Carolus nodded.

"I wanted your opinion on my level of success with the combination I have made of Ortiz root cream, sithabalm and the Drecon's bane paste.". He sounded quite self-conscious as he spoke and the Sorceress laughed gently.

'so that is what you are going to call your latest concoction is it? Drecon's bane. Is that lotion, tincture and paste? We must devise a stamp for the pots. How came you by that name?".

For a moment the old man looked puzzled, then he said slowly, "I am not sure. I think I saw a drawing in one of Beneva's old books. Yes, I am positive I did, but whether that was here, or there, I can't recall.".

He held the door open for the Sorceress, who nodded shortly at his oblique referral to Sanctuary and his role there as a spy for the Guardians past and so the Sorceress and the Apothecary set off on their late night visit to sickroom and nursery.

Ikella had relaxed the traditions somewhat, so that of late she no longer kept Guards at her door. She had needed far too much freedom in her work, as the Infirmary was relocated and enlarged in preparation for this very time, when she would be able to accept large numbers of novice Healers. However, she needed to let the Inner Guard know where she was, so she stopped in at their offices and was mildly amused to see Driss pale and sweating as she moved painfully about the room, marking the location of the Night Watch on a large black painted board, using the code that Shiarjha had so painstakingly taught her.

"Are you not well girl?" Ikella asked, her tone outwardly solicitous, but the curl of her lip embodied a level of malice that made Carolus grumble under his breath.

The Guard reluctantly confessed, "Just something I ate, my Deshun.". And, for the sake of convention, the Sorceress swallowed her somewhat unseemly amusement.

They took a lamp along the new corridors, which still lacked some of the facilities that had been planned. The sickroom which they intended visiting lay discreetly in the old quarters, well removed from the casual bustle of ordinary life.

As they turned the nursery corner, Ikella hesitated, yet Carolus had swept past her and, as he was holding the lamp, she simply raised an eyebrow in exasperation and followed him. The light dipped and waved ahead of her and then, as if the Apothecary had only just realised her absence, it stopped where the passage broke through into the old corridors, which oddly seemed to be much wider than those in the new complex.

Carolus was poised outside the sickroom and as she approached, he laid one silencing finger to his lips, which stayed a tart remark before she launched it.

The echoes of their passage died away and then they heard the low murmur of voices talking. One was particularly anxious and carried plainly to where Carolus and Ikella waited, breath held for fear of disturbing the moment.

"No Olneth!" said Daro sharply. "You must never give up. You will see your wife again, I promise, even if I don't know how to arrange it. She will be free one day, as will all of your Clan. Your work is not wasted, it is not.".

Ikella would have intervened, but Carolus held her arm, quieting her almost with a touch.

"Wait!".

The word carried on a breath to reverberate in her head and so they sat on one of the low benches provided for sickroom visitors, to see what scrape her precocious child had got himself into.

Daro's voice said coaxingly, "Tell me what you remember Olneth. I am only little, but I have the ear of the Sorceress, she is my mother you see.".

There was a gasp and then Olneth spoke. His words, though slow and slurred by his injuries, came clearly to the listeners in the darkened corridor.

"Oh, I see. You are that babe?" Olneth chuckled then choked a little, which brought his audience to their toes in mild alarm, but then came sounds which told the listeners that a small boy had thought to raise the man on his pillows and offer him a drink.

Carolus nodded approvingly, but then Daro spoke again.

"Why does everyone call me "that babe"? I will be seven Rotations old at Jentaroth, I am half way to a man and have more brains than most.".

His tone was not boastful, just matter of fact, but the comment wrung a startled giggle from his mother, who was hastily hushed as the conversation wore on.

"Well.". Olneth spoke, considering his every word.

"Your mother was trying to save the whole of Caranchar, all by herself and she had to work a great spell. I don't understand the manner of it, for I am only a man. She called the Winds to remove the Sand that had buried Caranchar. She made them take it away, so that the people could find and bury the dead properly. Without her courage, a great sickness would have poisoned the water and killed everyone who lived there!".

"By Hadda's ghost!" swore the impressionable boy (who had only just learned this ritual oath from his guard).

"I didn't know that Mother was that brave.". However, not to be diverted from his original question, he repeated, "But, why "that babe"?".

Olneth groaned, but it was with obvious amusement in his voice that he told the rest of the story. Daro was entranced.

"I can't imagine my mother taking off all her clothes in the open.".

He said conversationally and Carolus, feeling the Sorceress stiffen at his side, repeated the single finger admonition for silence and she subsided.

There was deep respect in Olneth's voice as he explained.

"I was once Captain of Guard to Soloria, late Sorceress of Beloved memory and she told me that some things in magic have to be prayed for, others have to be asked for, still more are conjured by the use of potions and artefacts, but the most powerful magic is natural magic. That takes courage, faith, the proper approach and the power of command. Your mother put all her faith in what she knew, removed her clothes so that she was open to all her senses and showed her trust in the One by committing herself and you, to the Higher Powers.".

"Me?" asked Daro doubtfully and Olneth gave a rich chuckle as he said, "Oh yes my lad. You screamed the cavern down. Louder and louder you cried, setting the whole town's nerves and every crystal this side of the Onyx Sands jangling. Every child from the town cried with you, so the Healers took you out to your mother and she strapped you to her bosom and continued to spell-cast. I.". said Olneth with great satisfaction, "Never thought in my life to witness such a thing, but I did, aye and lived to tell the tale.".

Daro's voice was awed as he said softly, "And I helped her, for she carried me in her arms right through it.".

The boy's voice had grown low and reverent, then Olneth said sleepily.

"I think you should go back to bed Master Daro. I am too weak to defend myself against your mother should she take against me and you she would spank if she found you out of bed so late.".

There was a muffled response and the listeners fled, totally convinced that both of their charges were on the mend.

The Rotation sped towards its end. Crops were harvested, Felmin homesteads corralled their beasts and settled down to get through the Storm Season. The cities of the Greeeyn took in as much produce as they could and then shut and barred their Gates and in the Opal Sands a miracle occurred.

Olneth had recovered almost completely, thanks to Carolus's ointments and intense spell-casting from Ikella. Even his eye had been saved, though he said that it sometimes stung him and wept when the light first touched it. Eventually, the Apothecary decided that the scars on his body were well enough healed, though privately he detected a melancholy that caused him to wonder if the man had lost his nerve.

However, he persisted until eventually Olneth moved into the tent in the pasture, now vacated by Rowin the Weaver and his wife, Viness. They had taken a large, airy house in the village that served Selesh and shared its name. The house, part of the development built by Errish, had become vacant and it gave the young people enough privacy while they worked on the huge order placed by the Infirmary within Selesh proper. New uniforms for the Healer Guild were paramount and, made in all sizes, they required an independent weaver who could devote his time to one type of cloth.

They had visited nearly all the Sands now, collecting dyes for their wares and had stayed for a ninenight with Sanra who, having returned to the Carnelian Sands for the Skythe Harvest, had rewarded them with a new fertility treatment in return for delivering more remedies to the Healer Hall. Seven ninenights after their return, Viness had presented herself at the doors to the Infirmary and, almost as Hanna welcomed her, announced, "I was sick this morning. I felt sick about dawn and then I was indeed sick, very sick. I have no pain, no fever, but I feel restless and my clothes feel restrictive.".

Hanna, a little uncertainly, said she would fetch Solana, as she was the resident Zurias Healer and the tall Nishan woman agreed, but continued to sit smiling at nothing in particular, her hands clasped loosely in her lap. Hanna fled to find Solana.

The elderly Healer nodded and came straight into the room where Viness sat.

She made a few notes on a wax tablet and enquired about loss of appetite, gains in weight and then said gently, "The cycle of Jenta? Is it stilled in you long?" leaning forward to pat Viness's arm as the woman raised her face, smiling and tear-stained at the same time.

"Praise the One and all his works!" the little Healer cried, before she went to tell the Community that Viness and Rowin had conceived the child they so desired.

However, that End of Rotation was especially hard. Families crowded into the undercroft, leaving their houses in the village secured against the winter. Rowin and Viness accompanied them and suddenly Selesh was full to overflowing with people fighting for room to conduct their lives and businesses. People were moody, grumbling about the cold and the small rooms, while the lack of privacy and stress was mounting to intolerable levels when, midway through a ninenight that had taken two small children to the Sands, Rowin appeared at the Infirmary door. Ikella was shocked at the transformation in the man. his shoulders slumped, he was grey with fatigue, his eyes were dark and unfathomable. He nodded to the Sorceress who was dressing a badly scalded hand belonging to a kitchen drudge.

"My Deshun.", he saluted her formally.

It was plain that he was not comfortable in such exalted company, but Ikella smiled at him, trying to put him at his ease.

"Rowin, how far progressed is the weaving of our cloth? I am so excited, I love new clothes.". she exclaimed and the man's tired eyes lit up.

"I have this morning completely finished the work. The loom stands empty, the shuttles are unwound and there is but one Colour remaining to dye. However, Viness is very troubled. I caught her crying last night, which is why I am here. We should not be bothering you at all, but the ninenights fly and still she has not felt the baby move.".

He looked at Ikella unflinchingly and continued.

"We already lost one child at this time and dared not tell my father. He is convinced that Viness is barren. He hates her anyway because I thwarted his plan to marry me to another Weaver's daughter in Sibrill.

"Can a Healer tell if the child is live, or if it will live if the mother has felt no movement?".

His eyes were huge in his face, a quiver of emotion ticked in his cheek and Ikella sighed as the drudge departed, bobbing her thanks.

"If a woman has miscarried before, then she is more likely to do so again.".

She explained carefully, while her trained hands methodically packed a few items into a basket.

"However, there is more against her than you know. Viness served at Sanctuary in the far north, where, as now, the prolonged cold of the permanent winter disrupts all normal cycles. Furthermore.". , her face grew grim as she said softly , "Not a lot is known about the Nishanawa. They are apparently a sub-set of a Clan that no longer exists and as you know they keep themselves private, serve only the Temple of the Winds or Sanctuary, where of course your wife has been subjected to the influence of magic. That is why when the Nishan came to Sanctuary to serve they were never returned to the outside world!".

She saw the man pale and reached out, amazing herself with her new found willingness to communicate by touch. She felt him gird himself against bad news, then he asked, his voice strained with emotion, "Then what are we to do? If the baby dies inside her again, I fear for her life, her sanity. She has cried and cried until she vomited this morning. She knows my father will demand I put her from me and take a childbearing woman to get me an heir. He holds my inheritance in trust and there is only me left to follow my Grandfather's craft!".

He turned piteous eyes on Ikella and then said roughly, "I apologise, I should not have come. What can you do? You couldn't even understand her pain.".

He turned away, striking out blindly against the wall as he went back to the undercroft, sobbing in frustration.

Ikella leant against the wall, her face remote as she contemplated the pain of losing Daro and presently she went and collected him from the nursery.

He was delighted to accompany her to the Infirmary and walked quietly at her heels as she toured the two wards that had patients in them. She listened to him as he cheerfully greeted old friends, remonstrated with him when he climbed up onto blind Duvell's bed, until she saw the tenderness with which he held Duvell's head still so that she could examine his eyes, which were acutely painful.

She watched him touching, talking, smiling, soothing and something in her said, "Carolus, this is Carolus's doing.", but she would much rather he learned the ways of an Apothecary than a transport driver, though she couldn't quite dismiss the wild thought of "Healer".

Presently she drew Daro to one side and said calmly, "Daro, Carolus and I know how you helped Olneth conquer his despair when he was so badly injured. We also know that you like to help other people. Would you help me talk to Viness and Rowin? You know them I think , the weaver and his wife. They are very sad at the moment and I need them to think positively, because if Viness gets too sad it might hurt her baby.".

The child considered for a moment, then he said in a puzzled voice, "Viness hasn't got a baby!".

He sounded rather indignant and Ikella groaned as she realised the wealth of trouble she had just wished on herself.

'shall we go and see them and find out?".

She suggested and willingly Daro placed his hand in hers and they went into Ikella's private corridor to the undercroft.

Because of his work, Rowin had elected to live in the old weaving rooms which, though full of archaic machinery, were draught-proof and warm. They had two large rooms to live in, which had once been home to many bolts of material, but the young couple had made them bright, cheery and functional as well. They were seated together, holding hands when Ikella clapped her hands at the open doorway and they turned, astonishment writ large on both faces.

Ikella took in the woebegone expression that Viness turned to her and said briskly, "Daro, I can't answer any of your questions about weaving or the looms that Weavers use. Why don't you ask Journeyman Rowin here and let him show you the looms, while I talk to Viness?".

She held her breath, but the boy responded to the cue beautifully. He said cheerfully, "Oh, I should love that, can you show me some of the new material you have woven too?".

Confused and a little embarrassed, Rowin leapt to his feet and soon, heads together, they were poring over a loom in the corner of the room.

Viness showed her mettle then, exclaiming enthusiastically, "Oh my Deshun, that is what I want for him , a son or a daughter to bring up in the knowledge of the work. With Rowin weaving and I running the dye house, what more could we want?".

Ikella then saw, with a little pang of jealousy, how it was for her people and, though she could never share her life in the same way, she understood their grief.

By the time she and Viness rejoined Rowin and Daro, she had run her Healer's hands and eyes over the woman and could find nothing to alarm her. However, the practice of many Rotations told her that often a mother knows that her child is dead or deformed long before the Healer, so she kept her voice authoritative and practical and was relieved to see Rowin much restored to his previous good humour. They sat chatting and Viness produced a cool sherbet drink for Daro and offered wine to Ikella, who noticed that neither of her hosts partook of such refreshment themselves.

Her enquiring eyebrow produced the reaction that she wanted, for Rowin said abruptly, "Only when Viness has a live baby, boy or girl, will wine pass my lips again.".

This was followed by Viness's softly spoken exclamation.

"I must take care of my baby!".

Daro didn't need the reminder of a lifting eyebrow to prompt him. He glanced around and then demanded, "Where's this baby you all keep talking about? Can I see it? I like babies!".

There was a howl of laughter from Rowin, an uncertain giggle from Viness and a prim smile from the Sorceress, who had spent half an hour en route to the young couple's temporary abode explaining the facts of life to Daro, using the Apothecary's Zeglur herd as a basic example.

Viness signalled Daro to sit at her feet and said simply, "Like all mothers, I keep my baby safe and hidden inside me. When the baby has grown large enough to survive in the outside world, I will give birth to it.".

Daro, now totally entering into the small intrigue that Ikella had plotted with him, saw that Viness no longer looked so anxious and that Rowin had relaxed, lying full length on a couch, a grin on his face, at what he perceived to be the

Sorceress's discomfiture. Greatly daring, Daro looked at the gentle swell of Viness's pregnant belly and asked, "Is that where you keep your baby? He will be nice and warm this winter.".

Plainly touched by this ingenuous speech, Viness appealed silently to the Sorceress who nodded with approval.

Surely, Ikella prayed, this must re-engage the mother with her child again? Surely the One couldn't allow the loss of another small life so soon?

Viness took Daro's small hand in hers and said quietly, "You may touch very gently. The baby is asleep right now, but he will soon wake up and then you can feel him kicking.".

Ikella, glancing at Daro, saw a sudden compression of the child's lips then Viness lifted his hand and laid it on her pregnant belly. Daro flushed with pleasure suddenly and then looked down, apologising, "I am so sorry Viness, I seem to have woken your baby up, he kicked me quite hard just then.".

Hearing the astonished gasp from Viness, Ikella knew it to be true and almost missed the whisper, "I didn't mean to Mother!".

It was some time before the cries of delight, the excited jostle of parents and Healer had subsided and Ikella turned her attention to a suspiciously subdued Daro.

Now hoisted on a Guard's shoulders, they had returned to his nursery door. For a moment, as they parted, his mother eyed him analytically.

"I suppose that all it needed was for Rowin and Viness to relax..." said the Sorceress as she smoothed the curls at the nape of her small son's neck.

"And I suppose that you planned to perform magic and again I was there to help you!".

Daro retorted, one eyebrow mimicking a familiar expression of her own. Too tired to try and follow the twists and turns of her precocious son's fertile imagination and definitely too slow to react to such a challenge, Ikella sighed and kissed him before taking her wary mind to bed.

Excerpt from the Chronicles of Carolus
In the hand of Brannith, scribe.

Nearly eight Rotations later, I am called to record the words of my Master, Carolus the Apothecary. I have attended him in many strange places, but few stranger than a tent in an underground pasture, but here he seems happy enough, though his words fill me with foreboding.

"It is Winter again and the stresses and strains of these clouded Rotations affect everyman. We are kept close to Selesh as the skies darken and the nights draw in, until the beginning of one day runs into the next with barely a flicker of colour in the sky.

Women grow pale and anxious in this season, men grow lethargic and diffident, children if they survive their sickly infancies grow shrill and quarrelsome with restricted activity.

Thankfully, this Summer we broke through into unexplored territory. Deep in the heart of Torrenesh, Selesh has again revealed herself to be as capricious as any woman. One minute one believes that you know her, in all her moods and fancies and the next you are forced to admit that you didn't know a third of her. I know, I speak in riddles, but that is a privilege of age, though I have never tried to figure how old I am, in case I frighten myself to death!

In this case, the Master Builder simply wanted to enlarge a storage facility, so that more grain could be kept for the Winter. He had calculated the dimension of a service corridor, when one of his men pointed out that there was a large discrepancy in the figuring. Two sides of an existing corridor (which had once formed part of old Selesh, the original fortress), didn't match up. When they continued on their explorations, they broke through into an immense room.

This provided enough excitement in one day for a ninenight. Everyone in the settlement came in to see for themselves and in the end the Guardians had to impose order, setting a guard on the room and all its contents. Once it was cleared to Beneva's satisfaction, they uncovered a doorway and a maze of corridors and rooms enough to keep the Guard busy for two Rotations. It was obvious that this part of the old settlement had been occupied by people of high status and immediately nothing would have it, but young Master Daro and that lad Ahnell must move from their old nursery and take up residence in what our Deshun calls the eyrie.

It is very high indeed, the best rooms have cunningly set window openings covered by smithed shutters, commanding glorious views out of Torrenesh and I can't but sympathise with the lads, for now they are both in their fifteenth Rotation, they need room, privacy and their own company in which to grow to manhood.

However, tell that to an overprotective, overworked, Sorceress and she will fire off all kind of reasons why her only chick should not fly the nest!

At the moment, a trial period has been negotiated, in which the lads may try more independent living. Daro has his own Guards and Ahnell to protect him and his mother dearly needs the rooms his nursery previously occupied, so they have come to a truce on that matter, but I sense storm clouds building between them.

She has a reluctance to let him choose his Way and watches him constantly. He says he must seek his destiny, with the fine flourish of the young and insensitive and I feel a pressure building between them, that bodes ill for anyone's peace of mind or body if it reaches boiling point. I know it is the privilege of the very old to worry about the future of the very young, but today, seeing his mutinous face with that curious "set in Opal, " quality that so enchanted us in his infancy, I actually find myself anticipating some head-on clash with terror.

Given this day of the fifteenth Rotation after Partition, by Carolus of the Nine Sands.

Chapter 19 - Foreboding.

It was unlike Daro to accept anyone's advice, but he eventually understood, that to triumph over his removals, might cost him Ikella's rather grudging permission. Daro's urge to parade his removal to the tramp of Inesh feet, had been ruthlessly suppressed by Carolus. Persuading him to behave more circumspectly, quietly sending Nadra and her team ahead of him and carrying his own bedding and a few treasured items to his new quarters had been harder, but he had, as advised, acted before his foster mother could change her mind.

He climbed the long staircase that wound up through Torrenesh, in a blur of anticipation and opened the door on a scene of pandemonium. Nadra was directing drudges to re-create the rooms he had just left behind. He stared at her in dismay, for nothing could have been further from his mind.

"No!".

His voice lashed out like a whip and seeing Nadra blench he instinctively crossed the room and took her hands gently in his.

"No, Nadra.", he repeated gently. "This is not a nursery. My mother does not hold sway here. These rooms are mine and I will decide how they are to be dressed. If I was not the son of the Sorceress, I would have left my family home before now, been fostered with another Clan to learn a trade and another culture.".

He frowned suddenly, saying almost to himself.

"Aye and been a better man for it!".

Nadra's smile faded, her head dropped submissively and, sorry for his short temper, Daro raised her hands to his lips and kissed them tenderly.

"Little mother.".

His baby name for her was spoken with great affection, but still with that implacability of one whose decision had been made.

"You have to accept that this is the day that one fledgling flies the nest.".

He led her gently to the old nursing chair that she had cradled him in so very many times.

"I have enough rooms here for one to be set aside for all my old playthings, aye and a bed for you should you ever need one. However, I hear that you have other plans too!".

He stood, tall and tanned, a little on the slender side, but with that promise of strength to come in the breadth of his shoulders and the sleekness of his thighs.

She glanced up at him and said softly.

"Yes, you are right Daro, the Ways must again change and my place with them too, for both of you are nearly full grown and I must seek other employment.".

She looked down at her hands a little flustered and then continued.

"I never thought to find another after I lost my first husband to the Storm. Yet, now I have to make a decision, I am fearful of doing so.".

Daro crouched beside her chair and said firmly.

"Nadra, when you came to nurse both myself and Ahnell, no-one knew what the future held. I wouldn't have survived without your care, Ahnell has in you the mother that he always wanted and yet no-one has thought about your needs. My mother told me that you are of her household now. She promises to care for you, all the days of your life.", He paused and said with a self-conscious swallow, "Followed by me if necessary. If you have no-one to return to, why not stay here?. You don't have to accept Beven's proposal, but I think you should consider it. He is a good man and he genuinely cares a great deal for you.".

He paused conscious of her blush and then said with a chuckle.

"I see Beven is to be congratulated. Will you marry him?"

She shook her head.

"I am not able to Master Beven would lose his Sandrights if he marries a Felmin woman, but I would keep his house, help him in some new enterprise, for he wishes to retire from his smithy.".

He studied her curiously.

"I think you used to run an inn before you came here, didn't you?".

Nadra grew shy under his interested scrutiny. His was a life far removed from such a basic existence, although she had grown to love him, perhaps better than her own small babies buried in the Sands of Caranchar beside her first husband.

"Well, I won't speak evil of those who has gone to the Sands.", she murmured softly. "Elco did his best, but I had to work to support the children and often all of us, for he had more ideas than skills.", Her face softened as she remembered her husband, the dreamer, the poet and eventually the hero, who had died trying to save a neighbour from the Storm.

"Let him rest love.", She patted Daro's hand and for a moment Daro saw the heartbreak of her life and knew himself to be part of it.

"Well, I want to talk about your new life.", he persisted gently and then she heard the sounds of feet approaching and struggled upright in the chair, her face pinched and anxious.

"What have you done you dreadful boy?".

She was piteous.

"Look at me young Master. We are not ready to receive visitors yet, your rooms are not prepared, your sleeping couch has not yet arrived and me in all my dirt!".

Daro raised her easily and turned her towards the private bathing room that was his pride and joy.

"Go then little mother, go and bathe. You will find everything you need and an attendant as well. Then we will meet in my great room and you shall see what those who love you have prepared.".

Uncertainly, Nadra went into the bathing room and froze transfixed, for her attendant was none other than Ikella herself. Half a sector later though, she was calmed and bathed. Almost a lifetime of reminiscences had broken the ice and she had come to understand that her service to Ikella's household was truly valued and was about to be repaid in an extra-ordinary way. Therefore, when she entered Daro's great room to see most of the Sorceress's private household gathered, she was immured to whatever plan Daro had concocted for her.

Ahnell came over and hugged her, Daro pulled out a chair that plainly showed her to be the guest of honour and, although she fretted to organise "her boy's" rooms for the last time, she sat quietly sipping a full-bodied wine that had been set out for guests in what she knew to be the Sorceress's own precious sand-paste tumblers.

When eventually a second group of guests arrived, she stared in amazement at the man who had tentatively offered for her hand. Gone was the bushy beard, his wildly flourishing hair had been tamed, thinned and braided. He wore sparkling Opalwear robes and his Hukvah bore the braid of a Master Smith. With him came his inseparable companions, Master Patris in his finest, Rowbet, Somner and Ivinish, followed by Carolus the Apothecary and Brannith, his clerk. Nadra stared at the little scribe in bewilderment, but then Ikella raised a hand for attention.

"Today I have come to thank Nadra for her service to my household.", There was an air of formality in her voice and Nadra drew a little worried crease between her brows as Ikella continued.

"Although this gathering is being held at my son's request and far too early in his life in my humble opinion, I concur completely with him that we owe Nadra a debt of gratitude for her Rotations of service.".

There it was, a flat, unequivocal statement that told all present that the latent friction that everyone had sensed between Daro and herself really existed and was not in their imaginations. Daro frowned and looked at his feet as his mother continued briskly.

"Taking two fosterlings to breast is above the call of duty and for this Nadra I will support you in food, drink and housing. You will be shod and clothed at my expense and I award you the freedom of Selesh to do with as you will.", Nadra stared in astonishment at her Sorceress and, belatedly, Ikella remembered her manners and took Nadra's hand.

"For many Rotations I have heard my son call you "Little Mother" and feel I can't permit this to continue without adopting you formally into my household and into the Clan. Honoured Little Mother, will you take the Colour of the Clan, hold to our Ways, serve Selesh faithfully and adopt the name bin Selesh?".

Nadra gasped in mute disbelief then, catching the gleam of a smile from both her nurslings, bowed her head submissively and was raised to her feet as Daro congratulated her.

That was not all. Still struggling to come to terms with the change in her status, Nadra nearly passed out when Beven cleared his throat and addressed himself to Ikella.

"Lady.", He used the form of address that Clansmen used to the Head of the Clan. "It is the desire of my heart that I be permitted to address Nadra bin Selesh, of your household and press my suit for marriage.".

There was immense dignity in the man and he faced Ikella squarely and paused, ready for her deliberations.

"Can you support a wife Beven?".

Ikella was all solemnity, but for the amused tic at the corner of her mouth. She continued, carefully enumerating Nadra's needs.

"She must have a clean, well-secured house. She has been used to high status fittings and fixtures in such a home. She will require a bathing room, at least one bedroom, separate living rooms and a good kitchen.", The Sorceress was emphatic.

"She is used to sewing by a good light and more than used to the various implements of cooking and housekeeping that my household favours. She needs a good diet, a range of activities to stop her getting bored and the comfort of someone to talk to when the weather turns stormy.".

Her face was calm, but her eyes were hard as she said softly.

"Nadra had a wealth of sorrow to forget when she came here in my service. I wouldn't wish on her any more of those sorrows!".

Beven stiffly bowed, then said impulsively.

"Lady, all she has and more will I lay at her feet if she consents to our marriage. As Master Smith and a Clansman, I am well provided for and willing to work longer to gain if you think my offer lacking. It is my intention to let my Journeyman Farandel take over the running of the Forge, so that I have the time to spend with my wife. I already own two homes, one within and one without Selesh and will sell them to buy anything Nadra sets her heart on. I had looked at taking one of the inns in the village so that I could have work and time for her together, but until I know her answer and have your approval, my hands are tied.".

Ikella looked from the blushing Nadra to the hopeful groom and said lightly, but meaningfully.

"Oh, well you have my permission of course, though that seems to count for little these days!".

and Daro blushed unnoticed as Nadra nodded and congratulations filled the air.

There was a pause in the chattering, but before Ikella could take advantage of it and take her leave, Carolus prodded his clerk into action. The odd, reclusive, little man stepped forward at his Master's bidding and the room quietened as he cleared his throat self-consciously.

"Lady, Masters and gentles all.", He addressed the company in a strangely rich voice for such a scrawny body. He flourished a scroll and read from it, with great attention to detail.

"It is the bride gift of my Master's that I am empowered to read aloud this day.", he announced and Beven stared as the young clerk continued.

"In equal partnership, Carolus of the Nine Sands and the company of Four Free Men, holding the free right of trade at the inn known as the "Cross-Eyed Zeglur" in the village of Selesh within the Opal Sands of her most indulgent Lady Ikella te Syrene, do surrender all right in the same free trade to Nadra bin Selesh upon her marriage to Beven ap Minidrahl, Master Smith of the Forge Selesh. The property, living and trade will revert to the said Carolus and partners upon relinquishment of Beven ap Minidrahl and his wife through age or infirmity, or retirement of interest. The contract of service to be enacted upon the marriage of the persons named within this document and agreements to be signed thereinafter.".

"It would seem.", said the Sorceress somewhat inconsequentially. "That we are all to have a new life and calling! All I need to do is to take up goat herding and perhaps we will all be happy!".

However, although the company present heard her complaint, no-one took any notice, all being aware of the habitual conflict between growing children and their parents. Yet a small frisson of foreboding shivered over the observant Apothecary when he noted the sudden pallor and the compression of his protégée's finely moulded mouth, as if Daro fought a sudden urge to reply to his mothers goading.

Soon enough the company disbursed, Nadra departing in a flurry of good wishes on the arm of her betrothed, Carolus and his friends to their flourishing business in the underground pastures and Ikella to her responsibilities in the Healer Foundation that she had started more than nine Rotations past.

She walked slowly back from Daro's apartments, noting the ongoing work around her as men carrying plaster buckets and spreaders came to work on the dusty, time-begrimed passages that linked the older settlement to the new. She entered her workroom in an odd frame of mind. Somehow, the little celebration that she had just attended at Daro's urgent plea had unsettled her, left her feeling depressed, somewhat cut out of her son's life.

Giving herself an admonitory shake, she picked up the list of journeyman Healers who would leave Selesh at the Zenitheon Gather to progress through the Sands of the Union on Song Walk. This, the last stage of their training, would bring them back to Selesh to qualify as fully trained Healers. This Song Walk, twenty-seven girls would set out, intending to sing their vows and demonstrate their accomplishments before the Council of Nine and herself four Rotations hence. Reflecting, Ikella realised with a pang, that Daro himself would be twenty Rotations old before they returned, if indeed they all survived to do so, she wondered what Daro would have achieved by then and she scowled ferociously as she re-visited the cause of their estrangement.

Daro wanted to travel and she didn't think him ready to do so. She hooked a stool from beneath a workbench and sat, the list of journeymen in her hand still. She considered him rash, unable to deal with the results of his impetuosity and she thought glumly that she knew why, which was of little comfort to her.

She laid the list down, knowing that all the names on it referred to sensible girls, who quite apart from the fact that they had been drawn from a group who understood how to make camp, how to find food and cook it, were also possessed of a link to the Source which would enable them to perform acts of small magic that would keep them safe in the desert, or heal themselves when damage couldn't be forestalled.

She sighed and frowned as she considered sending Daro abroad and shuddered, realising that her son didn't even know what most edible plants looked like, let alone how to avoid harmful ones. She doubted that he could follow the tranches or "water-paths" of their arid environment and if he knew how to put up a shelter, she didn't know how he had acquired the knowledge.

She raised her head and glowered into the mirror on the wall. It was all her own fault, she decided, knowing indeed that she had been overly protective of her foundling.

His strange meatless diet provoked much of her concern, she decided. He had been frail as a baby, slow to wean, reacting easily to animal products, making it hard for them to raise him to normal active health. His diet still lacked the proteins that a growing boy needed and he often looked pale and drawn, but he ate well, taking nourishment from many of the strange fruits and vegetables that Carolus and his friends found in the surrounding markets, at huge expense.

She continued to brood, counting off the pros and cons of their situation absently. If she had not followed the call of her Sands on the night of the Storm, Daro would never have been born alive. If she had not protected him and her Healers with a spell of some ancient power, none of them would have survived to come back to Selesh. If she had not been the Sorceress, head of the Guild of Healers, he might not have survived his sickly first half Rotation of life and if Carolus had not arrived in the nick of time to save him after a near deadly reaction to animal products and inform their knowledge of this strange allergy, they could never have saved him to come to near adult status. Surely, she reasoned, that was reinforcement for her argument. Daro needed extra care and as she was in the position to provide such care, then he should not unreasonably put himself in danger just to flaunt his own right to self-determination.

"No!".

 she decided. "He is much too immature to be able to decide such things. He must settle for having his own suite in which to explore his independence, here in the safety of Selesh.".

Her decision made, she stood abruptly and went out into the Infirmary, determined not to dwell on the hazards of mothering a young man, determined to put Daro from her mind.

However hard she worked that afternoon, the Sorceress was subtly conscious of Daro's presence. Even as she stripped her working clothes off and rubbed her aching back, she sensed him, staring out of his apartment's windows across the great escarpment of Torrenesh high above her, resentful and restless. She went swiftly into the private washdown installed in her workroom to shower the grime of her day away. Afterward, towelling herself roughly dry, she put on clean work wear and made her way out across the Gathering Square to the underground pasture, seeking Carolus.

The Apothecary was just leaving his companions and exhibited no surprise at seeing Ikella looking for him. He flashed her a quick smile and explained that he was just going to call in on Olneth, resident in the tent that had become established in the great pasture.

Ikella paused while he collected his medical scrip before accompanying him, paying lively attention to the richness of the grazing, the domesticity of the animals who grazed there, exclaiming in delight over a cloud of fluttering insects that rose above the Apothecary's treasured garden.

They came to the tent around which she noted several stakes supporting circular hand woven symbols. Her eyebrows rose in mute enquiry, until Carolus stepped forward and tapped a woven circle lightly. A melodious jingle arose, from a myriad of tiny bells which hung from the ribbons below the weaving and the Healer Sorceress immediately realised how this guarantee of privacy, had helped Olneth recover from the terrible disfiguring injuries that had brought him here.

Suddenly, silently, Olneth appeared in the entrance. She could only glimpse the outline of his head, for even in this private place, he wore his hukvah, ever ready to withdraw his ruined face from casual inspection. However, there was a bright gleam in the one eye she could see and the corner of his mouth twitched in a rueful smile as he bade them welcome.

"Had I known you were coming to see me Lady.", he murmured. "I would have provided wine!".

Ikella laughed easily at his courtier's manner then blushed at the warmth in his voice.

"No matter Olneth.", her Apothecary spoke lightly. "For we brought our own!"

He brought his hand out from behind his back and there was indeed a wineskin dangling there although Ikella had not seen him pick one up! She must have looked at him askance, for he murmured quietly.

"I have to look at his eye, it has become painful and I am glad you are here for I would appreciate your opinion.", He turned away to collect some pottery goblets and busied himself pouring wine.

Olneth sighed and reached up, reluctantly removing his hukvah, revealing that far from being horrendously scarred, his face, so tragically damaged before the Healer Hall opened, was strangely smooth and apparently unblemished.

Ikella frowned, as she tried to grasp what troubled her about his appearance and then realised that the two sides of his face simply didn't match. The new skin that had grown to replace the scarred area still had the appearance of childhood, the lack of sun made it unnaturally pale and there was patently a lack of elasticity around the eye. He bore her fiercely diagnostic stare unflinchingly, but his hands clenched and a muscle at the corner of his mouth jumped.

She spoke gently.

"Oh, well done Carolus. You two have achieved great wonders with that.", She leant forward.

"May I touch your face Olneth?" She asked him respectfully, at his silent nod, she examined him methodically.

She began by assessing his sensitivity, testing the tautness of the skin over his cheekbones, then probing the eye socket itself. She released his head abruptly and cast about for a chair in which her patient could sit. Carolus brought one across the tent, which she had somewhat absently noticed as being very well appointed. There was a curtained sleeping area, a table, chairs, even a low divan piled with scrolls and book bags.

The Apothecary met her eyes as he encouraged Olneth to drink his wine and sit, facing Ikella. Then, at a nod from her, he came behind the chair and adjusted the position of Olneth's head, tilting it back, firmly bracing it against his own chest.

Ikella stood with her head inclined. Her eyes took on an intent inwardly focussed look, as her aura sprang around her. She had caught the whisper of a songspell, even as she examined Olneth. The fleeting touch of the Source sang in her blood as she ran her analytical gaze over the repairs to his face and she swiftly revisited the map of new skin, new flesh, down, down to the very bones around his eye socket. She reached out an empowered hand, almost unaware of the cadences that had formed in her mind, her throat, as she tenderly stroked the man's mouth, cheek, nose and eyelids.

Carolus stood rock steady. His firm hands supported Olneth who quivered under Ikella's seeking fingers. He moaned softly panting as she found the tightness and gentled it into relaxing. His face was changing under her hands, moulding to the resonance of her voice, reforming under the skilled tutelage of magic. The sound of her voice informing his damaged nerve cells brought them dancing back to life and his tear ducts, destroyed by the Drecon's vicious acidic venom, stretched, reconnected and bathed the Sorceress's hands as Olneth wept with relief.

The songspell died away. Her hands were disengaging and the Source was withdrawing from her, when Ikella came to herself again and, strength spent, sank onto the divan, displacing a couple of scrolls as she did so. Making sure that Olneth was alright, Carolus swiftly brought a goblet of wine to Ikella and stood over her until she drank it.

Olneth sat up, rubbing his face cautiously, then he blinked rapidly for a moment and rubbed his eye carefully.

"Thank you Lady, thank you. My face doesn't feel so tight and my eye has stopped hurting. I am sure that my eye is wet again, but it has not been that way for so long that I forget what it feels like!".

He broke off abruptly wiping a tearing eye with his sleeve, then Carolus silently placed a small, polished copper sheet in his hand and the man reluctantly looked at his reflection in stunned amazement.

"But, but…" Olneth struggled to understand what Ikella had done. "My face is my face again.", He eventually managed to say and the weary Sorceress smiled at his disbelief.

"Your wounds were so savage and poisoned that all the layers had to recover, one at a time. Each part of your face had to be free of poisoned tissue to heal and that has been a long process. Once that was achieved the new flesh had to bond totally with the old, bone to bone, muscle to muscle before I could manipulate it. Put simply, the time was right tonight, but it has to be said that it took five full Rotations for your body to heal and another five for your mind to accept what has happened to you.".

She sipped her wine, idly reading the scroll she was handling and then froze in surprise.

"Olneth!" She exclaimed. "How is it that you have a report here from Trebizond that has only just reached Seris Beneva's ears? Her spymaster has only just conveyed its contents to her!".

Even as she spoke, realisation dawned and she touched her forehead delicately, in the gesture that demonstrated enlightenment.

"Oh, Carolus! My wits are lacking! I came to berate you for not taking Daro as Apothecary apprentice and instead I find you are Beneva's spymaster!".

She looked at Carolus witheringly, but he shook his head and chuckling appreciatively, simply indicated Olneth, who smiling, rose and sketched a bow.

"That is what you are supposed to think my Deshun!" The old Apothecary was obviously delighted at the success of his subterfuge, saying happily. "There are some who would notice my comings and goings and one in particular who has already indicated her lack of liking for me!"

This oblique reference to Adruna drew his attention back to Olneth and his face softened as he turned to his friend, who stared wonderingly into the burnished copper mirror as if transfixed.

"Do you reckon young Daro would make an apprentice Apothecary?".

Olneth gave a muffled snort of derision. Ikella stared at Carolus as the Sybillsce continued, amusement on his face and in his voice.

"I'd sooner give that scamp a job as a spy than subject your patients to torture at his hands!".

"Oh yes.", replied Carolus. "Do you remember the night Daro stole that herd of coatan, right from under the nose of the shepherd?" The Apothecary grinned wickedly as Olneth thoughtfully picked up the story.

"Yes, that was well done. He got them to market without loss, sold them at a ridiculously high price and took the money back to the man as compensation for his loss. He took them right up Torrenesh and over the old paths to Quinnox to avoid discovery as well. Bright boy, very inventive and a really good liar!"

His placid recitation of Daro's dubious talents and the fact that she had known nothing of this escapade, really hit home as Ikella stared at him in mounting horror.

Chapter 20 - A Pulse of Power

In the quiet tent, Ikella sat forward, her expression unreadable, her body language indicative of subdued anger. Olneth eyed her warily as Carolus commented..

"Growing lads have to keep themselves occupied somehow!"

This only served to provoke Ikella, who lashed out caustically.

"You knew of this and did nothing?",Carolus shifted awkwardly and immediately Ikella pounced.

"Yes?" The ominous voice purred and an icy chill touched Olneth's neck. Rising silently, he distanced himself from her anger, but the inexorable voice followed him, to his cooking fire, where he squatted, preparing a drink.

"Yes, I see it now.", Ikella rose to pace up and down. "You knew, yet you let him risk his life with never a word?"

She threw up her hands in disgust, sitting heavily once more.

"In the name of masculine conspiracy I suppose?"

Her scorn was absolute as she turned a withering glance on both men, who studiously avoided her gaze. In ringing condemnation, she declared, "Men! I despair of them.", and sat, drumming her fingers on the divan before saying curtly.

"Well, at least he is back safely.".

At this, Carolus replied uncomfortably.

"Perhaps I should explain. It happened when Suraya left to train with Kerisima.", there was a long silence while Ikella digested this, eventually, her voice icy, she spluttered into outraged speech.

"That was six Rotations ago! They were only nine! Children with no knowledge of the world!", she blazed angrily, 'Since the day that cracked brained episode with the Drecon's Claw nearly killed him, Daro has been guarded, day and night. How did such an idea occur to him? How did he come to do this thing? Why was I never told of this?".

However, there was an odd note of pride in her voice, as she thought of Daro taking it into his head to go adventuring. She sank back against the divan, feebly fending off a fit of giggles, exclaiming, "Oh no, Carolus, it is too bad of you.", She was shaking her head in disbelief, sure that the Apothecary was teasing her as she said uncertainly, "You don't really expect me to believe that child took a herd of coatan over Torrenesh? To the markets? On his own? I can't believe this! Its just a wild fantasy of yours surely?".

However, finally she did believe it and nothing would do but she had to have the whole tale.

Trying to make light of it, Carolus knew that Ikella's unnerving ability to detect subterfuge, made her a dangerous adversary. He leant back, watching Olneth from the corner of a veiled eye, as befitting a Master Spy, he was economical with the truth.

"Well.", He mused, "I don't think I can shed any light on what drove Daro to go "wandering.", He considered the subject, aware of green eyes blazing from the divan, adding cautiously, "He seemed to believe that you had a preference for Suraya. He was very excited as we packed the litters and bitterly disappointed when you left him behind!"

He made no apology. Facts were facts and should have been faced long ago. His voice sharpened.

"He gave Suraya his Dolcan, to keep her company, thinking that she might miss home, but Miss High and Mighty never even thanked him. He was devastated and I know he misses Usticus still.".

The censure in the old man's voice left Ikella in no doubt as to who Carolus championed. Olneth placed a pan on the trivet over the fire, which flickered, outside in the darkened pasture. The Apothecary sighed, glancing at the Sorceress, who was plainly digesting some uncomfortable thoughts of her own.

"Perhaps Suraya didn't know how much Daro loved the Dolcan.", She spoke gruffly, plainly unconvinced by her own argument, but Carolus retorted sharply.

"I disagree. Suraya, certainly knew how much Daro loved Usticus! She on the other hand, was bored, jealous and spiteful. I witnessed it myself!".

Carolus dropped his eyes in the simpering attitude adopted by Suraya, as he mimicked her gappy toothless lisp.

"Oh, poor boy .", The unmistakeable tones of the sixth Sorceress Elect were so accurate, that Ikella had the disquieting sensation that the girl was hiding behind her old friend.

"My poor, poor boy.", the faithful rendition continued slyly.

"Is your Mother leaving you behind? All on your own without any company? I, of course shall have both Guardians and Shiarjha attending me! I am going to be the centre of attention as Deshun Kerisima welcomes me. What a shame! You'll miss it all, as well as Usticus of course!"

The malicious note in the voice was all too believable and Ikella winced, understanding the impact this must have had on a lonely, impressionable boy. She remembered her own brothers, wondering if Bedick or Ruanneth had thought her arrogant in her excitement? However, neither candidates or outsiders ever knew of the strange distortion of time that would return them from training, as young as they began, to discover that their lives in magic had taken them far beyond the normal human lifespan of all they had known or loved. She might even outlive Daro, such was the penalty demanded for her power and soberly she considered this.

Carolus continued the story as Olneth served the sweetdrink silently, sketching the lonely child wandering the settlement.

"As you know, a ninenight later Selesh was in quarantine. Few escaped the red fever, the guard was halved, unable to keep up with him. Nadra, nursed Ahnell, until she succumbed herself. I ran from bed to bed for ninenights, not knowing of his plans right up to the night of Zenitheon, which was barely celebrated!".

The Sorceress listened silently, as he recalled tracking the truant, with Jashell and Diras.

"Though we only admitted those who had previously had the fever, sufficient numbers Gathered for him to get away unnoticed. He chose his moment well.", The Sorceress closed her eyes in mute despair, visualising Daro's adventure. Slipping past the guard, mingling with pilgrims. Sneaking off with the herd while their owner slept, before taking them onward and upward over Torrenesh itself. She forbore questions, accepting the story as it was told and only spoke once, observing Carolus closely, as she asked simply.

"Why?".

Carolus glanced down saying quietly.

"I don't know what Suraya said to provoke him, only that Shiarjha interrupted them, before Daro lost his temper. I remember the litters leaving, the boy sobbing, utterly distraught because he had given Usticus to one who didn't appreciate the gift.".

His words painted such a picture of misery, that Ikella whispered, "Poor boy!".

Colouring faintly, she lifted her head to share an intimate confidence with the Apothecary.

"There were signs I couldn't ignore Carolus. She had to be removed from these Sands before the tides of Jenta came upon her. She has to learn to control her powers, before they control her!".

The Apothecary nodded, saying shortly.

"It is a pity that she wasn't taught to control her spiteful tongue earlier. Does she understand that she will have no chance to apologise later? That...", his voice died away in pain, but Ikella ruthlessly picked up the train of thought effortlessly.

"That he will go to the Sands long before she can torment him? Of course not Carolus. That knowledge is too destructive to release and that is one thing that will never change!"

He nodded soberly and the subject was closed.

Ikella stood in answer to the Summoning Bell, as it rang out across the Gathering Square and Carolus watched her go back to her novices, wishing that she had as much time to devote to her son's welfare.

He sat, brooding over the dregs of his drink considering that he had acquitted himself well. He hadn't resorted to lying, he had given an acceptable explanation and most particularly he hadn't told Ikella of the last words he had heard Suraya say to a devastated Daro.

"Never mind boy! She won't miss you. After all, you are only a man. I, on the other hand am already a Sorceress - elect. When I return as Sorceress, you will bend the knee to me!"

The sweet spiteful voice added venomously, "How sad! I will be Sorceress and you? You will be nothing!".

Carolus told Ikella nothing of the long nights holding his enraged Songchild, listening to the single minded refrain.

"I will never be nothing! I am Daro bin Selesh. Son of the Sorceress, Ikella te Syrene. Warden of the Winds and Guardian of the Ways!"

He remembered the most telling statement of all, as Daro drifted off to sleep.

"I will show her. I will show them all, even if I have to become a Sandsinger to do so.", and the old man shivered apprehensively, bidding Olneth a "Good Night" and slowly making his way to his quarters. However, it was a long time before the troubled Apothecary slept.

High in his Eyrie, Daro paced restlessly, tired yet energised at the same time. He didn't understand it, but put it down to his new rooms or his new sense of freedom. He had spent his day arranging their accommodation to suit their needs. A suite each with the great room and his study in between them, leading to a large ante-chamber, the stairs and access back into the main complex. He was bent on exploring, but while guards and drudges organised, he hadn't been able to and he waited impatiently for Ahnell to return from his own days business. However, Ahnell was unwilling to talk, saying that he needed to think about things first and proved unresponsive to Daro's teasing.

"What troubles you my friend? You can speak in confidence, we understand.", soothed Daro in mock "Healerspeak. "Now take a deep breath, try again.".

He patted Ahnell's shoulder, adding sweetly, "Would you care to lie down? You can tell me your troubles. I can send for a soul searcher if you need one.".

He ducked as Ahnell laughingly swatted at him. "Fool!" He threw an arm round Daro's shoulder affectionately.

"Just don't let "She who must be obeyed, " hear you mock her Healers!", he warned as they made themselves comfortable.

Daro, throwing himself down on a divan, rolled over, raising his head on one arm, looking into his friends flushed face. Plainly about to broach a subject close to his heart, Ahnell hesitated until he sat up, giving him his full attention. The back of Daro's neck tickled, a sensation he had begun to associate with unpleasant experiences, but he remained quiet, as Ahnell sank to the floor cross-legged and tucking his feet under him, began to speak.

"I am told that a Clansmen of high rank has offered to adopt me!". The statement so simply spoken acted like a bucket of icy water on Daro's spirits. He and Ahnell had been brought up together almost from birth. They had been raised like brothers, behaved and felt like brothers and now, were they to be separated?

Daro rose, bleak faced saying brusquely.

"Is it already full night? The One take it! I am hungry and the kitchens will be closed!". His stomach growled softly as he crossed to the door and opening it, called over his shoulder.

"Doesn't the Infirmary have a night kitchen? You know the place, it is where the old storerooms were. I remember that they often have racks of fruit stored there. Let's go see and find out if the duty cook won't let us have some. We can bring it back here and you can tell me all about it then.".

He knew that he was putting off the moment, that he should listen to his friend, but his feet had taken him onto the stairway, on and down, Ahnell clattering along in his wake.

'shush! I don't want Diras or her mob alarmed.", Daro cautioned, as they turned into the corridor linking the Eyrie to the settlement. Guiltily, Ahnell stopped outside the night kitchen.

The door was shut!, Ahnell grinned and crossing the corridor confidently turned the handle, but the door was locked. A passing drudge spoke softly.

"The night kitchen doesn't open until fourth watch masters. You can collect fruit from the rear storeroom if you don't mind serving yourselves?.".

He fumbled in his pocket for a key and handed it to Daro, saying only.

"I must run this ice block to Healer Mina, she needs it urgently. It will be melting by the time I get there. Leave the key on the hook in the Guards cubbyhole Sirs.".

Daro grinned as the man departed at a run and seconds later they stood in the storeroom.

It was cool and dark. For a moment they paused, letting their eyes adjust to the night glow that burned faintly high on the sloping roof of the oddly shaped chamber, before they saw the piquantly scented fruit which surrounded them.

"Holy Surrandel!".

Daro's amazement was comical, as he surveyed the quantities stored there. Knowing that his friend had little understanding of crop production, Ahnell spoke up.

"They are fruit picking everyday on Torrenesh, I helped unload some of these I am sure.", He broke off with a whoop, hastily silenced by Daro, as he spotted a favourite.

"Look Daro, lushens.".

As he pointed dramatically to the large ovoids balanced on the back of a high rack, his hand brushed one and the inevitable happened. Fruit spilled everywhere and laughing and cursing, he and Daro played "retrieval", for the next ten sectors, but thankfully nobody came to find out what was going on.

They carefully selected a number of different fruit, but as they were about to leave, one of the lushens, precariously balanced on top of a couple of pelaquins, rolled, fell backwards down a gap and disappeared from view.

They both eyed the prominent gap ominously, then Daro sighed, handed the bag in which they had placed their own selection to Ahnell and saying simply.

"I know! I got us into this and I am the smallest.", he ducked beneath the framework supporting the fruit.

Sliding, then wriggling, he pushed his way into a surprisingly large gap, behind the storage racks.

Seconds later, he rose, clutching the fruit, sorrow on his face.

"Albinus take it.

I'm afraid it is split. Shall we add it to the haul?".

As he spoke, he leant back against the roughly plastered wall, muttering.

"I wonder where they keep the ice? A small bit and we could make cold drinks with some of this.".

He shouldered back into the wall, straightening himself, in preparation to return. There was a dull click and in front of Ahnell's bemused gaze, the wall behind Daro pivoted and the boy disappeared!

Reacting automatically, Ahnell squeezed through to the gap, where the blankly innocent wall, had swung shut. Controlling his panic, he pounded the wall in the hope of triggering whatever mechanism operated it. A muffled voice commanded coolly.

'stop that you idiot. I am behind the "door" if that is what it is and I have no light at all. I am not going to risk being flattened by any movement you provoke. Settle down and let me explore with my hands. I might be able to open it from in here.".

Quite unnerved, Ahnell slid to sit on the cold stone floor, listening to the muffled taps and rustling noises, coming from the secret entranceway. After what seemed to be an intolerably long time, there came a long murmur of "Aah", from Daro, a sort of fumbling movement and the door pivoted again to reveal a grinning boy.

Daro was glowing with triumph as he emerged.

"This is famous!", he exclaimed and nothing would have it, but he sneaked out into the dimly lit corridor to find a spare glow basket and examine his find.

Ahnell groaned as Daro lit the glow and returned into the passage he had discovered.

With the light bobbing ahead of him, Ahnell traipsed in Daro's wake.

"It wasn't even interesting.", he thought, glancing about him at the evidence of neglect.

"Its not been used in my lifetime either.". Ahnell was certain that they were disturbing the dust fall of aeons.

Daro seemed to be climbing now, for the light was definitely ascending steeply, then he stopped abruptly, raising the glow above his head. It was a dead end and Ahnell, a little below Daro see that ahead of them, the steep staircase was blocked by a huge rock.

Daro's shoulders slumped in disappointment as he turned at the top of a steep flight of stairs, carved into the natural rock, every tread lip bowed dangerously. Descending moodily, he scowled at the ancient passageway, all his energy dissipated by disappointment.

"I don't understand why anyone would hide this.", he exclaimed, taking a greenheart from Ahnell and biting into its strange furry skin savagely.

He continued to lament as he devoured another hungrily, accepting Ahnell's division of the spoils without question.

"This goes nowhere! I can't work it out either. The passage is too short and the stairs too steep to connect with anywhere that is currently in use.", he frowned, saying suddenly , "Perhaps the stairs were too badly worn to repair! If they led somewhere that was no longer in use, they might have sealed the top, with that rock. Or had it sealed for them by some roof fall!".

His eyes shone briefly as Ahnell commented in reply.

"Ten teams of Biron with Zeglurs to assist couldn't move that boulder, though I'd like to see them try!".

Daro chuckled at the thought and they sat in companionable silence, each imagining a use for this odd place until Daro yawned, then stiffened in alarm as faintly, through the walls he "felt", a stirring, a sensation such as he had never experienced.

He had sensed rather than seen, that the light from the glow basket was fading. His sudden unreasonable hunger had been assuaged and he was beginning to feel cold and uncomfortable, so he stood up and because there were only three steps to the top, he decided to exercise his legs by climbing back to examine the blockage. .

He found his legs trembling unaccountably, then heard the scraping sounds of Ahnell following him and only then did he see that the light of the glow had paled to a sickly hue. There was a brilliance from beyond the barrier, revealing the adze marks where the stone must have been worked to fit, what he now perceived to be some sort of entrance.

He pressed his face up against the boulder and peered one eyed into the depths beyond.

"Its some sort of chamber I think, but not somewhere I recognize.", This hoarse whisper reached Ahnell who climbed up to join him, both boys sitting on a larger platform which extended to right and left of the staircase, as if, once, there had been a small chamber, or perhaps a linking passage at the top.

Even as he spoke there came a swell of sound, so strange yet familiar, that Daro sank back from where he had crouched, peering through the gap around the barrier. Fixing Ahnell with a fierce stare, Daro laid a silencing finger to his lips. Ahnell obeyed unquestioningly, he was too frightened to risk discovery.

Daro however, sat head on one side, blissfully unaware of his friends terror, as the strange cadences rose to surround them with a wall of energy. Ahnell, who was once again kneeling to try and identify the chamber beyond, was astonished by Daro's reaction. He sat cross-legged, skin flushed and glowing. His eyes dazed, his lips moving in silent accompaniment to the chant that swelled, faded, only to rise again.

Bewildered, Ahnell tried to block his ears, but the sound swirled through them, throbbing into their bones, their brains until Ahnell finally broke free and turned to clutch at Daro, who was glowing!

Palely opalescent, his eyes open, but unfocussed, Ahnell finally understood that his friend was deep in thrall to the chant. It echoed and multiplied, strand upon strand in some mystical threnody, until Ahnell revolted.

Suddenly, he realised that what he heard was not for his ears, no and not for Daro's either. Somehow they had strayed into a holy place, a dangerous place, for now he could identify one of the voices.

"Ikella.".

He only breathed her name, but it roused Daro, who stumbled to his feet, bathed in sweat.

Ahnell, simultaneously realising that the sound had died away, grasped his friend's arm, almost recoiling from the heat that Daro gave off. Swiftly and softly, Ahnell spoke under his breath.

"Daro, we are leaving. We have to get out of here, quickly and quietly. This is no place for men, believe me and if you don't want Ikella putting us to the knife, I suggest we forget what we have found and heard. Do you hear me.".

Daro, a bewildered expression on his face, didn't argue. Following a relieved Ahnell, who secured all evidence of their midnight feast and helped his shaking companion down to the pivoting wall, which he closed behind them with a sigh of regret. Stepping cautiously they found themselves alone in the fruit store.

Ahnell, steadying Daro, slipped through the gap under the racks and cautiously regained the empty corridor outside, where they returned the key,(as instructed), before turning their feet towards the Eyrie once more.

As they passed along the passage, the light increased rapidly and there was a burst of sound to their left. Amazed, they peered out across a crowded Gathering Square, where it was obviously broad daylight and two apprentices were being chased out of the forge by a beaming Beven, as he joined in the ritual celebrations for their journeyman Rotation.

"What time is this Ahnell?", came the confused voice of his companion and Ahnell recalling the strokes of the Summoning Bell said slowly, unbelievingly.

"Two strokes after Height of Sun!". Then in some alarm as they ran up their own private staircase.

"Daro, I don't know where we were, but we seem to have been there all night and for most of the next day. I don't know what happened to us, but I don't like it at all. Are you sure you feel alright? I am exhausted!".

Daro turned a bright laughing face to him.

"I never felt so good in all my life.", He declared solemnly and Ahnell saw that he meant every word he spoke.

He stood taller, his eyes bright with excitement, his mouth turned up optimistically.

Ahnell, stunned by the change in his friend, followed his brisk footsteps toward Daro's suite, to see with astonishment that a woman hovered at Daro's door, pacing gracefully as the boys came to a full stop in the passageway.

"Hello gorgeous..", Daro's voice purred soft and suggestively in Ahnell's ear. Keeping sotto voce, Daro growled softly.

"Where have you been all my life?".

Suddenly feeling abandoned, surplus to requirement, Ahnell turned and slipped discreetly away.

Chapter 21 - Declaration of Intent.

When Daro woke, it was nearly Sunfall. He yawned, feeling at least ten inches taller, almost as though his skin fitted at long last. Positively glowing with health, he stretched until sleep lost its hold and rose, ravenously hungry and curious to find out more about "his" hidden stairs. He went to shower without looking for his mysterious visitor. He knew she had gone, although the ideas that she had left with him would haunt many a dream to come. He dressed rapidly then, absently towelling his hair, peered into the large mirror that had influenced his choice of room, staring at his reflection, bewildered by the apparent metamorphosis that had taken place.

His eyes, which had always seemed to alternate between greeny grey and blue, had suddenly "settled.", (although such a word was hardly appropriate to describe the unsettling orbs that stared back at him.). He studied them, a scintillating turquoise comprised of tiny flecks of green, gold and blue and blinked in surprise, grinning. He had a lean tanned face, a strong masculine jaw, which he fingered, impatient at the thought of shaving. Combing the dark tangle of hair from his face, he glimpsed in his eyes, the golden flames that flickered in their depths. Absurdly reminded of the fire Opal that Ikella liked him to wear, his hand hovered over its box, but he rejected the idea as his stomach grumbled in protest. Smiling, he left, startling Nimah and Diras as he clattered down the stairs, heading towards the refectory.

As he came to the bottom of the staircase, the door to the Square opened to admit Ahnell. He seemed a little reticent, but smiled as they headed towards supper.

"You alright?" Ahnell asked gruffly and Daro grinned sunnily.

"Never better!", he replied, without elaboration and stood aside to let a stream of Healers pass. He caught a flicker of interest from some of them, then Mina approached and Daro stepped in to escort her. She gave him a startled glance, then said sweetly.

"Daro, I don't know what you've been up to, but I'd make sure Ikella never finds out!".

Merry eyes met his innocently and she took his arm, chuckling at his shocked expression.

He had barely recovered his composure and seated himself where Ahnell had captured both the end of a refectory table and the attention of a servitor, when another of his "differences" became obvious. After listening to the menu, he said cautiously.

"I eat no animal products at all! It is difficult, but you mustn't use serving implements that have touched milk, meat, or animal fat of any kind either.", He smiled up at the worried man.

"I like all vegetables. Fungi, roots, nuts, fruit and grains. I am sure that Nadra has already warned the kitchen staff and if you tell the Master Cook, he will know my needs.".

He smiled sunnily at the man's concerned expression and said impulsively.

"Don't worry, I know what suits me. There are enough Healers here to put me right and I am sure you will manage!"

The man gave a tentative smile and went to fetch a Cook.

An immaculate vision in white robes approached, wax tablet and enscrasure in hand.

"Good Sunfall Master's.", his velvety voice purred, a brilliant smile splitting his dark skin and Daro leapt to his feet, grasping him in a hug of pure delight.

"Master Ombuya! How came you here? When did you arrive?".

The Kora - Mai Cook grinned at Daro, gesturing him to sit again.

"I arrived yesterday.", His bass voice rumbled placidly. "My Lady Nahamida follows, so I must prepare for her.".

Realising that journeyman Healers must be about to return from Song Walk, Daro frowned, trying to remember the Kora - Mai candidates, to no avail. So putting the thought to one side, he asked hopefully, "Onopente stew?", and Ombuya consulted a list of ingredients and approved, suggesting extra dishes.

"Sarr grains with roast fungi? Stuffed lenqua leaves and a ripe pelanquin with honeycream to follow?", he queried and Daro rolled his eyes and sighed with anticipation. Ahnell, remembering Ombuya's skill, ordered the same and the cook, returned to his kitchens chuckling.

They worked through the traditional dishes of the Onyx Sands, with minute attention to every crumb, hardly noticing their fellows leaving until their servitor brought a snowberry quencher to wash the meal down, when Ahnell sighed softly.

"Wow! That will be a meal to remember, when I join my new family!" and Daro, jolted out of his self-indulgent mood, sat up, finished the last of his drink and said apologetically, "Oh, Bless the One, I quite forgot your news! Shall we go up to Zenith Point? We can talk privately there.". He stood and Ahnell rose to join him, swiftly following the others out into the Gathering Square, where Healers and novices waited to attend Sunfall prayers. Despite the gathering gloom, they took the track up Torrenesh, walking silently, engrossed in their own thoughts. The climb was hard on full stomachs and they stopped half-way to the plateau at Zenith Point, purchasing the last posy of Jenta's Star's from a small girl. She plainly knew who Daro was, for she murmured quietly.

"The Guardians have only just left Sirs, You could catch them if you ran really fast.".

Daro thanked her gravely, saying only.

"Thank you Carris. I shall, but later.", He turned his particularly sweet smile on the child, asking gently, "Is everything well with you and yours?".

The child's eyes filled with tears as she said in a small, broken voice, "Today feels as though nothing will ever be right again, but Deshun Ikella is very kind. She has taken my mother as her servant in memory of Noni Trinet. She told us that she can bear anything Tarrin does, so long as she has my grandmother's skill with her hair!".

She sketched a wobbly smile and Daro remembered little spare bodied Trinet, working her own brand of magic on his mother's clothes and hair. Saddened by her loss, he clasped her shoulder warmly and said softly.

"Hers were the first hands to cut my own hair Carris. As a mark of respect for your Grandmother, I will take my oath, not to cut my hair this Rotation"

While the dumbfounded child stood staring after them, they moved briskly onward, Ahnell commenting acidly.

"By which time you will have succeeded in adopting the baby Biron look that 'she who forbids it", deplores!".

"Holy Oath! Sworn to respect the memory of Trinet!", Daro protested, but he held back as Ahnell found the marker for his late father, Donnish and watched silently as his companion perform the small duties accorded to the dead. The name stone, set with a facsimile of the late Headman's obesh to show his rank in life was washed, the flowers set in place and Ahnell settled back on his heels to "talk", to his father, as Daro walked to the semi-circular boundary wall that surmounted a sheer forty span drop above the Gate in the Rock and sat brooding.

Both boys displaced from their own people, had lived all their lives in Selesh and neither had ever known their parents. Daro, resting his elbow on a rock, thought mournfully, "At least Ahnell knows what happened and why, but what about me? I don't even know my father's name! I don't know why my mother went into the Sands to birth me. Didn't she want to live?"

He tried to control his thoughts but they skittered on and on and he suddenly saw that he would always be asking the same questions. What, why and who?

"What do I know of my family? Nothing!", His mother's line was untraceable. She had gone to the Sands with her story. As for why, he couldn't begin to understand that!

"Why would a woman in labour walk into such an epic Storm? Was she seeking death for herself?

"Or for me?", he agonised, then his mind drifted to the last enquiry.

"Who? Who is my father? Did my mother even know?" and surprised by how much that thought hurt, found himself considering sympathetically the fate of an unmarried girl and an unplanned pregnancy.

Only last Rotation, the dire consequences of lovemaking, (and Ikella's reaction should he be caught in the act), had been impressed upon Daro by his Songfathers, so firmly that he had voluntarily foresworn the company of women before he had even kissed one! Now he grinned at his own naiveté, then wondered if he would ever find love. He rested against his rock, legs dangling over the wall, reflecting. Though close to his Songfathers, he found himself bereft. Cheated out of the right to know who his father was, or had been.

"All I want is a description, someone's memory of him, but I don't even have that.", he cried inwardly, the pain of his loss unbearably sharp.

A chill breeze touched him, soothing his eyes, which unaccountably stung and almost as if he was present, he heard Carolus saying gently.

"Listen always. It is the duty of the young to learn and the solemn cause of the Elder to teach. There will come a time when we take our Long Walk, to join our companions sleeping in the Sands. Until that time, you will never be alone. Listen to the one that saved you, listen to the other, who brought your mother to the place from which you could be saved. Listen to me, for I have watched over you, contributing in my own way to your continued survival!".

He remembered how the old man had grasped his shoulders, turning his face into the light, observing him through unexpectedly shrewd and sympathetic eyes.

"I too, was different Daro.", Carolus announced and the quality of understanding in his voice, had stayed Daro, made him listen, though he had wanted to go, out of the Apothecaries apartment. Out of Selesh, out of the Sands. Anywhere, where he wasn't different, followed, spied on, talked about!

"I remember a time, when my beliefs were held up to ridicule, by other members of the Clan.", Daro stared at him uncomprehendingly.

"There is no point in going into all that now.", his Songfather continued softly.

"save to say that a rash comment, fuelled by the belief that none but I was right, cost me the last Rotations of my mother's life and took me away, cast out, forever a wanderer!".

His face suddenly worked and Daro saw an immeasurable sorrow there. Something that no-one could put right for Carolus and he looked away, not sure how to react, as a single tear tracked unnoticed down the lined old face.

There was a silence, then the Apothecary sighed, saying only.

"Never mind me boy, you have a life to lead and you must do as you see fit, but remember this. Listen, every day, in the stillness of dawn, in the calm of night, listen. One day you will hear a Voice and when you do, you will know what to do with your life.".

Daro smiled at him, laying his hand on the old man's arm affectionately.

"Songfather, you sound like one of those old prophets I heard about. Are you adding prophecy to prescriptions?".

Carolus tutted under his breath as he moved away, to tidy the small table in his room, where Daro had surprised him nodding over his game of Nine Winds. The old man tilted his head, looking at Daro gravely, his fingers straying amongst the carefully arranged tiles.

"Which prophets were those my boy?". He asked in a carefully neutral voice, as Daro opened the door and turned to go, unaware of the pain etched in Carolus's eyes.

"Oh, I forget now.", Daro's voice floated back through the open door as he departed. "They were called Sandsingers, or something like that. See you at Supper!", but he hadn't and now night was falling, he had a decision to make and Ahnell clapping him on the shoulder, nearly frightened the wits out of him.

His friend settled beside him on the parapet, listening to the night watch trooping up the track from Selesh Minoria below the great massif on which they were poised. Then, as the night lent him anonymity, Ahnell spoke softly.

"Beven and Nadra want to adopt me and give me an apprenticeship as well!", he announced proudly.

"They have another apprentice. Both of us articled to Brew Master Oswin, who was himself, Duvell's apprentice way back. He holds the Mastery at Caranchar and I will be studying three days of the nine with Carolus too.".

Daro thought for a moment, mildly intrigued.

"What's Carolus teaching you?", he probed and Ahnell screwed up his face in disgust, then admitted, I'm not sure, but it seems that there is a lot of stuff a brewer has to know about cleaning brew pans, sterilising equipment and then knowing which substances work together and which don't.", he sighed, but brightened, saying happily.

"Mira, turns journeyman this Zenitheon. I am to join Master Oswin then and Mira will stay until next Rotation, to get us settled in Selesh Minoria. Beven will have a full year's service from a journeyman brewer, (with his bottling rights), which will give them a fine start!".

Daro considered, "That makes sense.", he offered cautiously, "You would have a Rotation under your belt, it would be better for Mira to travel his round during Summer, when there is plenty of work for Brewers, but I thought that the Zenithion intake was restricted to Clansmen.", He paused unwilling to go further, but Ahnell sighed happily.

"I know, mongrel child of Inesh and Sand Sworn!".

Once it had hurt, but Ikella, dismissing the drudge who had made the comment, had taken the trouble to explain to the boy that he had inherited the best of both his parents, courage, defiance and high intelligence.

"Anyway.", he continued. "Beven and Nadra said they wanted to adopt me as soon as they "Hop the trave" and Deshun Ikella simply nodded, gave her permission and then.", he paused for dramatic effect, his eyes shining. as he said breathlessly, "She stamped my application, my indentures and said she would pay for anything I needed, until I am formally adopted and that she considers me a Clansman born. She even told me, that Ahnell app Minidrahl sounds a fine name to her!".

A blissful silence fell and Daro, heard the happiness in his companions voice and couldn't begrudge him his joy.

In companionable silence, they made their way down the steep incline that led them on to the harvesters track back towards Selesh. As they reached the main track, Daro paused, certain that he heard his name and Jashell stepped from the shadows.

Possessed of a powerful natural awareness of others (honed to a fine art by Olneth) he controlled his reactions superbly, although Ahnell jumped out of his skin, shooting the Commander of the Guard a suspicious glare, as she fell into step beside them.

"Trouble?", he enquired, with a worried frown at Daro, who chose to ignore it.

"No, just a message for Master Daro.", The tall shadow of the Inesh crossed the light from the lantern at the Gate in the Rock as they were passed in by the Night Watch.

"I saw you go up to Zenith Point as I came up from the barracks earlier, so when I was asked to send for Daro, I took the liberty of telling our Deshun, that I had seen you going to the Memory Wall.".

Daro nodded shortly. He supposed that he didn't really mind Ikella knowing where he was, it was just irksome that so many people thought him so incapable of staying out of trouble, that they took pains to report his every move!

He cleared his throat irritably.

"And?".

Jashell stepped into the light, her face impervious to his questioning stare, she seemed serenely unaware of the rebellion churning in his breast.

"If you return before Night Prayers, will you call on her in her study?".

It was a command, couched in a request, but both boys silently wondered if their incursion into the hidden stairwell had been discovered and if so, what would the penalty be.

'shall I come with you?".

Ahnell began, but Daro said smoothly, interrupting before Ahnell could make any reference that Jashell could pick up on.

"No, that's alright! I haven't made my duty calls on her for three days now. I expect she just wants to know how we are getting on.".

The Guard commander's eyes rested on him contemplatively, but she said nothing more, just sketching her ritual salute, fingers to forehead, then to heart, as she stood aside and let them pass, following their passage with narrowed eyes, face impassive, fooled by no-one, particularly not by Daro.

They entered the complex, through the Household door and Ahnell hesitated as Daro started up Ikella's private stairs.

"You go on Ahnell. We'll talk in the morning!".

Disappointed, Ahnell called back sarcastically, "By your command Lord Daro!" and disappeared, leaving Daro to calm his flustered appearance and wonder what she wanted him for.

He had almost convinced himself that she just wanted to catch up on his progress, but one glance at her face told him otherwise. She was sitting cross-legged on a cushion, her eyes glittered dangerously and he could feel the tension in the air before she snapped irritably at him.

"Where have you been young man?"

He said mildly, "I went with Ahnell to the Memory Wall to make offerings to Donnesh.".

Not placated in the least, , she snapped, "Why? It is not his memorial day, nor his Nameday, neither is it Ahnell's and why does he need your company?

Can't the boy stand on his own two feet, or didn't I provide enough for him to do?". Daro sighed.

"He wanted to make his reverences I suppose. I didn't ask him, but I think it has to do with Nadra and Beven adopting him!".

He spoke rather sharply, his temper aroused by Ikella's obvious lack of understanding.

"Perhaps he didn't want to accept so much, without giving thanks and "talking" to his fathers spirit. You know Ahnell as well as I do Mother, he respects Donnesh's memory.".

"Then he should give thanks at Night Prayers.", she said moodily staring at the fireplace, as though willing the glowstone chips laid, to burst into flame. As the thought crossed his mind, her eyes locked on his and Daro wondered wildly, if she could read his mind.

She replied to his thoughts, absently.

"Sometimes I can and if I wanted the fire to burn it would! No, I don't read your mind deliberately, there's seldom anything worth reading. Nasty, dirty places the minds of juvenile males!".

She rose stiffly and Daro held his breath for fear she would topple. It was clear from her demeanour that she was cross and wouldn't accept his help, but thankfully, as the blood returned to her extremities, she steadied.

"How old do you think I am Daro?". she asked abruptly. Taken by surprise, he prevaricated by mumbling, until she repeated the question, hazarding an answer that left her chuckling mirthlessly, as she parodied his reply.

"Sixty Rotations? Sixty two? Yes, yes. A very pretty tongued courtier you would make! If that was aimed at getting new hangings for the Eyrie, I suppose you'd better have them! Foolish boy, think! You already know that Healers are long-lived because of their connection to the Source.".

He paled saying hurriedly, "What are you saying Mother? That I must lose you soon?"

His voice cracked unnervingly and he thought furiously, "Why does it keep doing that?" and blushed furiously. Ikella grinned sardonically as she continued.

"No Daro. That is not what I need you to understand. The answer to my question is this. I was already one hundred and twenty Rotations old, when I found you!", she announced bleakly.

"I will be one hundred and thirty-seven Rotations on my next name-day and because I am a Sorceress, because of the constant use of magic, I may even outlive you!"

"There, she had said it.", she thought, watching as Daro struggled to take this in. She spoke shortly.

"That information is secret, Daro bin Selesh!"

Her hand rose and Daro felt a whisper of pressure on his lips, as she described a complex symbol in the air. It gleamed silver and disappeared. She fixed him with brilliant unwavering eyes.

"Must I then outlive one with no ambition, no gainful employment or skill? As Guardian of the Way, that is unthinkable. As Leader of the Clan that adopted you, it is untenable! Even if you only want to become a farmer, a cobbler, or a smith, you must aspire to something, but what I should like to know, is it to be?".

He was silent for a moment, digesting this. It was the very opening he wanted, but had he the courage to take it? He moistened his lips and spoke.

"I do have ambitions, though you may not like them!"

He clenched his hands, his jaw, trying to give some dignity to his words, but to his everlasting shame, his voice wavered, turning into a squeak. He had to breathe deeply to dispel the stab of fury that rose to his throat and tried again. Louder this time, trying to "fill" his voice out, aiming for authority, achieving only anger.

"I want to be like you! I want the power to help our world.", he stated, meaning every word he spoke, then she laughed.

He stood four-square to her, his eyes fixed on her face, as she creased with laughter. Now his looming headache rose, into his throat, face, eyes and then through his flushing skin. He gasped as though she had struck him, then outside the wind suddenly moaned. Heat blossomed through his body, as he surveyed the Sorceress, who quite obviously was still having difficulty mastering her features, or controlling her mirth, until she spoke.

"Daro!", she exclaimed in scandalised tones. "You can't aspire to magic, you're a man! Men can't interact with the Source, that's heresy and I never, repeat NEVER, want to hear you say such things again!"

She was perfectly serious now, frowning at him forbiddingly.

"We heal by using the link with the Source. A rare gift only accessible to certain women once the tides of Jenta are visited upon them. This is physically impossible for a man, who can't have an *othervoice*, understand sympathetic resonance, (because our men can't sing), or initiate a Healing field. You bewilder me utterly. Where are these powers that you want going to come from?"

Her voice had grown gentler as she tried to shield him from disappointment, but it was the wrong tactic altogether. Daro stiffened, aware of strength blooming, as he spoke in a voice strangely confident, though not yet his own.

"Perhaps the powers I seek centre not only in the Source but in the Sands?".

This premise, like many another heresy, was so reasonable that it was shocking. Ikella stared at him mutely, realising belatedly how angry... No! How totally furious he was. He stood over her, tall and limber, his head thrown back, his expression bitterly contemptuous. His mouth thinned as he taunted her.

"What is this?", he questioned, "Myst - cat got your tongue? Got nothing to add to the argument? You must be really old, you're losing your touch Mother!".

A roll of thunder reverberated across Torrenesh, startling her as Daro's voice, scarcely less thunderous exclaimed.

"What is it with you women? Given a little power, you'll lay claim to all of it! Get a little long in the tooth and you'll see us go to the Sands powerless. Well, that is going to change, because I'm going to change it!".

He crossed to a window and crouched, peering up at the slit of sky, visible through the cleft over the Gathering Square, chanting in a low rough growl.

"Ayez. Here comes one walking in the night, who shall cause the return of the Sun to his lands.", He paused, turning back to perch on the sill, facing Ikella, white faced with fear, sweating with rage.

"Someone said that about me and told me what I could become, who I must become and though I love and honour you Mother, you nor any other is going to stop me!"

He held up an imperious hand to stop her speaking.

"I believe her and so I will work towards my destiny Mother, I shall not be a spy, nor an Apothecary. I will be a Sandsinger!".

At this she managed to say, "But…" as the thunder rolled and the lightening seethed outside.

He stalked to the door, the set of his shoulders immutable, his face turned away from her. The timbers seemed to shiver beneath her man-child's hand as he savagely wrenched it open. The air seemed as thick and oppressive as the glowering expression on his face as he turned away, then, almost as if Daro had personally inscribed it across sky a vivid streak of lightening lit his features briefly.

Ikella was transfixed. The imperious tilt of his head, the sweep of his brow, the Opal flickers in his eyes… and suddenly she recognized where she had seen that face before and the Rotations peeled away. Heart hammering, Ikella "saw" once more the image from the caverns beneath Caranchar! The breath strangled in her throat as her questing brain struggled to take in what she had heard, what she had seen, then Daro fled.

In the corridor outside, the echo of feet approached. Ikella's head was pounding and she shrank back in her chair with her hands pressed to her cheeks, almost unable to contemplate any more confrontations. The footsteps halted and she was aware of a figure in the doorway. Then the pressure in her head, the ringing in her ears faded away, unlike the storm. Sighing, at the continuing bad weather, she returned to her reading, as a defiant teenager withdrew to his Eyrie, cutting himself off from his anxious Songfather, his curious foster brother and the woman who whispered at his door.

Chapter 22 - Shadow of the Past

The storm rumbled around Torrenesh and its range all night, breaking out into the Sands in the early hours, leaving fearful communities in its wake.

In Selesh Minoria there were uneasy stirrings. The villagers presented themselves before morning Gather, tired and fretful, they wanted audience with the Sorceress and waited impatiently until Diras, Commander of the morning Watch dispatched a messenger to Ikella's study.

She returned swiftly, saying curtly.

"Our Deshun is engaged in Council business and can't be disturbed. Last night's storm was caused by hotter air which might return, but the Winds pose no threat. Your rooms are always at your disposal, should you feel a need to join the Community. However, your duties are bound to be affected by the rituals of the Prayer Circle and you should consider very carefully before you take action.".

The villagers shuffled, muttering amongst themselves, until one of their Elders spoke up.

"It is not cold enough to give up work for the Rotation. We have those tender plants to get under cover in the special beds that Master Carolus has provided in his garden. We still have the late harvest to gather. If the winds don't rise, we'd lose too many crops. Let them pray for our safety, we'll get on with the task of feeding all of us!"

The deputation left, almost as abruptly as they'd arrived and Diras smiled wearily as they departed. She was tired herself and the villagers had certainly been frightened by last night's events.

Everyone had been restive. The air crackled and hummed. Lightening arced in sizzling streams, lacing wide gulley's with furious flashes of fire and the shattered skeleton of a greenfruit tree hung askew. Thunder prowled the desert, growling above Selesh. Around the turn of the Middle Watch, there had been a torrential downpour, as if the world wept with frustration. Diras smiled at this fanciful thought and went back to her duties.

A muddy puddle filled the narrow main street of Selesh Minoria, Plants and pets along with small children thought the water wonderful, but the Headwoman, remembering the mud slides that had buried half her village in the Great Storm was unimpressed. She spoke to the villagers as they returned to their plantings.

"I agree, it would be impossible. Both routines would suffer, the Community's ways are important, but, they are as dependent on the food we grow, as we are on their hospitality during the Winter. We have to open up far more of old Selesh if we must co-exist "

She paused, then said quietly.

"If the storms return, we will look at the rooms we discussed working on much earlier. There is a set that we could convert into store rooms and shops, another week of this worry and they will be knocking on our doors for help.".

Turning to the local guides, she raised the matter uppermost in her mind.

"Niva, Merans, can you take a look at the tranches on the lower track for me? They are going to be full of water. I fear a sand slip under Emblem Rock if we don't "draw" them.".

She walked into the village briskly, scattering playful children, considering what to do next and went in search of Errish, who had shown enormous interest in the water courses previously, Finding him ruefully considering the small torrent flowing down the centre of her village. They conferred briefly, aware that Ikella, ever watchful, could be using her powers to scrutinise the villagers reaction to her suggestions.

In fact, Ikella was not doing anything of the sort. She was closeted with Beneva in the Djellim, doing what all worried mothers do, confiding in a friend.

Beneva had been reading a crumbling scroll with Shiarjha as the Sorceress arrived. Shiarjha taking one look at Ikella's taut mouth and irritable disposition, promptly rose, bobbed a curtsy and swiftly absented herself, taking the parchment with her.

Ikella frowned, before announcing bitterly, "That boy will be the death of me!", in answer to her fellow Guardian's mute look of enquiry.

Her fellow Guardian spoke softly.

"Better to spread your sorrow, than to hold them to yourself.", Ikella snorted derisively and Beneva saw the depth of her concern as she announced, "I would be private with you Beneva!"

She paused, then raised an empowered hand towards the double doors. A gaseous stream of light flickered around the frame, followed by a subtle "snick" and the doors were not only sealed, but rendered impervious to even the most innocent eavesdropping, for what Ikella had to say was momentous indeed.

"I had quite a dispute with young Daro last night.".

The Sorceress strode across the floor, hooking a chair from a study table and sitting heavily. She waited for a moment, but getting no response from Beneva, continued.

"I know he feels bereft by Nadra's retirement and Ahnell's adoption, but he has come up with the most extraordinary idea. I have to bring it to your attention, because I am convinced that he too strays into heresy and when I confronted his beliefs, he flew into such a passion that my own anger frightened me!".

Beneva stared at her for a moment, then said, in an illuminated tone of voice.

"Thunder and lightening, rain but no wind!".

Ikella nodded shortly. "That might have been my vile mood. You know I could do it as a student, but I thought those times were long past!", she grimaced ruefully.

As she told Beneva of the cryptic prophecy quoted by Daro the previous night and his ambition to seek power himself, she grew pale and thoughtful and Beneva watching her, with the same unnerving stillness, that Ikella remembered from her far off childhood at Sanctuary, sighed deeply.

Ikella said slowly, "There is worse! I feel he may already be able to channel something dark. When he threw himself out of my study in a fine old rage, I completely forgot what he had been there for. Mind you, I had a positively dreadful headache at the time, which could account for it.", looking at her hands dubiously and then said abruptly, "Do you think he has been influenced by someone? Could he have encountered...?", she couldn't bring herself to say the name, so Beneva said it for her.

"Feydora!".

They sat silently, recalling the strange revelations, the stranger "visitation", from a woman, claiming to be a powerful mage from the past[1], until Ikella dourly commented.

"Selesh is so vast, that anything could be hidden away here? Sashandra thought it possible for us to share it with a hitherto unknown Clan, without either of us ever meeting!. How can I police his life, or stop him getting wild ideas if he remains here and insists on exploring?"

She threw up her hands in despair at the thought of so much immature masculine pride contained in one slight body.

"The One only knows what manner of prognostications he has encountered. I strongly suspect that it was these terrible beliefs that led to the Cataclysm myself. Beneva, I may have to get him fostered. He certainly needs to have some occupation that will get his head out of this mischief. I shall get him off Sands to stop him hankering after the power no man can wield!".

Beneva, who had been listening attentively interrupted.

"You appear to think that it was your reaction to Daro's temper that sparked the storm last night?".

She sounded curiously like Jocasta, dry wit to the fore and the Sorceress lifted a haughty eyebrow.

"What else fits the bill?", she enquired acidly and was shocked by Beneva's reply.

"Perhaps the elements were reflecting another's contradictory mood?"

She smiled at her own sly suggestion, but Ikella's jaw dropped, then tensed, even as a cautious tap at the door interrupted them.

She whispered, "No Beneva! What are you suggesting?", but the librarian had raised a beckoning hand and the doors flew open admitting Mina and Shiarjha.

To Ikella's perturbation, Mina, went to the flickering field of energy that kept the Council Chamber sealed. As she approached, Beneva made a sliding movement of her left hand and at the same time there was a quick shimmer of movement from her right. Ikella heard, rather than saw the opening of the Sanctuary Chest and stared at Beneva in surprise. Her fellow Guardian however, seemed quite unconcerned, waiting for Mina to emerge, before she lifted her hands in the gesture that would close the Chest and re-seal the Chamber.

---

[1] Dawn of Darkness © 2010 Julia Cæsar

Mina came to the table and quietly placed a small pouch into Beneva's hands, before withdrawing to the far side of the Djellim, hands folded into her sleeves, in the attitude of contemplation.

Beneva loosened the drawstring that kept the mouth of the pouch closed and as it opened, Ikella gasped, staring down at what lay on the polished surface in amazement.

"Deo support me!", she breathed the prayer softly, for lying there were a pair of silver bracelets, exactly the same as those that graced both her own and Beneva's wrists.

"Yes. The third gauntlets of power, for we have need of another Guardian now!", Beneva said solemnly and Ikella's wrists tingled, as their own insignia materialised. Beneva smiled at her bewilderment.

"Once we are three, you, or another Guardian can call the gauntlets to your wrists instantly. It is our greatest defence against dark power and enables the power of three.", she explained, adding gently, "Will you summon Jashell and Indeera for me? I will summon Carolus. Mina is also of the High Council. Dorra and Beven will represent the Clan. I need two representatives of other Clans as well, so Diras will fetch Nahamida's cook and Olneth.".

She chose not to enlighten Ikella further, but walked Shiarjha to the Council Chamber and smiling sent her in to sit separately as the Inesh summoned set out chairs, facing the strange light patch on the Djellim floor, that had never responded to cleaning.

Ikella went through the motions in a dream. She watched the others troop in and then saw Beneva had somehow arranged for the Great Book of Rule on its lectern to stand in the circle of light.

She shook her head. She had not seen it arrive, nor had she seen the Honour Guard that should have accompanied it, but it was there, all the witnesses had arrived and Beneva had, with a wave of her hand, seen that both Ikella and she were clothed in their formal silver robes.

Beneva raised a hand and silence fell as the group observed her solemnity.

She began to speak.

"In our Way, Guardianship has always been bestowed on those who have the power, the wisdom and the experience to assume the wristlets. We don't seek to change this Way, merely to adapt it to our changing circumstances.".

There was a hum of assent then Beneva raised a hand and called Jashell and Indeera to her side. They conferred in soft murmurs and then both warrior guards went to the Council Chamber and escorted Shiarjha, who came light footed, to stand facing the Guardians.

The Sorceress - Elect smiled gravely, gracefully bowing her head in submission and held out her hands. Beneva regarded her steadily, as she began the ritual.

"In the presence of Seris Ikella, Guardian of the Way and of Seris Beneva, Guardian of Knowledge, members of the High Council of Selesh, the High Priestess of the Inesh and representatives of the Rightful Clan Council of the

Amethyst Sands and a Clan sworn Master Craftsmen representative of the Onyx Sands, I, Seris Beneva call upon this gathering to witness a Calling.".

As Shiarjha looked into Ikella's eyes apologetically, as though she was silently saying, "I didn't mean this to happen Mother!", then the third pair of gauntlets leapt to embrace Shiarjha's slender wrists.

The three of them stood in a circle of light, it positively poured out of the domed ceiling of the Djellim, lighting up the three pairs of gauntlets, flaring along ceremonially tattooed hands linking them mystically with the Great Book of Rule. Silently a page turned, the Summoning Bell sounded and with that small intrusion, the mood was broken.

Amidst a flurry of congratulation, Beneva said dryly.

"Now that is going to confuse everyone, but Seris Miriniva was also called to Sanctuary as a novice, from the Amber Sands I believe. She never left Sanctuary after her potential was spotted. Another left to take up the Staff of the Sands on her behalf. However, this is different yet again, Shiarjha could well take the Staff in her turn. Remember what Jocasta told us, the gauntlets can only choose the one that can wield them!".

Seriously Carolus said.

"However, there are those who would say that too much power seems vested in the Opal Sands these days and I should guard against too much in the way of celebration, although all those present can but feel great pleasure in the settlement of the matter.", He visibly expanded as he said comfortably.

"I far prefer my troubles to come in three's and packaged so pleasantly, who is going to hold against this choice?".

They all chuckled as Shiarjha blushed at the compliment and then Beneva said brusquely.

"I am sorry Shiarjha, I must convene a Council of Guardians immediately. Celebrations will have to wait until later. In fact…"

She turned imperiously on the gathering.

"Until it is necessary, I believe any announcement would be premature, so could you keep this between yourselves in the immediate future?"

There was a small rumble of assent, although Master Ombuya looked particularly disappointed, until Beneva said soothingly, "You shall be present when we tell Nahamida that there was a Kora Mai witness to the Calling, Ombuya.".

His brilliant white teeth flashed in a smile of delight as the party of witnesses were permitted to depart and Beneva gently steered her companions into the Council Chamber, with a wave of an empowered hand.

Behind them in the outer Djellim, the glow from an ancient circle dulled, the Book of Rule on its lectern disappeared, the glows in the ceiling paled. All that remained for a magic-user to sense was a tingle in the atmosphere and a subtle perfume, as the Council of Guardians began.

In the Council Chamber, Beneva busied herself with selecting a wax tablet, a sharp enscrasure, one of the new type "styli" that Master Woodsmith Arkneth had made and settled before Shiarjha a couple of really ancient scrolls.

Ikella sat, still somewhat dumbfounded by Shiarjha's new Calling, but cautiously pleased that the great depths of the child's personality had been recognised at Sanctuary. Shiarjha was calm, studiously referencing a few points in the scroll that Ikella recognised as the one that Beneva and she had been studying earlier and then Beneva spoke.

"Shiarjha and Miriniva studied a lot of the older scrolls that came into our possession during recent Rotations.", She stated flatly.

"That was largely because I found a lot of references to an artefact of enormous power, that they as Guardian and Guardian-designate of power, had to know about. Seris Jocasta ordered an intense search for this artefact prior to the Storm.".

Ikella's interest stirred, galling though it was to know that her own Elect had certainly known of her Calling and had chosen not to speak of it. She glanced at Shiarjha, who was gazing at her, a worried little crease between her brows and impulsively Ikella grinned. Beneva looked up at them, then said tartly.

"When you two finish grinning like a pair of well-fed Myst-cats?" and they returned to the subject in hand. Shiarjha carefully unwinding the primary scroll-stick, revealed a long line of script, the like of which Ikella had only seen at Sanctuary. She peered at the scroll doubtfully.

"Can either of you really understand it?", she asked curiously and Shiarjha smiled at her warmly.

"Oh yes. This is the old script, used well before Cataclysm. It is not symbolic, like our current lettering, but it is very neat, takes up less room and conveys a great deal in a little space. Miriniva understood it better than I, but she showed me a way of relaxing my eyes and brain, so that what appears to be jumbled script, sorts itself out in my mind. You understand that it is not plain writing, nor is it magic, it is a sort of code, which hides a secret so great that they couldn't let it fall into the wrong hands. It relates to an artefact that would one day be needed, in order to save our world from a second Cataclysm!".

Ikella regarded her sharply.

"What artefact? What second Cataclysm and who, for the sake of the One are they?".

Shiarjha regarded her sombrely, then answering her questions in the order that they had been presented, she said quietly.

"The artefact is known as the Tapestry of Tten, it is likely, though not certain that the Great Storm might have been prevented had we known about it, or how to use it and they my revered Mother, were mages of a far different sort, known as Sandsingers!".

Ikella said faintly. "Deo me! Did they really exist then?", but her heart already knew the answer. She stood shakily and cane to peer at the scroll over Shiarjha's shoulder.

"So where is this Tapestry? Does it say anything about them losing it? Is there a description of it?"

Shiarjha considered carefully, before answering.

"There is no description, other than it is beautiful, composed of every Colour in the Sands and embodies more magical power than all of us together, commands today. It was not lost by them either. It was made by one of them and left, so that we might escape their fate!".

Ikella digested that then asked, "How would we know how to use it? Do we know if there are instructions, should we find it? Or was that Storm our second Cataclysm? The One defend us from anything more!"

She came to a glum silence and Beneva said cautiously.

"We still have all the scrolls from this Chamber to go through. Carolus can also read this script and his scribe Brannith is well versed in it. If we enrol their help, we could really make progress. I have some theories of my own about this Tapestry. It may even be hidden here, because it would seem that the Opal Sand has always held the skilled Weavers and much of the ancient cloth, holds their strange spells within it. I don't believe that our Storm was this second Cataclysm. That event is still to come!", she spoke with conviction and Ikella eyed her sourly, as the Librarian scrabbled through another scroll, muttering under her breath.

"Where is that prophecy Shiarjha? I had it here a moment ago.".

The new Guardian bent her head over her scrolls again, diligently searching for the start of a particular line. A few minutes later she held up a hand.

"I have it here.".

She read from it slowly, while Ikella's heart turned to stone.

"One comes, who walking in the night, shall yet shine the light upon his people!"

With every word she pronounced , Ikella's horror grew.

"His? His people? Shiarjha, Beneva, for the sake of the One! You speak heresy, you are worse than my son, who is just an ignorant man! Men can't use magic! Men can't access the Source!"

Then Beneva said gravely.

"Oh no my Sister, there you are most grievously wrong, for the greatest of all Sandsingers was a man called Darius!".

On the table, Beneva gently laid a beautiful enamelled picture. Ikella took in a huge steadying breath to fortify herself, then gazed helplessly, on the face of the man, in whose thrall she had hung, as he honoured her, affixing to her Staff, a pair of flawless crystal wings.

Chapter 23 - Revelations in Amethyst

Despite the enhanced concern of his mother, having declared his intentions, Daro settled down to his solitary state with no further mention of magic. As the Rotation turned onward, he supported Ahnell through his adoption and even took the customary "friends walk", to the Guild Masters Brewery when Ahnell was apprenticed. Now, the only time he saw his childhood companion was when Ahnell attended classes with Carolus.

However, Ikella let well alone, for it seemed to her, that so long as her calls on Daro's time and attention were minimal, they could, at least co-exist without contention, although she would have wished him to pursue a more creative lifestyle.

Zenitheon that Rotation, was marked by the marriage of Nadra and Beven, to which everyone from Selesh Minoria had come, partly because they wanted to taste the new brew that had been imported from Caranchar for the purpose and partly because no great celebrations of this sort had happened within the community of Selesh itself since the Great Storm. The villagers of Selesh Minoria, preferred the low-key celebrations of their own devising, held by the Headwoman out below Emblem Rock, but for a Clansmen of Beven's standing, it was only right and proper for Selesh to be the centre of the festivities.

The Inesh solemnly oiled the trave of the Gate in the Rock on a daily basis, timing these activities to coincide with the daily comings and goings of the Master Builder. His men were setting out a comfortable home where he and Mina would live, a short distance from his aggrea, (builders yard). He endured the good natured teasing, although he would have preferred to spare Mina's blushes.

"Jashell and Indeera seem to have acquired a taste for marriage ceremonies. They have begun a real campaign of nagging both poor Errish and now me!", grumbled Mina as she handed the daily report to Ikella. They were checking supplies as Winter would be on them all too soon. Distracted, Ikella only just caught the end of the complaint and turned to stare at her friend in surprise.

"Don't let them bother you Mina.", she advised and then stopped to peer at the Senior Healer, who was blushing.

"Errish wishes to be a father, but I can't continue Healing and make babies!", she said earnestly and Ikella was forced to admit that she was right. Completely unaware of the effect her announcement would have on Ikella's plans, Mina continued thoughtfully.

"I would like to make this my last Jentaroth as Senior Healer and concentrate on preparing for our marriage, next Spring.".

At last, conscious of the consternation she had caused, Mina protested.

"Deshun, Errish completed the repairs of Selesh, before he asked for me. We were so intent, on making everything safe, on opening the school, the Infirmary, the Hall of Sorcery that we took no notice of our own needs. The School has been open for nine Rotations, during which he has extended Selesh to nearly double its size, making it possible for Beneva to continue the work of Sanctuary.".

Ikella nodded seriously, unprepared for the pain in Mina's voice as she declared.

"This will be the seventeenth Jentaroth since the Storm. If we had married straight away, my own daughter could well be on Song Walk, instead of which, I may never bear a child, for my best Rotations are behind me!".

Appalled at her own insensitivity, her lack of perception, Ikella sighed and subsided into a chair, drawing another opposite for Mina, saying gently, "I am sorry Mina. I forget how time passes...", she broke off abruptly, not wishing to make matters worse, but Mina completed the sentence with equanimity.

"For us ordinary mortals?" She smiled easily and with the bravura of a long friendship said mischievously.

"Watch who you are calling ordinary! I am Mina bin Selesh, Senior Healer of the Guild. I can remove your teeth painlessly, cure your corns, or if I am left to get more elderly and infirm, I could indulge myself in one of those Senior moments when I just can't remember how that spell song worked!".

Ikella burst out laughing.

"Mina, you are outrageous! I should forbid this marriage, I think Errish is a bad influence on you.", She chuckled at the thought of Mina losing her place in mid-spell song and then asked seriously.

"Who would you elect to serve in your stead?".

The little Healer had obviously given this some thought for she said unhesitatingly.

"I think that with her great knowledge of infertility, it has to be Sanra. It must be one of the Council of Nine, she has served us willingly and with her children grown she might like to serve here in my stead?"

Ikella nodded, saying softly.

"Yes, Derun has developed some interesting training for the blind. We could use his skills as well, make something for the men to get involved in, something that could better any blind persons life.".

Mina pursed her lips, thinking.

"How complex it becomes.", as she considered the Way life had been. Men unless trained in the traditional occupations ruled by the Guilds, simply stayed home, minded their children, grew a few crops or ran errands for their wives. However, of late even people like Derun, blind now for sixteen Rotations, had developed new Ways of doing things, ideas that could be passed on, ideas that could illuminate even the sighted! If the Guardian of the Ways was accepting change of this magnitude, then perhaps one day, she might be persuaded that her own son deserved a little more latitude.

The busy Healer thought as she bustled back to the Infirmary, but she wouldn't hold her breath in anticipation of that event!

The object of her mild concern was himself considering his future. Not however ensconced in his Eyrie, but sitting cross-legged at the top of an ancient stairwell, quite cut off from any part of his ordinary life. He was drifting, dreaming, bathed in the flow of power that seemed to permeate the walls here, listening to the empowered voices that launched the Source from which he fed like a starving man. In a Rotation he had grown to his full height and could now stand up to Jashell, eye to eye. His sudden maturity had taken his foster-mother by surprise, his masculinity disturbed her. He shocked giggles from the novice Healers and surprised glimpses of appreciation from his devoted Guards, who had been known to fight for the honour of serving him. However, he had shown no particular preference for anyone's company, just interacting as he must, but increasingly withdrawing, spending long hours in his Eyrie, studying. He explored the ancient settlement's honeycomb of disused rooms, sometimes taking food, glows and his latest finds into the stairwell, dreaming over them, bathed in the Source, as the Sands of his birth surged beneath his feet. He was aware of the piercing cold as the Winter set in, but somehow it didn't affect him as he sat listening to the practice of the Healers, then late at night the testing of the "Little Sisters of Sorcery", under the expert tutelage of the three Guardians. He felt at once apart from and yet intrinsically a part of this place and he took particular interest in the arrivals and departures from the training Halls, often following a new voice, testing his own ability by learning the chants word perfect, humming softly under his breath. Once or twice he had seen the concern on the faces of his Songfathers, but kept his thoughts carefully shielded, his face schooled to impassivity and those who caught a glimpse of that remote dreaming stranger in their midst were few and far between.

The Jentaroth of Daro's seventeenth Rotation came and went, Ahnell was well into his apprenticeship and living with Nadra, Beven and Mira, their journeyman, when Mina and Errish set the date of their wedding. Errish called into the "Cross-Eyed Zeglur", taking a convivial lunch, while ordering the beer for the feast.

"We are to marry, as soon as the chill is off the Sands and my men go back to work. We talked to the Lady and she agreed to perform the ceremony on the first day of Spring!".

"Well.", said Beven comfortably. "That gives the Brew Master plenty of notice, the women can get their finery planned and the Inesh can oil that trave again!"

His comment brought a wry chuckle from the Master Builder who had endured the ribald comments of the guards, since he and Mina announced their betrothal.

"That Gate is a marvel of engineering you know Beven.", Errish produced a wax tablet and a stylus from his pocket and the two men's heads drew together as they looked at the Master Builders sketches. He speculated happily, "There may have been some of those panels with numbers on, right through the complex. I took some from young Daro's Eyrie, before the Lady would let him move and others are starting to come to light. They are all metal, I reckon they operated some mechanism, but for the love of the One, I couldn't fathom it.",

He considered his drawing, head on one side. "More like Smith business than mine.", he confessed to the ex-Master Smith. "Want to take a look one day?".

Beven nodded, but ducked guiltily as Nadra said.

"Not until after we have the work finished here. I needed those rooms shuttered properly before we left for Selesh at Jentaroth. If Carolus can spare Ahnell for an extra day, then you can go and play with your friend dear.", she smiled up at her husband, who said ruefully, "See? I hope you know what you're doing. They're all tyrants at heart!".

The Master Builder left whistling jauntily. He wouldn't have to spread the word now he thought with great satisfaction. What Nadra didn't tell her cronies in the market, would go from Beven to his best customers, the Inesh who lived in the nearby barrack block. What they didn't spread, Ahnell would carry and even their friends in Caranchar would know the date of his marriage and have it noted before he got back through the Gate in the Rock! He went merrily on his way, mightily satisfied with this morning's work. Later, it crossed his mind, that to make the information 'shoot the Sands', he should have told Carolus and Olneth, who seemed to have contacts everywhere.

"However, tomorrow was a different day!" He thought, as he absentmindedly studied the schedule of work planned for the start of the Spring Rites, after the first quarter-day of the Rotation. His teeth gleamed in a smile as he thought that his life would certainly be different after his marriage, just how different he and all Selesh were about to find out.

Daro pored over a scroll, never considering his strange ability to understand even the most complicated of these remnants of the past. He found the line that he wanted and was engrossed in his reading, when a light footfall in the doorway alerted him to Ahnell's presence.

He carefully re-rolled it, aware of Ahnell's intense scrutiny, but offered no information. He looked up laughing, as Ahnell spoke.

"Hah! Caught in the act of real study! I hope Beneva counts her scrolls each night!"

Daro retorted rudely, "Huh! and I hope she doesn't!"

Ahnell came into Daro's great room, looking around him curious to see what Daro had altered since his last visit. It was a comfortable space, shelves lined one wall and the boy crossed to them, surveying childhood treasures with deep affection. He noted the number of additional scrolls and sand-tablets, but knowing how Daro could be prickly where his special interests lay, he said nothing.

Daro observed his friends progress with amusement, until Ahnell stopped at a fragment of tile. A blue grey ceramic, very thick, it reminded him of the natural slate bands on the borders of the Azure Sands. Ahnell bent over it, his brow creased as he queried, "That's odd. It's new isn't it?" and Daro picked the shard up and handed it to Ahnell.

"Oh!" Ahnell gazed down at it in consternation. "It had words on it a moment ago, I saw them!".

Daro laughed easily.

"Yes, it is very odd. I can't quite understand how that happens.", He retrieved the tile, saying thoughtfully. "There are many things about this piece that I find strange. One, of course is that the words seem to come and go.", He held the piece out to Ahnell again, who saw that indeed there were words on the triangular shape. They stood out in high relief now and Ahnell looked at them doubtfully.

"That's just darn weird.", He seemed a little unnerved and Daro cocked a contemplative eye at him, until Ahnell qualified the comment.

"When I saw that, I thought I could read it. Now the words are illegible! It must be some trick of the light. Or something other? The moment I held it, the words disappeared.", "I am very much afraid that is, "something other!"

Daro didn't hesitate. "It has the feel of old magic, but it is not complete, so it probably doesn't count as an artefact to go to Beneva.", He put the tile down on the table and as he let go of it, Ahnell said softly.

"Did you notice, when you hold it, the words were all shiny and glittering.

He sighed and turned away, saying.

"Its not fair! Your life seems so much more interesting than mine. I don't know why I thought that a home and a job would be better than exploring Selesh with you!".

His normally cheerful voice took on a tinge of self-pity.

"I suppose brewing is interesting, but there is just so much you can drink! Beer is part of life and needed, but....", His voice trailed off miserably and Daro jerked his head up, staring at Ahnell in surprise, until the boy burst out with the comment.

"...It is boring. Nothing I do at the Guild is especially hard, it just seems to take forever! Beven and Nadra are kind, but there's never a day without the same boring round of jobs to do. Mira is back by the way. He has completed this part of his round and has leave to stay with us during Jentaroth. He is going to stay on for the wedding because it was his journeyman brew that Errish chose for his guests. It will create great interest at the sign of the Cross Eyed Zeglur, because as his sponsor, Beven has the bottling rights to it. The Guild are very excited, Mira could get his Mastery very soon if he is that rare animal, a creative brewer, but I'm bored to death!".

Daro surveyed his friend in amazement. "Where did all that drive and determination go?"

he wondered and then an idea crossed his mind.

He sat, offering Ahnell a chair and lapsed into thought! For a long time he had considered trying to find a way, beyond the blockage that sealed his stairwell. Recently, when he had found the walls of his secret haunt quieted, he had pushed on the great stone barrier and felt it shift under his hand. Now he eyed his friend silently and thought.

"If Ahnell needs some excitement in his life, I could do with his help! I wonder. When everyone is occupied with this wedding feast, if we could slip away and explore the possibilities?".

Ahnell saw the flush of excitement dawn on Daro's face and leant forward expectantly.

"What now you madman?" He demanded, but even his jaw dropped as Daro outlined his plan.

The day before the wedding Carolus was restless. He took himself out into the underground pasture and walked around the new entrance way, examining the clever additions that the new Master Smith had made. He prowled, looking at the counterweights that held the door open or shut, peering through the high eyelet windows, which permitted a good view of the Gathering Square, while maintaining their own privacy and the special qualities of their unusual pasture.

Patris came to join him.

"Something up?", he queried. "Or have you also got pre-wedding nerves?"

The Apothecary eyed him sourly.

"Pre-wedding nerves indeed!" he snorted, brightening as he thought of Errish and Mina. As he spoke the couple in question crossed the Square, hand in hand, making purposefully for the Hall of the Healers. He scowled, heaving a huge sigh.

"Another dratted rehearsal I assume? Still all I have to do is hold the man's hukvah while he sells himself into slavery. Hello.", His tone brightened considerably.

"Here's Olneth. He's back early, I wasn't expecting him for another ninenight!"

He opened the door himself and the Master Spy slipped inside, unobtrusively tugging at Carolus's arm as he passed. Patris raised an eye as the two men hurried off to the tent in the far pasture, but didn't follow them. They patently had things to discuss and needed their privacy. He had long ago ceased to wonder what went on in the far pasture and his life seemed a lot more comfortable as a result.

Olneth however was far from comfortable. He was chattering with rage and Carolus was forced to slip a calming potion into the sweetdrink that he pressed on the man. Retiring to the bench seat they had made for themselves, he waited for Olneth to calm down before he enquired, "What's happened? I have seldom seen you so angry my friend.", and listened silently, as Olneth related the story.

"For Rotations I have been searching for news of my family.", he finally blurted out.

"Up to Partition, I had searched for Soloria's household in vain. I suppose I hadn't really accepted that our Sorceress could die. there were no witnesses. When I returned from Caranchar, where we met, Buerchan was devastated. Not one survivor remained. Only the Gattarene survived. As you know, I was off-Sands during the Storm and it took from my return until Jentaroth, to discover that Soloria's death was nothing to do with the Storm. For a long time I only had rumours to work with, but as witnesses gradually spoke up, I had to go undercover in my own Sands.".

Carolus stared at him. He was pale with fury, shaking with the ferocity of it and the Apothecary began discreetly to prepare another potion. Olneth suddenly smiled, a flash of white teeth in his tanned face. He held up a hand, forestalling the Apothecaries intervention.

"No my friend, I need this anger, for now I know! One day I will tell you how, but I have it on good report that the creature that your Lady calls the Gattarene is worse than that. She is a murderer, a mass murderer who has killed not only my Lady Soloria, but has massacred all her household, including my wife and our unborn child!'

He choked and turned his head to hide his tears, but Carolus reached out sustaining arms and the strong Sybillsce leaned against him, a storm of silent weeping shaking his body.

Eventually he recovered a little and Carolus listened as Olneth explained.

"My brother was a silver smith, much in demand for the delicacy of his work. When Telandra and I married, his bride token was a pair of identical lockets. Mine has a twist of her hair in it, hers has a twist of mine. I came back here hot-foot from the Onyx Sands because I found something that I recognised. I had hoped against hope that somehow Telandra had got out of our Sands before the Shunning. I had some idea that she might have been sold into slavery, taken to the Onyx Sands perhaps.", he lapsed into a brooding silence, until Carolus touched the back of his hand sympathetically.

"Prowling the slavers haunts, I met a man who sold me this!' He laid a tiny silver locket on the table, springing the catch as he did so. Inside were two twists of hair, one that was plaited like his own jet black locks, the other, a fine baby twist that he fingered in mute bewilderment.

"He told me that he had found a trench at the entrance to the Sherrol Pass and on investigation, had found numerous bodies.". Horror-struck eyes met those of the old man.

"He found, men, women, children, even babes in arms stripped naked. He searched them for identification, or so he told me.".

He cleared his throat saying faintly.

"He lied! He was no more than a grave-robber, a ghoul existing on the sorrows of the living, whom he callously deprived of their heritage. Just as he and his companions robbed the dead of Caranchar!".

He rose suddenly and went out into the pasture, seeking cool air. Returning after a few lurching moments, wiping his mouth. He smiled weakly.

"Sorry. I suddenly thought of the stench of Caranchar, the putrefaction we saw!" and sat, battling nausea, jaw clenched resolutely as he said. "He couldn't describe the woman who wore Telandra's locket but I knew it was hers.", He placed another on the table and clicked it open, lightly touching the curl of her hair nestled there, before continuing harshly.

"I don't believe he killed to get his loot. I think grave-robbing was an easy occupation for him, but it leaves so many unanswered questions. Was one of those babies ours? Was the woman who wore the locket my wife? Perhaps not, but, they were killed before the Gattarene came forth to steal our Sands. The trench was quite overt, right across the Sherrol pass and if I understand the Gattarene's mentality, that implies that the body of Soloria is probably there, for she would want her and her household in the dust under her feet as she returned in triumph.".

In the anguished silence that followed, Carolus looked at the lockets, eyeing askance the soldered links suspending a tiny silver vial from the catch of each chain, saying pointedly, "Poison is it? So one can follow the other if needed?'

Olneth looked around uneasily, before whispering.

"That's what anyone finding them was supposed to think, but in reality…"

He explained at length about Soloria's "back door Key" and Carolus sat for a while absorbing what he had been told. Then he leant forward murmuring conspiratorially, "Since you have shown me your secret, I will share mine, though you won't remember it.", and his eyes gleamed, magic in their depths.

He took Olneth's wrist in one hand, as he had done so many times while treating him, the other hand reached for Telandra's locket and the tiny curl of baby hair, both hands glowed suddenly and Carolus opened gleaming Opal eyes, compelling Olneth to lift his head and listen.

"Telandra lives.", His voice was low, the monotony of the entranced taking all expression from his face.

"Another took her locket and paid the price, but she carried a message, one that says "Your daughter lives, though not in the Sand of her birth. Telandra had twins and was so afraid that they would both be sent to the Reaper, that she gave the girl to a childless woman. She should have been wearing the locket, which would have identified her to you. Your son however has been taken as a slave in the Gattarene's household, where Telandra watches.", Olneth looked up.

"Someone to fight for, someone to search for.", said the Master Spy, hope in his voice once more.

"Yes indeed.", said the Apothecary, adding the post-hypnotic suggestion, "It was good of your old friend to search you out and pass on Telandra's message and her locket, wasn't it?".

Olneth looked at Carolus oddly, but replied evenly.

"It certainly was!" Then he added the grim afterthought.

"Even if he died for the privilege!".

Chapter 24 - Sacrilege

The day of Mina's Wedding dawned cool and comparatively clear. They had all become used to the sullen roll of cloud which obscured the sun, but today the clouds seemed silvery, steel instead of iron grey and Mina sighed happily. She sat while Nadra plaited flowers in her hair, thanking the One that Master Carolus had provided more than enough bride flowers as part of his marriage gift to her. The other part had been a sizeable section of his private garden, already dug, weeded and fertilised ready for planting. He had been very delicate about it, but his eyes had twinkled as she exclaimed in delight.

"Just ready for the seeds to be placed in their beds!"

She had blushed furiously at his dry comment.

"Precisely, I am so glad that you have given up active Healing for a while. It should help that little matter along very well I think!"

She thought happily about her husband to be. She had watched him go last night, framed in the doorway of the Hall, giggling students behind her, she had boldly lifted her hand in farewell as the Master Builder departed in a gaggle of his own men.

"I hope he didn't drink too much last night!" The anxious thought rose unbidden to her lips and Nadra, thinking nothing of it, reassured.

"He certainly didn't. Beven served them only brashban last night.", She referred to a new drink of Mira's devising. It tasted and looked like beer, but had only a tithing of beer's alcoholic content, being devised as the first drink for the very young, or a beer like substitute for those who couldn't tolerate alcohol for reason of age or infirmity. Mina grinned, "I shouldn't let Errish or his men know about that! They'd be mortified.", The conversation died away as Ikella, resplendent in her Guardian's robes entered the room, with Beneva in her wake.

"Mina, you look lovely, those pale blues and greens pick up your own colouring absolutely.", said Beneva appreciatively and Ikella held her breath, for once silenced by the natural magic that had transformed her ordinary little friend into a raving beauty.

"Yes, indeed.", The Sorceress agreed seriously and then smiled wistfully.

"This is indeed your day Mina and I for one only regret that time and circumstances have made your courtship longer than usual, but I wanted to give you my bride gift now, before we descend and mingle with the rest of your guests.".

She produced an Irix hide bag, so tiny that it just covered the palm of her hand and bewildered, Mina extended her own hand tentatively.

"Oh, for the sake of the One!" Beneva took the bag and gently canted it over her hand. The silver chain tumbled out first, followed by a narrow oval plaque. On the face of it, in delicate natural shades there was a picture of a man.

"Oh!" cried Mina half choking back a sob of joy. "It's Errish!"

She stared down at the lovely thing, noting the eyes set with gemstones, even the Builders tools in the hands and Errish's sigil stamped into the back. Her eyes glistened as Beneva said lightly, "Shiarjha caught his likeness well didn't she? This is the gift of the Guardians, you are bound to be showered with many other things today!", she smiled indulgently and Ikella took Mina's hand saying quietly.

"We found an ancient pendant and thought that you would like such a keepsake.", The Sorceress showed Mina a matching bag, "Do you want to see our gift to Errish?" and Mina nodded, dumbfounded as the Guardians displayed her own portrait in enamel work, set with gems depicting the flowers in her hair. Diplomatically, Ikella chose not to notice the bride's emotions and remarked practically, "We discovered a scroll showing the method and although these were made quite a different way, we know enough to revive that skill and soon we will have another craft to offer a Guild.".

Mina was entranced.

"Will you bless these my Deshun?" She asked quietly. "We should put these back into their bags and let Carolus look after them. It would make our ceremony unique don't you think?"

They left the shelter of their private rooms shortly thereafter, totally unaware that as Errish and Mina, hands traditionally bound together, stepped through the trave of the Gate in the Rock, Daro and Ahnell were committing an act that would make their Wedding Day truly memorable.

It was going to be easy, Daro said. He had organised all that they would need and a few other things besides.

"You never know, in some of the rooms I explored the floors were so dangerous that I had to tie myself to sconce mounts, doors, anything that would support my weight if the floor fell away!".

Ahnell gulped, his eyes round and alight with mixed excitement and apprehension. Daro continued loftily.

"Do as I say, when I say. There is no room for argument and none at all for errors of judgment!" He looked up anxiously, but Ahnell was transfixed.

"It will be an adventure to tell my grandchildren.", he enthused, but Daro held up a silencing hand, his face suddenly grave.

"Ahnell, no! You will never be able to tell anyone about this. It is a secret. Never to be revealed, or you will get both of us killed. You don't understand what I am searching for, or you wouldn't think that way at all.", He drummed his fingers on the table where they sat, in solitary splendour in the Eyrie.

"I had better tell you all of it.", he decided, with a heavy sigh, "We don't have much time. The Wedding will take place in a few moments, then there will be a Clan blessing in the Hall. It is then that we have the best opportunity to get into the little storeroom unseen. That corridor is so busy today, that I want to make sure that all the kitchen staff and drudges have left for the village.".

Ahnell eyed him uneasily.

"All of it?" he question suspiciously. "What are you trying to find.".

Daro considered for a moment, then leant forward, elbows on the table, his hands steepled against his forehead.

"Do you remember my telling you that it wasn't fair that only women had command of magic?"

Ahnell pulled a face.

"How could I forget it? It was monotonous. Don't tell me that you are still hung up on that?".

Daro grinned, it was no more than he deserved. However, time was running short, he anticipated no more than half the post noon break, before the duty cooks would return from the village to ready the ovens for supper and not everyone would be out of the way.

"Let me tell you then that I know differently now. I even have proof of what I say in writing.", Ahnell's eyes grew bigger as Daro continued softly.

"Men once had command of power too, my friend.", He announced this Sand-shattering fact confidently, so committed was he to this belief, but Ahnell looked at him in silent consternation, as Daro reached out and took down a scroll. He unrolled it carefully, feeling slightly self-conscious, but his voice was calm, his reasoning exact and as his finger ran along the line of mystical symbols, Ahnell saw them quiver and tumble, forming swiftly into words that obviously Daro could read. He surreptitiously crossed his fingers under the table and listened, fascinated in spite of his doubts.

"When Darius, first amongst Sandsingers saw flaming rocks fall from the skies over Selesh, he withdrew within the enclave. Together, with the freemen and the Fellmen, the Clan members and the Sandsworn, he offered shelter to the Highlands and Midlands, the people of the bays and waterways, the shores and the seas. He called them into the great Hall and there together they prayed for their lives. One volunteered to go forth, to carry a warning and Darius sent this messenger to Sanctuary, telling them to assemble the Tapestry of Tten, with which he would spin a great shield for Pelshar and its people. In precedence the Sands were sealed before he and his brothers and sisters in Magic departed to save our world.".

Daro's voice was hushed and Ahnell found that he was holding his breath as his foster-brother stopped reading.

Daro was emphatic.

"Brother's and Sisters in Magic!" he repeated softly, "therefore, my hearty, men have held power in the past and I believe it is my bounden duty to find the key to that power and feed it to my mother, by force if necessary! Just because she has been there at the right time and place does not mean that she and only she, can wield the power round here and besides I owe Suraya a lesson she won't forget!" and with that Ahnell had to be satisfied.

Daro, unconcerned with the embarrassment of questions that were fairly choking Ahnell had risen to his feet, glancing around the room. He reached out and took the piece of broken tile down, sliding it into his capacious backpack and then he was ready.

They left the Eyrie, silent and soft footed and passed unseen into the deserted corridors leading to the old kitchens and the store room.

Daro had taken the trouble to make another key for the fruit store. He rarely found anyone coming or going to it, but always checked the key rack in the guardroom before he approached the solid little door. Today, there was no guard, every key hung innocently in place and with nobody to disturb them, Daro used his key to open the fruit store. He slid inside, calling Ahnell impatiently, with a muffled "All clear.".

Disgusted to find himself trembling, Ahnell was astonished as they entered a room bare of produce and cleared of storage racks. Daro grinned at his baffled expression.

"By Hadda's ghost Ahnell! It doesn't take long to make you forget that fruit is only available in Summer does it? How do you think I have managed to come and go all Winter, working out the measurements of our stairway?"

He closed the door softly and to Ahnell's astonishment, locked it behind them.

"No-one is going to come here anyway, but if they did, they wouldn't be able to open the door. If I leave my key in place they will just think that the door got stuck over the Winter. By the time they have given it a few kicks, I will have heard them and we can slip away.".

Ahnell followed Daro as he confidently triggered the pivoting door that they had found by accident. Inside the musty corridor had been transformed. Daro had refilled old torch sconces, new wax candles were placed in niches. He had even equipped himself with a small cupboard in which flint and steel were stored.

Ahnell looked around more appreciatively. An old rug covered the platform at the top of the stairs, a basket wedged into a crevice, held more of the old fashioned torches, from which Daro could either replenish his stores, or, further his explorations. Ahnell shivered, but whether from fear or excitement, he couldn't tell.

The secret door was closing as he turned to meet Daro's challenging gaze.

"Why shut that as well?", he asked, annoyed with the quaver in his voice, but Daro didn't notice.

"Well, if someone got in, they wouldn't know we are here. Leave it open and Sundreth's Mines would be a mere pleasure trip!"

Ahnell had a sudden vision of Ikella condemning them both to a lifetime of labour, but looked with interest as Daro passed him, a loop of rope over his shoulder, his backpack at the ready.

They climbed up to the point at which the stairs were blocked and Daro held up a hand for silence.

Ahnell sank down on the top step, his heart had been pounding so hard that he hadn't heard the voices lifted in celebration. He looked in bewilderment at Daro, who stood poised by the great capstone that blocked any further progress.

"That's coming from the Hall of the Healers.", he blurted out and Daro looked at him witheringly.

"Yes, I worked that out two Rotations ago, dolt!"

His voice although brusque was nevertheless affectionate and Ahnell grinned.

"Sorry, not always the sharpest stylus in the box!"

He caught the flash of Daro's teeth and then they quieted as Ikella's voice was suddenly lifted in blessing.

Ahnell jumped as Daro placed a round of bread in his hand.

"May as well have something to eat while we wait for them to go. I'll hear the doors from here and so they busied themselves, quietly. Daro told Ahnell how he had fallen foul of Ikella when he had addressed the matter with her. He didn't go into detail, but added odd comments as they finished their food. Daro had brought sweet peppers stuffed with Sarr grains, a fruit pie that they broke in two and bottled drink. Ahnell grimaced at these saying disgustedly, "Brashban? Daro, I'm not a coatan's get! I'm a brewer, I could make something with more of a kick in it last Rotation!".

"Yes, yes my little adventurer.", Daro interrupted rudely.

"You would also walk into danger half drunk if I let you. Have you completely lost your wits man, or left them with the Sarr grain mash, in your brew Hall?"

Ahnell fell silent, suddenly aware that this was not a game, that he and Daro were walking into extreme danger. He sobered abruptly.

"So what do you want me to look for?", he asked, turning his head to see that Daro was examining the oddly shaped piece of tile again.

The words stood out on it plainly and Daro was reading them, an odd, shuttered expression on his face, as the words were barely breathed.

"It's a riddle. I just thought I would look at it for a moment, while they leave the Hall and I recognised the words! How odd is that?".

"Well don't keep it to yourself my brother.", Ahnell challenged and Daro frowned.

"It's a riddle I think.", and read aloud.

"As Sandsingers come, so shall they go.
Do they hide in the Sands? Where the cold Winds blow?
Or, are they amongst us? You'll never know,
Until the dark moon rises.".

They sat, staring at each other, then at the shard of tile, until Ahnell asked quietly.

"Where did you find that Daro? Seems to me that you'd be better off searching there than trying to move that wretched stone, it probably weighs more than the Gate in the Rock and we might kill ourselves in the attempt!".

A rumbling thud echoed through the confines of their stairwell and Daro said in a relieved tone of voice.

"That's the door! Not only are the guests and celebrants gone, but so are the Guards.".

Ahnell asked curiously.

"Where do you think we come out then?".

Daro said airily.

"Somewhere at the back of the Syndarial I suppose. Higher up, probably on the same level as the Eyrie! There may be abandoned study rooms and older corridors. I am hoping for one of those. I certainly don't want to come out anywhere risky!".

Ahnell persisted, trying to sound a note of caution.

"How do you reckon to get past that stone then?"

Daro grinned wickedly, hoisting his bag and the rope over his shoulder again.

"About two ninenights ago, I shoved the stone when I tripped over something. It moved, almost enough for me to get through the gap, but it moved oddly, as if it somehow pivoted. When I let go of it, I realised that it had swung out from the top and I thought that if I had someone here as another pair of eyes, I might be able to work it out! The lower door pivots, so it kind of makes sense that the stone might. Obviously the risk is that the stone has no support on the other side, so hence the rope.".

He leant forward, over the sharp incline of the stairs and shook the rope out. At one end was an enormous loop, Daro slid the free end of the rope through this and then walking confidently out on to the very edge of the platform at the top of the staircase, he passed the free end of the rope through a metal loop that Ahnell had never noticed before. He ran down the stairs rope in hand and twisted it around a stanchion anchored in the shadows below and suddenly Ahnell saw what he was doing.

"Do you think it will hold that?" he asked, but Daro wasn't listening. He had picked up the doubled loop now and was urgently beckoning Ahnell. Together they leaned against the upper part of the capstone. Together they heaved until there was a little rattle of debris. Daro knelt, his hands searching until he removed a knife from his pack and ran the blade along the edges of the stone. Ahnell considered.

"There is definitely more light around the edges.", he informed his friend (sotto voce). Daro grunted assent, bracing himself against the wall and straining. There was a grating sound and to Ahnell's horror, the stone started to swing out. Daro muffled a roar of excitement and leapt, hanging on to the top of the stone as it swung away from them, notching the loop of the rope over the top of it and sliding it down, hastily securing it with a twist to a secondary stanchion revealed as the glare of lights from the chamber beyond penetrated their darkness.

"Ahnell. Can you see anything recognisable?" Daro was hopping up and down, his excitement quite blinding him to the danger they were in, but he plainly saw Ahnell's mute shake of the head, because he pushed impatiently at the stone again. It swung further and suddenly Ahnell felt sick. He knew those lights, at least he was sure he knew the shape of those lights, but his voice failed him and Daro pushed the stone away once more.

This time the most sonorous groan accompanied the movement and even Daro paused paling, but then the movement ceased and Daro said in tones of deep dismay.

"Oh Kastiss take it! I think it has stuck!"

To be true, Ahnell was glad of it, but Daro raged impotently, until he realised that both of them were slim enough to squeeze through, with care.

So it was that two dusty, sweat stained adventurers found themselves high above the Sacred Circle, standing horrified on the gallery rim surrounding the domed roof of the holiest place in Selesh.

Silently Daro tied a second rope to the rock, which canted high above the Sacred Circle and held the other out to Ahnell, who shook his head furiously, his eyes rolling with fear.

Daro hissed in urgent whispers.

"Don't be such a fool Ahnell. I am not asking you to get involved. I am trying to get you out of here.", He looped the rope around Ahnell and pointed.

"Look at the raked Healer seats.", He leant over the gallery railings cautiously.

"I can swing you over. All you have to do is hang on, walk your feet along the back to the highest seat, until you have your balance and can work along to the end. You can jump down into the side aisle from there, you are not going to end up in the Sacred Circle. You will be quite safe I can assure you.".

Ahnell was so frightened that it was about all he could do to follow Daro's directions, but shaking violently he allowed himself to be lowered, finally finding a cracked voice in order to tell his friend that he was safe and sitting on the warm hotfloor, his teeth chattering.

"Untie your rope then!" The cool voice struck him like a stone. "I am going to slide the main rope off the stone and see if it will swing back into place, once the rope isn't jamming it. I have quenched the glows in the passage, retrieved my key and shut the door once more. All I have to do is get myself down to you and I want to do that in a particular way!".

Ahnell felt dazed. He undid the rope and watched it slither away as Daro recoiled it. He sat dully preoccupied with the devout wish to return to Selesh Minoria and get very drunk. He had forgotten how frighteningly intense Daro could be and so he didn't see the precise moment that the great rock sprang back into place, or watch Daro descend from the gallery above.

He was stupefied, only aware of a prickling in his skin as Daro appeared by his side, dropping his bag and turning towards the Sacred Circle and the Great Book of Rule on its lectern. It was only then that he heard the faintest thread of music.

He sat upright, his mouth opened to call Daro, but it was already too late.

His friend stood in the sacred Circle, where no man strayed on pain of death.

Chapter 25 - Sent into Exile.

If the Great Hall of the Healers seemed to be holding its breath, certainly Ahnell app Minidrahl was. He had risen on to his knees, his face pressed against the railing that separated the Sacred Circle from the place of the ordinary people, staring with sorrowing eyes as Daro made a deep reverence to the Holy Book of Rule. He walked calmly to the stepped plinth on which the lectern stood and paused as another page turned. There was a taut expectancy overhanging this most sacred of places, yet Daro had suddenly found his feet, moving gracefully towards some predestined future, with a surety beyond his years. Ahnell stared at his friend, his foster, no his blood brother, in a mixture of wonder, awe and fear, for Daro was glowing.

He stepped onto the plinth of the lectern, as if to read, but as he raised his hands, Ahnell saw an aura blossomed around the boy and the Book. A page turned by itself, then a few more, gently, invitingly. A shimmering arpeggio sounded, a soft swell of notes, but detecting no obvious source, Ahnell turned back, to see Daro lift his head and sing.

The sound of that first stanza both terrified and enraptured. It soared delicately into the cavernous roof of the Hall, sending in its wake the firebright glints of Daro's aura. The notes throbbed in a throat unpractised at this art, trembled on the tongue of the Singer and fled into the heights of the Hall, setting the glows dancing.

Ahnell saw the passion, the joy, the reverence with which Daro sang. He heard him school the vibrato of a particularly high note, steadying his breathing, controlling the power that positively shook the very air around them. He witnessed the sudden flares of brilliant colours streaming around Daro, who stood with hands uplifted in wonder. As the last notes soared aloft, Ahnell knew he heard the release of constraint, the shackles of silence falling away and he trembled as Daro's voice found its maturity, its focus, its real power, culminating in a whispered prayer of self-dedication.

Daro stood, looking at his hands as though he had never seen them before. His eyes were like fire, his face at once grave and triumphant and as he stood solemn and convinced, Ikella stepped out of the shadows behind him.

She palely glimmered, dressed as she was in the silver robes of Guardianship, but there was nothing light or silvery about the voice that lashed the stillness of the moment.

"Daro bin Selesh, Ahnell app Minidrahl surrender yourselves and follow me in silence. The One may forgive you for this act of sacrilege, but be certain, I never shall!".

Daro turned to her, his hands mutely appealing for mercy, but she tilted her head imperiously, compressing her lips. Daro's heart sank, but he crossed to where Ahnell cowered and drew him to his feet, an arm round his shivering shoulders.

They turned onto the side aisle and Ikella fiercely drew back the curtains that concealed her private entrance at the side of the Hall. They never once looked at each other. Pale and clammy with shock, eyes downcast they followed the furious Sorceress as she took the corridor to the Djellim.

Driss arriving at the guardroom, to take up her Sunfall duty, saw them pass in miserable silence and summoned Nitra, her new second.

"For the love of the One. Go, quickly and quietly. I don't know what is going on, but Master Daro and Ahnell are in grave trouble. Get Beneva and Shiarjha away from the crush and tell them that I think they should return, before Ikella kills them. Fetch his Songfather's and find Jashell!"

The girl departed at the run and Driss gritted her teeth in frustration. She couldn't leave her post, but a second later, she saw Indeera crossing the Gathering Square and her hands flickered and danced as she signalled her concerns.

Ikella inclined her head to Sorrill as the party entered the Djellim and made purposefully for the shielded Council Chamber. She took no notice as Sorrill peered after them perceptively, but went directly to the Council Chamber and with an angry wave of her hand, passed into it, closing the sound proof barrier behind Daro and Ahnell with a furious flourish.

She rounded on them, incandescent with fury, her finger pointed directly at Daro.

"I have loved you as my own son! Yet you! You are the viper in our midst!"

He was so appalled by her repudiation of him, that he quailed and Ahnell saw that indeed their case was lost, there would be no forgiveness, no understanding. A certain calm fell on him and he stopped quaking and pulled himself upright, prepared to defend Daro, though how he could, never even crossed his mind. Daro, however, was ahead of him.

"Ahnell had no way of knowing what I planned to do.", He spoke clearly, without resentment, just stating his case. Ikella ignored him.

"Ahnell knows that if he keeps dubious company, he may be blamed for their crimes.", She spoke coldly.

"Ahnell had no choice about the company he kept, seeing that you brought him here as a hostage!" Daro jeered defiantly.

Two movements of Ikella's hand later and Ahnell found himself sitting in the outer Djellim. There was a guard on the door and he was too exhausted to question the arrangement. He could see through the barrier, but although inside the Council Chamber the angry exchanges continued, he could hear nothing. He stood, to stretch his legs and adjust his clothing and in his mind, he heard Ikella's voice. Devoid of feeling, icily disdainful she remarked.

"The prisoner should remain seated!"

Ahnell sat.

Daro faced her fury.

"I meant no sacrilege, no disrespect and Ahnell couldn't have known that the Book called me. I didn't know it myself, it just happened!"

If she heard him, she didn't react to what he said. Her green eyes glittered dangerously as she paced backward and forward.

"You say that the Book called you? How did it call you? We have had it in our possession for hundreds of Rotations and yet, no Guardian, no Sorceress has ever been able to read from it! How dare you infer that a mere man can interact with the most sacred of our relics? That is another act of sacrilege to count against you.".

There was a fine dew at her forehead, she was breathing hard, but her eyes bored inexorably into his and his mouth was dry.

"I don't know how I knew what to do.", He finally blurted, reluctant even to think about the unusual way that he and Ahnell had gained access to the Hall.

"Something inside me "clicked" and I could sing as I have ever longed to do. It just happened. I readily confess to being fascinated by the concept of using magic myself, after our arguments I can hardly deny that, but ...""

"Enough!", said the Sorceress wearily, "Don't you realise, you stupid, stupid boy that your "fascination" is to be the death of both of you! It is the penalty I must demand!"

Her son stared at her sombrely.

"Must?" He probed delicately. "I assume that this means a public death?"

His tone was light, almost bantering, but Ikella shivered. She stared at him, as though at a stranger and his head drooped a little.

"Yes, I can see that it does!" He was strangely accepting, a sort of resigned tranquillity had settled on him.

"Can't you let Ahnell go?" He pleaded with her. "He didn't know, he is guilty only of staying with me, he didn't enter the Circle and he did try to dissuade me.".

Ikella sighed. "Daro, if you understand anything about ruling other people, you have to know that I can't let one of you carry the punishment for the other. You were both there, you both know what you did, you may also know why, I don't, but it would be folly for me to try and choose who is the more guilty. No, you must both die, though how I shall bear it I don't know!".

The bleakness of this statement shocked Ikella herself, but her voice didn't waver and with a sigh Daro saw that there was no turning her.

"Ah.", He turned away and lifted his pack, pulling the drawstring to open it.

"Then I'd better tell you where my investigations have taken me, before you have us stoned! Might one ask where we will be punished? Zenith Point seems fairly appropriate, not too far to cart the remains to dump them in the Great Divide! "

His calculated brutality caused only the clenching of her hands and not naturally an unkind boy, he gave it up and withdrew the broken tile piece, deliberately clearing his mind, trying to make the words on it show and show they did.

He faced her across the table, the oddly angled mirror in the corner reflecting Ahnell's worried face, as he sat alone in the Djellim.

"I found this, about ten ninenights ago. The symbols on it made no sense until I was showing it to Ahnell and then I found I could read them.".

He was dimly aware of others entering the Djellim and his mother's scowl, but he continued bravely.

"It is a poem about the Sandsingers.", His claim fell on deaf ears. Ikella was staring at the tile scornfully.

"You amaze me!" She pronounced sarcastically. "That pretty piece of pottery came here with me, Daro. I brought it from a Wanderer, a beggar who frequented the fairs at Shilinch, where I grew up, more Rotations ago than I care to think. Those dots are not symbols, they are patterns. Just the fancy of the tile maker, a pretty fancy, but not words. They have no meaning, you are obsessed!"

Daro was suddenly enraged. He wanted to show her, but she wouldn't look. He tried to say that she should give it to Beneva, but the words stuck in his throat.

"You aren't going to listen are you?" He snapped, his eyes blazing with fury. "You are just too proud to admit that you too, can learn something new. You would prefer me and Ahnell to go to our deaths in silence, than listen to something you might not like!"

He hefted the tile in his hand.

"Well then, mother dear. You and your kind can go to perdition your own Way.", said the boy, silky smooth fury, awash in his voice, "but, never say I didn't try to warn you!"

For a moment, his rage left him incandescent, burning with an intensity that lit up the Council Chamber, then he threw the tile, straight into and through Jocasta's Door!"

Ikella, cloaked in her aura, saw the missile arc towards the precious mirror and made a complicated pass with her left hand. The portal wavered and appeared to shatter as a glass might have done and then just the frame was there and the boy was staring aghast at what his own temper had done.

Suddenly Ahnell was beside him again, whimpering in bewilderment. Beneva, Shiarjha, Carolus, Patris and half a cohort of Inesh were crowding the doorway and Ikella was pronouncing sentence.

"Daro bin Selesh, guilty of sacrilege by reason of attempting to enter the Sacred Circle. Ahnell app Minidrahl, guilty of sacrilege by reason of aiding and abetting Daro bin Selesh in this most terrible of crimes. I have the power over your lives and deaths and I pronounce your lives forfeit.".

The stony face didn't alter by a flicker or inflection, but incredibly the implacable voice said.

"However, I also find Daro bin Selesh, not answerable to the death penalty, due to his suffering from mental obsessions, beyond his control. I therefore sentence both of you to a period of no less than three Rotations exile, during which you will seek out the Healers of every Sand, save that of the Gattarene. From them you will retrieve one cure for obsession native to their Sands. You will bring me the written evidence that you have undertaken each treatment.

You will also bring me the means to effect such a cure by the fourth celebration of Spring Rites from today.

You may take with you common provisions of suitable foods, clothing and any other necessities to support life. You will spend the rest of this night preparing to depart in silence and under guard. You will leave the Gate in the Rock at first light, returning here with your proofs together, at the appointed time, or not at all. I have spoken to you privately on this and not to the shame of the Clan or your families. This is not only my mercy to you, but to them. Remember, my mercy only extends for the length of your silence. Yours in particular Daro bin Selesh. Do I make myself clear?".

The night passed, awkward with shared pain and stilted by the enjoined silence. Daro and Ahnell, fluent in the hand code of the Inesh, didn't dare to discuss private matters in their presence.

They endured the tearful farewell permitted to Ahnell by his adopted parents, who promised to let Tuennis know that he had been sent to accompany Daro on a journey for Ikella. They sensed the disgrace, but thankfully didn't ask questions and departed having seen Ahnell equipped with clothes and notes of exchange.

Diras sniffed in misery, as Daro told her goodbye, saying that ordinary guard duties would bore her to death. Patris, Rowbet and Somner came to the Eyrie with a wickedly curved knife, which slid unobtrusively into a boot. They brought with them a medicine scrip from Carolus, who they said was dealing with a seriously ill Zeglur and who would see him in the morning.

Daro nodded bleakly, he seemed calm and resigned to his exile, but he looked hurt as the old man's message was delivered.

"I've let him down.", He said quietly. "Tell him that I never meant to hurt him, I will be back I promise!"

It was Ivinish, catching up with the others as they left that voiced all their concerns.

"Master Carolus is a lot older than we realised at first.", The gruff beast handler pressed a hide jacket on both boys. "It isn't a question of whether you return but when. His journey to the Sands is not that far away and you may return to find him gone!"

Daro suddenly felt tears prick his eyes and the beast handler nodded, saying.

"I'll tell him!" as the room emptied again.

However, in the first light of one of the darkest mornings since the Storm, Daro and Ahnell were accompanied through the Gate by Diras, her Chapter of Guard and Ikella.

Tethered outside were two Zeglurs, one of which had a wax tablet tied to its pannier.

Curiously the Sorceress had Diras read the tablet out loud and Daro, close to tears of contrition, heard the words in his Songfather's voice.

"These animals are destined for onward transmission to Malos in the Malachite Sands. They have been kept separate from my heard which is all sick, so would you take them with you? they need to be delivered to an inn called the Half Armoured.".

The Sorceress sniffed suspiciously, but a glance at the underground pasture door showed a yellow disc in the door, the traditional warning of infection, so she said.

"You may lead the animals. You know what I have decreed, I should not have to repeat it here. Go, out of my Sands, maintain your silence on the subject and I will maintain my discretion. Remember, Daro, you are to obtain proof that you have undergone the treatment for this obsession and then you can return, together, or not at all! Ahnell, you are to witness that my son obeys me in this, if he does not, then I beg you, don't return to Selesh, it would mean your death.".

She paused and then handed Daro a pouch.

"Show my sigil to get all that you need to sustain life. If you get bored, then I pray you, turn your mind from Sandsingers to finding something that we need to find urgently. The detail is all in this book that Beneva has stitched together for you. Go now my son and turn your life into something worthwhile.".

She resisted the temptation to reach out to him, but he saw her eyes glisten and raised a hand in the sketch of a farewell. Ahnell retrieved the halter of the nearest Zeglur and they turned away, taking the trail toward Caranchar and the Low Pass into the Azure Sands.

High above them where the memory wall edged the plateau over the Gate in the Rock, three figures watched them go. Jashell, dark and brooding, Indeera gentle and concerned and the Apothecary.

Carolus watched as the boys guided the Zeglurs on to the trail and stood, steady and calm, though his eyes looked haunted. In his minds eye was another time, another being sent into exile and then there was music, glorious, hopeful and yet poignant. A man's voice, golden tenor, power throbbing in its depths, soaring melody in its heights and he remembered. The pain of leaving this place, the half terror, half excitement, the exhortation of the Voice to return at the appointed time and place, or not at all.

He felt the Voice, it vibrated through him as he watched his Songchild leaving and then he heard Indeera's encouraging tones. "Master Carolus, he will return, you must believe it. The Light of the Sun will one day return!".

PART THREE - TRAIL OF TEARS

Chapter 26 - "Ichta Selunsanni.".

Jashell and Diras crossed the Gathering Square and paused to stand in the doorway of the underground pastures, passing the time of day with Carolus. He was assisting a kitchen drudge to wheel a barrow of vegetables, from the winter growing fields, as they arrived. They all chuckled as the urchin wobbled his way across to the kitchens and Jashell, eyeing a particularly well fleshed gourd, said sadly.

"I really miss Master Ombuya, but I suppose Deshun Nahamida's need was greater than ours now "Ichta Selunsanni" wanders the Sands.", The Apothecary looked at her oddly, then said tentatively.

"Ichta Selunsanni?" The Apothecary questioned, "Do I understand that you are talking about Daro?", he gave Jashell a measuring glance, his eyes bright with speculation. "Does the Lady know that her scamp has been given such a noble name?", he asked innocently, "I'm afraid "The Light of the Sun", has a long Way to travel before she will smile on him again!".

Diras turned mournful eyes on Carolus.

"Do you have any news of him? It might cheer the Watch to know that he is safe.".

Carolus sighed and sat on a nearby hand-cart. He seemed to be considering the question, as he tucked his jacket in firmly and re-dispersing small possessions about his pockets, cleared his throat and said cautiously.

"Well…" . He drew the word out, looking thoughtfully at Jashell, who met his gaze with equanimity.

"The last I heard was from Anempor, although they over - Wintered at Darnesh. I took their orders to Caranchar a ninenight ago and the girl who collected them, told me that they went to consult with Solana, while she was visiting Anempor. I heard he will go on to Scartel with her, continuing through to Malos, where Deschima is drumming up support for our school. It seems like a good idea to me! What better advertisement for Selesh could there be, but the presence of the visiting son of Seris Ikella?".

Diras snorted. saying darkly.

"That is until they discover that he is in exile!"

Carolus raised his eyebrows.

"Why should they discover what is known to only a few? Only what the Lady is pleased to refer to as her Inner Circle know about it. She didn't even tell Mina and Errish until they asked where Daro was. All anyone is to be told, is that he travels for his mother. If all goes well, he will return to us within the space of a Song Walk. I hope for his sake that he has by that time grown out of this obsession that so frightens Ikella.".

Jashell stared at him speculatively, then said quietly and deliberately.

"Or has learned to be more circumspect in thought, speech and behaviour?".

Carolus replied, his voice and features grave.

"Or has achieved his ambitions!".

Solemnly and with true meaning the Inesh warriors touched fingers to head, heart and lips in silent invocation of the One's great mercy, whether for themselves, Daro, or all who inhabited their shadowed corner of the Universe, only the One would know.

Carolus watched them going back to their duties, remaining where he was, leaning against the wall, chewing a straw placidly. After a few minutes, Olneth slipped out behind him, a mug in his hands which he passed to Carolus.

"Here, something for your grumpiness!"

Carolus, bridled at the accusation, but he took the drink and sipped it appreciatively.

"Thank you, not that I am grumpy, any more than you are.", He said stiffly and Olneth grinned as he suggested, "What about taking a couple of Zeglurs over to Malos? We ought to find a couple of ours rested up at the "Half Armour". I think Beven does business over there, so we might get a commission out of the trip, particularly if there is a return of some sort.". He gazed innocently up at the Master Spy and Olneth nodded.

"Aye, I could do with a stretch.", he remarked, treating the long overland haul flippantly and Carolus finished his drink more cheerfully, saying, "We'll need permission to stir before tithing Day, but if I pay ours in advance, I can't see there being many objections.", He stood and shook himself all over, stamping as he limbered up, celebrating their forthcoming trip and Olneth laughed.

"You're as bad as your own daft Zeglurs.", slapping Carolus on the back, Olneth retreated to start preparations and Carolus went to get travel passes..

He found Ikella in the large exercise Hall, supervising a game in a circle of third Rotation Healers. She was watching a child sized pillow being hesitantly manipulated, by students using only their empowered *othervoice*. As he approached however, the girl due to "catch" the pillow, caught sight of a man in their midst and forgot her cue, allowing the pillow to fall. Amidst a chorus of groans Ikella said calmly.

"Serillia! Now you have dropped the precious child into the bath in which you were to wash his wounds, I will leave you to explain to his parents what killed their newborn! I must talk to our Apothecary on a matter of Infirmary business!"

Shoulders shaking, she led Carolus to a nearby bench and sat gravely, but Carolus saw the quirk of her lips as she turned from the flustered girl.

"She'll recover.", said the Sorceress heartlessly, "She's inclined to overreact at the moment.", to which the old man said gently.

"Try oil of Jenta's star on her. During the shadows of Jenta, it should relieve the hottest temper, calm the nerves and actually make the tides of Jenta, less painful, less wearing on the girl in question.".

Ikella smiled.

"Thank you Master Apothecary.", She spoke warmly and Carolus said happily.

"I have plenty in store, in fact, that is what I came to talk to you about. I have business that takes me to Malos. I have supplies to drop off at Caranchar, then I would like to travel off-Sands with your permission. Is there anything that I can do for you, while I take the stores needed to the northeast?".

She shook her head.

"I don't think so.", She hesitated, a worried little frown creasing her brow.

"Deschima didn't mention a problem when I spoke to her. Does she know that you're coming?" Her voice tailed off as if she was too tired to worry about Carolus and his reasons for travelling, this early in the New Rotation. He picked up her hand, noting the lack of the usual lustrous tone of her skin and hair.

"I think that you have Winter-chill.", he pronounced gravely.

"You seem tired to the point of lethargy. Why not try one of Nadra's new products? She and Tiriteth, her serving girl, decided to ask Jashell and Sorrill how they kept looking so good in the winter months. Now Beven says that they will break him, because they offered to trade drink for remedies that combat tiring complexions, or dull hair. They have tinctures for the eyes and anything they can waggle at a man.", he grinned cheerfully, saying lightly, "I think Beven is more concerned with that, rather than the cost of purchasing bottles, jars, stoppers, or vials in which to put their creams and lotions. However, I can recommend them wholeheartedly.".

Ikella looked at him sombrely.

"I am just an old woman, missing my son! I am just tired of trying to balance the needs of a world, against my own. However, I must, I suppose let you go, if only to replenish your pots and sell Nadra's lotions, but it will cost you a jar of cream for my dry skin, something to refresh my hair and news of Daro, if you can get any.", she stared at her feet, crossed neatly at the ankles, until Carolus got out his purse and jingled it.

"What?" She stared at him. "Oh, I suppose you need money for travelling, go and see Dorra, she will give you provisions, Shiarjha will write you a permit.", She slipped a ring from her finger and passed it to him.

"Put that in your scrip and present it if you need help or shelter. Send it back to me if you need more assistance and I will send Diras and her Chapter of Guard. They have precious little to do, while Daro is abroad in othersands.".

Her voice had grown lower, pain filled and the eyes she lifted to his were swimming with unshed tears.

"Do you see what the mere thought of that boy does to me? Have you a cure for a broken heart in your scrip Master Carolus?".

The Apothecary watched as she rose and strode back to the group of Healers to be and his face grew long as he watched her, demonstrating her own skill and power, as the young women clustered around her skirts.

"Why?", he questioned savagely. "Why should such a woman choose between magic and motherhood?", he paused wondering to himself. Why not give the joy of Voice to one singularly unsuited for any other occupation? Let a woman like Ikella, have a man who adored her, children aplenty and real happiness.

"Pah, I understand nothing about the working of the Way!", he said crossly and strode out of the hall, a tall wiry figure, his hair framing a stern face. A passing servitor seeing his bleak eyes, reported back to the kitchens that he thought Master Carolus had crossed the Lady, for judging by the expression on his face, Carolus was in a very bad temper. No-one dared to comment, when in the early hours of the morning, Olneth and Carolus slipped out of the Gate in the Rock, leading two Zeglurs and two pack mules, heavily laden.

Daro, happily unaware of the deepening depression that his absence was causing, lay, as Solana had commanded, half immersed in the Sands of the Azure desert. As the name implied, there was a blued monotony to everything here and an unusual saltiness which irritated his skin. He had slathered it with Shallin oil, which worked well, but after he had used their small stock, he had sought a Healer's help. It had amused the Sorceress Tirjella greatly, when she discovered that the tall strangers working as grooms in her stables, were none other than the fosterlings of her Sister in Sorcery.

She had been delicate about the manner in which she questioned Daro, seeing him stiffen when she teased him about running away and he had appreciated the way that she had sent a young Healer with more cream for his skin and a casual invitation for both of them to join her retinue at Anempor, where she was recruiting more novices for Ikella's school. He had picked up the unguent, wondering how she knew that he needed to consult her Senior Healer, but now he wished he never had.

His chest was aching, his mouth was dry and Solana was busy poring over fragmentary writings, scrolls that she said she had found in the cavern riddled walls of the ancient crater of Scartel, where she lived.

"Keep still! All the syndralls have to be in the correct place if this is to work.", Her voice was gruff and Daro eyed the odd assortment of items that she had placed down the long length of his naked body with acute distaste. There were shaped stones, which said Solana, cackling in aged merriment, were said to resemble the inner organs of his body. Then there were threads of various colours laid over him, like a net used by farmers to trap fly-bys. He wondered how in Hadda's Hall he was going to get free of all this rubbish.

Perhaps his expression gave him away, but Solana said seriously.

"You claim obsession young lord and you ask Solana for something to break that obsession. I have lived for many Rotations and have only rarely left my Sands and every time I do, there is a disaster of kinds.".

She moved closer, holding a bottle in her hand and Daro eyed her nervously. He had agreed not to talk, this was part of his treatment she said.

"Don't fill your mind with endless chatter, send your friend away for the day. Solana works best alone with her patients.".

Daro gently eased the crick in his neck, as Solana turned to pick up a lighted taper. He felt sweat break out on his brow, but only a moment before he had felt cold!

"Think young man, only think the thoughts that brought you here. Think only of those, hear them in your head, taste them in your mouth, but speak of them nothing, for Solana seeks only to remove unhealthy reactions to such thoughts. The thoughts themselves and the subject of those thoughts is not at fault. Your reaction to them is what we seek to put in check, to straighten or confine.".

Her voice had a gentle monotony to it, like the colour of this blue Sand. He relaxed, laying his head back and gazing at her impassively as she set light to the network of threads she had so lovingly draped over him.

In his mind he was leaping to his feet, screaming in fear and beating at the flames. In reality, he lay, still and naked, half his body hidden beneath a pile of blue sand, which weighed him down and immobilised him. Under his head, Solana had placed an ancient sheet of Opal weave and suddenly, Daro felt as though his hands were burying themselves in Opal Sand. He concentrated, lifting the Sand, pouring it over the flaming threads, cooling and soothing himself.

Languidly he stretched out a hand and suddenly Solana was there again, now he could focus on the room. They were deep in Anempor, in a room of such elegance and luxury as he had never before experienced.

He was lying on a bed, cushioned in pillows of such softness that he thought he could melt into them.

Solana's voice roused his wandering wits.

"Such a thing I have never before seen. She was commenting in a low voice to someone who annoyingly remained just out of his sight.

"I followed all the instructions, down to the last item. The young lord was adamant. "Whatever it took, " he said. So I took the cloth and the Sand and I let him think I had fired the threads which represented the threads of his obsession.".

In a hasty aside she said to her hidden companion.

"Of course the flame was only that of the taper, brought hear to his skin to spark the obsession. Suddenly, his hands are full of Opal Sand, though where that came from the One only knows. He stayed totally calm, but he doused the flames and then..."

The other voice was male, familiar, but Daro was drifting, stood in a great circle singing and the arms of the Opal were around him.

In the morning, he awoke feeling strangely refreshed and went to find Ahnell. However, he was not in the room allotted to him and to Daro's dismay, it appeared that his foster-brother had not returned the evening before.

He answered the questions of the Household Guard, but found himself unable to think of these men as much of a protecting force, besides his memory of the Inesh women that his mother favoured. He took a belated breakfast and bathed before visiting Solana again. He was troubled about his experience during treatment, but the Healer gently reassured him.

"I don't think that you have very much to worry about.", She spoke seriously, not belittling his fears.

"The treatment that you undertook will have aligned all your pulses, which can explain your notion that something was burning you. Fire is a very potent symbol in dreams and it may mean that your obsession will in some way threaten your life, but I think you are in control of it. Very much in control and that control you rightly ascribe to the Sands of your birth. In your dream, you say that the Sands saved you, so hold on to that, because if a young man, far from home and uncertain if he will be received back, still feels so strongly about his Sands, then all is well with your psyche.".

Daro didn't remember telling her of the schism between himself and Ikella, but undoubtedly, all that they talked about were sealed into silence and Solana was ancient in her skill and knowledge. He relaxed and heard Ahnell laughing easily, as one of the Guard brought him in to Daro.

He stood, smiling in relief and wondered at the sudden cloud on Solana's face, but kissed her hands respectfully, as he ran out to his travel companion.

However, Ahnell's first words dampened his enthusiasm immediately.

"Daro!", said that worthy unrepentantly. "I have met the woman I am going to marry.".

In the cool of the early morning four travellers turned their two Zeglurs and a pair of borrowed pack mules north. Sitting perched on her Spring supplies was Solana. Always tiny, she clung on determinedly, shifting uncertainly like a Dolcan trying to ride a hound. Beside her, decorously perched on a saddled mule rode a pretty red-haired girl of the eastern Zurias. She had huge grey eyes, creamy skin and was in Ahnell's eyes, all that he ever wanted in life. The two boys rode the taller Zeglurs, riding bareback, only their blanket rolls to protect them from the spiny backs of the animals. However, these Zeglurs were well rested and very well fed, having spent the Winter housed in Darnesh, which had very good stabling. The Zurias had equines bred for battle, the warlike Clansmen protecting their borders with patrols that rode hard. The Zeglurs had been admired and cosseted, turned out into Spring pasture at Anempor and were fat and comfortable to ride. So they journeyed, northward, on to Scartel and a short break, before making for Malos and an inn called the "Half Armour.",

Chapter 27 - Solana's Children

Daro and Ahnell were surprised, when instead of turning into the main street of the large village nestled into the extinct crater of Scartel, Solana turned aside and took a narrow precipitous track, that wound higher, ascending the back wall of the caldera.

Daro kicked his Zeglur on and joined Solana in the lead, leaving Ahnell and Sararrh to follow as they could, for the track was narrowing as it climbed and there would be no room to make mistakes, or indulge in the frequent caresses that passed between them. He grinned sardonically, thinking, "If this terrain doesn't make this sweeting turn back, then she is more than I take her for.", He blushed as Solana turned a critical look in his direction.

She spoke quietly, although she didn't have to, Sararrh's mule had baulked at the climb and the young couple had dismounted to lead their animals and even as he looked back at them, they paused to kiss passionately. The Healers voice was gently amused.

"It is in the nature of man to find his opposite and equal. Don't begrudge your friend his joy. First love is very special and only the cruel destroy what they can't share. Your part now is to help them, guide them and not be jealous of what they have. Life and love is too short for that!"

Thus admonished, Daro turned his back on the lovers and followed the old Healer on to a wide plateau, onto which a large cavern mouth opened.

They reined in beside a hitching rail and as their animals came to a grateful halt, a gaggle of children emerged, behind a tall man, who chivvied them into a neat line.

He stepped forward with a ready, engaging smile and held out his hands to Solana, gently assisting her to dismount from her mule. He busied himself, organising a work party to take Solana's panniers , during which time, Daro leapt down from his Zeglur and collected his blanket roll and saddlebags. He could see Ahnell and Sararrh on the track below, they would be on him in a moment and strangely uncomfortable in their presence, he strode after Solana.

She was engaged in answering a chorus of older youngsters, who were demanding news of those she had accompanied to Anempor.

"No Ario, I don't know if S

Selkis, or any of the others that went with her will be successful. We have to wait until Zenitheon, when all Healers gather to Selesh. In the meantime, our five are in the care of Deshun Tirjella, who is taking them back to our own novice hall at Darnesh. She has agreed to give them some basic training and take them off-Sands at the right time, as they are in the protection of the Clan.".

She glanced around at the dawdling children, who still hung around her, finally clapping her hands abruptly, chivvying them back to their chores, crossly saying.

"Come along there, we have work to do, mouths to fill, unless you expect me to sit and plait my fingers, I would get on with your own work and let those that can, get on with theirs.".

Thus scolded, the slender girl who was posing most of the questions departed, but the others stayed, staring at Daro.

Solana had absently picked up a sand tablet and looking at it, used a flickering finger code to beckoned the tall man to her.

Suddenly Daro understood her helper's silence. He was deaf, probably mute as well. He had noticed Ario limping on a built up shoe and now as he looked carefully around, he could see the differences. There were the solemn faces of children who couldn't see, the giggles of a pair who were chasing each other across the floor on crutches, the whispers of the three who laboured at a desk, using twisted arms to support pestle and mortar as they ground herbs for the Healers use.

Solana interrupted his train of thought.

"I see that you care for children young lord, but don't let them see your pity. They don't need it. They have a permanent home here with me, they have food, clothing, warmth and work. What more could they need?".

Daro faced her. She stood only shoulder high to him and he found himself gazing down into hazel eyes, that shone with a clarity of view that only comes with age.

"Love?" he suggested and Solana flushed.

"I give them companionship, one with the other and with me. I brought Orto up since he was abandoned here. He hears nothing clearly and speaks very badly, but we understand each other. He would defend us to the death. A friend and his wife give him a room in the village now he is full grown. He runs errands and shops for us and tends our fields. The others work there in good weather and here in bad. They sleep here mainly, they have there pick of rooms and they are better cared for than begging on the streets. So, my love is of the practical kind. I don't let people tell them that they can't do ordinary things. I show them the way to get around their difficulties, their differences. I don't indulge them in temper tantrums and shows of frustration and I don't indulge myself in pity and mawkish sentiment, that way I would only cripple them and myself.".

The defiant voice dropped.

"Not all of them survive what brings them here. I have watched many go to the Sands and will see many more who can't survive a sickly infancy. Nevertheless, I have learned that those that are left need me more at such times, so I love in my own way, but I don't cling to them, or allow them to cling to me!".

He thought he understood and said so and suddenly Solana grew animated again. She was obviously busy, but happily took Daro's arm and showed him her home, returning to the main cave and the curious gaze of the children, who were waiting silently for their evening meal. The elderly Healer continued chatting.

"So, now you have met Solana's children. There are only twelve of them at the moment, five have left to become Healers themselves, so the others miss them badly.".

Daro noted how the children sat, grouped together on pillows and cushions. Now work was over, a few had treasured toys in their hands. He readily helped pull a couple of benches into place, greeting Ahnell and Sararrh, as they arrived with Orto and watched unashamedly as Orto questioned Solana, with a swift flicker of hands, where three guests could be housed for the night. As Solana explained who Daro and his friends were, he recognised most of the signage Orto's eyebrows rose, then he turned a smiling face towards Daro and bowing deeply. Daro grinned and signed slowly, "I am delighted to meet you.", and as he had hoped, after a seconds hesitation, Orto grinned appreciatively, signing.

"Thank you. I forgot, you have Inesh at Selesh. How wonderful that you learned their code. I was taught it by the Nishanawa. They are Clan cousins you know.".

Solana smiled, flashing a heartfelt "thank you", as Orto guided Daro, Ahnell and Sararrh to the herb scented store rooms, where comfortable cushions made generous beds.

Daro was amazed and intrigued by Scartel. It had the feel of Selesh about it, yet Solana had encouraged bright colours, gaily patterned weavings and against the blue-black basalt rock of the crater walls, the effect was warm and friendly, a cheerful home for the children.

They gathered together to eat. Simple fare with no hint of meat or other animal product for Daro to worry about and then they sat around the flickering firelight in the main cavern and told stories of their travels.

Solana told the children of the night of the Great Storm and how she had been there when Daro was born. He listened avidly, for Ikella had told him little of his mother, her beauty, her death. He listened attentively to the stories of the world before the Storm and like the others he first doubted and then wondered at the description of a world without dense cloud cover, a world of warmth and bright sunshine. He slept well that night and woke refreshed and positive, determined to follow his dream, wherever it led him, for he now knew what he wanted to achieve.

He broke his fast with the Healer. Orto and the children having departed earlier for the strip fields they managed. The aging Healer shook her head when he offered her some money for her hospitality, but relented when he suggested buying a few special foods for the children. She smiled, but said little to Ahnell and Sararrh as they shyly joined them, hand in hand and Daro forced himself to be gentle with them too, which earned a nod of approbation as they stood to leave.

Solana faced Daro solemnly.

"I have here your certificate for Seris Ikella.", She paused, then deliberately placed a hand on his arm, in a warm familiar gesture.

"She didn't desire your exile you know that. She could have exacted a far worse penalty, but stayed her hand, because she loves you. Now it is for you to follow your destiny, but never forget that it was she who saved all of us, brought you safe to the point where you could be free of her.".

Daro stared at the old wise woman and wondered if that was what he truly wanted.

"To be free of Ikella? How could he be free of the only woman he had called mother?"

Solana suddenly chuckled.

"By finding your own Way and taking it, whatever that Way be!".

She was still laughing at his bewilderment as the group of three travelled onward and into the Malachite Sands.

Ahnell caught up with him, kicking his reluctant Zeglur into a trot as soon as he reasonably could.

"That was a weird evening he remarked conversationally. "What a group! Not one of those children was fully fit, how on earth does she cope, she must be nearly as old as Carolus anyway.".

Suddenly, Daro felt ashamed of his friend, of himself. Ahnell had remained aloof all the previous evening and Daro had assumed that it was because he was with Sararrh and was bored with the lack of entertainment. However, now he realised how uneasy Ahnell had been around the disabled youngsters and he spoke rather sharply.

"I saw nothing weird, just a gaggle of orphans having fun, at home with their friends and those who support them.".

Ahnell stared at him.

"I meant no offense Daro, it was just a bit difficult. I didn't want to offend anyone, but I just didn't know where to look. I have never met so many children with such severe sickness before. Did you know that two of them died this Winter? That kid Ario told me and one of those was her sister!"

Daro slowed down, glancing at Ahnell. He hadn't realised that Ahnell had spoken to any of the children and his friend grinned.

"She was hanging around Sararrh and I saw that she was fascinated with the bead earrings that I made for her.".

This was news to Daro and he gradually fell back so that they were all riding abreast. Ahnell continued cheerfully.

"She finally asked if she could look at them and Sharr took them off and handed them to her!" His eyebrows raised comically and Daro heard the unspoken comment.

"Women!" and smiled.

Sararrh took up the story in a soft husky voice.

"I was waiting for her to ask if she could try them on, but no. Miss Busy Fingers wanted to see how they were made!".

Daro turned to her in surprise, seeking a qualification for the name she had applied to Ario.

"Look.", Sararrh gestured to her ears impatiently and Daro stared blankly, until Sararrh reached up and unclasped the delicate turquoise jewel. She handed it to Daro with a flourish and Daro bent over the ornament in surprise.

Ahnell picked up the thread again, guiding his Zeglur down through the straggling forestation that typified the Fringes of this the most northerly desert.

"I made Nadra an Opal blaze to go on a chain, which I gifted her the day my adoption was announced and I gave a pair of ear jewels to Mina on her wedding day, I am thinking that I might try to get transferred either to the Forge, or to Nirak, the Silver Smith Hall when we get back. Anyway, that was not what we were trying to tell you.", "I learned some of the smith techniques from that man Olneth. He says his brother was a Master Silver Smith and he is himself used to the wearing of a light armour made of many metal links, so he learned the tricks of repair. I went to the Forge with Beven and he showed me how to fashion a wire into such jewellery and how to secure beads on the wire.", He grew very off-hand as he remarked.

His face grew very serious, his voice quite tentative as he said.

"I think Ario has an ability quite outside my understanding and I didn't know what to say to Solana.".

Daro reined in.

"Go on.", He spoke abruptly, not liking the way this conversation was going.

"Well.", said Sararrh, reigning in beside him, "She had no access to a forge and yet she made those turquoise ear jewels overnight!"

Ahnell stated quietly.

"It took me three attempts to draw a fine enough wire to thread beads on. Then all the beads had to be graded and pierced. I included nine joinings and those require constant heat and sub-silver to meld the wire into its new shape and yet a little girl can learn this skill overnight?" He added slowly.

"Daro, many of those children were found wandering. Do you think them to be the children of the Sealed? Could they be Wanderers themselves?".

His trepidation was genuine and Daro was at a loss to know how to answer him, but Sararrh said equably.

"My love, does it matter? She wanted to see how something was made, she then, by whatever means, copied them in turquoise and gave them to me as a thank you for the plaiting of her hair and a little womanly kindness! Don't you two make something of this that it is not. I want her to make more ear jewels and send Orto to the market at Caranchar. He could make a very good living for Solana, much more than he would get from his fields.", and leaving the boys absorbing her swift grasp of Solana's needs and the practical ability to see how a difference could be made, they kicked their Zeglurs forward and along the trail to Malos.

Chapter 28 - Sand Walking

They travelled for hours, through an immense silent forest, heading towards a valley filled with lush green plants. They rode single file, along paths carved in clean white ground, a faint perfume rising as they trotted onto some tough low growing vegetation.

Daro was still thinking about Solana, when the track they were on, broadened out and he got his first glimpse of the Malachite Sands.

He was so astonished that he came to a lumbering stop and just sat atop his Zeglur, staring. The sands were a range of deepening greens, not level, but undulating into the distance. He looked suspiciously at the appearance of "ripples" and as Sararrh and Ahnell joined him, he questioned.

"Quicksand do you think?

Ahnell looked dubious, but Sararrh grinned happily and said comfortably.

"Never! That my dear Daro is a type of sand that Ahnell's Nadra would give her eye teeth to get her hands on. He tells me that she prepares skin creams and lotions?"

Daro grinned. She was friendly and quite kind as well he decided. It was nice to be treated like a brother again, although the memories he had of Suraya alongside Ahnell and himself were of a more abrasive relationship.

"Yes, I could be about to enjoy knowing you!" He thought as Sararrh explained.

"That sand is so fine, that it is used to rub many things smooth. It is graded and you have to know what you are doing with it, but if it is coated on to sheeting with tempered glue, you can use it to rub rough skin back to smooth again. Works wonders on heels and elbows.".

She grinned impishly at Daro and displayed a perfectly rounded dimpled elbow, with no hint of roughness. Daro blushed but his eyes caressed the brief display of golden flesh and he changed the subject swiftly.

"We will need to earn some money, is that something that you could do Ahnell? I know that you have watched and helped Nadra. What do you think?".

Ahnell spoke gloomily.

"I think that we would need a license to extract Deshun Deschima's Sand. I also think that unless you know how to extract any impurities in it, you could be looking for a long time before we found any clean enough to trust, though of course the glue isn't a problem. We can get masses of that easily, by boiling down the bark of these trees.", His face clouded again and Daro said testily.

"Oh what now? I suppose you just remembered another problem?"

Ahnell nodded.

"Mmmh. It stinks and I don't know what to do about that. Women like things that smell good and pitch glue absolutely reeks!".

Sararrh giggled at them and both of them turned irritable eyes on her.

"Why not use cover-ground? It has a really strong clean scent, if you mix it with most things the only thing you will smell is the extract from that!".

So it was that Sararrh persuaded them to stop and camp, make a fire and get out an old shirt of Ahnell's, that he had washed and put aside for rags.

It was quite pleasant really, Daro heaped armfuls of the short flowering plants for Sararrh's use. Ahnell chopped firewood. Sararrh tore strips of cloth and set Ahnell to split softwood twigs. Daro carried a bucket down to the Sands and walked until he found a place that was covered in a myriad of ripples. He patiently scraped off the surface sand, looking at the strangely dull level revealed, then he scooped out a bucket full, before returning.

They laboured over the making of the glue, which had to be released from the leaves of several plants and as Ahnell describe filled the air with an acrid pungency, that wet the eyes and cleared the nostrils.

Sararrh patted the clean sand down on to a board she had found and Daro and Ahnell diplomatically went for a walk, when Sararrh began to experiment with the glue.

Daro grinned at Ahnell.

"Hadda's balls! I didn't know anyone who could swear as badly as Sorrill!" He said admiringly and Ahnell chuckled.

"I will have to teach her not to do that in front of Beven.", He commented.

"I suspect that he thinks all women are delicate little creatures to be cherished and protected.".

Daro spoke ruefully.

"He hasn't met my mother in a bad mood then!" and a companionable chuckle filled the air as they returned to Sararrh.

For two nights longer they worked on the "Sand sticks" and then Sararrh said that she had endured quite enough of the gruelling task of dipping slender strips of fabric into the glue, smoothing them around the twigs. This was eye-watering work, the acrid fumes of the glue making nostrils stream and quiver. The sticks dried quite quickly, hung on a line drawn from a blanket and stiffened with glue. They each had an allotted task and Sararrh, who had invited Daro to use her short-form name in the most sisterly of manners, had laughed at his lack of dexterity with the sticky twigs, but had simultaneously stopped him taking offense by showing him how to grease his fingers so that they wouldn't stick to the material. Once the base sticks had dried, it was Ahnell's job to dip the sticks back into the second glue, which Sararrh had coloured and scented. They had hollowed out a log so old that it had almost turned to stone and split it lengthwise. One half formed a bath for the glue, the other a repository for the Sand and soon Daro and Ahnell had the skill of rolling the dampened sticks in the Sand, making sure that every part of them was coated, before they were once again threaded and hung up to dry. Whether it was the nature of the task, or just the companionship, Daro started to relax and as he did so, his movements became more assured, less awkward and he was genuinely regretful when they loaded the Sand -sticks into their panniers and broke camp.

They turned on to the road to Malos and arrived as if planned on market day. Everywhere people bustled and talked, bartered and shouted at their servants to

"Bring more blue thread, " or "Move along there Masters", as they gawked at the enormous Gresshe men as they rolled barrels and cheeses, carried bedding and bales into place.

Daro had to shout to be heard across the throng.

"Where would we get a pitch to sell our Sand Sticks?"

The man whom he had addressed, shoved his flat hat onto the back of his head and looked around him in a harassed manner.

"Sand-sticks?" He patently didn't know what they were talking about, so Sararrh explained, producing a sensation of outrage in Daro, as she once again displayed her elegantly smoothed elbows. Blushing, the marketeer said slowly.

"Well now missy, that do sound like a thing that might sell along of some folks from the Opal Sands. They be an Apothecary and his assistant, but they stock some beautification stuff. If they permit it…", but he was talking to himself as Ahnell and Daro spotted Carolus and Olneth, positively surrounded by clamouring women.

As Daro was enfolded in his Songfather's embrace, he realised that either he had grown a hand height's taller, or Carolus was shrinking. He hugged the old man generously, then slapped him on the back. Ahnell was hugging Olneth, who looked at him a little askance before smiling and grasping his wrists in the familiar gesture of the Sybillsce.

"We have been waiting ninenights for you. Where have you been holed up?" Olneth indicated a stool for Sararrh, grabbed a mouthful of drink and threw a pot of unguent to Carolus who had drawn Daro into their stall and was serving an imposing matron. Daro took in a long look at his Songfather. He thought sombrely of the Edict posted on the Gate in the Rock, which said that if anyone gave sustenance or shelter, money or clothing to convicted felons expelled from Selesh, that they too would be expelled and wondered if indeed Ikella would be delighted to see this reunion.

He took a mouthful of drink from the mug that Olneth passed to him and came spluttering to the realisation that in these strange green Sands, the local habit was to take their wine hot and spiced.

Suddenly, home and Selesh seemed very far away and he wondered if indeed he would ever return to the only place he had called home.

A hand came down on his shoulder and Carolus said reprovingly.

"I thought you had goods to sell. Young Ahnell gives this girl all the credit, but it seems to me that all of you could use some experience running a stall, as well as some cream for sore fingers.".

He fumbled under the counter and produced a range of empty pots, too large for his potions, he had plainly acquired them to sell on and with relief, Ahnell and Sararrh made room on the gaily draped table, on which Olneth was laying out more stock. Sararrh filled the pots with her Sand-sticks, ranging them along the back, in order of height. She had noticed several Clanswomen approaching and happily explained to the tall pale haired group, what her Sand-sticks would do for them. Again and again her dimpled elbows, her silken smoothed heels were uncovered and Daro found himself sweating, hot-eyed and aching as the buying frenzy began.

Ahnell was happily oblivious of the effect his woman was having on Daro and joined in uproariously when some of Deschima's Guard arrived. They were the tallest, fairest and the strongest in the Clan and their honoured position as personal bodyguards to Deschima, gave then the honorary title of Maiden. However, watching their open camaraderie with half the eligible males in sight, Daro came to the embittered decision that very few of these women actually deserved that honorific and the thought came unbidden to his mind that perhaps his own celibacy was to blame for this uncomfortable position he now occupied.

He was so engaged in mentally berating himself over this point, that he jumped out of his skin when Carolus clapped him on the shoulder.

"That's it for the day my boy.", His Songfather grinned at him, "Your girl has done well for you. She has already sold all of your Sand-sticks and we have bought the rights to her process from her. Olneth is persuaded that there could be a roaring trade in them. He thinks that he can work out an easier method of production and that if we start to offer a variety of colours, of abrasive quality, there are other applications for them. Anyway, your girl is someone quite admirable, for she said that she wouldn't consider our investment unless a proportion of the sales was made over to a group she calls, "Solana's Children". She has done a very tight deal with young Olneth, he has to send grain, meat and fruit to these children at their orphanage in Scartel. She wants proofs of sales every half Rotation and yet I still think there is money to be made!"

Daro stared at his Songfather.

"Had he actually heard Carolus praising a bossy woman for her business acumen?"

He snorted in disgust. He personally never intended to let a woman rule him again, what with Ikella, Nadra, Diras and her crew and now Sararrh, or Sharr as she liked to be called!

"Thank the One that she is Ahnell's girl, not mine.", He found himself muttering, at which comment, Carolus smiled and went away whistling cheerfully.

They slept that night in the old stables that Olneth and Carolus had hired out as a store cum workshop. It was basic, but comfortable and roomy, another plus was that Daro could bunk down with Olneth and was spared the sound of Ahnell and Sararrh's lovemaking.

Olneth grinned at him from the comfortable pallet bed he had made for himself.

"We'll eat well tonight.", He promised. "They have a kind of nut and root stew here that even Master Ombuya would envy. They use many different varieties of bean, a type of tuber that they can bake, boil or steam and lots of leaf greens. I took a lot of time to make a list of the best foods available to import to Selesh and when we leave here next week, we will need every animal we can lay hands on to take back plenty of plants for the gardens and seed for next Rotation.".

Daro sighed, they would be on foot from now on he thought, but then no other exile had ever been offered the comforts of home as far as he knew. He examined his boots critically and Olneth said comfortingly.

"Carolus has arranged for you to carry on here for another ninenight after we leave, until Derana can get here. She has been visiting the northern territory, taking medications out to the mining communities. We have no more market days after tomorrow, we can even take in a little sightseeing and some entertainment ourselves before we must start packing and clearing all our stuff out, ready for the road.".

Daro wasn't sure what constituted entertainment to this normally constrained and taciturn man, but he caught the twinkle in Olneth's eye and readily agreed to accompany him the following day and yawning, snuggled into the furs that decorated Olneth's bed.

He dozed for an hour and was just falling into a deeper sleep when he heard the creak of a floorboard and came instantly awake. A fully clad Olneth was gliding silently out of the room and suddenly, all the old suspicions against the Sybillsce that Daro had heard in his lifetime, reared up in his mind.

Where could the Master Spy be going in the dead of night? Were they in danger? Did Carolus know that Olneth was abroad at night?

All these thoughts and more flashed through Daro's mind as he swung silently clear of the bed-clothes and slid into his boots. He had remained almost fully clad, feeling the chill that comes with intense fatigue, but now he was grateful as he swung a short dark cloak around him and slid cautiously after Olneth.

At the top of the ladder to the lower floor, Daro hesitated, then using a technique he had seen builders use, he grasped both of the side rails and instead of facing inward, he simply slid down, holding his breath, conscious that both his hands were at risk of any protruding splinters or nails. Luckily, although his palms burned momentarily, he suffered no ill effects and he was able to break his landing sufficiently for there only to be a slight rustle as he landed in the straw strewn stable. One of the Zeglurs, stabled nearby snorted softly as it browsed in its manger and Daro froze into immobility while his eyes sought to adjust to the dim greenness of the night.

The stable half-door was opening softly as he paused in the shadows and to Daro's surprise Carolus's unmistakeable shape was briefly framed against the greenly black of the night sky, as he passed, apparently unaware of Daro's presence out, under the lamp that burned in the courtyard outside. Cautiously, Daro slipped after him, sliding eel-like through the lower half of the door, which had thankfully remained slightly ajar.

Outside, the Gresshe habit of hanging lamps to light up every doorway, nearly proved his undoing, for there was very little cover for him to shelter in and he had to keep a close watch on Olneth, who walked stealthily to the corner of the stable yard before he looked back. It was very strange, he didn't seem to be aware of Carolus at all and he gave no sign of having seen Daro either and so they processed. Olneth, careful not to attract attention, darting from shadow to shadow, leading Carolus who made no attempt to hide his presence at all, followed by Daro, heart hammering, dry of mouth, not knowing where they went and terrified in case his clumsiness led them all into danger.

They passed several establishments that were still open. Olneth didn't seem to notice them, Carolus just ignored them and Daro took a wondering look at the outrageous costumes and behaviour of the women who crowded around the doors and windows, importuning any man within their encompassing gaze. Olneth had kept to the other side of the street and their unusual caravan seemed not to attract any attention. Daro was getting more and more curious, when Olneth suddenly ducked aside and entered a low walled passageway.

Deciding that to follow further might be madness, Daro refreshed his memory of a return path, while he flattened himself against the meagre shadows of yet another courtyard wall. He severely doubted his ability to retrace his steps if Olneth led them deeper into the intricate maze that was Malos. He was already uncomfortable with the concept of living in a city built above Sands, with most of the buildings constructed from wood.

As he hesitated in the shadows, Carolus turned and facing him directly put a finger to his lips for silence and beckoned urgently. Daro stared for a second, he had been so careful, so quiet, but the old man grew positively animated, his gestures insistent, so he stood and carefully walked forward. When he was ten paces away, Carolus stepped into the light and to Daro's disgust, tapped the back of one hand in the Inesh gesture that indicated the beginning of a hand-code conversation.

"Keep close. Don't alert him. I hold you responsible afterwards!"

So fast and nimble were the old man's hands, that Daro had to concentrate to follow this and his bewilderment must have shown, for Carolus gestured.

"Did you think I didn't know what you two were saying?"

It was as if the Apothecary's voice had sounded in Daro's mind. At once, Daro fully understood the deviousness of the old man and face flaming, jumped back into the shadows as Olneth, returned to the mouth of the alleyway and peered back uncertainly.

He seemed not to be aware of his travel companion, stood only five paces in front of him and having made a cautious survey of the street, he retreated into the narrow passage once more.

Daro raised his shoulders, shrugging in complete bewilderment, but obviously Carolus saw the movement, for after an irritable flap of the hand, telling Daro in no uncertain terms to sink back into deeper cover, his hands showed again and he signed a brief, shocking, piece of information to the watching boy.

"He is sleep-walking. Don't wake him!".

Instantly Daro remembered one of Ikella's second Rotation Healers. He had forgotten her name, but he recalled the absolute shock and devastation that had run through Selesh when the girl had been found lying at the foot of the stairs to the second Rotation dormitory, in the middle of the night. He heard the story from a very subdued Diras, who had known the girl and liked her.

"She was quite dead when her dormitory mates found her.", Diras had told him heavily.

The young Chapter commander seemed drawn and confessed that she felt responsible for not setting a floor guard in the novice Hall itself.

"Had I known that she regularly walked in her sleep, I would have advised Somishen Shiarjha to allow a patrol in the dormitory wing, but apparently the child's parents thought that history would count against her gaining entry to the school and decided not to tell anyone. Healer Mina tells me that her injuries were light, but that she probably died of shock! If a sleep-walker is roused abruptly, it can also affect their mental health as well. What a terrible waste and so easily prevented!".

He considered the fact, that the subject of this episode was a full grown man, armed and trained in almost every discipline of covert surveillance and hand to hand fighting and his blood ran cold.

Sneaking a look at his Songfather, he saw that Carolus was poised across the way from the alley now, still as the wall against which he leant. A dark flicker of movement was all that betrayed Olneth as he left the shadow of the alley and doubled back along the street, passing Daro at a brisk trot, before turning left and clattering down steps to the next terrace of housing. Instantly, Carolus followed and as he came to the steps, he gave a brief nod and Daro was almost forced to run, in order to keep up with him. He slipped silently down the second flight of steps in his Songfather's wake and obeyed the quick flash of hand commands.

"Stay back!", followed by, "Go right, then follow.".

Daro obeyed, overtaking Carolus and sliding through the shadows behind Olneth. He wasn't sure when he knew finally that he was alone, but suddenly that sense of Carolus was gone and Daro suddenly, unaccountably felt deserted. He crouched, concentrating all his efforts on following the tall, sibilant shadow that was Olneth and was relieved when the Sybillsce finally appeared to have reached his destination. He stopped in the gloom cast by a huge tree and watched as Olneth quartered the rough ground ahead of him.

He watched carefully as his quarry conducted a hunt of his own, tracking back and forth, moving slowly, with extreme caution. Daro had just slid a little further forward in an attempt to see what Olneth was doing, when he became aware that he was no longer alone and restraining his screaming nerves, relentlessly battening down the urge to scream and run, he turned his head to meet the bright friendly gaze of one of Deschima's "Maidens".

She put a finger to her lips and then indicated that he should move back and then he sensed rather than saw his Songfather's presence.

The Maiden sank silently down, where Daro had been crouched and while he slipped back to Carolus, she watched Olneth intently.

Carolus drew Daro back into the shelter of a wall, then he signed.

"Well done. I will tell all later!", before sliding down the wall to sit at its base. Daro joined him, watching as a cohort of Maidens, all wearing dark green, their silver half armour discarded to ensure silence, arrived and spread out along the edge of the parkland that Olneth had led them to.

Olneth was still searching the scrub surrounding the area and Carolus watched as the Master Spy paused, wiping his brow, seemingly distraught.

He stood, his head bowed, chest heaving and as Daro watched, he cried out, sobbing a name, over and over again, his brow furrowed in agony, his tormented eyes burning.

Daro was aghast. Had Olneth wakened? Into what tortured dreamscape was his friend staring? He must have made some sound or moved, for suddenly Carolus put out a quieting hand and whispered softly.

"Not long now. He always comes here, always weeps.".

Daro was repelled by the analytical tone of his Songfather's voice.

"If his dream is so bad, so torturous, surely it would be better to wake the poor man.", he thought, watching as Olneth took out something from an inner pocket.

The cloud cover here was not quite so thick as it was in the Opal Sands and there was a pale green glimmer in the air, possibly from the many lights that the Gresshe burned in their city. Against this Olneth's face seemed absorbed as he gazed down at his hands, one finger seemed to be caressing something and then the storm broke and he threw his head back and howled.

Daro started to his feet, even as Carolus rose and calmly steadily walked to his friend and gathered him under a protecting arm. Daro fell in beside him and they gently drew him away and walked back to the stable yard.

Olneth stumbled along, allowing them to gently guide his faltering footsteps. He seemed oblivious of his surroundings and Daro understood that he was still, in a way, asleep. He was certainly unaware of the air of subdued expectancy that filled the yard as they arrived and Daro stared around as a score or more Maidens rubbed down sweating Zeglurs.

Carolus drew him inside, closing the door firmly on the midnight bustle and with Daro's assistance, persuaded Olneth, in a low persistent voice that he should go to bed.

Daro followed the Sybillsce up the ladder and didn't make a move to divert the man from his usual bed. He crawled wearily into the covers and Daro feeling strangely protective of this silent sufferer, carefully tucked the furs around him.

He was tired himself, but very curious, so he slipped down the ladder again and went into the main room of the lower floor, pausing in amazement as he saw a throng of Maidens, surrounding Deschima, Sorceress of these Sands and a couple of travelling Healers.

Derana he knew, having broken his wrist in the distant past. This member of the Council of Nine had travelled to set the bones at Ikella's urgent request and she smiled at him, saying in a wondering voice.

"Daro! I really can't believe that I assisted at your birth! How many Rotations have you now?".

He had made his obeisance to Deschima, who nodded to him gravely, making him aware that she was most likely to know of his exile. He had not expected to feel embarrassed, because in his own mind, he had done nothing to cause such a furore, but undoubtedly his mother would have warned her Sisters-in-Sorcery of their argument, his threats and unaccountably he felt ashamed of his temper and awkward in the presence of the Sorceress.

He sat down at the table with Derana and another Healer in a pale green cloak and speaking softly and seriously calculated.

"I left just before my seventeenth Rotation, so this Jentaroth will be my second away from home and my eighteenth. I am getting old very quickly.", They enjoyed the gentle chuckle this comment aroused and then the Healer in the pale green put back her hood, revealing the high forehead and flat planes of a typical Quexoni Healer. She smiled at him thoughtfully and said comfortably.

"You were about this big when last I changed your wrapper, young man!", to Daro's acute embarrassment, but he bore it in good measure, saying gently.

"Then in that case I had better go back to bed, before anybody here wants to get back into bad habits!".

Amid the cheerful buzz of conversation, Carolus drew Daro aside.

"Andria is the Soul Searcher of the Tourmaline and member of the Council of Nine, so I was able to inveigle her away to treat Olneth, by dint of asking her here on Council business. Derana assures me that there is plenty of that to cover my tracks. I already told them both of your Sand-walk, though they don't know the reason behind it. They simply think that you are seeking medical help, but don't want Ikella to know or worry. Don't let on to Olneth when you go up to bed. He always sleeps badly anyway, but he needs his rest, before he finds out that we managed to find the gang of child-traffickers he has been searching for. I must ask you to put this by his bed.".

He handed Daro a small but elaborately decorated locket and as Daro took it, somehow he released the clip and two locks of hair were revealed. Daro looked at them quizzically and Carolus explained.

"This is Olneth's hair.", Daro touched the neat curl lightly. "The lockets were a bride-gift to Olneth and Telandra when they married. She was pregnant at the time of Partition and we still lack proof of her continued survival, but one thing is sure. She gave birth to twinlings, one a boy remains in the Amethyst. The other, a girl, seems to have left the Sands before Partition and has been sold into slavery. Olneth tracked her to Malos, quite accidentally, but has not been able to follow her further. It has quite unhinged the man.".

Daro ran his forefinger lightly over the tiny curl and as he did so, he heard a strange sound, a chord of some music which struck at the soul. It was as if some instrument sang, a warm thrumming roll of notes.

He bent his head concentrating all of his senses on the sound. It pulsed and thudded, but was not a drum, for it carried notes that throbbed in a glittering ascent of sound and then it stopped and he was left, staring at the locket in amazed fascination.

"I thought you might like to hear that.", said his Songfather enigmatically. "Now my boy, don't you think that you should go to bed?"

With much to think about, Daro took his farewells and joined Olneth, crawling into the pallet bed with a groan, but not before he had carefully wound the precious locket round Olneth's hand as he lay relaxed and strangely vulnerable in sleep.

Chapter 29 – The Waking of the Sands.

When Daro awoke, Olneth was gone. Regretting the nomadic existence that he had inflicted on himself and those who travelled with him, he rolled out of bed and prepared to investigate.

He had realised last night, that Deschima knew rather more about Carolus and Olneth's comings and goings than he did and from there it was not difficult to reach the conclusion, that this stable formed part of the Sorceresses Hall of Rule.

Recalling the Maidens and their familiarity with these surroundings, he re-dressed, (wrinkling his nose at the staleness of his clothing) and wondered whose bed he slept in. However, before he could hazard a guess, he smelt food cooking and his stomach growled softly. Sliding down the ladder rapidly, Daro found Carolus lavishing honey onto the local sourdough pancakes.

His Songfather glanced up at him.

"Sit you down and eat! Nothing like a few pancakes to revive a man!" He commented, pushing a bowl of the steaming, fragrant delicacies to Daro's side of the table and flicking a plate out of a nearby rack with his other hand.

Conversation dwindled to a few murmurs, as they ate companionably, then Carolus announced.

!I took the liberty of introducing Ahnell and his lady over at the Hold of the Maidens. They took your washing with theirs and will return after they have bathed. Olneth left with Derana and Andria, well before dawn. He is going into retreat with Andria for a day or two.".

His strangely brilliant eyes caught Daro's look of concern and he said gently.

"Olneth needs treatment for this obsession of his. To find his daughter and his wife is his whole reason for living and while I understand that motivation, if he doesn't get it under control, he will lose his life in the attempt.".

He had glanced down at his hands as he spoke and Daro was astonished to see Olneth's lockets under his palm.

Carolus looked up, catching Daro's eyes with his and sighed deeply.

"These seem to form the focus of his search. He says, they draw him to places. He hears strange music and believes Telandra's locket to be enchanted, leading him to his child.".

The old man sounded intrigued, rather than disbelieving, so Daro said easily.

"Yes, I heard it too, last night when you showed me the locket. Didn't you?".

Carolus nodded softly rising from his chair, with a finger to his lips signalling discretion.

"We are not in our own Sands now my boy.", He admonished. "Use extreme caution when discussing this sort of thing, these Sands are not awake to your needs.".

Daro looked at him perplexed. Carolus had heard the strumming glissando himself and yet he was cautioning Daro about talking out loud about his own abilities.

"Olneth thinks the child is calling him. He suspects the girl is in terrible danger and has wondered if in fact she may be of the House of Sorcery, perhaps the true heir to his Sands. Whatever it turns out to be, he must be persuaded that to take the chances he has taken, in an attempt to find her, might imperil her more and so Andria, Chief amongst Soul Searchers has agreed to treat him first and then to treat you.".

Daro mopped his plate clean of honey, with the last pancake and said deliberately.

"I don't need any treatment Songfather. I just need to find something and at the moment I don't know what that is. My mother wants me to try and find the Tapestry of Tten, which she thinks will save the world. I want to find a way to help her, but she shuts me out, even though I have already helped her.".

Carolus sighed, peering at Daro through narrowed eyes.

"Daro, I know that you believe that you need to find your own Way, but how can you have helped a Sorceress? Did you tell her that you think you helped her?".

Daro grinned suddenly.

"Oh yes.", He admitted. "She was not impressed, but Mina, Solana, even Mother told me, that I screamed so much when she first enchanted the Winds, that she had to strap me to her body, before she could summon them.".

At Carolus's blank stare, he continued defiantly.

"If you don't believe me, ask Olneth, he was there too!" He warmed to his theme then.

"Apparently, the same thing happened when they returned to Selesh. I screamed the place down until she carried me while spell-casting. Shiarjha told me that Mother..." his voice dropped dramatically, with just a hint of hysterical giggle in it, as he continued, "...Stripped stark naked in order to enchant the Winds. She told me that it was the oldest and Highest form of natural magic to paint symbols on your naked body and make yourself most vulnerable in order to command a greater power!".

Carolus said nothing, but his mouth thinned disapprovingly, as Daro continued.

"I remember other times when I helped her without her even knowing.", At this the Apothecary lent forward, his hands clasped together and a rapt, attentive look came over his face as his Songchild listed events on his fingers.

"She worried about Viness and her baby. I was about six Rotations when she asked me to help her. She wanted to see if Viness's unborn child would quicken. I was allowed to put my hand on Viness's belly, so I woke the baby up for them. When I was about eight Rotations, we had that sudden outbreak of red fever in the north. Mother was about to take Suraya off-Sands, to train in the Tourmaline and she was delayed, tracking the spread of the fever. She only just got off-Sands when Ahnell and half Diras's Chapter went down with it, remember?"

Carolus looked at him oddly then and Daro suddenly said.

"I was determined that I would show Suraya that she wouldn't be the only one with power when she grows up. I went up to Zenitheon Point after Nahamida celebrated the Solstice and I stood with many others who had come to honour their dead. While I was there, I heard someone tell me that I needed to go out into the Sands.".

He didn't seem to notice the hissing breath that Carolus had drawn and he said quietly.

"As you know, I went out to the pasture lands and there I found a patch of sand and I touched it.", his head came up and he turned dancing turquoise and gold eyes on his Songfather.

"The Sand spoke to me, it seemed to swell, to blossom in my hand and a voice told me that I could command that sand, shape it, hold it, be one with it. I thought of the red fever and how I wanted it gone from my Sands, washed clear from the tranches that had carried it south and the sand cried and moaned and made promises to me. Then the evening breezes came and I remembered Nahamida's prayer for the cleansing of the Sand and I repeated it, word for word and the Sand obeyed. The next day, the temperature dropped, the red fever reduced and never returned. I promised myself that after Zenitheon, I would go and see if the villages were getting better, so the following night, when the market closed and all were packing to go home, I took the coatans and went north to investigate.", his bright eyes never blinked as he said gently.

"You know this to be true my Songfather, you were there. You and Olneth, Jashell and Diras followed me all the way, to Shilinch and back. I suppose you told Mother?!

Carolus blushed and blinked and then chuckled.

"Well, not until we had to and that was when you were fifteen, so some time ago now!"

His gravity returned as he said.

"What now? Do you understand what you are doing? There is a choice ahead of you and you don't have to make it. I think that you know far more than you should about the past of our world, you are certainly moving along a path that has not been taken for many Rotations. Along that path there are many dangers and at the end of this Way, the choice you make may determine your life, or even if you live. However, you have already begun a process, a process that will change you and all around you irrevocably. Daro (whose name means a new beginning), can either remain as he is, or continue to wake the Sands, in which case, our world will change again and might even survive a fate which has hung over it for millennia.".

The old man's voice was very soft, very gentle and Daro looked at him, taking in the poignancy of his words, the tenderness of his expression and he said sharply.

"What do you know Songfather? Why do you know about these things?" to which Carolus replied quietly.

"When the Storm struck Pelshar, a great protective power that has kept our world safe for centuries, was diverted to repair the Source. When that happened, the repository on the Heights of Surrandel, that you know as Sanctuary fell. When Guardian Jocasta's powers, Guardian Beneva and the repository of knowledge was transferred to Selesh, the Messenger of Sanctuary went with them. You know me as Carolus of the Nine Sands, but I have been in the service of Sanctuary, for more Rotations than many another lives.".

Daro looked at him for a long moment and then he asked solemnly, "Can you advise me? Where must I travel? How can I wake the other Sands? Do I even need to wake other Sands? and how do I find someone who can tell me more about the Sandsingers? Why their Way ended so abruptly?".

Carolus seemed to retreat, for a moment he looked austere, chilled and then he sighed and reached into a capacious pocket, withdrawing a small, hide bound volume. Its crinkled pages were of a fine, almost translucent material, the script sharply defined, the tiny embellishments so finely executed that even Daro drew in his breath. He reached out a tentative finger and Carolus smiled sadly and relinquished the book, with a loving pat. Daro picked it up, turning a page, already absorbed as the writing seemed to unscramble itself under his tracing finger.

"If there be evidence of a deep connection with the three powers that govern each Sand, that of the Source, that of the Wind and finally the Sands themselves, then shall the one who believes in a greater power, bring themselves to the Great Hall of Tirjhinar and offer his most precious possession in exchange for the power of the Sands. In taking the Oath, must each candidate be prepared, mentally, physically and spiritually for the most profound change, for from that time, they will be bound to the Sand that they command and that Sand to those who command it. Through their veins will run the Sand and the Source, in their Voice shall be the command of life and death, the power of the Wind. The first, shall Sings the Opal and have the command of all in his Voice..".

Daro's voice trailed off uncertainly and he lifted his hand from the book, passing it back to Carolus, who blocked the movement with his hand.

"No my dear boy. No. I have held this too many Rotations, waiting for the one who could read it. Now I pass it into your care, for you have more right to it than I. You must stay a while and consult with Derana and Andria, they will have treatments to offer you. Take them, retrieve the written form and make sure you learn every one by heart as you travel through the order of the Sands. You will need to know them word perfect before your journey ends.'

His voice dropped for a moment, as though he looked inward, at some picture that Daro couldn't see and then he brightened again.

"Forgive an old, tired man my son and travel only with hope in your pocket. I will miss you, miss the mysteries in this book, which has guided me for as long as I can recall. Now it will guide you, bring you safely back from Sand Waking, in the knowledge that all the Sand that is your destiny is in the Opal Desert, at home, in Selesh.".

From that time Daro felt a detachment settle over him. He had felt this same calm sense of purpose as he first launched his voice into the high reaches of the Hall of the Healers and had wondered at it, then. He knew with certainty that where he walked, no man had walked since before Cataclysm. He felt peculiarly alone and it was with relief that he went to Derana's small Hall, undergoing firstly a treatment that left both his hands encased in a plaster made from the soft green Malachite Sands, with such a wistful, pensive expression on his face, that Derana whispered her doubts to Andria, saying that Daro was still a child, too young to be obsessed.

Andria, measuring the long lithe length of limb, the broadening chest and taut belly laid before her, doubted privately that she would ever behold such a potent symbol of masculinity in her sight again and said so, to Derana's blushing face, until the Malachite Healer found the ancient remedies written form and copied it for Daro to take back to Ikella.

In the treatment room Daro lay, supremely detached as Derana gently removed the Malachite encasement. He looked at his hands, seemingly unaware of Andria's open appreciation of his body. Stretching deliciously, he finally made his way to the Healers bathing pool to remove every last grain of the Malachite from his skin. However, it whispered to him, singing of tall trees and fertile Fringes, high mountains and the shimmering dunes that stretched to the horizon.

He submitted willingly to Andria's hands. His eyes danced inexplicably flickering with subtle glints of green, as she poured the palely glistening Tourmaline Sand into a large bowl and encouraged him to work his feet into it. She spoke the ritual words from a scroll of such antiquity that she flinched as she unrolled it, then invoking the Source she carefully followed a notation that he presumed to guide her *othervoice*.

The sand shifted under his feet, awakening a memory of huge plains, sparsely grassed, a high mountain lake, a sheet of pale green and pale barked trees, their slender growth and short stature speaking of great height. He felt the tingle of the sand beneath his feet and then it was over and he was waking to anxious faces, hot sweet drinks and a strangely aching chest.

He accepted the written confirmation of his treatment, the records of both Healers and, as if walking in a dream world returned to Malos, to discover that his Songfather and Olneth had already departed for Selesh, anxious to be further South when Winter returned. So it was, Sand after Sand, treatment after treatment, until in the heat of their third Rotation away, with only one Sand to travel that Sararrh fell ill.

Chapter 30 - The Dream.

Daro was dreaming, or at least, thought he was. He stood on high rolling dunes, far into this desert, where no recognizable landmarks were visible. He wiped the sweat from his brow before taking the last two steps to the crest of the dune, where he rested, refusing to worry about Ikella's reactions should she find out that he was back in the Opal Sands, from which she had banished him, almost four Rotations ago.

He was seeking once more, the footprints that had led him here. Night after night, a dream that repeated itself, never varying, never resolved, an endless repetitive search, up dunes and down, across the many Sands of his world, following an invisible companion. In the early Rotations of his exile, he had come to believe that he was following in the footsteps of his unknown father, seeing only the footprints, never the man, not even his shadow. Then there was the music, driving the dream, a never ending ripple of notes, cascading with his running feet, a relentless thudding rhythm, echoing his wildly beating heart and the Voice. The voice that mocked and cajoled, the voice that summoned and demanded, the voice that alternately consoled and sobbed with his own despair.

He crouched to examine these new footprints, seeing with bewilderment, that the constant companion of his nights, had been joined by two others. He stood slowly, peering into gathering gloom, although he knew from the debilitating heat, that the sun stood off the Sands at its zenith, despite the lumbering roll of cloud, that hid it from his world. He strained his eyes, following the trace that told of three ahead of him and suddenly hopeful of identifying, the one he had followed for the length of his life, set off in pursuit.

The shadows lengthened and still he staggered onward. His legs leaden with exhaustion, eyes straining to see the faint foot marks he followed, but now, despite his thirst, his mind sapping fatigue, he couldn't have stopped if he had wanted to. Through an area where the wind played havoc with the tracks he followed, into an expanse of eerie silence he stumbled. Not sure if he was dreaming or awake, the voice called him, the thudding rhythm pounded in his veins and then he was clutching at rock, Opal rock and his hands traced the entrance to a cavern and he woke to a low querulous enquiry.

"Daro? Daro is that you? Oh, thank the One you found us.".

They lay, cocooned in each other's arms and as he came fully to his senses, Daro hissed at the piteous picture they made. Gone was the graceful youth that was his best friend Ahnell, gone was the tempestuous red head with the creamy skin, that had so aroused him, leaving him weak and tremulous in her presence.

What faced him was as shocking a sight as he had ever seen. Sararrh was a shadow of her former self. Always slender, she was now skeletal, her eyes huge and dark, that lustrous, fiery hair, barely distinguishable as it clung to her skull, its thin, dry strands, barely enough to cover it. Hastily opening his flask, he bent over them, supporting first Sararrh and then Ahnell, gently trickling a little moisture on to their lips, anxious not to choke them, as he reversed their dehydration. Counting three mouthfuls apiece, he shared the precious remnant of his water with them, before stowing the flask away and returning to Ahnell.

His stomach lurched as he saw the tell-tale signs of Stoneskin Fever in his friend as well. The stark white patches on his face and upper arms, the drawn gauntness of his features, the hugeness of eyes. He opened his mouth to commiserate, but Ahnell's eyes flashed a warning, a frail old man's hand was laid imploringly on his and Daro saw, in the brief shake of his head, that Ahnell didn't want Sararrh to know, how ill he was.

Daro forced himself to smile and be calm, tend to his friend's needs and not react to the despair in Ahnell's eyes. He dampened his scarf, gently wiping Sararrh's face, appalled at how sunken her cheeks were, struck to the bone by the tenderness of the smile she bestowed on him, devastated by her bravery as she glanced at Ahnell to make sure he was resting, before whispering brokenly.

"Daro, I am so sorry, I couldn't make him stay away! Telani, the Healer at the hospice warned me, but I think he has it too.".

It was too long a speech for her. The words came haltingly, slurring on the lips as she struggled to say on a gasp.

"Sssh! Don't tell him, he couldn't bear it, to be so close to home..." her agonized whisper died away and Daro glanced at Ahnell and saw that he was awake and that he had heard and understood.

He raised a weak smile, just breathing the words.

"Mi amaney"(my love) and Daro unaccountably felt tears prick his eyes and a lump form in his throat.

There was so little he could do, except be with them, so he willed his restless legs to quiet, his frustrated anger at the unfairness of it all, to drain from him, as he sat cautiously folding his long body down on to the ground at the base of the back wall of the cavern. He arranged the travel pack he had slung across his chest, so that it pillowed his back and as his friends did, lapsed into exhausted somnolence.

He awoke in the night, cold and thirsty and carefully unwound himself from where he had slumped. Now he could take notice of his surroundings, but not before he gently checked on Sararrh and Ahnell. He bent over Ahnell first, noting the strange mottling of his skin, knowing full well that the rare fever would have already penetrated his feet and calves, that his thighs would be by now taut and inflexible as the disease welded skin and bone together.

Only that dawn, Telani had spoken quietly to him, giving him small packets of preparations that would greatly relieve their pain.

He remembered her words, her patience with his stupidity.

"It is so rare, no-one knows exactly what causes it, but we think that some people might carry a chance of getting it from birth. If we could but know, who those people were, we would stand a chance of reducing the numbers hugely, but there is nothing to show, nothing to tell us that one man's occupation is another man's death.".

He had stared at her blankly and Telani bit her lip.

"O forgive me.", She had smiled at him tentatively. "Whenever I saw you before, you were surrounded by Healers, by the Sisters of Sorcery. For some reason, I had assumed that you knew about the perils of certain employments. Let me explain and don't worry, I'm not one of your mother's most gifted students, I'll keep it simple!".

She grinned at him conspiratorially and he remembered laughing with her, but this disease was no laughing matter and he wondered at Telani's ability to see humour in anything, for her day to day service to the One, was spent in nursing terminally ill and dying patients. However, she had made the explanation simple and painfully clear to him.

"Many occupations carry their own risks. For example, if you don't like being round sick people, or are afraid of getting ill, you'd make a very poor Healer! Some occupations bring you in contact with things that you might ordinarily, never handle. For example, to cure leather, tanners use substances that the ordinary person would never come in contact with. I have treated men and women, pledged to that skill, who had to be released from their indentures, because something in their bodies reacted to the elements that they were handling. To say that their occupation was killing them, is but one way of putting it. Perhaps Sararrh caught Stoneskin fever by exposure to some element that her body was never intended to contact. Ahnell could certainly have contracted it, simply by prolonged or intimate skin contact while Sararrh was infectious. Do you know of any unusual elements that Sararrh could have handled?".

At the time, Daro hadn't thought clearly, but now a memory was stirred by the sheer look of exhaustion in both their young faces and he shivered. He was seeing them again, in the High Fell Forest, boiling plant solutions to make glue for sand-sticks, locked in each others arms at night and guilt blossomed, flushing his face with hot blood, filling his mind with angry, self-condemnatory words.

He choked them back, thrusting the thought away as Ahnell shifted painfully, sitting forward stiffly, groaning softly as the pain hit him. He gasped.

"Help me up Daro, I need to move.".

Daro, carefully supported his childhood friend outside, busying himself doing nothing, while Ahnell relieved himself behind a nearby screening of low branches.

They stood in the Sands that they both loved and Ahnell asked curiously.

"Did you ever hear the legend about the waterfall in Tirjhinar?".

Sararrh was still sleeping, so Daro humoured Ahnell and came to lean against a convenient pile of rocks at the entrance to the shallow cave, sure that he would hear her stir, if she did.

"Probably, but not recently. Remind me.".

Ahnell complied, though his voice was rusty and he was coughing throughout the short tale.

"I think it was Diras who told it to me, when Trinet got sick and not even your mother could save her. Apparently there is a place called Tirjhinar, where a miraculous waterfall pours day and night, into a basin, which has no drain. It never overflows, it never runs dry and the waterfall has miraculous properties too.".

He stirred uneasily and Daro saw that he was suffering great pain, but Ahnell waved him aside, determined to tell his story, so Daro let him continue.

"Do you remember telling me that you wanted to become a Sandsinger?" Ahnell turned and looked deep into Daro's eyes.

"Daro, Tirjhinar is the lost city of the Sandsingers.", Ahnell's voice was lifted in a travesty of the old gaiety he had shared with Daro. His voice cracked a little hysterically as he performed a sketchy bow, waving one uncertain arm in the direction of the cave, making a trumpeting call, the other hand pressed to his mouth in a mocking imitation of the horns used at great celebrations.

"Ta Ta. Behold the Cavern of the Fall.", his voice had risen with the sting of poignancy.

"Sararrh worked it out. We've found Tirjhinar, we found the waterfall, but we lack the Sandsinger! Isn't it rich? We found Tirjhinar, but we can't get in!" It was then that the damn burst and he wept, clinging hopelessly to life, to Daro, to hope and watching it slip remorselessly out of his grasp.

Daro held him, felt his tears fall on his hands, felt Ahnell's weakened body shaking with sobs and felt first helpless, then suddenly furiously angry. With fate, with this destiny he had spent four Rotations denying and finally with himself for letting this happen.

He restrained his anger long enough to take an exhausted Ahnell to the back of the shallow cavern, laying him down beside Sararrh, who to his awakening senses, seemed to have slipped beyond normal sleep. He fussed for a moment, tucking his own cloak around them and then he very deliberately turned his attention on the cave.

It was enormously high in the centre, with an oddly angled entrance, that seemed designed to conceal itself in the sheer rock Opal cliff in which it had formed. Sand had drifted right to the very back wall and not in inconsiderable amounts either, for it positively filled the central cavern, as if heaped on something like a platform. Heart thumping, Daro stared upward into the cavern, shrouded in darkness and wished that he had more light, with which to see what he knew would be there, for he remembered all too well, the whispered accounts of where he had been born, told to him like some fairytale, when as a child he had been unable to sleep at night.

He walked reluctantly to a substantial sand drift and gently probed the side of it and it was as he thought, solid. He gently brushed the surface away, half horrified at the thought that he might uncover his own mother's body, half disappointed when the basin he revealed gradually was empty of anything but a covering of a strange crystalline material, which bore Ikella's own sigil, as confirmation of all she had told him.

The light had grown subtly, night shifting into greyed out day and he stretched, standing upright once more, looking out into the Sands, seeing as

Ikella must once have done, the dawn of another darkened day and the Irix herd, grazing. He clicked his fingers gently encouraging and one of the dams, heavy in milk trotted confidently to him and allowed him to take a liberal cupful for Sararrh and Ahnell. He fondled her and her calf, half unbelieving, half revelling in the fact that not one thing that Ikella had told him, was less than the truth, but for some reason, he still couldn't bring himself to look up, to see the last proof, the waterfall of Tirjhinar, frozen in time, just waiting for a potential Sandsinger to release it once more.

Not until the light, such as it was, had grown sufficiently to reveal the eerie shimmer of a clear, glassy cascade, suspended over the raised basin that now dominated his view, would Daro bring himself to look at it. He stood, careful not to disturb Sararrh, for she was far beyond his rudimentary nursing skills now. During their fitful night, he seemed to recall winding the liniment soaked bandages that Telani had supplied round Sararrh's frail legs. He knew that he had fended off Ahnell's feeble attempts to resist the same treatment and it was with a wry grimace that his childhood playmate greeted the day and his sweetheart's collapse. He watched Daro mutely, as he gently straightened her clothes, removing the evidence of her increasing lack of control over her bodily functions and weakly complained.

"What we really need is someone to turn on that water, I could just do with a nice cup of Stemmis and a bath!".

It was just like Ahnell to demonstrate a thoroughly irreverent sense of humour in the face of circumstances and Daro grinned at him, reminded suddenly, with incredible poignancy of the faint whisper that Ahnell had dared, just after Ikella had confronted Daro, as the cadences of his voice still hung on the air of the Hall of the Healers.

"Daro.", He had whispered urgently. "Daro, I told you that taking lessons from Zeglurs wouldn't impress your mother!"

Their eyes locked, each knowing that the other thought.

"I love you my brother.", Then without turning his gaze away, holding Ahnell's eyes with his, Daro reached up and touched the suspended crystalline form and with a mighty thundering roar, the waterfall of Tirjhinar softened and cascaded into the very basin in which Daro had been born.

The icy flow of it shocked him. He stood, poised on the brink of it, soaked to the waist by the fine spray as it roared into the bowl. He could feel the colour drain from his face, but he was entranced, bewitched and to Ahnell, it seemed suddenly as though his friend was surrounded by an aura of such power, that he nearly forgot to breathe.

Daro reached forward, cupped his hand and collected some water, bringing it to Ahnell, somehow with his eyes still focussed on Ahnell's. He spoke and Ahnell blinked for Daro's voice had changed, matured and settled into a certainty of tone, that rang and chimed off the rocks in this strange cavern.

"Drink this Ahnell.", Daro said quietly, but in a voice that brooked no dissent.

"It will refresh you better than anything else I know.", Obediently, Ahnell bent his head to Daro's hand and drinking from it reverently, sliding inexorably from pain into dreams.

Chapter 31 - The Awakening

Daro stood, hands supporting Ahnell's sagging body as he literally fell asleep in his arms. He lifted him gently, relishing the ease with which he could do so and tenderly lowered him into the pool. Now the roaring torrent slowed, the force of its initial battering reduced and as Daro cradled Ahnell against him, he found the water warmer as it swirled delicately around their bodies.

He sank gratefully into the pool and was able to sit, back supported by the sides. This enabled him to pull Ahnell against him and their he sat, feeling a subtle tingle spreading through his tired body, until he was able to re-engage with his surroundings.

Nearby, cocooned in her blankets Sararrh still slept and Daro began to consider how he would rouse and dry Ahnell, before he immersed Sararrh in what he hoped were healing waters.

He considered Ahnell's claims.

"The waterfall at Tirjhinar can cure many incurable conditions, or so the legends say. All we lack is a Sandsinger to make them work.", The words came clearly to his mind as though Ahnell had spoken them himself and Daro turned his head to look at his friend, who leant against him, a lost dreaming expression on his face.

Daro's thoughts lingered on their condition. As Telani had explained, Stoneskin fever started with a desperate fatigue ,night sweats and a high fever. These symptoms might then suddenly disappear for some time, before re-emerging with appalling cramps, the typical mottling of the skin and increasing disability, caused as the skin and muscle turned to a bony substance. He imagined the fear, the inability to control one's own body and the painful lingering death at the end of terrible suffering and he knew that whatever they faced, he would face with them, whatever it took.

The problem was, he simply didn't know where to start. He moistened his lips, wondering what form of words he should use to beg the One for help, for how could he approach those who had once populated this place? It was ancient, lost in the Sands of a far distant time. Even the history of the Sandsingers had been lost, or deliberately relegated to an almost mythical status and certainly, there were no Sandsingers left to answer his questions, had he known to whom he should address them. He sank into a morose silence, while he considered the next avenue of approach.

When a slightly amused voice spoke, so softly that he wondered if he was hallucinating, he sat forward, staring wildly around for the source of the sound.

"Ichta Selunsanni, why struggle alone? Why don't you simply ask your questions, instead of talking to yourself?".

Controlling the impulse to run screaming from this place, never to return, Daro tried valiantly to marshal his thoughts, only to subside into ineffectual silence. After a pause the voice continued.

"Didn't your Songfather tell you to listen for a voice to tell you what to do? Why then, are you so surprised that it should be here that you are summoned? Selesh may not be the centre of all power, your Way and theirs must work together, but this is our place, our home and yours if you pass the testing.".

Daro lifted his head.

"Testing?" He questioned, his voice hoarse and quivering with emotion and the Voice said quietly.

"Did you think that all you had to do, to become a Sandsinger, was to endure nearly twenty Rotations of living in luxury? Did it never occur to you that to obtain great power, you must first lose something that you treasure? Even your foster-mother had to give up any chance of love, marriage or motherhood to achieve her status. Your own mother knowingly sacrificed her life to bear you in this place, just to give you a chance to become the most powerful mage ever known to Pelshar.".

Daro digested this quietly, then, he knew what he must do and slid away from Ahnell, making sure that he was safely wedged against the side of the shallow pool, before he slowly stood up, directly under the downpour.

"Make me whole, fit and worthy to serve.", He prayed, hands uplifted to the water. "Take from me the obsessive nature that so distressed my friends and make me worthy of the task.".

He felt the water's embrace, the strange sensation that he was being changed, moulded to a Way he didn't yet quite understand and then realising that even a Sandsinger couldn't immediately know the answer to everything, he felt the water suddenly warming him, soothing him and he felt himself quieting, his confidence returning.

Ahnell stirred and sat up smiling.

"I'm all wet.", He seemed bemused, but fairly comfortable and Daro, fearing to break the effect that their impromptu bath had imposed on them, bent to his side and asked softly.

"Are you in any pain? Should I help you out and get you dried off?"

His friend nodded, trying to get his feet under him, giving a low chuckle as he failed to find any purchase.

Daro hoisted him easily, shocked by how light and insubstantial Ahnell seemed in his arms, but cheered by the fact that the pain seemed to have receded, he dried him, made him laugh by reminding him of their boyhood water fights in their bathing room and finally left him, wearing his sleeping blanket over a hastily draped drying cloth, while he carefully rinsed out his clothing and draped it on the rocks outside to dry.

He cautiously inspected Sararrh, before going to his own travel pack for the healing preparations and dressing Ahnell's withered legs. Returning to his pack to stow away a gouche full of medication, he took the opportunity to whisper quietly.

"Would Sararrh benefit from being immersed in the pool?".

Equally quietly the Voice in his mind said.

"How can you doubt it? Strip her of her clothing and re-wrap her in a blanket. Slide her into the pool, the water will be very warm for she is in the first cold of death. She is far down a path from which you can't return her, but she does not need to suffer pain, or disability. Death is not always the end of everything, sometimes it is a beginning. Your own mother knew this truth and embraced it for your sake. Now you must embrace it for theirs. When the woman has received the power of the water, you will feel her fever drop, her pain leave her. Then, you must enter the glory that is Tirjhinar to find your destiny and end their suffering.".

Slowly, not sure if he understood all that had been said, Daro tended to Sararrh, doing all that had been asked of him. Finally, he took his own comb from his pack and gently disentangled the girl's hair, letting it swirl into the pool, noting the fire-bright strands reviving under his clumsy ministrations and then she stirred and her hand moved under his.

"Ahnell?"

She murmured, her voice husky and Daro raised her, so that her anxious eyes could see across the cavern, to where his friend rested against the back wall.

"You have both been bathed in the waters.", Daro said tentatively, not quite sure that he should raise their hopes of a cure any further, but Sararrh held up a silencing hand.

"Then we have been blessed indeed.", She whispered and her eyes went again to Ahnell.

"Don't let him suffer Ichspeller.", She begged, "I could stand anything but to see him suffer.".

Daro said urgently.

"What did you call me? What does it mean?"

The Voice in his head said patiently.

"Ichspeller. An ancient honorific, applied to a male Sandsinger by his Sandsworn followers. Sheispeller, is the feminine variation of the title, applied to a female Sandsinger in the same way. However, your devotees are a little precipitate. You are not yet entitled to that honorific, being only Ichta Selunsanni, Sandsinger Designate, the Son of the Light returning.".

Daro stood stock – still, suddenly aware that his heart was pounding, there was a subtle change in the light, a shimmer in the atmosphere as the back wall of the cavern dissolved and Tirjhinar stood revealed.

He was only dimly aware of lifting Sararrh in his arms as he moved forward into the lofty dimness of the ancient Hall. Ahnell dragged himself to his feet, still swathed in his blanket and staggered after him, an expression of rapt awe on his face. Every wall glittered as the carvings revealed the Opal beneath the coppery coloured rock face. Everywhere, narrow seams of light flickered and flared into life as Daro approached until they entered a broad concourse set with great sheets of opal, behind which were apparently concealed niches. Two or three stood open and here, gratefully Daro paused, lowering Sararrh on to the couch which occupied the centre of the small room. She smiled up at him, then he was aware of the figure limping in his wake and ran back to assist Ahnell, who sank down to lie alongside Sararrh gratefully and so they camped. Daro running outside to collect dry clothes, travel packs, blankets and the little food and water that they still had, before returning to the awe inspiring interior that seemed to wrap him in its welcoming embrace.

Sararrh and Ahnell seemed too exhausted to eat and so he carefully divided their remaining food for the morning, covered the pair of them where they lay and took his own blankets to the next alcove and slept. He woke to the sound of running water and leaving his couch, stepped out into the concourse, to discover a fountain playing in the semi-circular area in front of their rooms. Ahnell was awake, leaning on an elbow, staring around him in bewilderment.

Daro immediately thought wistfully that what he really needed to locate for all of them was a necessary and a wash-down, then some food, before he went in search of a library and the cure for his friends sickness.

Even as he thought the need, a light showed to his left, a door swung open and the very facilities he sought were revealed. He carefully helped Ahnell, but after only ten paces, it was clear that his friend was becoming too weak to walk and Daro was forced to carry him the last few paces and stay to make him comfortable.

Ahnell stared around him.

"Such a wonderful place.", He sighed wistfully. "Will we be able to explore it later do you think Daro? I am so tired, I don't even think I could stay awake long enough for breakfast!"

Daro considered the answer carefully.

"If you are well enough, I don't think there is anyone here to object.", He spoke cautiously and then Ahnell asked curiously.

"Who then are you talking to? I hear you whispering to yourself sometimes. I am sorry that we are such bad company.", Daro looked sharply at his wan face and wry expression and wondered if he should tell Ahnell about his guide. A chuckle of pure amusement greeted this and suddenly Daro felt surrounded by affection, not just Ahnell's, he now knew that his guide had some connection with him too and he relaxed, jumping out of his skin a moment later when the voice he had heard in his head, boomed all around him.

"My name young man is unimportant, but suffice it to say that I exist to train those who would follow the path to power, a far greater power than your world knows today. I have had the training of many over the Rotations of this world and I am responsible for this city, sleeping until the coming of the next Opal Sandsinger. Your name I believe is Ahnell ap Minidrahl of the Shalhanhi and your companion is Sararrh te Dinnavage of the Zurias?".

Ahnell looked helplessly at Daro and then said breathlessly.

"Yes your honour.", in a thin, weak shred of sound, that left Daro in shivering anticipation of imminent collapse.

"We honour your devotion to Ichta Selunsanni.", The voice was grave and formal. "I will tell you all about the city, though I regret that neither of you are well enough to travel through its immensity. You must rest, conserve your strength awhile, during which time your needs will be met.".

Ahnell looked amazed, but simply too tired to take in anything as Daro carried him back to join Sararrh.

However, waiting for them at their cubicle there was a tray containing steaming cups of Stemmis, platters of fruit and a bread roll liberally spread with honey. Daro split a ripe greenfruit with his friend, carefully chopped up another and used the honey to sweeten the flesh for Sararrh, but his heart was heavy as he left them dozing and turned away to explore.

He could hear the voice carefully explaining the many levels on which Tirjhinar was built as he walked quietly towards the high metal railings that separated some great edifice from the general walkway and as his hand touched the gate, he was amazed to hear the voice in his mind again.

"This is Cathedral Cavern, you may not enter there yet, for you have much to learn before you will be ready to attempt the Vow.", He peered through the elaborately wrought metal gates into the remote heights beyond, straining to see if, in any way this place, obviously dedicated to ritual beliefs, matched up with Selesh.

The remote voice said, with satisfied amusement.

"How could it not, seeing that I designed both!" and the hair stood up on Daro's neck.

The voice mused to itself.

"Academically bright, totally untutored and sadly been in the company of women for far too long. You didn't come a moment too soon Candidate!"

At this speculation, Daro took very great care of his thoughts as he noticed a bright light burning a little way ahead of him, in a room, still within a short distance from Cathedral Cavern and near to where his friends slept.

Daro entered the study, for such it obviously was. Shelves lined every wall and contained many strange objects, other than the familiar scrolls and wax tablets. He put his hands firmly behind his back, for the One only knew what damage he might do to these fragile, ancient things. He stood for a while in bewilderment, studying some strangely shaped blocks of gemstone, before eventually deciding that although they seemed to be nothing more than a wealthy child's building blocks, their very presence in this ancient Hall of Mages, meant that they might very well have a purpose that he couldn't divine without much training and as he turned away to look at the desk facing him, the voice remarked drily.

"Very wise!".

Daro ignored it, carefully examining the desk with his eyes. He leant forward to study a discarded tablet, but could make nothing of the inscription from this angle . He cautiously slid behind the desk and was peering at the ornate lettering, when the voice intruded yet again.

"You have come all this way, why don't you sit down. Your studies have to start soon, so why not now?".

Absent-mindedly, Daro obeyed and as he did so, he felt his head swim, there was a rushing sensation in his blood and as he struggled to his feet in sudden fright, a door he had not even noticed opened and a young vigorous man strode in.

Daro gaped at him and the man chuckled.

"Shocking isn't it? Now, sit down before you fall on your face and take a deep breath.", Daro subsided obediently and the man stepped forward, into the pool of light and Daro sighed as he saw the glimmer around him.

"You are not really present are you?" He sounded wistful and his companion looked at his solemn face and said comfortingly.

"No, I am afraid that I can't be with you in person, but judging by the way you reacted, my presence can indeed be felt. I am glad that the sensitivity in you is strong, for you must first be aware of the changes that will affect not only you, but everyone you encounter, if you succeed in your quest. A Sandsinger bears awesome responsibilities, to match his powers and you will be the very first of a new breed of our kind and therefore you bear a great burden, for there will be no-one to share your fears or joys with. Our Way is not something that we actively sought, for we were born to power. Always in contact with the Source, never alone, able to share amongst us our joys, our knowledge, until one of our kind stepped aside from his power and corrupted our Way, teaching irresponsibility and indolence to his siblings.".

Daro sat, his face alight with interest and his visitor continued soberly.

"We were so busy, trying to correct the faults within our own society, that we couldn't act together when a great peril demanded that we did. That is how our time suffered an event that now threatens to repeat itself and it is to prevent the destruction of Pelshar that our kind must once again summon our strength and act as one.".

Daro stared at him uncomprehendingly and his companion smiled gently.

"Ah, you have not yet been awakened to the Source, though I imagine that you have a some time connected with it, within the Hall of Sorcery at Selesh?".

Daro thought of his stolen moments, sitting on his secret stair, feeling the sensation of power tingling on his skin and he nodded, sighing as he recalled the camaraderie of his friendship with Ahnell.

"I felt as though I was being stroked by something warm, something that I felt familiar with.", He spoke simply, trying to convey his yearning to connect with such power.

His companion spoke contemptuously.

"Women's meddling.", He challenged and Daro was suddenly aware that his hair was lifting, some crackling energy ran along his flesh, touched his throat and suffusing his skin. He stared incredulously at his visitor, who shimmered and glowed, a living man of pure Opal.

"Ichta Selunsanni, Daro of the House Selesh, awaken to your full potential!" and the Source flared within him and Tirjhinar awoke.

Chapter 32 - Song for Sararrh.

In the outside world time passed and the fourth anniversary of Daro's exile was less than a ninenight away. In the settlement of Selesh a deep unease permeated the very rocks. Drudges whispered and scurried about their work, the Healers watched the Sorceress and wondered what would happen next and seemingly imperturbable the Inesh wove their way through every known access point to the settlement, in case of trouble. What sort of trouble no one of them could specify, but it hung in the air, winding its way into every waking moment and many of their most provoking dreams.

It had been a hard Winter. There had been ice storms in the wake of a Rotation that Ikella would have preferred to forget, for the Infirmary and training Hall, had been infected by a new fever. Arriving with the onset of Winter and primarily affecting the school of Healers, victims suffered soaring temperatures, swollen joints, followed by a painful rash. In far too many, what followed was either violent convulsions, coma and death, or a sudden inability to breathe, coma and death. They had exhausted every remedy known and tried some pretty innovative ones, before the illness burnt itself out.

The training Halls were silenced. Bereft and sobbing parents clung to the place and an acute depression settled over Mount Torrenesh clinging like some foul miasma, encouraging a feeling of impending doom amongst the survivors.

As Winter passed, many of the local villagers clung to their Winter quarters, too frightened to emerge, even though Selesh was overcrowded. A sense of barely concealed panic, permeated the place, even those who had never seen Seleus, their Sun, long hidden by impenetrable cloud, muttered fervent prayers for it to return.

Shiarjha sat in the Djellim, quietly listing the roll of the Clan dead, in order to prepare for the annual Rite of Zenitheon and her heart ached as she sanded the scroll to which she had just added the name of Errish, their Master Builder and Troneth his son, just two Rotations old. How his mother had survived the grief, she didn't know, but Mina was a shadow of her former self, keeping apart, returning to work in the Infirmary only now, as Spring Rites approached.

Ikella had worked herself and everyone else to the bone, sitting up, night after night with her students, holding dying hands as they cried for their mothers and accompanying far too many to the burial grounds of the Sands. This Rotation had seen her grow more bitter, introspective and the current atmosphere was doing nothing to improve upon her already uncertain temper.

Knowing that the Sorceress had other troubles, Shiarjha sighed, contemplating one in particular.

A student Healer, nearing the end of her training. In less than a half-Rotation, Ikella had to decide what to do with Jalni, who, while stubbornly determined to become a Healer, was simultaneously conducting a campaign of self-destruction. Even now, this late in her training, Ikella was forced to consider removing her undoubted Talent, before unleashing her on the unsuspecting Sands. Then, Shiarjha considered ruefully, there was the problem of Daro.

There had been little word of him of late, even Ikella, who professed disinterest in the progress of her wayward son, had taken to interviewing messengers privately. They knew that he had completed his tour of the Sands, because Nahamida had let them know when he departed the Onyx Desert, but since then they had no word of him and Ikella had grown nervously defensive, anticipating the ruination of the Spring Rites Festival, if Daro returned in the same rebellious spirit in which he had left.

Sighing, Shiarjha shook the sand from the dry scroll carefully and laid it aside, hoping that there would be no more names to add to the toll this Rotation and turned to see Beneva's scribe leaving the Council Chamber silently. He acknowledged her interest with a slight bow and left without comment and intrigued, Shiarjha rose and taking the precious addition to the Book of the Dead, went to lodge it in the Council Chamber.

Ikella and Beneva stood looking into the glass known as Jocasta's Door. They were apparently watching their Apothecary packing a batch of medications and Shiarjha, came to join them, saying quietly.

"More trouble?" at which Ikella snorted irritably.

"Pah! Men trouble mainly I suspect. Carolus, Olneth and Brannith have requested permission to travel to Malos. Tonight if you please! Which means in reality, they can't face the friction when our wandering boy returns!".

Her scowl was so ferocious that Shiarjha didn't doubt for a moment that the Sorceress had hit the nail on the head. She continued sniping viciously.

"As usual, they present their regrets. As usual, Carolus needs travel funds and as usual, he intends to be away about three circuits of Jenta, which means that I shall be without an Apothecary until we are planting outside again.", Her irritation overflowed as the man in the frame of Jocasta's Door, ironically raised his cap and sketched a bow of farewell, as though he knew her to be watching. Driven to fury by the man's insouciance, Ikella positively snarled.

"By Hadda's Hall. He for one, certainly intends that I should greet Daro's return alone and unsupported! Well, he needn't think that I shall spare his precious Songchild on his account!"

She crossly gathered some papers up and swung around to face her Sister Guardians.

"Oh, Hadda hang all men high!" She exclaimed. "I am going to go and think about Jalni and what to do with her! I must have been mad to entertain any of this nonsense. Men, children, are they any different? I for one can't tell them apart!"

On that note, she swept past and left the Djellim. Shiarjha and Beneva eyed each other, but neither smiled. They knew trouble when they saw it and they certainly saw it approaching on the heels of First Spring Rite.

In Mina's eerily empty chambers, the Healer bent over a single bed, firmly smoothing the covers into place and refusing to look at the basket in the corner that still brimmed with Troneth's clothes. She would find a home for them soon, she promised herself and crossed to where a child's nightlight burned, playing out the chain that supported the smithwork vessel, until she had lowered it sufficiently to tend the glow that burned within.

She knew it was stupid, but the light had not been snuffed since Troneth went to the Sands with only a whimper to mark his passing. She had been numbed by the grief of losing Errish. He had been so well all his life. Never suffering even the mildest of infant ills in childhood, so they had assumed, that he was unlikely to catch this new fever.

"How wrong could a Healer be?" She questioned herself ironically. When Errish came home at lunchtime with a mild chill, she had not even suspected that he had Joint Fever. The terrible shock of finding her soulmate, her love, the father of her child, lying still and pale, cold and dead, as she returned from her evening rounds had nearly unhinged her. If she had not had Troneth to live for, she might very well have chosen to die then. Had she known that within a circuit of Jenta, her darling boy would succumb as well, she couldn't have carried on, but the One had sustained her, carried her broken heart, until her own body healed and then thankfully brought her back to her life's work again, mentally whole although physically weakened.

She caught a glimpse of herself in the copper panel that Beven had made for her bride-gift and for a second, she thought she caught a glimpse of Errish behind her, wide grin in a berry-brown face, curling hair just starting to grey, but of course, he was gone and she set her jaw.

She wouldn't fail him, life still beckoned and suddenly convinced that she had the solution to one problem at least, she smiled to herself and let herself out into the wide corridor and made her way to Ikella's study.

The Sorceress allowed a scroll to reform as Mina entered her rooms and the Healer looked around in astonishment.

"It is unlike Beneva to permit so many scrolls out of the Djellim at once!" Mina hazarded and was rewarded with a scowl of fierce concentration.

"These I discovered in Daro's library would you believe? I found them when Nadra pestered me to let her clean the place and prepare for their return. Of course, the one she wants back will return under her roof, but she would have it, that Daro would also be welcomed with clean rooms. Beneva doesn't even know these exist and frankly, I dread to think what she will say or do when she reads them!" was the rejoinder and then she relented, scooping up an old rush basket and filling it with scrolls and freeing a chair for Mina's use.

"Are you well?" Ikella enquired sharply and Mina nodded.

"I will live.", She spoke wryly and Ikella said with rough sympathy.

"I can't imagine bearing even a tenth of your pain my dear, but if at any time you need to retreat, we will all understand. I wanted to ask you to take up your old duties again, but I hardly think it fair at this time, what do you feel you would like to do?".

She looked at Mina steadily before stating quietly.

"I have not one student fit or ready to send on Song Walk this Zenitheon.", This admission was enough to leave Mina staring in shocked immobility, as the Sorceress, hunched forward, hands knitted together, fingers white at the knuckles, evidence of great stress, as she continued soberly.

"I would have at least five sets ready but none are well enough. Not one of that Rotation escaped the fever. As yet, we don't know if there are long term repercussions of that sickness to face. Out of sheer common -sense I must keep them back until next Rotation. I must make sure they are fully fit again, mentally and physically, before I send them forth. In the meantime, the Senior dormitory is filled with the remains of one Rotations intake and the rest of the school is empty. I have two students still in segregation and Eshima, my Sister in Sorcery nears the end of her Way and needs her Senior Healer home. I have yet to break the news to Sanra, I wanted to speak with you first.".

Mina nodded slowly.

"Sanra has been Senior for the Guild for the last four Rotations. How will she feel if I simply take up my position again?"

There was the faintest lilt of curiosity in her voice and Ikella grinned.

"Relieved I should think. She definitely has the skills and the experience, but she lacks confidence in her own virtues and she is nervous around the students. It isn't really her fault, she never had that many students to deal with before and then she has rather run up against …" Her voice tailed away and Mina pounced.

"Jalni?" she demanded incredulously.

"Jalni!" Ikella agreed, then sighed. "I don't know what to do with that child. She is very strong in the craft, but there is a shift in her energy patterns which puzzles me and angers others. She has been so unloved by her parents family it is a disgrace and now she has found her feet, she is lashing out at everyone who tries to help her. Worst still, she lost so many classmates in this sickness, that she is potentially more of a hazard than a Healer.".

Mina drew a breath.

"Well.", She spoke diffidently. "I actually came to talk to you about Jalni.".

The Sorceress leant forward, her face alight with interest.

"Go on.", She encouraged and so they talked, heads together, planning late into the night.

In Tirjhinar, Daro eased the knotted muscles at the back of his neck. It seemed like a lifetime since he had time to go and look at Sararrh and Ahnell and he sighed, acutely aware that his head ached, his eyes were sore and he needed to stretch, to move his body.

He had listened for what seemed like Rotations to his mentor, wondering how he could possibly be expected to learn so much in such a short time. He surprised himself though, faithfully repeating the names of Sandsingers past, allotting them correctly to their Sands and jumped when the tolerant, amused voice returned to his mind.

"Your progress is quite acceptable under normal conditions.", It soothed and then dropped the bombshell.

"However, you have but two nights longer before the Oathtaking and you must be very sure that you can remember the form before I will let you pass into Cathedral Cavern. I want you therefore, to rest your head a while. You can tend to your friends, but I advise you to eat only sparingly yourself. In this next day, you will be subjected to sensations that will leave you nauseated, if you have eaten before we start.".

Daro stood, moodily swinging his arms, trying to waken deaden muscles.

"I'm not sure I like the sound of that. I'm tired of being hungry, cold and thirsty.", He grumbled, turning down the light over the desk as he had been taught, with a wave of a hand.

He made for the door of the study, but was stopped in his tracks.

"Books, sand-tablets, scrolls.", Scolded the voice.

Daro, turned back, growling resentfully.

"You're worse than my mother!"

However, he lifted his hand and thought carefully about the order of the scrolls, then the sand-tablets and lastly the small books, which obediently rose from the stack on the table and put themselves away. Tidying completed, Daro would have left the room, but the voice, annoyingly prompted.

"Obedience!".

Daro flushed then, standing squarely in front of the desk, nodded in the direction of the enormous chair that stood behind it and said in a bored tone of voice.

"My obedience to the Opal, to the One and these Sands.", He stepped back and discovered that he was not alone.

Again the insubstantial figure appeared and Daro mentally groaned. His narrowed eyes took in the calm expression on his companions face and suddenly daring, he spoke sharply.

"Oh for the One's sake!" he snapped irritably. "I have worked since I arrived. I haven't even had one short break. I have learned all that you can teach me in that time and I need to sleep, I don't even know what to call you!".

He was too weary to care about the opalescence that had flooded into his companions eyes, until he felt the strength drain out of his legs and a terrible pressure forced him to his knees. His next breath was strangled at birth, as a silky soft, but unutterably dangerous voice said softly.

"Ichta Selunsanni, you can call me Ichspeller! If you want to survive long enough to try on my cloak for size, you will stop this mutinous posturing. Your friends have not lain down their lives to bring you this far, for you to throw it all away. Show them some respect! You will also pay your respect to me, to the Sand in which you were born and obedience to the One we serve, or your training is at an end. Now!".

Daro felt his chest tightening, turned dizzily away from the Opal flare that lit his face and shuddered in terror. He felt ashamed of his outburst, but he was so tired, so very, very, tired. He gulped miserably as he felt his hair stirred by an ephemeral touch, then his mentor said gently.

"I forget how the changes sap the strength. I am sorry to be so strict, but there is so little time left, in which to prepare you. Our world is so terribly damaged, that I forgot that you don't have any of our advantages and the Source is much diminished. I will do what I can to balance your strength and inform you while you sleep.".

The glowing spectral shape, reached out a hand and from it a stream of sparks leapt, surrounding Daro in a cocoon of warmth and peace. His skin tingled, then abruptly he felt the opal cloth of his robe shifting, changing and he stood, stark naked in a pile of Opal Sand. He smiled, remembering how he had quenched the flames that Solana had woven around him, only three Rotations back and a dry voice said.

"I am surprised that they left you free to return, if you could do that then. You are an enigma my child, but I am relieved to say that we are more than half-way there.".

Daro remembered nothing more coherent about his training, assuming that he had just fallen asleep, but during the following days, he somehow came to a new sense of purpose and he awoke perfectly refreshed, no longer suffering from the terrible lassitude of mental and physical exhaustion.

On the last day, he went early to check on Ahnell, pausing as he recognised the waxy pallor of imminent death on Sararrh. She slept most of the time now and he stood looking down at her in grief, until a whispering voice asked.

"Brother, why do you take so long to undertake your Vow? Sararrh hasn't got another full day unless you help us. Yesterday, she nearly choked. I can't persuade her to eat, when drinking is almost too much for her. She is in so much pain and all I can do is to rock her, wipe her tears and pray to the One to help you, help us. Please Daro, please for the One's sake stop her pain.".

Daro stared at Ahnell, for the voice was that of a very old man. He seemed to have shrunk into himself and Daro was stricken with a terrible thought. Their time and his seemed out of step. How long had he been studying? How long had they been suffering? He was not comforted as his mentor's voice said quietly.

"Their suffering has neither increased nor diminished since their arrival here. They won't suffer as though they were in the outside world, but we can't take that pain from them either.".

He was horrified and thought fiercely.

"How long have I been here? How long have I been studying?"

The voice said so softly that he could only just hear it.

"While time outside Tirjhinar has passed normally, for every ninenight that you have been here, I have condensed ten Rotations of knowledge so that your understanding of your power and position would allow you to succeed in your allotted task. This, is to prevent another Cataclysm leading to the destruction of our world. Whatever was done was necessary and done by consent.", Daro stared down at the frail old man that was his friend Ahnell and suddenly understood that his friends had known of their impending deaths and had decided that their part in his life was to assist him to get here. He knew suddenly, that they had also known that they would never leave Tirjhinar alive and the grief of it threatened to unman him completely for a moment.

He considered his choice of action carefully as he lifted Ahnell into the wash-down and made him comfortable for the day. As always a flagon of fresh fruit juice and some flat bread with cheese sat on the low table, but today, when Daro returned, Sararrh was wearing the most beautiful Azure blue robe. There were fresh flowers in her newly washed hair and he suddenly understood. This was the day, the day he would take his Vow and release his friends from their torment.

Ahnell said gently, in that cracked whisper he had come to use.

"I am too ill to go on much longer. Please Daro, go and study. The sooner you accomplish what you came for, the sooner Sararrh's pain will stop.", Daro heard the finality, the acceptance in Ahnell's voice and realised that his friend was so much wiser than he. There had been no references to Daro healing them, no request to assist them back to Selesh and humbled he reluctantly bathed and prepared himself, putting on the simple Opalweave robe, before checking on Ahnell again.

This time Ahnell reached out a withered hand to grip Daro's fiercely, before he turned away, curling himself protectively around his love, whispering to her.

"Hold on my love. Hold on, I am with you, I will be here always.".

Daro, feeling terribly the exclusion of that gesture, rose silently and padded away to the study.

Today was tedious, he studied with care the scrolls he had retrieved as he journeyed, remembering his journeys and how the Healers had willingly parted with ancient cures to help him achieve his goal. He recalled how only recently Tisanna, herbalist of the Amethyst Sands, who had never returned to her own desert after Partition, had made the journey from Selesh to Tearchan, ostensibly to help Telani, whose own Song Walk had been so rudely interrupted by the Storm and his own birth. She too, had brought an ancient tablet covered in the runic script that had become familiar to him now and with the tiniest amount of pure Amethyst Sand, had performed the incantation that would set his feet firmly on the way to taking his Vow. However, he reflected dully, he could do nothing without the cure of the Opal Sand itself and that he lacked, for Mina had not been available to add her skills to those performed upon him by the other Healers present at his birth.

"That is understood my child.", Said his mentor in his ear and Daro's head lifted in apprehension, but he was not present.

"Now you are ready.", The voice said gently. "You have finally accepted your own fallibility! In order to succeed in this attempt, your greatest mantra is the word fallibility. No-one of us is perfect, we all forget something, make mistakes or simply don't think things through carefully enough. For those who lead the plain and ordinary life, those mistakes can be disastrous enough, for those of us with power, those mistakes can affect a whole world. Your strength is your belief that you were born to do more than the average and the courage to face the dangers that such a destiny brings. Your weakness is the arrogance of youth and only age will cure that.".

"Is my learning incomplete if I lack the cure of the Opal.", Daro asked humbly, but his mentor chuckled.

"My dear boy. I am the Opal and I will take you through that part myself, but we must hurry, for the Sands of time run out and tonight you will Sing your Vow and take the Opal Staff, or die in the attempt.".

Daro sat very still, his blood chilled to the bone as he listened to the bright, remorseless voice filling his mind with aeons of knowledge. A brilliant light surrounded them both and they seemed to be locked in some ceaseless communion of minds, two faces absorbed and introspective, the power surging about them endlessly, until with a shiver, Daro rose and went bleak faced to the Cathedral Cavern.

It was dimly lit. A single glow hung centrally above a lectern on which stood a great book. Daro walked slowly towards it, conscious only of a thready whisper arising around him. He first thought of ghostly voices, but finally identified it as the wind and he called softly.

"Mirayen, wind of my Sands, attend me in my hour of need.", It ruffled his hair and sighed along his skin and he smiled, mouthing silently. "Welcome.".

He remembered his instructions and paused at the top of the central aisle for a long moment, eyeing a great throne like chair that stood to the back of this Hall's Sacred Circle. In the back panel there was an Opal below which was a cartouche, which he couldn't decipher from here. Controlling his wandering mind with difficulty, he faced the chair and bowing his head in a profound obeisance, said softly.

"I pledge my obedience before the One and all his witnesses, to Tirjhinar and its Guardians, to these Sands and its people and to the Winds and all their works. In obedience to the Way of the Singers, I pledge my life, my honour, my all.".

There was a flicker of light, streaming down on the book and Daro walked slowly forward, mounting two steps, to stand at the lectern. Around and below him, he knew there was no-one, but there was an intangible feeling that hundreds of others surrounded him and wrapt in their warmth, he raised his hands and the book obediently opened.

Daro read slowly.

"The Vow I take this day, binds me to my Sands. Though I may travel, my power and my Sand is one thing, absolute, indissoluble. Through the Source and the wakened Sand, I commit myself to the service of the One and his works. To the spirit of this Sand and all its peoples, to the Sands of this world, whose protector I hope to be.

As I hope for a lifetime of rule, so do I pledge in return to surrender any interest in ....", This was what he had been warned about he thought straining to make sense of any of the words that followed and then he realised his mentor was speaking softly.

"The surrender of some part of you that is of significant importance to you, is essential. This is the only time that you will have to consider what you will offer in return for your powers. Be very careful, you will hear the music in a moment, as your Oathtaking begins. You can only have three attempts, if you fail you will join these others who have tried and failed.".

A pale light filled the arena and Daro suddenly realised why he felt surrounded, for he was, by the bodies of his predecessors and as he shuddered, wondering wildly what he could offer, that had enough significance to be acceptable, the music began.

It cascaded like rippling water from the very walls of this immense darkened Hall, shivering along his skin, prickling every nerve in his body, sitting him quivering in an agony of anticipation as he leaned on the lectern and sang.

His voice soared, a clear golden tenor, uplifted on a background of pulsating power and he couldn't help but sway to the rhythms contained within him. He didn't need to look at the words now, he knew the Vow, had somehow known it all his life and his body flushed and singing with the joy of it grew visibly taller as he sought to verbalise what he would exchange for this joy, this completeness of being.

He considered as he came to the point in the music and then remembering the days and nights of torment that he had suffered over Sararrh, he offered his love for her, humbly and with a sense of contrition in the words.

He didn't know what to expect, but what he didn't expect was to hear his mentor's voice saying scornfully.

"Puppy love? Frustrated desire for another's chosen mate. Unacceptable. Try again!".

The music started yet again and again he struggled not just to contain his joy at feeling so at peace with himself and the universe as he sang, but to think of something he treasured that he could give up for this. Tentatively he offered his lifelong friendship with Ahnell and again, in despair, he heard his mentor say, albeit gently.

"You can't give away something that is not wholly yours to give!" and the music reached a crescendo as he began tremulously to sing for the third and last time.

At the point of surrender, he felt suddenly calm and collected, suffused with the exultation of a deep connection with the Source, no longer afraid, he laid himself at the feet of the Book of Rule and sang simply a pledge to endure with the same courage displayed by his friends, whatever was acceptable in exchange for the power to release Sararrh and Ahnell from their pain and permit him to fulfil his destiny. It had been his fixed objective for so long that he was incapable of considering anything else and it was with a sense of shock that he realised that the music had ended and that he was still alive, on his feet and gleaming with an aura of such power, he felt light-headed.

The lights were raising, the shadows dispelled and with them the ghosts of those past candidates. Seized with sudden fervour, he knelt at the foot of the lectern and was still there when the voice in his ear spoke again.

"Stand up Ichspeller. Time to indulge yourself later. Your friends need your care now!"

Daro stood, then ran lightly out of the gates, down the great concourse and into Sararrh and Ahnell's niche, pausing in shocked sorrow as he realised that Sararrh was in convulsions. Ahnell was holding her, crooning gently, but his frantic eyes found Daro's and his jaw literally dropped.

Had Daro been able to look into a mirror he would have understood it, for he had gained a lightly opalescent sheen to his skin, his eyes were like twin fire Opals and an aura shot with flickers of living Opal stood around him.

"Help me Daro.", Ahnell pleaded and Daro extending a hand over Sararrh, grew still as he searched for the living flame of her personality within this shuddering shell, in vain. A thready whisper of voice said quietly.

"You can stop her pain, release her spirit, but you can't bring her back. She was far beyond help when you first arrived here.".

Sorrowfully, Daro explained this to Ahnell, who held her sobbing, until Daro touched his arm and said gently.

"Brother, you can't wish more pain upon her. The bright spark of her life has fled from this affliction, you can't doom her body to ceaseless suffering, let her go my friend, let me Sing her to sleep.".

So it was, that in the dim recesses of Tirjhinar, that a Sandsinger's voice was heard once more and against the accompaniment of a rising wind, Daro sent the bright spirit of Sararrh forth into the Sands in which she would be eternally honoured.

Chapter 33 - The Reckoning.

There was a deep impenetrable silence in the great halls of Tirjhinar. In the desert that surrounded it, a wind prowled incessantly moaning its lament for Sararrh and in Cathedral Cavern Daro knelt in prayer, holding on to his memories of a red-haired girl with merry eyes, creamy skin, the courage and tenacity of a Myst-cat. He smiled faintly as he remembered her challenges to both Ahnell and himself. How she had taunted them, two lads from the deep desert lands of the Opal, neither with any experience of running water and he pictured her, sitting on a rock at the side of a stream, soaked to the skin like some wild untamed urchin, calling to them cheekily.

"Come on cowards, jump in and get cleaned up. Its cold, wet and lovely and the last one in is a Dolcan!".

He offered that precious memory of her as a living memorial and he heard the whisper of his mentor.

"She lies with the Honoured Few. Those who have performed a service in their lives, far above and beyond the call of their own station or Way. Sararrh will be remembered with so many more in the constant prayers of Sunfall, here in Tirjhinar. Your existence as Opal Sandsinger is a tribute to your friends' courage and endurance. Make it your duty to give thanks for that, every day of your life.".

Daro said abruptly, not really expecting any reply.

"Well, that might not be too long. First Rites of Spring should be getting under way tonight if my calculations are correct and I must go and face my mother. Though I can tell you that the wind is getting very rough and I don't really fancy having another row with her when I can't fulfil the terms and conditions of my exile. She will probably kill me anyway.".

He knew that he was deliberately prolonging the moment in which he would have to release Ahnell from his pain and say goodbye to the friend and brother whose bravery and honour he had constantly undervalued.

The voice in his mind said gently.

"You have no need to fear her. Mother's constantly relent of their intentions. What you may not appreciate is that she can't physically harm you now. She is as far removed in power from your status, as the beggar on the street corner is removed from hers. Even though she is a Guardian, her power pales into insignificance besides your own.".

Daro was silent for a long time, before he whispered faintly.

"Will there be others like me? Sandsingers I mean, I don't want to be alone always.".

He heard the merest sigh, then the voice replied gravely.

"There will be other Sandsingers, for you have woken the Sands. However, they will never be like you. No Sandsinger will ever exceed your Talent. Like your mother you have acceded to the Opal and as the senior Sand, yours is the superiority of power, of knowledge and responsibility. You will lead the other

Sandsingers, train them as I have trained you, rule them where necessary, but guide them always.".

There was a sorrow in the voice now and Daro's suspicions quickened. He viewed what he knew, running through the information with a speed of recall that surprised and pleased him.

His mind protested mildly, but the information he sought was not there. He framed his question cautiously.

"Will I live long enough to complete my task?" He asked and the wind from the desert seemed to shriek and moan through the ancient corridors as the voice came wearily to his ears for the last time.

"A Sandsinger is immortal Daro. You will live until the Source is extinguished. Whether you fulfil your destiny or not, you will live for as long as the One decrees. No accident, no disease, no heartbreak can destroy you. Until the Source fails, you are immortal.".

The wind whined in desolation and Daro looked up, staring at the great throne in the Sacred Circle.

"Get used to it.", He told himself. "You wanted this.".

He rose and went to read the cartouche on the chair back. It gleamed, golden lettering on an Opal panel, he bent forward and red it.

"Daro bin Selesh, First Son of the House Syrene. Lord of the Opal, Ichspeller Selunsanni.".

He raised his head and said softly.

"Who are you? What if I need your help again?", but answer came there none.

He walked away, more alone than he could bear and found Ahnell.

He had quieted now. The howl of pure agony that had accompanied Sararrh's gentle death had hung in the air, its memory still haunting their quiet cubicle. Daro saw that his friends travel packs had been removed, a low table now only supported a sconce where glows produced a soft white light to alleviate the gloom. Sararrh's body lay, released from pain, the youth had come back into her face and she looked calm, at peace.

Ahnell had lain beside her, holding her hand in his and he looked up at Daro silently.

"I sorrow for your loss. Sararrh was wonderful, brave, thoughtful, tolerant and so beautiful. You should rejoice in her life, her love.".

"I know.", Ahnell sighed and said thoughtfully, a trace of his old boyhood humour colouring his voice.

"I thought I might have to fight you over her, once you learned to see her as she was.", His voice trembled on the edge of tears as he said.

"I knew she would choose one of us, I just can't believe it was me.", He caught his breath, biting on his lip as a wave of emotion shook him.

"Don't leave me, Daro, Daro, don't leave me to die alone!".

Daro felt the stirring of an old anger. Borne on the back of his own pain, he felt it grow as he hastened to reassure Ahnell.

"Never.", He promised. "I will stay with you until the end!"

For a short while Ahnell dozed against Sararrh, his breath was laboured, his pallor increasing as Daro wished a damp towel into being and wiped his clammy forehead. Reached for a non-existent comb which appeared in his hand as he thought of it and combed his friend's hair.

Ahnell murmured wonderingly.

"I can't believe it, you are a Sandsinger, just as you dreamed and I saw it first.", He shifted restlessly as the pain increased and then said thoughtfully.

"Do you remember Usticus? The night he escaped and I couldn't sleep? You let me sleep in your bed then and told me stories of all the things you would do when you were Sandsinger.", His eyes crinkled at the memory and a smile touched his face.

"Let me get comfortable and then you can tell me more!".

So it continued, the sun they couldn't see, sank below the horizon. The clouds scudded across the skies of Pelshar and the winds moaned despairingly. They spent Sunfall reminiscing and with the memories Daro's anger grew. Ahnell finally checked himself on a cry of pain, caught Daro's hand to his mouth and kissed it, hot tears falling as he whispered brokenly.

"Enough Ichspeller, enough my friend, for I have lived twice my lifetime today. Once in reality, once in memory and I can't bear more. I think I always knew that life would be a short one, but I am happy and fulfilled. Take my messages home to those I loved. Tell my mother that she bore me in pain for the honour of both Clans, tell Nadra how much I loved and respected both her and Beven. Tell them all, tell them.", his voice was ragged, cracking with emotion, but he raised a hand to Daro's glowing eyes and said faintly.

"Daro my brother, let not the reckoning prey on your mind. Sararrh and I might have gone to the Sands without achieving anything. Our deaths are not on your conscience, rather they were a price to pay in some great Universal reckoning. There is always a price to pay Daro, always, but I paid mine with love and pride. Now Sing to me, send me to Sararrh before the Sands of my courage run out.".

Daro grew very still, he deliberately engaged his connection with the Source, seeing in the gleam of Ahnell's eyes that he recognised his part in Daro's history and was satisfied. He gently lifted and curved Ahnell's hands in his and Sang.

He Sang the colours of the Sands they had seen together, the hot breath of the Cynabarr Sands, to the cool of the Eternal snows. He sang prairies and rivulets, highlands and seas, he Sang Pelshar as it once was, as it would be again and he Sang his friend into the peaceful embrace of the Sands he had honoured with his being and only stopped at Ahnell's last breath.

A howl of grief filled the halls of Tirjhinar. Stopping for nothing Daro ran from the Hall of the Honoured Few to the entrance, seeing with strangely blurred eyes the billowing Sands of the Opal, roused to fury by his grief. He had stepped through the entrance into the cavern of his birth before he even considered that he still didn't know what price had been exacted from him. He could see no further than the loss of his friends.

He tried to bite back the angry words he found streaming through his mind as he strode out of Tirjhinar, seeking a path back to Selesh, where he would be exacting some reckoning from his foster-mother for doubting him, for laughing at him. He could hear the howling of the Wind, feel the Sands buffeting him, but in the Sands it was pitch black.

"Odd.", he thought and taking another step out of the cavern, fell head-long over a rock that came to his knee's in height, a rock he hadn't seen.

The scream of terror, poised on the brink of insanity that was ripped from his very being as he realised what a savage price he had paid for his power, should have been heard in Selesh, but it was lost in the deep growl of thunder, the ear splitting crack of lightening and the feverish scream of the Winds, as the Sorceress hastily ushered every living soul in Selesh into the shelter of the Hall of the Healers and the Gate in the Rock was closed against the Storm that licked at the heels of retribution.

If events could herald a Second Age of Mystery, those that took place at Selesh, during the First Rite of Spring this Rotation, would certainly qualify. Born in a Storm so apocalyptic as to defy description, Daro, (an orphan adopted by our Sorceress), was eventually exiled (in his seventeenth Rotation of life), for reasons I cannot divulge here.

In the three Rotations since, an uneasy peace descended on the Healer Hall and the School of Sorcery, for nothing was so provoking as Daro's presence. However, on the night of his return, (in my own absence), another Storm struck at the heart of our Sands, threatening Selesh, where everyone sheltered behind barred gates, hiding from the force of nature that was my Songchild in all his anger.

It seems that determined to understand the High Magic of the past, Daro has fallen headlong into the trap from which mortal man has been protected, by obedience to the Way, and to the rule of the Guardians. Now, he has unleashed the power, there is no other like the boy whose life entwines inextricably with mine. I am told on the night of his return, the rocks of the desert rang. In the cities of the Greeeyn, men spoke fearfully, as their women found the quiet depths of the city shelters, and built defences for their children. In the Fringe settlements, Felmin traders, farmers and builders, huddled into cellars, or underground caverns.

Even the heights of the Central Plateau seemed to draw in, as dim echoes of a forgotten Age, raged across the Opal Sands towards our settlement. The Healers, the Sorceress, and the Guardians all tell me that they felt a change in the magical field from which they derive their power. As "The Source" blossomed from gentle flow to raging torrent, a witness travelling our borders, saw a dim glow, as if the memory of the lost city of the Sandsingers was sketched on the horizon, where it once stood.

Tirjhinar, created a thousand Rotations ago, by mages using the magical power of the othervoice, has been a closed subject even in the Mother House of Sorcery. Now, in a society which barely survived the Storm in which he was born, Daro has returned to confound conventional wisdom, and set the House of Sorcery on its ears.

Witnesses report a man running, fire in his eyes, whirlwinds at his heels, lightening at his fingertips. Frightened inhabitants fled to hide, even Mount Torrenesh shrank from this vision, or so the outposts report, and still he ran on.

A growl of thunder greeted him as he came to the Gate in the Rock, finding it locked and barred against him, then he was surrounded by an eerie flickering light. A silvery blue sheen masked his features, and as if irritated beyond control, he raised a hand and struck out angrily. My witness tells me that his hand only encountered air, for in some despair, he had turned away from the Gate, but out of his hand came a ball of lightening. It streamed, hissing from his hand in a terrifying arc of power, roaring toward the Gate, where momentarily, the incandescence lit up the smouldering fury etched on Daro's face. I have no doubt that it was my Songchild and no other that committed the unthinkable, for from his hand, a lightening bolt struck, and with an awesome groan the iron clad Gate, leapt in its housing, toppled and fell, to a thunderous roar which rang round the Gathering Square below.

As my witness fled to raise the alarm, Daro strode forward, lightening flickering in his eyes.

Approaching the doors to the Healer Hall in a trance, he apparently stopped outside, ear pressed against the door, listening for a familiar voice. Even as my witness gathered her Command and disposed them to protect those within, Daro lifted his head, and smiled, a smile born of some intent other than joy. I am told that he felt for the metal hasps of the doors, pausing only a fraction, before he cried out,

"Ikella, come forth Sorceress! I am returned. Now let us see who really wields the power in Selesh!".

Nothing other was said, nothing other was done to forewarn those who watched from the shadows. He simply tapped the door with his fingertips, once, twice, and...

To find out more read Another Shade of Mystery, details overleaf.

The Tapestry of Tten - Book 3 by Julia Cæsar

"Another Shade of Mystery."

Having exiled Daro for his obsession with the ancient mages of their secret past, life is still far from peaceful in Selesh. The aging Sorceress has found no relief from troublesome children, for she has given refuge to Jalni. The girl, hotly pursued into the heart of the community, has an intriguing (though erratic) command of power. Admitted as a novice, Jalni commits a catalogue of crimes, and is on probation when Daro returns empowered, to challenge his foster-mother's long held beliefs.

Determined to ignore the personal price he has paid for his power, the Opal Sandsinger takes Jalni as his guide, and sets out to save the children of Scartel. Encountering Myst-cats, Wanderers, Storm horses and a mysterious mentor, Daro must also find his feet in a strange new world, looking for "Another Shade of Mystery", to help him understand, "The Song of Sorcery".

"The Tapestry of Tten", a gripping series of Fantasy Fiction novels by Julia Caesar is published by Arima Publishing. To order, please visit our website, http://www.arimapublishing.co.uk , or write to us at,

arima publishing
ASK House
Northgate Avenue
Bury St Edmunds
Suffolk
IP32 6BB
UK

The Tapestry of Tten - Book 4

Song of Sorcery.

Returning from Scartel to safety, Daro and Jalni are shaken by the death of a child. As Daro questions his faith in magic, Jalni decides that if he can face the past of a world, she can face her own, and slips away unseen.

En route to Jerritol, followed by an old friend, she encounters Orto and decides to help him find the Tapestry of Tten. At the Temple of the Winds there's no trace of the relic, but the Oracle predicts, Jalni will become, "Mother to the Tenth Wind."

Jalni goes into retreat, but when the Sorceress Tirjella is poisoned, she usurps Sandsinger powers and saves her. Returning to Selesh, Jalni can predict Ikella's reaction, but Daro's she couldn't have foreseen in a thousand Rotations!

Empathise with Jalni's struggle to control her own destiny. Watch Daro confront the limitations of his power, and smile as Jalni finds love. Does it last? Read the sequel, "Sword of Honour" to find out.

"The Tapestry of Tten", a gripping series of Fantasy Fiction novels by Julia Caesar is published by Arima Publishing. To order, please visit our website, http://www.arimapublishing.co.uk , or write to us at,

Arima publishing
ASK House
Northgate Avenue
Bury St Edmunds
Suffolk
IP32 6BB
UK

RNIB Talking Books - A message from the Author.

A proportion of the purchase price of this book, is being donated by the author to RNIB, The Royal National Institute for Blind and Partially Sighted People, and will be directed to their National Library Service which runs the Talking Book Service and the Learning and Skills Library. These provide visually Impaired people with an accessible source of entertainment and education, through the conversion of books into an audio format, known as DAISY (Digitally Accessible Information System). This is a unique system that allows navigation of audio books.

The resulting CD's dropping through the letterbox are a powerful tool in the battle for equality, giving blind and partially sighted people access to thousands of books which were previously not available. This lifeline service is invaluable to some tens of thousands of people across the UK.

"You have already supported this significant service simply by buying my book, but if you want to help further the aim of making it possible for all books to become accessible to Visually Impaired Readers, or need information about the RNIB Please call their helpline on

0303 123 9999 or visit www.rnib.org.uk

Thank you for your support,
Julia Cæsar

Where can you find out more about the Tapestry of Tten and get regular updates about forthcoming books?

Why not visit
www.sandsingers.co.uk

The official home of The Tapestry of Tten, and find out more about the fascinating world of Pelshar. Get a feel for this troubled planet, find out about the Clans, the culture, and the ideas that drove Julia to write the series. Find out about the parallels between our world and theirs, follow the characters, study the maps and see where they lead.

Website designed and maintained by our friends at
Red Dragon I.T. Ltd

+44 1303 723456   **www.rdit.co.uk**

www.ingramcontent.com/pod-product-compliance
Lightning Source LLC
Chambersburg PA
CBHW071129260626
47162CB00003B/724